Changing the Subject

Kate Abley

For Alex and Tom

Acknowledgements

First and foremost, my thanks go to Ian Abley, who has put up with me clicking away and not earning any proper money. I am also deeply grateful to Alex Cameron for designing the book jacket and Graham Barnfield for giving me ISBNs for free. A massive thank you goes to John Davey, who did his best to teach me editing. The inimitable Sandy Starr was kind enough to read 'the science part' but there really was no helping me. Two people took the time to read my drafts, be my critical friend and gave me great advice, some of which I took; Hilary Bailey and Michael Moorcock thank you for everything.

Author's note.

The speech attributed to the fictional Charles Windsor herein is an amalgam of words that the real-life Heir to the actual British throne in fact said in speeches taken from his website.

The names Hilary Bailey, Alfred Bester, Angela Carter and Michael Moorcock belong to real authors who are well worth reading.

Great Boots

"So, this is illegal immigration," said Sue, "…Thank you, Yunis," and Yunis smiled. She let herself be completely charmed one last time. "…If you're ever in Chingford,"

And now that they would probably never see each other again it was safe to sigh into a proper hug. They even kissed, then they smiled some more. One great boot hit the jetty and she steadied herself before she lifted the second to stand on something solid, if not a little rickety, for the first time in about ten days. He handed over the hold-all and she nodded.

"Good luck," said Yunis and he walked into the wheelhouse and ground the boat back into the black. Sue walked towards the bar she could see at the end of the jetty, found the pace for the great boots and walked with her head up having another bloody revelation. She was that woman, that woman with the long blonde hair and the great boots, a great stride and a hold-all over her shoulder. Taut-faced-tight-arsed and confidently walking along a jetty somewhere warm towards a bar. She looked just like that woman in the shampoo advert. Mind you, that woman's hold-all was probably full of the swim-suit and evening dress she would need for the next cutaways. Not like hers. Her bag was loose and lumpy. The contents exposed what was too much backstory for a shampoo advert. Probably too much backstory for her. One-minute sitting on the Seven-Oh-Five reading in the Metro about Bloody Brexit; next minute, well

1

next year, an 'illegal' bombshell cum lab rat with great boots. But she was definitely worth it. In all that time no-one had mentioned actual numbers, that's how big they were.

She needed a drink and luckily she was now at the bar. A neon ad for a beer she'd never heard of lit a few odd tables and chairs and a couple of what? Fishermen? She tossed her head to let the breeze tussle her locks. Felt the grease and grime on her skull. Could do with some actual shampoo, and deodorant. She hadn't had a wash of any kind for...well over a week, that was for sure. There was no point asking for cider or even gin, the place was basic. Having, much more recently than one would think, completed her daughter's GCSE Spanish exam coursework to Grade Nine standard she was able to order a cold beer with ease. She herself had done French.

She sat down outside under the advert, almost but not quite forgetting that she would look great in a strong light, and realised that she had started wondering again, as soon as she hit dry land. She had stopped wondering for a good three months. Too angry and frightened probably, too busy with escaping. Her own sister.

Now she felt safe enough to wonder again. But she hadn't always been a wonderer, had she. When had all this started? Not with the metamorphosis and all the silly business that went with it. Before that. And would the other stuff have happened if she hadn't started wondering in the first place? When was it? When the letter came? No, it was before that, but not much before. It was that morning. Yes, that Tuesday, no Monday morning. Her beer had appeared and she hadn't said 'Gracias'. She took a sip. She had a lot of time for Moslems now but drinking was great. That was it. When she had that other face, that was when.

That face had not been so different really. It was like a sculptor was making this face but instead of pushing wet clay with his thumbs from her mouth up and out to form her cheekbones he had pushed down. Then he had got bored or the phone rang and he hadn't smoothed her off or made sure she was symmetrical. But it was the same face really. She had pored over this face for hours and so had other people. It had been measured and prodded and samples had, sometimes under great duress, been taken. It had been kissed too. She winced. Oh dear. There was indeed no fool like an old fool, even if they could pass for a sixth former.

She tried to properly think about her old face. It hadn't been a bad face. Did she miss that face? She had looked fifty. Plenty of hair, not like Julie, Julie's hair was definitely starting to get thinner, and you could see her scalp at the crown. But that was probably the stress. She used to do that, didn't she; almost unconsciously and almost all the time. Compare herself to her friends, family, work colleagues, people she saw in the street. And in foolish moments models and actresses too. Yes, she used to do that a lot. How many hours would all those milliseconds of physical comparisons with other women add up to? Never mind men. Women were worse. What else could she have been thinking about?

She'd had a few permanent furrows on her brow and Sue ran her fingers over her forehead as she squinted into the Monday morning mirror back in Chingford not even a year ago. Deeper wrinkles, definitely getting deeper. Not laughter lines anymore. More than Jan…even though her sister Jan was nearly four years junior, she looked ten years younger. Mind you. Jan was rich; money for facials, money for a personal trainer, money for enough sleep, money not

3

to worry constantly about money. Money to think she could treat other people like lab rats, even her own sister.

The breeze in whatever country Yunis had dropped her off in was warm but quite strong and a shiver ran down her spine. She had never so much as slapped anyone. But she had truly belted Jan over the head with that jug in the hospital. And when she didn't fall immediately, she had belted her again. With the hope that she wasn't dead and another nip from her glass, Sue pushed Jan's flickering eyes as she fell from her mind.

In that old mirror back in Chingford the shiver of deeper and older resentments temporarily ironed out a couple of lines as her eyes narrowed. Jan wore too much makeup; it clogged her pores and made her look washed out. But Sue still had fewer wrinkles than her best friend Julie, Julie had loads and they were both Fifty-Eight. And Linda, her second-best friend. Linda smoked. Sue's crêpe covered hands moved down to beside her eyes and the crow's feet felt deeper too. Less than Julie, more than Jan, less than Linda. Good skin, not too blotchy, not too red, better than Linda-and-Julie.

It took a moment to recognise the old feeling; guilt ebbed up from her belly and into her mind. Comparing looks with Julie was wrong. Julie was always tired, from getting up at three in the morning to put her mum back to bed. Or traipsing from work to the hospital and then the shops. That was why she'd said yes to all this business in the first place. If Alzheimer's was genetic then Julie might be screaming down the street in her nighty one day. Julie had aged ten years looking after her mum, more, and, had she put her in a Home by then?

Yes, her mum was already in the Home because Julie was finally coming out on Friday, or was it the Friday after? No, it was that Friday wasn't it, the day after Brexit. That had been the first surprise, the first big event for her hadn't it? Time wise, if you put everything in order, which she hadn't had time for. Still didn't really. She had to wait for Albin. She took a swig of the unknown but rather tasty beer.

The mood that night in the pub had been odd really. All those people quiet from getting what they had voted for. The Elizabeth was definitely a Brexit pub. It was like they had all won the lottery and didn't want their friends to know or something. No, not like that. A strange atmosphere. Subdued. Was it because it had been such a close-run thing?

Everyone had close ties with someone who had voted the other way. There was less than two percent in it. Perhaps they didn't want to rub it in. Not that anyone she knew had properly fallen out over it.

Was it because no one expected it? The papers, the TV, the polls, they all said they would lose. Was it because of the campaigners? The winning side had been 'led' by a bunch of politicians that no one, not even the Brexit voters in the Elizabeth, really liked or trusted. They were still Politicians.

Was it because the drinkers in the Elizabeth just weren't used to getting their way? Tory or Labour, it didn't make any difference, no one ever listened to people like them. Sue didn't know why it had been so strange in there. But except for the odd bit of laughter maybe the mood had been dampened in some way.

Was it the silent self-suspicion that they might actually be Racist like all the 'Remoaner' journalists were screaming in the London her parents had run away from?

But that word Remoaner hadn't happened yet had it? Had it? She hadn't been home since March and those last few months had been a bit chaotic.

Had she voted Brexit because she was Racist? She would have to wonder on that some more.

Anyway, Julie had forgotten to vote because her mum had had a bad few weeks and the girls were Remainers.

Julie had looked about Seventy that night. Sue had actually felt guilty that her own mum had died quickly. Now she felt guilty that she had run away and left her best friend to carry on, day in day out, without her.

She took another gulp of beer and looked shamefully down at the great boots. This slow, what had Julie called it after a few Gins, 'living death' of Alzheimer's disease, was killing part of Julie as well as her mum. Julie had been despairing. One minute a glimpse of the old feisty (to put it politely) woman who had brought her up and then hours and hours of confusion, panic, not knowing who anyone was or what was going on.

Sue rallied and sat up under the neon used to the fact that her breasts would come with her. Julie's mum and Julie were why Sue was here, sort of. She had wanted to help hadn't she. It was not her fault that the drug trials had gone wrong or right or whatever. It was not her fault she was on the run from her own bloody sister and that horrible, bloated, greedy 'Big Pharmer' she had married.

She didn't want it but the image of that red-faced Fat Bastard with his lank and slimy hair, this time dressed like an actual farmer; complete with a piece of straw dangling from his thin purply lips, flashed across her consciousness like a subliminal frame spliced into an advert for shampoo.

It was not her fault that she now looked better than Jan. Jan was always the pretty sister 'till Steve came along and made Sue, the clever one, feel beautiful. Then 'till he made her feel ugly, worn out, old. That dreadful picture he did of her in the kitchen, all purples and orange. Bastard. She hadn't seen the father of her children for years but she bet he was aging gracefully, craggy handsome and salt and pepper hair. She hoped he was bald.

Sue sighed, swigged and refocused on the year-old image a thousand miles away or more; her old face so different from the one she felt inside. Inside she was just her. Was that a turkey neck? There were definitely signs of a turkey neck and she turned her head to get a profile in the Chingford mirror, yes, a turkey neck was coming. Was there an exercise you could do for turkey neck? Claire had a definite turkey neck now and someone should tell her. Not her though, she was her third-best friend so she didn't know her well enough for that. It would come over as bitchy if she said it. Like when she had tried to tell Belinda about the nose hair. Jowls too, Claire. Sue checked her own face for jowls. Her cheeks were definitely threatening downwardly, but not yet. She looked forty-nine, maybe fifty? Not bad for pushing Fifty-Eight. And she started with the primer.

In the Spanish speaking bar, she took a last swig of the cold beer and lit a cigarette. Then she caught sight of some bloke out of the corner of her eye and spontaneously sniffed and wiped her nose with the back of her hand to put him off, just in case.

She was busy with remembering. Was that all, a year? It felt like longer. Much longer. Maybe it was two. She remembered trying to remember something. That was it. People didn't used to wear so much foundation the last time she was twenty, did they? Even twenty-year olds wore lots of slap nowadays and Sue couldn't remember wearing so much at the same age? Was that Feminism? Or that post-war gloom that took so long to lift in Chingford? Or just her? Maybe she just hadn't been paying attention? She couldn't remember if Julie or Linda wore lots of foundation back then either. She could have sworn it was just for parties and going out. Yes, foundation had been for work interviews and nights out back in the day surely? Not every day, not to 'stay in the game'? She was going to ask on Friday when they met up. She hadn't, Julie had too much on her mind already. Any way it didn't seem fair she thought, and she rubbed in the primer.

Those women at work didn't need foundation, they were young. Didn't they realise that they were beautiful? Of course they didn't, her daughters were a constant reminder of that. And it didn't matter how many times she told them that they were beautiful, they just couldn't see it. They would stand in front of the hall mirror nearly every morning from the age of what, twelve? Jo more than Sam, with that worried look at bum; shape and size, tum; shape and size; legs; length and shape, knees, ankles, and in summer heels and toes, and face.

All that staring at their face; shape, size, eyes, mouth, nose, under eyes, chin, cheeks. And all the while looking like works of art. Better. She had needed to wear makeup, she looked fifty in make-up. She sighed again and reached for the foundation that combatted the ten signs of aging. That was a lot of signs, what were they? Wrinkles, jowls, turkey neck…what else…thinking 'she'll break her neck in those boots'? She had thought that hadn't she, and she smiled as she smoked her cigarette in the bar out of the advert and looked down at her great boots that did not in the slightest bit pinch, honestly, she was in no pain whatsoever, none.

On the train that same morning not even a year ago she had noticed that she was the only 'older woman' in her carriage. There were plenty of older men and lots of young men and women. But only she looked like someone's mum. It was the same at work. Where had all the women her age gone? Was the London bubble actually a force field that pushed women who looked over Fifty back into the suburbs.

She sighed again and wondered why she was wondering all those things that morning? She hadn't wondered anything for…for a very long time. No. She didn't used to wonder at all really. So why now? Or then? Work at Murphy Hobbs had been hell for months, bloody Emma. Taut-faced-tight-arsed 'going forward' bloody Emma. She'd learn. She wondered if Emma still lived at home, like Jo. Her Jo. She wondered if they were the same age? Could bloody Emma put a load of washing on? More wondering. Sue went back to her Metro and was comforted to find that nothing except Brexit was happening anywhere in the world. A bit about immigrants was all she could remember, or was it migrants?

Her recent experiences had confused her, she had travelled through a lot of countries recently, stuck in the back of a lorry for most of the time and unable to see where she was going. So she had taken to imagining the routes. In the fog of all that cigarette smoke she had visualised all the roads and tunnels that ran over Europe like veins and arteries. Seen her and her companions as cells flowing through the circulation of a continent. She had trouble remembering the old way of seeing things back home. Were they rules; Immigrants were economic, Migrants were humanitarian? That was it. But home was Britain so there were more rules. Illegal immigrants were the worst. Working legal immigrants in private accommodation were just about acceptable, especially Doctors and Nurses. Non-working legal immigrants and those in Council Housing were generally bad. Migrants were mainly good. Well, not good exactly, deserving. And Europeans, no, Western Europeans, Canadians, Australians, New Zealanders and Americans were technically from other places but didn't count as Immigrants or Migrants. Immigrants were generally black or brown or poor, no not poor - unskilled. Migrants could be any colour. And the Only-technically-Immigrants were generally white and skilled. Yes, that was it.

And Immigrants and Migrants were two separate issues to be discussed as such at all times. But add a 'tion' or two and Immigration and Migration was another matter altogether; there was too much. That was how the Metro covered the issue, all the papers really, the telly too, and the Government. Everyone. No-one had to spell it out. Everyone just knew. Different people on the move got different labels according to the unspoken rules.

But when she said it, people called her Racist. So, either the whole country from the top to the bottom wasn't Racist including her and she was just using the wrong terminology? Or, the whole country, including her, was secretly Racist and she was being impolite for bringing it up? Or? Was it and/or; Andy was right when he was drunk in the Elizabeth that night and we were all Special Constables now? She heard his Actual-Proper-Policeman's drawl, saw his fingers counting off, out in the beer garden for a cheeky fag,

"Do not state your personal opinion on anything controversial, report anything suspicious and leave the rest to the Police, Experts, People on Telly, People with Columns in the Papers and Celebrities?" Andy was a Metropolitan Policeman. But that didn't mean everything about him was resentful and corrupt did it?

She was an illegal immigrant now of course. Or did being light electricals designer make her a migrant? She wasn't wicked. Mind you, she wasn't squeaky clean, possibly a murderer of her own sister. And Yunis, such a nice man, was technically a people and drug-trafficker wasn't he. But they were different from the ones in the Metro. Sue and Yunis had back stories.

That bloke was still staring at her. Still staring at a young woman in great shape and boots who had turned up off the sea in his local bar. If he was trying to be alluring, he was being very subtle about it because he sat with his legs open and his belly out. He reached and sipped his beer without taking his eyes away. But she was busy. Busy remembering Tesco's and nagging feet.

No! it hadn't been that morning! It was the Friday before. It was that Emma. Bloody Emma…in that bloody design meeting. Was her memory going? No, that was one of the tests. She'd always had a terrible memory, like dad. He'd have had Alzheimer's by now if he hadn't died of heart disease. Angela had said. Not like Jan, Jan had always remembered every little itty-bitty thing. What was that thing she'd blurted out in the hospital-cell? Something about seconds when they were kids. How did that justify locking her up! Who'd want seconds of mum's mince anyway?

Maybe it was the genes? Jan didn't have them, did she, Hah! Almost cried in that bloody clinic. Still, she really did hope she wasn't dead.

That was it, she had wondered why Emma had not been alone in rolling her eyes in that bloody meeting. Sue had done a perfectly presentable presentation. Her graphics had popped up and down and along and around like they were supposed to do. Yes, some of her ideas were so old that everybody else there thought that they were new. But she had replaced the old boxes and arrows with bubbles that floated over the screen. She had changed the odd word; 'elegance' 'style' were okay, but 'life-style' had been replaced by 'choose', not 'choice'- 'choice' was out now, or 'identity'. Kettles could be 'aspirational' again now but any sort of 'trim' except a 'retro-chic' one had to be an 'accent'. And she had said 'user focused', twice. The designs were always good, she was a very good designer. It was a shame that wasn't enough.

The upgrade coffee makers were both beautiful and undercut the competition. Their partner's capsules were still selling well indicating that the product was being used. Not just a desperate idea for an expensive enough Christmas present, 'I knew you liked coffee' - who didn't like coffee, that became a box in the loft or eBay's 'never used'. But as soon as she had said 'experience tells us that there will be seasonal variations in actual use', which was so true it was almost not worth saying but it was a presentation so she had to, nearly everyone in the meeting had rolled their eyes. And bloody Emma had flattened her mouth into a 'what do you expect' to Geoff from marketing before raising the over plucked eyebrows on her taut face and smiling sweetly back at Sue.

No-one challenged her, no-one lingered with anyone else at the end of the meeting but somehow Sue knew that she had been undermined and she couldn't work out why. It had really upset her. She had forgotten to go to Tescos on the way home. The letter hadn't come till Monday.

Yes, that was it, then they had to get a takeaway and she had had to have a bubble bath. It was only a little thing but it was a big thing.

Sue stretched her neck back in the chair under the neon wherever she was now; a bath. A long hot bath. Would there be a bath or a shower in the safe house? Was it a safe house? Or just a holiday let? Albin had said 'safe' house but how far did MI5 or 6's reach extend nowadays? Sue couldn't be bothered to try and conjecture on the relationship between Government cuts, international property prices and post-Cold-War geopolitics. But a bath would be nice.

It had been a rough sea. But Yunis was an excellent sailor, fourth generation, so were the crew. It was a shame the Somali fishing trade had been destroyed after all that time. Such a nice man. Wasted on people and drug trafficking. But what else could he do, except become a pirate? His little boat couldn't compete with the huge First World fishing trawlers. She hoped his mother-in-law would get better. A flicker of a smile went through her lips as she remembered their first proper conversation just off the Canary Islands. She had been angry because he had said he would drop her off there. He had been angry because he didn't want to take her all the way across the Atlantic either. She had said something about illegal immigration, about it being the other way round. He had said something about the UK being for most immigrants their third or fourth choice.

13

She had been offended. He had charmed her out of her mood and into a proper conversation about homesickness. She missed those girls.

It had turned out to be a very productive bubble bath as it happened. She had worked out the stain after about a twenty-minute soak. She had said 'experience'. Thirty years previously she had been deeply unhappy when she learned that the ideas of the older generation were outmoded and irrelevant. She had worked so hard to be the first person in her family ever to go to uni. More than that, she had loved some of those old ideas. Her dad had helped her look for and find beauty on countless Sunday afternoons. The first time she had felt that Lost-it-doesn't-matter feeling, that So-this-is-beauty feeling was looking at that Rubens. How old had she been? Six? Seven? Jan had never really forgiven her of course. Jan had giggled at the titties while Sue and her dad had made a connection that would last until he died. Maybe that was why Jan had found it so easy to hurt her own sister later on?

She really needed to get back home and see it again. That Rubens. The picture she could remember wasn't that good. Her memory was not as perfect as that picture. She needed to get back and see it again. Back home.

Mr Smith, her art teacher at school, had helped her try and make beauty. Helped her develop a relationship between her hand, her eye and her brush. That's what he used to say. And she had been good, really good. But of course she hadn't been able to see that either. Her painting or her great figure. She still had those old sketch books somewhere. Mr Smith had seen her talent and spent hours on her. A fifty-year old man leaning over a lithe seventeen-year-old girl alone in a school art studio, that wouldn't happen now. He hadn't been 'like that' though.

Mr Smith had taught her line and form and shape and space. He had shown her prints and told her where to spend her Sundays. Because he loved art. Then she had got to college and discovered from her lecturers, if she could ever find one, that those ideas belonged to a social class that hated her, used those ideas to keep her down. What's more, it was up to her to discover new ideas that could replace centuries of thought and work. She'd had a Good-Comp education, but still?

At the time she had wondered how beauty rules could belong to just one set of people but apparently it was all relative anyway. There wasn't just one truth or just one beauty and the truth and beauty she had been indoctrinated into was oppressive. That's what they said. It all gave her a headache. She hadn't minded having 'false consciousness'. She loved those Old Masters, Rubens especially. What was wrong with those old ideas? Look what they made.

Mind you, in the late '70s everyone had been so depressed or fed up or angry that any kind of truth or beauty at all had been kind of sneered at. Naive, that's what people used to call her, if they bothered to say anything from under their bad haircuts or Velvet Underground berets. Nappy pins in their ears. Sue could not remember the '60s because she wasn't there. The '60s never happened in Chingford. Then, at eighteen she found herself surrounded by people who had apparently found the whole decade exhausting. If anyone was riled enough to argue with her it was to rant about how irrelevant and awful the old ideas were, and the people who went with them. No wonder she never made it past her foundation year.

Now there were more old ideas but they were rubbish too apparently. The older generation were not to be trusted with ideas and she was deeply unhappy about it again. Now that she was the older generation. Not that she was any more, except she was really.

But she hadn't known that in the bubble bath. In the bubble bath she had remembered back to when she first looked eighteen, actually eighteen. Back then people had rolled their eyes at her all the time because she had been eighteen, well nineteen and a woman, no, a girl, that's what they called her, and trying to tell a bunch of men that women didn't have to ask their husbands if they wanted to buy a new kettle every ten years if they were lucky. She had worn that light blue suit with the shoulder pads and done her brown hair with Jan's curling tongs to try and look older. To look like she belonged to the new era.

Well, she did belong to the new era, she had voted for Norman Tebitt with an enthusiasm she couldn't remember, couldn't even imagine possessing. Had she really been that zealous? Aspirational? Kept the secret of the ballot from the love of her life in case he disapproved? Not that he was that interested in politics, Steve. Mind you, she had only bothered voting in the last election because of Brexit. That Ian Duncan Smith didn't even sound Scottish, so annoying. Everyone called him by his initials and IDS; sounded like a venereal disease. He was alright over Brexit of course, except for that NHS money business. Heartless.

She had had heart, and soul. And all to push for proper market research to a bunch of outmoded old men who had fought in the War and damn well invented electric kettles, which would sell themselves no matter what colour they were because they were the best in the world and would last a lifetime, and they weren't going to be told what to do by a working-class-girl without a degree in fine art. Bloody Emma had a degree, but she couldn't bloody draw, could she.

Sue had sucked up to another Geoff, a Geoff who was probably dead now. Geoff had commissioned the market research. Geoff had found out that kettles were seen as modern and labour saving and colour and design were important and that women generally consulted their husbands before buying one. It had got easier in the '80s and '90s, being a woman at work as well as autonomously buying a kettle. Then it had got harder again, being a woman. Kettles, even well-designed ones, were as cheap as chips. Cheaper if you bought organic chips, probably.

A kettle would have cost the best part of a hundred pounds in today's money. She said the words slowly in her head: Nineteen-seventy-nine. She had been drawing kettles, and the odd toaster, for forty years. Kettles and toasters and coffee makers, it had been her idea to market kettles and toasters together in matching modern colours, back in the day. If it hadn't've been for Jo, getting pregnant with Jo, and then Sam. She'd left it late enough as it was, not by today's standards, but back then having your first child at twenty-nine got you special treatment and something written on your notes. Steve had known what that meant. Bastard.

And the mergers. So many mergers. Still drawing kettles. She'd probably be a director by now. But that was then and this was now and the bath water was getting cold. In the bar another shiver ran down her spine and she pulled up the collar of her jacket as she had learned to do on the boat. What day was it now? She would have to wait for Albin to find out.

That bloke at the next table wasn't going away but she couldn't ask him what day it was, even if she had done all of Sam's Spanish coursework. She took another swig of beer and burped emphatically. It would put him off a bit, but with a bum like hers not completely.

Jo had taken the figure thing really well, not Sam though. Sam didn't take anything well. Never had. Sam knew she was an accident. Steve had only wanted one. If that. But wasn't everyone an accident, Samantha, wasn't everyone?

Sue wondered why she found it so easy to think that all of a sudden. She drank some more beer and ordered another with her finger like she had seen in the advert she was in now. It wasn't that easy to think, come to think of it, especially when she was so far away and could do nothing about it. She loved those girls and didn't know how they were feeling, what they were doing, how were they coping? And Jo's knee! She rubbed her oh so smooth forehead and stared out at the black sea and the black sky. The barman came out to take her glass and she ordered another beer.

She could still hear the sea but it was just a gentle shampoo advert swish now. Not the massive tumult of undulating mountains toppling onto them on that tiny boat in the middle of the ocean. Days and days of nothing but huge belts and swirls of grey and black above and below and all around. Every step was a swaggering and a falling kind of leap up or down or sideways and usually all three in various random sequences. Walls, floors ceilings all suddenly rushing up and trying to smack her. Or sliding away or down without warning leaving her in mid-air. Constantly trying to work out which way was up and then giving in and going with it. A real work out that her young body had actually benefited from in the end. A standard Fifty-Eight-year old woman who owned a yoga mat but never seemed to have the time to go to a class would have been black, blue and aching from head to foot. And Yunis really was an excellent sailor. But it was still properly scary.

Now that same ocean just lapped at the land, breathing gently like a big man sleeping soundly. She sighed and the warm swell in her belly washed up without bidding, but she had got re-used to that now. She allowed the warm wet feelings drift over her until her nipples tingled. There was something arousing in being young and firm all by itself. The pleasure of being desired was it? Not for her genes or what she could do for some Doctor's or Researcher's career. Desired purely. The memory she'd cultivated in that first lonely hospital room unfolded into her, all of her. The sight of her own thigh wrapped around Alfie's back. Young flexible, soft legs, her legs, contrasted against his dark and supple skin. Her fingers seemed to get more sensitive to her cold beer glass while she let herself remember the smoothness of his skin against hers. So much better than Steve. She sighed and swigged and stretched her legs. Great boots. They fit perfectly.

Not Invisible Any More

Her feet had throbbed in Tesco's, even in brogues. It had been a long day facilitating bloody Emma's own bloody fault. Was that really the same day as the letter? Must've been. Emma was gone by the next Monday. A lot had happened since then.

She lingered with the cauliflowers seeing why Medusa had got such a kick out of her affliction. He, poor boy half her age, was way off at the cheese. But he had not so nonchalantly turned his mini trolley and was heading her way with a glint in his young, rather small and beady eye. He was only trying to liven up a boring attempt at healthy eating, poor boy. And maybe get an experience or two, enough to justify the hat. It was a silly hat, not a trilby and not a pork pie. Fine Art had taught her about that innocent Greek girl turned into The Monster Medusa through no fault of her own and everyone who looked at her petrified with a disgusted expression stuck on their face. Poor girl should've had to wait for years for that.

The poor boy was taking in her rather passable silhouette, passable enough for a young man in a silly hat to take a detour in Tesco's. Maybe he needed glasses but they didn't go with the headgear? What could the hard done by and hardened woman do but learn to enjoy it. Not just look like a monster, be one. Take pleasure in the inevitable.

And Sue could appreciate it all the more when her libido had evaporated. When that warm pool of longing that ebbed and flowed constantly down in her belly was a memory. It was strange how she hadn't missed it till it came back.

He was only three feet away when she was perfectly ready to drink in the transformation. That look of cheeky flirtation turning rapidly into the horrified discovery worthy of Oedipus when he found out he had been doing the deed with his mum. He un-petrified and suddenly desperately needed some coriander. He would just have to put it down to experience.

Ho-hum-hum-drum ooh two for one on green beans again. Good news. Jo liked green beans. Now, fruit to keep Sam's pale complexion clear- and something nice for pud'.

God. Great boots and advertising standard location or not, she missed them so badly. And the everyday. Routine that had kept her so busy and so stifled for so long. Not that she had felt stifled really. She loved being a mum. Missed it. Missed it badly. She might be home in two days.

Had she thought about that other thing, which happened at the time? No, she'd been too full of that unintentional Oedipus boy and the other thing that happened in Tesco's was more usual and she had been used to it. The other thing was that she had been standing in the self-service checkout queue looking for her compact shopping bag in her handbag and a young woman had pushed past her and gone to the next available till with an apple and a bottle of water. Then, while she was there looking at the young woman a young man had walked past her and gone to the next available till with a loaf of bread and some eggs. Both of them oblivious. Like she was invisible. She had actually been invisible to them.

At the time she had let all sorts of things wash almost unnoticed through and out of her brain that had other more important things to retain; they had no idea what responsibility was, no conception of just how much a foot could throb. Was her time less precious? And the mild annoyance had melded with a minor twang of aggravation at herself for not saying, "Excuse me, there is a queue." It was her job to say that now. Also when someone dropped litter, "Excuse me you dropped something." If she didn't take on that responsibility, who would? If no-one told younger people how to queue and not drop their litter the whole world might end up like the inner London her parents believed they had evacuated after the War. Left it to the immigrants they had said. 'Dirty, full of litter and immigrants, dirty immigrants,' that what her parents had said. And she had just agreed with them hadn't she, openly at first and then more and more quietly until her daughters, and political correctness, had shouted her views down into an unremembered thought or two in Tesco's.

Now though, illegally migrated into God knows where, on the run from God knows who, stared at by the man that she had decided was a fisherman, she sighed with a deep longing to be invisible again. An invisible middle-aged woman on her way home via Tesco's. Keeping her views about immigrants to herself. On her way home to her girls. All grown up but still at home.

Who was she kidding? She had loved it. Loved touching her toes and dancing and looking fantastic. She hadn't remembered looking that fantastic last time but then no-one that age knew they were beautiful did they. Well a few did and no-one liked them. And she had spent, what fifty pounds a month, on day-cream and night-cream and primer and firming-gel, tried Plumpers, Serums and lingered longer each time on magazine adverts for injections.

How many times a week had she wished she was twenty years younger back then? Or even ten? Wished she could get away with that dress or those shoes? Wished her face was still smooth? Wished that bloody Emma didn't eye her job like a bloody vulture waiting? Wished that pain in her elbow, or her hip or whatever it was that was aching that particular morning would just shake out in ten minutes like it used to? Wished to be attractive to...to who exactly was a bit vague? She knew from the magazines that the correct answer was wanting to be attractive to herself and that it was a bit true. Who else exactly? A man? Other women? The boss, whoever he was? So many mergers. Bloody Emma?

And she had loved looking eighteen again, gone a bit wild. Oh dear. And Jo had been horrified and Sam had said nothing. Her girls with the mum who looked like their younger sister. How were they coping? Were they coping at all?

Another huge torrent of missing her lovely girls battered her into a large swig of beer. Not like when Jo left home, it had been hard on her and Sam but she had known the day would come and Jo was good at calling home. And popping round. And then she was back again of course. And

Sue's could console her, say things about fish in the sea and feed her daughter again.

"Can I just get in the front door love…and put this lot away…and maybe get a cup of tea?"

She missed them, both of them, so badly. How could she be their mum from here? They still needed her, didn't they? Not like before. But still. Look at Julie, she had missed her mum even though her mum was still there, technically. And didn't she still miss her own mum, long gone now? And she needed them, her girls, needed to see them, see they were okay, happy, healthy.

"Sorry Mum," and Jo maneuvered round her making tea while Sue got the frozen stuff into the freezer. A real double act. Sue side stepped to the fridge while sticking out her bum to let Jo stand up from under the sink, stretch sideways for the milk and wince.

"You have got to get that knee seen to, any news from the hospital? THERE'S FRUIT IN THE BOWL!"

"That's what I wanted to tell you, "Jo said beneath the thunder of a huge thing that had been so sweet as a child coming down the stairs. "…There's a letter from the Doctor's for you." And she managed to step back without too much pain as Sam careered towards the fresh apples.

"Me?" said Sue. Sam looked at her and then the fruit and grunted questioningly. "…Yes they're washed…must be my smear reminder." Now Sam winced and lumbered back upstairs with four apples, a banana and two satsumas, the peels and cores of which would only reappear when the smell reached the first-floor landing.

Jo wasn't going to let it go and flapped the envelope at her mum once she was sat down with her tea and she had stretched out her leg under the table. The letter was too fat for a smear reminder. Jo was too young to be giving her that look. Sue raised her eyebrows in maternal 'now now young lady' mode and the cheeky mare raised her eyebrows back. She had seen her mum snot nose crying in this kitchen. She had done the tea and tissue s and you're-better-off-without-him talking. She had slapped her father's face for him. She had slapped that no good ex 's face for him too and moved back home. And she had cried. She had a right to raise her eyebrows. Sue took the envelope and tore; it was probably a breast screening appointment with lots of what is breast screening leaflets.

"Who are 'Fielding and Hardy Medical Solutions...stronger, longer'?" Jo reached for the letter but Sue didn't let go and kept reading, Jo checked the envelope, it was definitely from the doctors, it had the Trust logo on and the toner was running out.

"What's 'my profile' I thought that was Facebook?"

"Give me that," said Jo and her mum let her take it from her hand this time. "...'Dear Susan Duggen' ...There is nothing to worry about... As you remember in May of last year you took part in a research questionnaire to look into the prevalence of Alzheimer's and other age-related diseases' ...?" She looked at her mum quizzically, her mum looked at her quizzically before raising her eyebrows.

"Oh yes that...I filled out a questionnaire at the doctors when I went in for my elbow...usual things...have you had heart disease, liver disease, diabetes? Tick boxes...something about chicken pox?"

"What's wrong with your elbow? You never told me?"

"It's a bit stiff, that's all...if I told you about every ache and pain at my age we'd be here till Christmas." Jo was not happy but she read on,

" … 'age related diseases… as you know the En-Aich-Ess works in partnership with various research…Care-dot-data?...research….public benefit …resources… we are writing to you because your care-dot-data profile is suitable for a trial ….aging population…Alzheimer's and other age related diseases… your participation in the 'Tip of my Tongue' study?' Did you do that Mum?"

"Oh yes, well I was dropping some bits off at the charity shop one Saturday and a man in a tabard asked me…how do they know that, the En-Aich-Ess? I gave the sample to that age charity? ...and you know, Heather…Julie's mum…and she was so exhausted and sad with it all and I thought it might help…it was only a swab, you know a giant cotton bud and signing a form." Jo looked suspicious, deeply suspicious "… It's a good cause Jo, a cure for Alzheimer's that'd be amazing, you might be grateful one day." Jo didn't want to think about her mother's getting even older and she read on,

"'…more detailed study… care-dot-data…brain…Dee-En-Ay …research…new drugs…gene therapy…a dedicated counsellor will be ringing… important advances'…Don't do it!" and she put the letter on the table emphatically and Sue picked it up again. Jo picked up the forms it came with, lots of forms. The usual name, date of birth…medical conditions. "…You'd think that if they've got all this on some mega database in the sky you wouldn't have to keep filling out all these forms…" and then Sue took them back. Jo picked up the letter again defiantly, "…It says here… 'agree that neither the En-Aich-Ess, nor any of its partners accepts any liability'…what is this? Don't do it! Liability! Bloody cheek!" and she kept reading and rubbed her knee. Sue took the letter back again and then put it down and her went head to one side,

"Do you want a hot bath?"

"Had one," Jo said and stopped rubbing, looking at her mum's wondering face. "…But seriously Mum, you're not a bloody guinea-pig…could do with a massage." And she blinked like the lovely little girl she had always been. Sue smiled and got up to get her a fresh cookie while it was still a bit warm.

She needed another beer, this time the barman dragged his feet and sneered at her when he put it on the table. It would appear that three was her limit in his eyes. In her eyes she hadn't been out in ages. Locked up for God knows how long. And then that lorry. Yunis, and his crew were all teetotal too obviously. Muslims. She'd never met any actual Muslims before and had been greatly relieved to find out that they were just like normal people except that they didn't drink.

That bloke, who was most likely Catholic, was still there looking at her as well. He just drank his drink and looked at her. Not bored at all. Sue had forgotten what that was like. She had only been out properly that once since the metamorphosis and had been so full of herself and her pert bosoms and the warm feeling back bubbling in her belly that she hadn't noticed other people. Apart from… Oh dear.

She was alone in a strange land, carrying an obviously fake passport and being looked at by a man whose employer appeared to have neglected his equal op's training refresher. Should she be worried? Perhaps he was just curious? Not many women drink alone out of doors in any nations of the world. Back home she always made sure she got to the Elizabeth after Julie and Linda. In fact, before this business, she had never been out by herself?

Did he even know he was doing it? Was it still okay to ogle women where he came from? Which was here presumably. Did he assume by her clothes or the fact she was alone in a bar that she was fair game? Was he waiting to see if someone was coming to claim her?

Of course, it could be that he understood by her demeanour that she did not wish to be disturbed, appreciated that an eighteen-year old woman who looked like a shampoo advert would not necessarily be looking for the company of a thirty-five-year-old man who obviously enjoyed his food? He was simply respecting her autonomy but he just happening to be looking this way? Was the reason he was looking at her because she had inadvertently sat in his regular seat? Curious about a mysterious woman getting off a boat late at night? Was he waiting for her to get drunk? Was he Albin? Was he a spy from Zabtrex? She had thought that Jan and that vivisectionist of a husband were holding her without his Company's knowledge. Albin had said. But what if he didn't know something?

What if someone had alerted Zabtrex to her and they had decided to kidnap her for themselves? Or they were in on it from the start? What if another huge multinational was on her tail?

Whatever the answer, she knew it was her job to work out what it was and alter her behaviour to ensure that she was allowed to carry on drinking beer in a bar in peace. She wished briefly that the metamorphosis had been to change her sex. But then she wouldn't be her. She liked being her. If she had still looked like the old her, she might've been resented if she was seen at all. But she could've relaxed a bit more, she supposed.

Fuck it! She hadn't been out since...since for at least nine months, probably longer, and she could damn well have a beer in a bar in an indeterminate Spanish speaking country if she wanted. She had lived through the fucking '60s and '70s and even the bloody '80s and she wasn't going to go through all that trying to look like she was waiting for someone, or like she knew karate, or like someone's sister or a good girl or any of those this time round.

She wouldn't miss out on looking around a new place because she was too busy keeping her head down. Was that ogling bloke aware that she still had a pair of Levis older than him? If one of her daughters had not taken the opportunity provided by her absence to nick them because they were back in again apparently?

Oh, and yes, he was clearly incognisant of the fact that she did have that Woozy or Oozy or whatever it was and that nice Yunis had shown her how to take the safety catch off. Yes indeed, fuck it!

She lit a cigarette and stretched out her legs and considered whether she had indeed had enough beer while sipping off the froth. If only she had had chicken pox. Jan had had chicken pox. Hah. She smiled again and then felt the guilt rise, then subside. Her own sister. But she did hope she wasn't dead.

That old Monday she had only just got her jacket on the back of her chair at work, not even sat down when the dedicated counsellor from the NHS or Fielding and Hardy or both or something rang. Alfie his name was. Alfie, now she remembered. Oh dear. He had turned out a bit too dedicated but there you go. His timing was great because she had needed something apparently constructive to do before Ten o'clock. She felt like she was being watched in the open plan office. Sorry 'workspace'. They didn't know what was coming. Especially bloody Emma. At Ten o'clock it would all kick off.

Sue sat down comfortably and had a nice long chat with Alfie, her dedicated counsellor without the slightest intention of volunteering for medical research. She let him regurgitate the contents of the letter as if she hadn't read it with a few 'Oh's' and 'yes'es to stretch it out. He seemed very keen to stress the partnership with the NHS. The Good-Ole-En-Aich-of-Ess. The real NHS involved waiting for an appointment, waiting for a referral, waiting for a consultation appointment, waiting for test appointments, waiting for test results, waiting for the test result appointment, then waiting for the treatment. This partnership was in far too much of a hurry. And he was just too pushy, like he was selling something. The NHS wasn't supposed to sell things. The NHS gave things, eventually. But she let him talk over her in a relaxed and convivial manner.

Oh dear. She hadn't just run away from the public-private thing had she, she'd run away from him. Or the idea of him at any rate. She was old enough to be his mother. But when they were together it looked like he was into school girls. He was her dedicated counsellor. It had been too much to deal with. If Alfie's dedication had tapered off sooner, she might'nt be sitting in a Spanish speaking bar with a fake passport and wanted in connection with murder, or attempted murder, she really did hope she was alive, while being ogled by some bloke in Spanish. Oh dear. Was that business with Alfie the last straw; what made her run away with Janet? Got her locked up? Her own sister. Her own, possibly dead, sister. She gestured for another beer and was served almost immediately.

"No, no I definitely haven't … m …all my friends, my kids, all their…it…mildly? No, I don't think…why is that import…oh okay…Yes, I can see th…Look. I can see that it's a small commitment for something that could make such a difference to so many people's lives, but I need to …and to my family…and work…I have a lot of questions…what are the risks…. okay yes face to face is better…okay," Alfie had a lot to say about privacy and security and computers in his long wind up. He gave her the distinct impression that she should be worried about privacy and security and computers. She couldn't oblige and be concerned about privacy and security and computers because a/ she was in an open plan workspace and trying to look oblivious and b/ she had pressed 'accept' a million times on phones and computers and nothing bad had ever happened, so she said, "…shall we talk about that when we meet? ... Yes…. Let… me… get… my…diary…yes…no that's not good for me…yes…half an hour later? ...yes…lovely…. okay I'll see you then…Yes…Bye Alfie." She didn't choose to share when she hung up but stood up and asked, "…Does anyone fancy a coffee?"

And there was a big blurry hand under her nose.

"You must be Sue, I'm Albin" She was shaking the big blurry hand. She had drunk more than she had realised, she hadn't been out in ages, Albin was here.

"Sorry, yes, I was miles away. Hello." And Albin sat down, appraised her so quickly she hardly noticed and ordered a beer with one finger. This was the first time that they had actually met and he looked younger than he had sounded on the phone. She appraised him at her leisure, once she had focused. She wondered if perhaps two was her limit after all.

Focusing took a little while and he had been talking about the revised plan for quite for some time before she tilted forward suddenly and said, "…I get it now! You're James Bond; the suit, the haircut, that watch. Oh and the shoes! Lovely shoes. It's the perfect disguise for a spy I must say." And she leaned back just as suddenly and beamed, almost literally and looked into his eyes. Given that he was actually going for a minor character out of Le Carre he was momentarily put off his stride, so before he could resume, she was able to pre-empt the, "…Quite," before he could actually say it. She grinned, "…I'm sorry, but I've been 'all at sea,'" and she waved her arms up and down to emphasise her point, "…for quite a while already and…what day is it by the way?" Albin smiled and said authoritatively and calmly,

"It's Thursday, you've been thr…"

"Thursday night," she smiled, "I haven't been out in ages, …and the date, what date is it?"

"The Twenty-Fourth. You've bee…"

"Of October?" He nodded,

"You've been through quite an experience haven't you Sue. How are you feeling?" He said 'how are you feeling' like women who don't like each other say 'how are you feeling' when they have to say it because something horrible has happened. Sue's back was actually put up. She also fell back and said,

"How do you think I feel?" A little more aggressively that she was used to, causing her to become momentarily confused at the sound of her own voice.

"I'm sorry. Of course, … I can't begin to imagine how difficult this has been for you…" Sue didn't listen for a bit because she was too busy frowning at Albin's lack of imagination, of course he could begin to imagine, a bit, surely. "…the important thing is that we've met finally now and we can start to get you home. It's been very difficult for you but…"

"You sound like you're picking up a dippy girlfriend who got on the wrong train," said Sue before she could stop herself. "…no, no, sorry. But really. I am actually old enough to be your mum and got out of Zurich without you so…"

"Yes, your initiative and bravery in successfully getting yourself to Puerto Rico during hurricane season is admirable," said Albin. So she was in Puerto Rico, very nice. "…any other interested parties have definitely been put off the scent, there are quite a few interested parties but your initiat…"

"Perhaps…Puerto Rico was a bit of a long way round but I was in a very difficult situation…"

"But you're safe now and back in British, safe hands. We are going to remain off the grid you so successfully circumvented, just to be safe. It really was a stroke of…"

"…circumnavigated more like. That's just the way it worked out, who are the interested parties anyway?"

"Oh the usual suspects, You-Ess, China, and of course Zabtrex. But they are all scrabbling around Europe trying to pick up your trail, it really was…"

"…Luck, that's all, and there were storms off the Canary Islands and we couldn't…and I've always wanted to go to the Canary Islands and you've got a…you never turned up at the hospital and I did manage to escape and I have found this whole thing…"

"Peeving?" And he smiled now.

"Yes, peeving, that's it peeving. No offence Albin but it might be as well to remember that I got myself out of Zurich without you and I am old enough to be your mum." Drunk people do repeat themselves.

"Yes of course Sue, you did…and everyone is full of admiration for you and what you are doing. Very brave and…public spirited." Sue frowned again; he had said public spirited like it was stupid. And him a public servant.

34

She had paid her taxes, for his bloody James Bond bloody suit and...but she must remember to be nice. She stopped frowning and tried to look intent. She saw him look a bit worried and turned down the intent. He was still talking, "...Time is, however, of the essence and...I assume you do want to be back in England for the results of the Public Inquiries, don't you?"

"Not really. I just want to see my kids. I don't see why I have to be there really? For the inquiries I mean...I'm not really that important am I. My Dee-En-Aye is a coincidence isn't it...a Dee-En-Aye lottery, that's all. I don't really understand why there needs to be a big results-of-the-inquiry thing. I mean... people are interested enough with just the facts, aren't they?"

"Not my department, I'm afraid. My job is to get you back to Blighty. Quietly." And he smiled ironically. She didn't ".... But you want to be back home as soon as possible?" Said the overtly tailored public servant. She did. She wanted to see her kids. "...can we get on with the plan now?" She nodded assent. "...Alrighty then: there is no direct flight and so we will fly to Houston, Texas, once there we will immediat...."

"Is there any news about my sister?"

"We'll cover that in the debriefing at the house. There is much you can tell us too. When we get to..." that was a bit heartless thought Sue,

"My sister. Jan. Is she alive?"

"Yes of course she's alive, she's fine?... Are you talking about that concussion? Your sister is in perfect health...a bit of a headache, that's all. Look, I need to give you an outline of the plan so that I know you agree and we can go," so Sue had not murdered, or attempted to murder, her sister. She sighed.

"That's a relief," she said and went back to resenting her little sister with a clear conscience.

"Yes, good. Once we're in London you will remain…"

"And the children. How are the children?"

"What chil…oh your children. Yes, they're fine and looking forward to seeing you home. In London you will be k…"

"AND they have had chickenpox…who's us, is there someone else here?

"No, no it's just me, we don't think you're in any real danger. Your sister and her husband are co-operating and appear to have been working independently…amateurs…Zabtrex is cooperating fully. I just need to inform you of…"

"Isn't everyone nowadays…. working independently…" Albin looked worried. "…Can't you tell me all this on the way to the house, what house is it anyway? Does it have a bath or a shower?"

"Er, I'm not sure, a bath I think, both? …I'd like to tell you now, if I may. I need to know that you know and understand the plan and that you agree…"

"Is that procedure? Do I need to agree?" Albin sighed,

"I need to know that you know and unders…"

"It is procedure, isn't it? Look, my new passport's rubbish, it wouldn't fool anyone at Dover, I've only just found out what country I'm in, the world and his wrinkly wife wants to kidnap me and all I've got is two sets of clothes, a few hundred euros and a woozy…I'm feeling woozy," she would keep her right to bear arms for a little while longer she realised. Why was that? "… I miss my girls, my best friend's mum's not well and I need to get back for work at some point to sort out the voluntary retirement thingy and I haven't had a decent cup of tea in ages so I damn well have to agree don't I. No choice." She had stopped talking but Albin was still chugging his beer.

"The car's over here." He said and the world lurched almost as much as it had on the boat on the way to it.

"I haven't been out in ages," she explained as Albin took her arm before realising that was a mistake and letting go. "…Is this your first time you know 'in the field'?"

"What? No, no. I've been in the service for…I'm Thirty-Five," but Sue wasn't listening because she was waving toodleloo in Spanish to the bloke who had ogled her. When in Rome.

No Deodorant

Debriefing was boring. Boring and frustrating. Sue had lived through the whole thing already and any questions she had like, "Where were you? You were supposed to be at the door at three o'clock if it wasn't for Yus...that security guard I'd still be in that room, or worse!" or "...Why couldn't you pick me up in Milan or somewhere?" were not answered. Nor did he answer any other sorts of questions really. Not even if he had had a pleasant flight. That can't have been an official secret and he must've flown, and even if he didn't, he could still have made conversation.

Still, Albin had sat back and let her sober up with a potter in the strange kitchen and make a cup of tea, even if the milk did taste funny. He appeared slightly bemused to begin with but then saw that Sue was more relaxed and talkative if he just let her get on with investigating cupboards and drawers as if she was getting her bearings in a holiday cottage.

It was a holiday villa, he told her that much. They would fly to the US tomorrow and from there to the UK. He did not hide his annoyance at having to come all the way to Puerto Rico. But she hadn't much choice, the people she had had to 'bribe' had already planned their trip. She had spent several days in the back of a lorry and Yunis couldn't drop her off at the Canary Islands as originally agreed because of the weather. It had been a rough trip.

"Have you ever tried to make flasks of coffee when there's a storm brewing? It's not easy…" And she left out the bit where Yunis had been impressed by her bringing the flask to the wheelhouse. How he had warmed to her when she had demonstrated a simple lower back strengthening exercise after she noticed him rubbing his 'trouble'. How they had laughed when a wave landed her on her bum for the first time. He was going straight and the drugs he was running were very expensive state of the art anti-inflammatories for his mother in law. His cousin Yusef, who worked as a security guard at the hospital in which Jan had imprisoned Sue, had intended to steal the drugs. Yunis simply drove up to the factory to pick up the drugs from whence he would drive down to his boat.

He was going through Italy to buy some legitimate leather goods to sell to tourists in the Caribbean, as well as pick up for his wife an anniversary hand-bag in Milan. Sue was simply added baggage on a trip that had been planned for months. She certainly left out the bit where his mother-in-law lived a few miles down the coast. She did hope she was feeling better. She had had an amazing life and deserved a peaceful and pain free retirement. Also, the bit where he had sold her the mini-Oozy at what was probably a very reasonable price when the storm had abated. "…This one sways a lot less, this kitchen." The kitchen was surprisingly well stocked for a safe house. Not just a tin opener and a couple of cups but all the things you would find in a normal kitchen. There was even a torch under the sink.

Albin appeared interested in the security guard until Sue made it clearly vague that he was just an immigrant who couldn't speak English or French and she had bribed him into getting her the money and the phone. She left out how he had felt sorry for her and helped her, even taken her to his place and rung his cousin when Albin hadn't shown up. Also, that it was her who had gone back and broken into the storage room and taken the drugs for his cousin Yunis's mother-in-law's foot.

Albin was more interested in where she had got the money from. She said she had paid him and another man who was coincidentally robbing the hospital with the Euros she, not Yusef, had been withdrawing from a cash machine near the hospital almost since her first day in Zurich. She had been suspicious of her sister as soon as Jan said they would go straight from the airport to the hospital when Jan had originally said they would go and stay at her house. At first, she had just thought a bit of cash might be handy if she decided to go home. Albin was strangely suspicious at that point,

"So Oskar had your passport and your mobile phone but not your cash card?"

"Oh, I always keep my cash card in my wash kit, and my wash kit in my handbag... In case I need to brush my teeth, or get I mugged. Only when I'm travelling. I travel a lot for work you know. Not like this but...I've got an old card in my purse. Just in case I get frog marched to the cashpoint like happened to the Director of Marketing at Delele's you know, they do those transparent kettles? Very nice product. Oskar's got my old card from an account I hardly use. I've still got mine, look" And she rummaged for a long time in her hold-all before showing it to him. That seemed to satisfy him.

She described how they had insisted more and more forcefully that she stay, until they locked her up. She couldn't say why she was suspicious to begin with, but she had been right, hadn't she? His staring more than he should made her a bit uncomfortable, but she understood it. She was 58 and looked like a school girl. She was young and attractive on the outside and could knock him up an omelette as good as his mum's. While she cooked and cleaned up, his eyes followed her around, well not her, her bum, which she had never thought of as her best feature, but there you go. She had missed pottering about in a kitchen and chatted away with a cloth in her hand even though there was nothing more to say and the kitchen was spotless.

"I wouldn't've slept with a messy kitchen downstairs," she said, "...and I'm sober now."

The water in the safe house wouldn't be hot until the morning and the wind was rather loud. But this land-lubbing bed was comfy, wide and stable. She would be able to roll over without having to wake up a little bit first. But she did not let herself go to sleep immediately. She had to try and figure out why she had done her contingency plan in the kitchen. Why she suspected Albin the same way she had suspected her sister. And she had been right about Jan, hadn't she? She also needed some wondering time.

She was in a safe villa in a proper bed with a proper spy who looked like James Bond looking after her. But it still felt to her like she couldn't relax. Maybe she was just used to being suspicious now. Why hadn't she told Albin about the Oozy? Why had she prepared the kitchen?

She had had good instincts about Jan, that's why she had got Yusef to take all that cash out in 300-euro withdrawals for a reasonable percentage. But she knew Jan. She was in safe hands now wasn't she? Why had she trusted Yusef and Yunis but now felt so uncomfortable with Albin? They were all involved in moving people about the globe unofficially. Yunis more unofficially, he took money from desperate people. She had read about people like him in the Metro. Although to be fair, his boat was in excellent condition and what he had described sounded a bit like a ferry service from one side of the Mediterranean to the other.

And he didn't do it much nowadays anyway. Now he was a family man. He had met Maria renting out his boat for a fishing trip just as he was beginning to go straight. It was love at first sight. The boy was four now. What did Yunis say his name was? Adam. Little Adam with the lovely eyes. Yunis had shown her a clip of him with his mother and grandmother on a beach on his phone. Both he and his wife came from long lines of fishermen. Now, both families had been forced out of the trade by 'Europe'. Maria's family had lost out from quotas in Spain and Yunis' family could not compete with the massive floating fish factories off the coast of Somalia.

Now, Maria's grandfather took tourists on tours around the Southern Coast of Spain, and so had Yunis in a manner of speaking. He had started his tours from Tunisia that's all. Until the 'bad bad men' had taken over.

Yunis only did unofficial ferrying as favours nowadays. Well paid favours it was true. But he was such a nice man. It really was a shame they weren't going to stay in touch.

But Albin? She didn't know anything about Albin. With anyone else she would have found out their backstory within five minutes of meeting them, but not Albin, which was also a stupid name by the way. But Albin was a UK Government employee, he was her rescuer. So why had she done that thing under the sink, been so careful about the Oozy?

She had learned rather late in the day to be suspicious of Government employees after the drugs trial gone wrong or right or whatever, but that wasn't it. He had missed their appointment in Zurich because of 'security issues'. He was purposefully blank. He didn't need to be that blank.

He was a bit condescending too. The way he explained the itinerary as if she was twelve or hard of hearing. Mind you, he was a professional having to deal with amateurs, was that it? When he looked at her, he didn't see her somehow. See beyond the shampoo advert blonde, through to her. That was a big flaw in a spy surely? Maybe he was fed up because he was 'acting down' or something. She decided she didn't like him but would try and be more trusting in the morning and let herself fall fast asleep in the proper bed.

Then there was a big hard hand in front of her face.

Albin was jolly and enthusiastically making toast when Sue shook into the kitchen at eight, with the sea salt that had caked in her nose washed out and fake tanned and dressed as planned.

"Feeling that beer now?" He joked and Sue glowered, her wet hair in strings round her head.

"Any tea?" She said and she opened the cupboard underneath the sink before sighing weakly.

"No problem," smiled Albin indulgently. He opened the cupboard over the counter and got out a cup before he put the kettle on. "...wasn't there a hairdryer in your room?"

"Huh?" He didn't bother repeating the question. She moaned faintly and then loud and he poured a little milk into the cup. She sat down,

"I'll have mine without milk...aren't you going to say anything about last night?" He didn't turn round, but began making another cup of tea without resentment. He was in a cheerful mood. She moaned again. "...I think there's sugar in the cupboard...no that one...at the back...behind the...that's it...two please." He rummaged through a couple of drawers to find another teaspoon. All the teaspoons seemed to be in different places.

"What about it...did you sleep okay?" No reply, just another grunt. "... Need a sugar boost ah,"

"No I bloody didn't sleep okay." He took the teabag out of the cup and left it on the side, "...aren't you going to put that in the bin?" She said hastily and gruffly. He did as he was told before turning around to put the tea on the table for the woman who had taken the safety catch off her Oozy.

44

His eyes widened and his hand went back to the cup of hot liquid.

"Don't! Put your hands behind your head and kneel down. Now!" He moved slowly and acquiesced.

"Okay, okay...you know I'm here to help don't you...I have a clear br..."

"Oh shut up Albin! I'm the one with the W... Oozy." His eyes swivelled up to look at her

"Sue you're shaking! ...you've been under a lot of str..."

"SHUT UP! Yes I'm bloody shaking and my aim is prob'ly rubbish so even if I don't want to I am liable to shoot you if you don't bloody...! Stress he says!"

"I don't understand...I..."

"Which bit of shut up don't you understand! ... I don't know what they told you at spy college but there is no such thing as a truth serum and why did you not think I wouldn't remember! 'This is a dream...you need to talk but you can't do it when you're awake you're talking in your dream'" She misquoted in an effeminate and patronising voice. "...I've been living on my wits for a while now...My dreams don't usually involve interrogations and needles. Did you take a sample of my blood?! ...There's beaches and sunshine and cocktails and...and what did you think I wasn't telling you anyway? There was nothing else to bloody say! My sister's a bitch and ... and my Dee-En-Aye is worth a lot of money...and no amount of Pee-Ar can put a positive spin on the way I have been treated. Any other kind of truth doesn't come out when you're drugged up any way." Albin sighed; he had certainly neglected to ask her if she had an Oozy concealed under the sink.

"Oh," he said, contrary to instructions but she let it go and moved round the kitchen table keeping the shivering Oozy more or less pointed at him

"…Oh, I felt like talking all right, it works that way! It felt good talking there's no denying it and what I said was sort of true, but it also sort of wasn't and…well the gun's a surprise isn't it…. you've wasted taxpayers' money on serums…But there's no deodorant? No! … what is this any way? You are Em-Eye-Five or Six aren't you?" Albin nodded while Sue picked the strip of gaffer tape dangling off the edge of the table and kicked him flat onto the floor in her great boots.

Since she had not felt entirely comfortable with Albin last night, she had pottered around the kitchen hiding her Oozy next to a roll of gaffer tape, a torch, just in case, and some kitchen scissors. In the unlikely event that a spy on a mission wanted to find a dustpan she had placed a tea-towel over the entire precautionary kit. She knew she might be a bit paranoid but she had learned not to be trusting and there was no harm in holding on to an Oozy just in case. Albin had got used to her opening and closing cupboards and blethering on like his mum the night before. While he made tea from ingredients and utensils she had spread in random drawers and cupboards, she had got out her Oozy and quickly cut the gaffer tape into strips hiding the noise with the grunts and groans of a genuine hangover.

"This isn't…." But the gaffer tape was over his mouth now. This woman had wrapped a lot of odd shaped parcels in her time, some for overseas. He wasn't going to get loose unless she wanted him to.

"So you thought you'd do a bit of freelance did you, is that it?" She said as she pulled his arms behind his back with all the skill of a person experienced in getting busy toddlers into jumpers and undressing lively drunks. Except this time she didn't care if he winced. He shook his head and snorted "...well there is a lot of money involved...thought you'd sell me back did you? Oh don't worry I'm not going to interrogate you, waste of bloody time." She probably overdid the gaffer tape but she was new to this sort of thing. "...You asked all the wrong questions...I would have told you things but you didn't ask me about them....and drugs company questions, not Government questions...well some Government questions but mainly drugs company ones." Sue mused as she straddled Albin. She frisked him with the deftness that can find a pink felt pen nib in the tiny pointless pocket of a pair of jeans before putting on a load of whites.

Of course, with all this public private-partnership business nowadays it was hard to tell what sort of question was which. She would probably have told him all about Yusef and Yunis and his mother-in-law and Maria and little Adam, but he didn't ask about them at all. All he wanted to know about was if she had talked to anyone about her 'condition' and her bloody sister. "...Actually, second thoughts; did Jan put you up to this? Or her husband? That blood sucking human vivisectionist bastard?" He shook his head and looked up at her pleadingly like a naughty child who hadn't done it this time.

She had his phone, his car keys, a small handgun and his wallet, leaned over and put them on the table. What next? She stood up over Albin and narrowed her eyes. A map, possibly a better passport, a map or a phone with an app or something, she couldn't bother Yunis again he had done enough already, and he had to look after his mother-in-law after the op, more money if possible, oh and deodorant, she was out of deodorant. Looking down at the thoroughly taped young man, she took a sip of tea,

"…lovely. Nothing like the first sip of tea in the morning," she lied because she took hers with milk and without sugar but had needed more time. She went upstairs to search his room. She had spent hours wondering why Albin had seen fit to interrogate her. It was perfectly possible that it was normal spy procedure and he fully intended to help her get home. It was also perfectly possible that it wasn't and he wasn't and she had to get away just in case.

His bag was packed on the bed and all she had to do was rummage through it. Car hire documents, a bit of cash, two American passports and two plane tickets to Houston. No others to London. Some 'trying too hard' sunglasses. She would wonder about using the tickets on the way. She took them with her with the full intention of dobbing him in as soon as possible.

A little silver box with rounded corners. She opened it and found a syringe and a little tube of red liquid. He had taken a sample of her blood. She threw it on the tiled floor and crushed it under a great boot. Analyse that. He was working for Zabtrex, or Oskar on his own, she was pretty sure now. He had failed to turn up the last time on purpose, probably.

Now what? Call 911? Puerto Rico was American wasn't it? Explain to the American authorities that she was a 58 year old domestic appliance designer who had undergone a clinical drugs trial into Alzheimer's disease which had nearly killed her but she had woken up in the body of a eighteen-year-old woman, become disillusioned with her own country's public private partnership and so gone to Switzerland with her sister who had locked her up so she had escaped with the help of illegal people traffickers and travelled Europe in the back of a lorry before sailing across the Atlantic to deliver some anti-inflationary drugs to a Puerto Rican national whose insurance wouldn't cover them before meeting someone she thought was a spy from her Government but he was probably working for her brother-in-law or a multi-national drugs conglomerate or both? They'd lock her up. And maybe Yunis too? Or Yunis's mother-in-law, and she wasn't well.

Angela, she could call Angela. Dr Carter was a respected medical ethicist with high up connections and they got on really well. She understood and explained the left-and-right handed Octopus of public and private and semi-public and semi-private bodies who were involved in Sue's 'condition'. Angela worked for the Medical and Health Research Council, which was semi-public, a quango. She'd been really helpful in London when she was getting better and then again when Yusef had finally got her the phone in Zurich, got her in touch with 'Security Services'.

49

Or Alfie? Alfie didn't know anyone. Angela was the only one who could explain things to people who could help back in London. I wasn't Angela's fault if the Security Services had gone freelance. This time, Angela could talk to the Department of Health people who had called her a national asset, they could talk to someone in America. She should go to the British Embassy and wait for it all to be sorted out.

But Albin? What if they believed Albin and not her? Albin had been referred to her by that man from Scotland Yard. Albin was a real spy who was working for or with Zabtrex or not and could tell people anything he liked and take her away again. In Zurich Jan and Oskar had got her certified on top of everything else and he could say at any time that she was mad. She would have to get home under her own steam and without anyone who might believe Albin knowing about it. Then she would call Angela.

She nipped back into the kitchen on the way out and picked up his valuables. He had wiggled himself up into a sitting position.

"I'll let someone know you're here as soon as I'm safe Albin, or far away enough, so it shouldn't be too long, bye." He was too busy snorting to hear.

A strong, warm wet breeze breathed into her as she blinked into the bright sunlight and looked up. The sky was all ready for a Baroque Annunciation. There were those grey-pink wispy clouds dotted around at tasteful intervals. Shafts of the purist sunlight pierced down to earth. And the sky was showing off a bit with how much azure it had at its disposal.

The house was quite high up on a mountain and she could see others around her. Underneath was different; a variety of greens and pinks that would have done an Impressionist proud. it was her first actual sight of 'tropical'. Lush. The grass, the trees, the shrubs, all of them were lush. Steaming. A diamond dew was evaporating in the valley below and fading up into the blue. She took in a big whiff of powerful, sweet and damp clean Puerto Rican air and got into the car.

She hadn't driven for ages, not since they built that new Tesco's oh so conveniently between the station and her front door. She put on the sunglasses. She had never driven an automatic before. She wondered what side of the road they drove on in Puerto Rico as she typed the words San Juan from the plane ticket into the satnav. A strip of black tarmac wove down between big leaved trees in front of her. She had to concentrate deeply in an unfamiliar car on the unfamiliar roads, which curved steeply. It was a scary drive and she had to say 'Siento' and smile for two near misses.

When the road flattened out and she neared the airport she kept veering onto the wrong side of the road every time she checked the satnav. Which meant her deep resentment for her little sister (who was not even nearly dead and was probably definitely working in cahoots with James Bond back there) had turned into full scale anger by the time she got to the airport. It was not the lady in the airport café's fault and she apologised after asking for a coffee and a pastry in too nasty a tone. Her own sister.

Jan had been more than just a total selfish cow this time. She had turned up in her designer shoes two weeks after the welts started clearing up, after the hard part - typical, and acted all concerned. Oskar was a specialist in anti-aging she had said. Yes, a specialist sadist. Her own sister. Jan had said all that stuff about the NHS. Appealed to the last time they had had a political discussion, when Sue had spouted on and Jan had sat and eaten one portion of mince at their mum's in about 1979; State monopolies. Inefficiencies. Lack of competition. Complacent. Too Many Managers. She hadn't thought that Jan had really been listening.

Sue had more or less forgotten she'd ever thought that way. And even back then, she was just showing off really. To be part of it all. The 'rolling back of the frontiers of the state' stuff seemed so long ago. But Jan had been listening and Sue had felt surprised and reassured. And Sue had augmented what she said with more up to date things herself; Emma's knee, A&E waiting times, Julie's mum, Whipps bloody Cross Hospital, the public private chaos when she got sick, nobody knowing what had happened to her. And Jan had used fear too, mentioned the C word a lot. She pushed Alfie's reassuring face into her mind with that stupid talk about getting run over by a bus tomorrow. Oh dear.

If it hadn't've been for Yusef, she might still be locked in that hospital room in Zurich, or worse. She fumed and bit into the pastry without tasting. The time Jan hit her too hard with that fire iron when she was Nine and Jan was Five and she had got the blame, fused effortlessly this more current betrayal. The time Jan had got her husband to lock Sue in a hospital room and experiment on her for her own selfish ends. Her smug rich husband with the good job who turned out to be a human vivisectionist.

Sue wasn't entirely blameless, looking younger, and therefore prettier, than Jan for the first time in their lives had felt good and maybe she had rubbed it in a bit, overdone the 'I hate being objectified' talk.

But Jan had been doing that to her for years from that bloody mansion with the bloody 'help' she couldn't get any 'good' of nowadays. And she did hate being objectified, she hadn't really understood what it meant till she had woken up looking 30 years younger and all those people had poked her, prodded her, talked about her as if she wasn't there...had treated her like an object. But she had also spent the best part of 40 years putting up with the 'I'm so skinny and eat so much...I'm sure they're making size Eights bigger than they used to' bullshit from her younger prettier sister.

Besides, looking older than your failure of an older sister who had married that good for nothing till he left her, oh she never said as much but it was always written all over her face, was no reason to kidnap her was it? Her own sister.

The pastry was gone without her even noticing. She gulped down her coffee as the tannoy announced her check in. Her own sister. Was she really in cahoots? Who with? If Albin was lying then she could still be 'at large' and looking for her? But he might have told the truth about that. The Swiss police must've been called when the alarm went off after she broke into that store-room for Yunis's mother-in-law's foot medicine. He didn't ask about that, why not? He had not asked anything about her health at all? She didn't know who was who or what was what and she would have to find out.

But first she had to get back to England without anyone noticing. She had done some crimes herself; she might be on a list. Then Albin might get out of the gaffer tape and report her…or come after her. She got panicky. She should not be here. She should be ringing the doctor again about her daughter's knee. She should be figuring out how to get Sam out of her room. She should not be flying out of Puerto Rico on a fake passport. She had not taken the hire car back to the depot. There were two guns under the back seat. She had broken lots of laws all over the place. She only had hand-luggage; didn't they get suspicious if you only had hand-luggage? Her hand luggage mainly contained passports, cash, and a man's wallet. She had forgotten to get deodorant.

Her heart was beating very fast and she knew she looked very guilty handing over her passport, which only made her heart beat faster. She could feel the sweat forming on her forehead. She hadn't felt that hot since the menopause. But the man at the gate only noticed her chest heaving. That sort of helped. Her fear morphed easily back into anger, and she snatched her passport back with a,

"Do you mind!" Something she would have never done thirty years ago. As she was walking away, she realised that she should have used an American accent to match the passport. But she could feel the official eyes on her bum and she swayed her hips a little bit more to be on the safe side. Hypocritical? Yes. Necessary under the circumstances? Also Yes.

Once on the plane she ordered a beer. It was 10:30 in the morning. She knew she was probably drinking too much at the moment but then again, she had eighteen-year-old liver. She knew she had to stop thinking about Jan, she could think about that later.

She began to doubt her instincts. Albin had not looked her in the eye but that was no reason was it? Lots of people didn't look other people in the eye and they were just shy or brought up that way. Truth serums and blood tests were probably MI5 or 6's procedures, they were spies after all. Perhaps he was just going to take her home? Perhaps she should not have gaffer taped him up so thoroughly? What if he dehydrated? Why hadn't he asked about her health? Back home the Government, in the form of doctors and nurses and Angela and even the Minister's something or other were always asking about her health. She had to stop thinking about Albin. He was young, he'd be fine. She had to think about herself and how she was going to get home.

She would need airfare. She had money but not enough for a flight from Houston to London. Where would five hundred and fifty euros get her? That's all she had left and she couldn't use her card or Albin or someone might find her, she had seen it in the films.

It wasn't a matter of picking which of her friends could help her. If it was Europe she would be able to rely on a large network of domestic-electrical related contacts. But Americans had never taken to electric kettles. Sue only knew one person in America.

Was he still in America? Yes, Jo had shown her that Facebook post. There was no-one else. Only Steve. She didn't want to think about Steve. Twenty-four years. Twenty-four years where she had worked her butt off, no time for her painting, no, it was all about him. Twenty-four years of drawing kettles and keeping the girls out of the way for his painting for what? As soon as he started selling he was off. Off with a Twenty-five-year-old who hadn't dropped out of Art School to draw kettles.

Sue gulped back a tear. Not because of Steve, not because of Meggie, she was a nice enough girl. Because of her. Why had she dropped out? Why had she had so little faith in herself, she was good, really good. She sucked in that revelation with another swig of beer at half-past-Ten in the morning. She had been good hadn't she. But this wasn't helping. She would have to ask Steve for help. She really didn't want to do that. He hadn't just left her. He had left his daughters too. Just upped sticks and left.

Jo was in the middle of her A-levels and Sam was only Nine but he felt stifled. Who does that? Stifled. She'd give him bloody stifled.

She really, really didn't want to ask Steve for help. She sighed and had finished her first beer by 10:45 in the morning. A bloke in the middle aisle was looking at her. He saw her notice and smiled. He looked nice. She smiled back. Perhaps she didn't have to ask for help from her ex?

As far as Steve was concerned she was a Fifty-Eight-year old brunette. Mother to his daughters, one of whom was blonde. Ooh she was good at sneaky. Drawing kettles, and the odd toaster, for years, staying in the game, requires sneaky. Look at how she let taut faced tight arsed bloody Emma get herself into that coffee maker mess. Look how

56

she got out of Zurich. And here. She would need to ring the girls, which was risky but would also be wonderful. To hear their voices. She welled up at the thought.

She sat up. She would call them on Albin's phone as soon as they landed. She could read his messages too. Maybe she could find out if he was a bad guy or not. She rummaged in her jacket pocket and got out the phone. 'Enter pin'. Why would a spy not have a pin? That was probably lesson one in Spy College. She sighed and put the phone back in her pocket. Then she took it out again and turned it off with a vague TV infused fear about tracing or something. Then she dropped it between the seats smiling sweetly at the businessman next to her. He rolled his eyes and didn't notice. She would have to buy a new phone in Houston. Two; one to phone 911 about Albin. Then she would phone her girls on another one and hear their voices and possibly find a way to get out of America without her having to ask Steve for help. The steward took away her glass and she stretched out her legs and fell asleep for the rest of the flight.

Meeting Up with the In-laws

Outside the phone outlet Sue pulled the phone out of the box like a junky in need of a fix. In a quiet corner of the airport concourse she was shaking as she dialled the only number she knew off by heart. There was a pause. The phone began to ring in an international purr. She heard a harassed late for something say,

"Hello."

"Hello…Sam…is that you?"

"Mum!?" Sue burst into tears.

"Yes Sam hello…how are you?" She could hear Sam's thunder on the stairs, she must be on the cordless. More tears came.

"Oh my God! Mum! Where are you? Are you okay!"

"Yes I'm fine Sam are you okay?"

"Yes yes we're fine. Oh My God! Jo! Jo! It's mum!... Mum...No. No don't get up, here."

"Hello mum?" It was Jo, more thundering in the background

"Hello Jo? What's wrong, why can't you get up?"

"Mum!? Where are you? Are you okay? It's okay it's okay I've just had my knee done that's all, Mum where are you?"

"Yes, yes I'm fine…You got your knee done!?" And Sue heard a click as Sam picked up the extension.

"Yes, at last. It's fine Mum. But Mum!?"

"How are you managing? They said you had to keep it up for…"

"Yes Mum I'm fine, Sam is looking after me…she can cook! But…"

"Mum, where are you? All sorts of people have been asking us…are you okay?" Said Sam. Sue took a deep breath and found her this-is-serious-but-manageable-no-more-discussion-now-you-have-to-listen-to-mum tone.

"I'm in…a safe place, it's a long story which I'll tell you soon, I'll be home soon but now I need to know that you two are okay, …" and she paused for a response.

"Yes Mum, we're fine," they chorused, if not actually reverting to do-as-you're-told then doing a great impression. Sue 's voice was a little shaky.

"Good, now, I need both of you to keep this conversation to yourselves for the time being. I'm afraid that the Em-Eye-Five or Six person who was sent to help me has gone freelance, …" and she paused for another affirmation. "…Good. Now I need to know who exactly has rung since…in the last couple of weeks…"

"God Mum who hasn't…Oskar of course, he seemed very worried, he said you were…"

"Pay no attention to that bastard…" She heard the shock of mum swearing, "…anyone else, a man called Albin J…Johnson?"

"No? …Ava someone? Angela, Some people from the En-Aich-Ess, Age You-Kay, Dee-Be-Eye-Ess, The Alzheimer's Association, Em-Ar-Cee, Aich-Cee-Aye, Cee-Aye-Gee…Gee-Tee-Aye-Cee, En-Eye-Gee…Journalists Mum…foreign ones as well…the police…security se…"

"Ava Jones yes, works for the Minister of Health. Tell her nothing… Angela good, anyone else, who from the En-Aich-Ess?" Any one could say they were from the En-Aich-Ess.

"Loads…lots of times…the police, they said that if you contacted…."

"Don't talk to the police until I get back…until I say okay…it's just…bad apples you know?" She did not tell them about the conversation with Andy. She hadn't told anyone about the conversation with Andy. Least of all Julie, his wife. She had just gone out into the garden and cried.

"Okay?   …Mum   they   said…   you   were psychotic…the trauma had…"

"No more than usual Samantha…Look I can't say I'm feeling great but I'm okay…My Dee-En-Aye is very valuable and your Auntie Jan has been very bad…. I'm afraid that people saying they're from the Government can't be trusted at the moment, there is a lot of money involved potentially…and a lot of Government…We can sort all this out once I'm home. Has anyone else tried to contact you?"

"No… I don't think…er…what about Angela, wanting to talk to both of us about your wishes and feelings, mental health, again, she's Government isn't she sort of?" It was very early in the morning.

"Okay. Angela? No that's not…she's nice…but? Not even Angela for the time being. Just in case. Look, I need to know if either of you have been in contact with your dad?" And she received a loyal collection of,

"What…no…why" s from her daughters.

"Good, well not good but you know what I…Right. Good. That's all I need to know at the moment…Sam…"

"Yes?"

"Well done for looking after Jo. I knew you could do it" This was a lie; she hadn't given Sam credit for anything except turning up for college nearly every day.

"I'm not doing anything really just…"

"But still, it's reassuring Sam, I should be there…" But this time Jo interrupted,

"No Mum, why should you? …I'm fine…You need to think about you…"

"Yes I know I know it's just I've missed you and you've had your knee done…it's such a relief to hear you, …" and Sue burst into tears again.

"Mum we're fine," came the weeping chorus down the phone from three thousand miles away. Sue gulped and sniffed,

"Sam, I need you to find my address book, it's in the dining table drawer," she could hear Sam was on the move, "…. Can you tell me Dad's number?"

"Are you going to call him? Mum?" Asked Jo confused.

"I've got to…I need his help. Don't worry," and Sam read out the number while Sue scribbled it down on the back of her old plane ticket.

"Thanks, I've got to go now girls," and she and they sobbed again, "…I'll be back soon. Your dad's going to help me…just if he phones for any reason say Sam has been away studying and you haven't heard from her in ages…or me," she could almost see their confused wet faces. "…I'll explain later," she said in the tone she used when she was late for work. She heard their sniffs and their acquiescence and their intention to talk to each other earnestly as soon as she hung up. This was reassuring, they had each other. "…I'll see you soon, very soon, a few days at the most."

"Yes, Mum, but…"

"Don't worry about me I'm a tough old bird," she said in her bedtime story voice.

"But Mum…"

"Don't worry, seriously. I'm getting quite good at getting out of situations. This one is easy; there's clean toilets and phones…I'll call you as soon as I can…don't tell anyone yet. Unless? If Julie calls you can talk to her…no, no don't, she's stressed enough as it is."

"She has already, she's very worried, everyone's so worried mum."

"Angela can help Mum, let us talk to her…"

"No. Not yet Jo. Just to be on the safe side…wait till I'm home…unless she calls okay? You can tell her I've rung and I am on my way home… I'm just being on the safe side you know…There's probably nothing to w... Oh ye of little faith. I'm on my way now girls and I'll call as soon as I can. I love you" Just as if she was off to work again.

"We love you Mum…look after yourself."

"We love you Mum…"

"Look after that knee." And she hung up before anyone who might be trying to trace the call could hear some really serious crying. She hadn't noticed the nice lady her real age walking towards her. She appeared at Sue's shoulder with a tissue. She looked at Sue and rummaged in a large black handbag to give her two more. The nice lady her age gave her a smile,

"It'll work out honey," she said to the to-all-the-world 18-year-old pretty girl crying in the airport and she walked away, pulling a small black wheeled suitcase behind her. And Sue choked out another gust of grief. She should be the nice lady her own age. She should be on a boring business trip, with a handbag full of tissues and no doubt a small sewing kit and some paracetamol. She had small black suitcase on wheels just like that one back home in Chingford.

All she had now was a cheap Italian hold-all full of fake passports, someone else's wallet, horrible sunglasses, a wedge of cash she'd just changed into not enough dollars to get her home and boots that might look great but really pinched her pinkie toes.

She should be a few hours away from home with a loathing for her own wobbly belly. She wanted her old achy hips back. That swimsuit dress. She wanted her girls. She wanted to moan about the state of the kitchen. What was Sam doing to her kitchen? She never washed up properly? She wanted Linda and Julie and a bottle of wine.

She was so lonely. She wanted perfect strangers to talk to the old inoffensive her about nothing in particular in familiar transport hubs. She had been away so long and simply walking along was so hard because she looked so different and it was hard to get used to or remember how it all worked. This youth was exhausting. She wanted to be with people who knew her. Not shampoo advert her but her, the inside her.

Just then a taut-faced-tight-arsed woman walked past and began a scan. She had the eyes that could in one swipe up and down accurately judge another woman's age, weight, social class, employment and relationship status. And then, while the other woman was looking back at her and thinking she had nice shoes or something, she could pull out some sort of stopper in the person who had not realised she was her opponent to fully or partially deflate her with a dismissive turn of the head or a sneer. Sue had been well into middle age and so had not been worth scanning for years. She wasn't having any of it now. She mouthed the words,

"Fuck off." Before the scanner eyes had time to look away. The girls would be fine. They were grown women and she had already left home and married by the time she was blah de blah blah.

She strode back towards the ticket place with her head up. Determined not to be self-conscious this time round. It was good for Sam, not the worry, but the responsibility. Sam had no room to grow up, neither did Jo really. All this would be good for them. Like when she was in the unit. They had really pulled together when she was ill.

They were two grown up women being cosseted by her. Stifled. She couldn't help it. But they were better off without her around all the time, weren't they? She needed to get home so could she finally get round to looking at downsizing and getting deposits together. They needed places of their own.

She pulled out the other phone and phoned 911. She spoke with a very posh English accent so there would be no ambiguity,

"Yes, I'd like the police please…. Yes? I thought you might like to know that there is a, a person from British Security services tied up at a house called 'Buena Vista' on Camino de Montaña in Puerto Rico, I don't know the full address. He can explain." And she hung up and threw the phone into a bin.

But she felt wiped out. That first phone call had been the hardest thing she had done in a long while. Harder than that last row with Jan when the anger could sustain her. Now she had to phone Steve. She was not ready. She would buy the ticket to New York and have bit of lunch if there was time. Then she would phone him.

What she really needed was a proper cup of tea. Did Texas milk taste funny too? She would find out. Then she would call Steve. Or cider? A nice cool glass of Julie's home-made cider. And deodorant, she needed more deodorant. And a fridge magnet. A Houston fridge magnet, she had not got one from Puerto Rico and regretted it already. Ticket first.

She slowed down to check her name on her newest passport so she could tell the ticket seller; Andrea McCauley, 1st of May 1994. Same birthday but she was 23. She put her passport back into her bag. There was a heavy hand on her shoulder, it stopped her in her tracks without any apparent effort, she turned her head. A man had his fat-fingered hand at the end of a charcoal suit on her shoulder, a big blubbery white man.

65

"Hello Sue," he said. She was too stunned to reply. It was Oskar. Blood sucking human vivisectionist Oskar.

"Come with me…Where's Albin?" He said hurriedly and did not take his hand off her shoulder. He was being menacing on purpose. He was strong under all that fat. Another hand appeared on her neck and it gave her a little but powerful squeeze before loosening and remaining. She looked back from the big slender black hand up a long charcoal check suited arm and long neck to the big oval black expressionless face. His big almond black eyes did not look at her. He had a new suit. A good one like Oskar's. To blend in in business class? Yusef was Oskar's security guard. She had a chance.

"Huh! What! Who's Sue? Who's Albin? Take your hands off…" She was speaking in an American accent and loud. But Oskar was pushing her forward now. Yusef was coming too but without any real force. So now she shouted,

"Hey get off me! Who are you!?" Just like in the films. She struggled against Oskar's grip.

"Come on Sue don't make a fuss, I'm going to help you, you need to come with me, you signed a contract remember, …" she was going to say something about duress then but,

"You okay Miss?" Another strange man was standing in front of her, he wasn't as big as the ones behind her with their hands on her shoulders.

"This man…He's…Get off me!" And she wriggled free of Oskar's hand.

"It's alright Sir, I've got this…this young lady needs to come with us she's…."

"What!? No!? Who are you?" And she really yelled this time, partly at the man in front of her and partly to the world in general, "Help me...this man is..." in the accent off the telly.

"Now stop it Sue," he said menacingly and then he laughed nervously at the stranger,

"You Cops or something?" Asked the stranger suspiciously,

"No, no nothing like that I'm her Doctor, she's my wife's... Sorry Sir, this girl...is my sister-in-law and she needs to..." but the smaller man heard a foreigner of about Fifty and saw a pretty American girl no more than Twenty with a big black man's hand on her shoulder and didn't move. A woman came up,

"You okay honey?" It was the nice woman her age again.

"My name's not Sue...I'm...Andrea...My name's Andrea...this man just attacked me!" And she burst into tears, American ones. People were slowing down and looking over. Then a security guard appeared. Yusef took his hand off her shoulder and stepped back into the gathering crowd.

"He just came up and grabbed me...he called me Sue...I'm Andrea!" The nice lady had her arm round her and the smaller man was standing between her and the big fat old man. The big fat old man looked at the security guard so that the security guard could see he had on a good suit, a very good suit,

"I'm sorry, sir, my name is Doctor Oskar Blutegel and this is my sister-in-law...Sue is...has mental health issues…she thinks she's a middle-aged woman from Chingford…. she needs to come home to Switzerland…her sister is very worried." Sue fumbled in her bag and produced her passport and showed it to the guard without letting go. The guard looked at the passport and then the big fat old man in the very good suit who now had panic in his eyes, "…yes, yes, Sue is a pet name…Andrea was named after her mother…we call her Sue," and he looked at her, "…Now come on Suzy you know you need to come with me don't you…Where's Albin, Suzy?"

"I don't know who this man is or what he is talking about…" she said each of the words in quite a good American accent but sounded English somehow. An American police officer arrived on the scene, "…Officer, officer, this man attacked me," she sounded more American again, "…he thinks I'm his sister-in-law," she couldn't say law in an American accent, no-one seemed to notice but she needed not to say law again. She needed to say as little as possible. She cried some more. The big fat old man in the very good suit looked frightened. But he still came over like a Bond Villain as far as the Houstonites were concerned. Sue tried to look small and young and American, the fear was real.

"Look officer, this has all got very…my name is Oskar Blutegel and my sister-in-law here is unwell, she needs to come home," he sighed and looked paternal. But the policeman wasn't looking at him, he was looking at the security guard and the security guard had decided that Oskar was a madman, and foreign.

68

"Okay sir, if you just come with me, you can explain everything nice and slow…young lady you okay?" Sue sniffed and nodded with the nice lady's arm around her shoulder.

"Suzy! Sue! Come on now…Sue! Look I've got a mental health assessment, it's in German but…if you just let me…I am senior research director at a major…Joseph! where is Joseph?" But Jan had been right about the help. 'Joseph' was strolling out of the busy airport in a very good suit in la-la-la-la-Amerika and the policeman was man handling Oskar away. The guard came up to Sue and asked,

"You okay?" She nodded. "…where are you headed? She pointed to the ticket counter. "…you need any help?" She shook her head,

"I just need to call my dad," she said in American and lifted her face so that the nice lady her age would let her go. She took a deep breath and made a weak smile. The guard looked around the concourse, for Yusef presumably. Her knees buckled. The guard caught her and smiled indulgently.

"Thank you," she said very quietly. "…I'm fine…I just need to buy my ticket…and call my dad," she held onto him and looked small and young and pretty for as long as she could. The nice lady her age took her weight and smiled. The guard walked away talking into his walkie-talkie. Then three people said,

"You sure you're okay?" In quick succession and she nodded and made a less weak smile and a quick sigh sort of movement like she had seen heroines in American films do. She put her wrinkle free hand on her smooth collar bone and said "…phew…thank you I'm fine…I just need to get…buy, buy my ticket. My flight is…I don't want to miss it. Get home to M…om and Dad," and she let everyone stroke her arm and smile in turn and walk away.

But Sue was not fine. She had had e-bloody-nough of all this nonsense. She looked around desperately for Yusef. He was gone. Had Yunis said something about an uncle in Florida? What was Oskar doing in Houston? He knew Albin. She was right to gaffer-tape him up. This vindication and a bit of anger was enough to get her to the ticket counter, buy a ticket to New York and a sandwich.

It was not until she was on the plane that she realised she had forgotten to buy deodorant and a fridge magnet.

Nor had she phoned her ex-husband. And she was running out of energy. Not physical energy; that body, her body was young and strong and recovered quickly, she had learned that in the back of the lorry and on the boat. And there were all the tests. No, she had run out of all the other sorts of energy. The energies she needed to get home. Fear and anger had probably got her this far but she was getting too tired to be angry or even frightened any more. The metamorphosis, the rashes, the pain, the tests, the reports, the threats of C…, Fielding and Hardy, all the independent Government agencies, the dependent Government agencies all making such a hoo-hah, her own sister, the escape, the lorry, the boat, Albin, missing Jo's knee operation, Oskar. It was all too much. She got out her sandwich and began to munch mechanically,

"You want a drink with that?"

"Yes please...diet coke please," drinking alcohol wouldn't really help. She had forgotten her accent! The steward didn't mind. She would make a dreadful spy. She paid the man. "...thank you."

"...and thank you," said the steward. She sighed. He was nice, nice bum too. The warm pools in her belly began to stir. Steve, she had to think about Steve. That put her off. She would be seeing him again in a few hours. Well she hoped she would because she needed him. Zabtrex or just Oskar was obviously still after her and she only had a few dollars left.

After having spent the last ten years cursing his name, then not thinking about him on purpose then forgetting not to think about him because she was just not thinking about Steve any more, she would have to think about him now. Bastard.

She sat back and munched and decided to start from the beginning and skip the bits she didn't like. She had met him in Art School in 1979. She was still in her Foundation Year but he was already a second year and wouldn't have spoken to her if it hadn't been for her hair. Her long chestnut hair.

He had fallen head over heels in love with her hair and her skin and her shape. And he was Twenty-one and everyone loved him and his gift for painting. Her included. She realised she was remembering the how we met and fell in love story. The story they had told when they met new people. When they were together. The how-he-left-me-and-I-never-want-anything-more-to-do-with-the-selfish-heartless-call-himself-a-father-bastard story was the only one she had visited in the last ten years. That story she had told to Linda and Julie and the gang.

But even that story she hadn't told for a few years, maybe even five. She was over him. She only felt a visceral pang when the girls said or did something that made her think they needed a father. But at those moments she thought about a father, not their father. Bastard. Now she had to ask him for help.

The two stories didn't fit. She had about an hour to try and mesh them together. It was hard. Neither story was particularly true. They were both sort of potted, cleaned-up, versions she, and once they, had used to…just share with other people. A sort of shortened, tidied up narrative to make sense of their being together, or not together. Everyone had a story, they had one too. Just to be sociable. Nobody wanted the messy, convoluted, inconsistent truth.

Not that he had been particularly sociable. Her mind skipped briefly to sitting in the Elizabeth with Julie and Andy before any of them had kids. While she and Julie wittered on easily, she could see Andy, still an innocent man then, out of the corner of her eyes doing his best to engage Steve, 'Monosyllabic Steve' as she later found out Andy called him, in some sort of conversation. He didn't like football. He didn't watch telly. All he did was paint and he didn't like talking about that. In fact, now she thought about it again their how we met and fell in love story had always been hers.

The sandwich was quite dry. She finished her coke and looked around for the steward. Did she really have to think about him? She would be seeing him soon enough, hopefully. What was the minimum thinking about Steve she had to do? Enough so as not to start screaming "Bastard! Bastard! I'll give you mature! Bastard!" with snot and tears pouring down her face when she saw him next. That'd been all she could manage the last few times. That would look odd coming from Sam. Sam just went quiet when things got confrontational and had hidden in her room for the entire break up, well ever since really. Was that why she never came out of her room? Still upset? Had Sue failed to rebuild their lives properly?

It wasn't fair. A person was entitled not to think about a person and all this business was making her think about him and she didn't want to and she had a perfect right. She had made her own story now. Not hers, theirs. The story of Sue and Jo and Sam and it didn't need him in it. It really didn't. They had made a lovely little life hadn't they. The steward appeared and requested some I.D. before he gave her the beer.

All those years drawing bloody kettles, not just drawing but pushing and fighting and playing office politics and getting harder and harder. To stay in the game. He never understood. He never thought about how she might like to sit at home and draw what she wanted while someone else brought home the money, cleaned the house, cooked the food, brought up the children. The truth was that the girls hadn't missed him that much. She had been a single parent from the beginning really. Their dad was like some sort of lodger. Linda had tried to tell her but she couldn't hear it back then.

Sue sat there in the National Gallery in front of The Judgement of Paris by Rubens for the umpteenth time. That painting had been there all her life and it had always inspired her. Sometimes because of its composition, sometimes the brushwork, sometimes the colour. Rarely, she would enter into a complete marvelling reverie, absorbing the whole amazing thing through not just her eyes, but through every pore of her, somehow.

Not that time. Forty-something, hair un-styled and overweight. Not even looking. Not even keeping one ear out for the girls. Not even trying to teach them anything. Just keeping them out of the rain and the way so Steve could finish a picture.

How old were they then? They were upset when he left of course but they hadn't had that much to do with him. He had sort of taken them to school for a few years but he never walked them all the way to the gate. Jo had said once that she felt he resented them. Sue had felt that sometimes too.

Not that she had had much time to feel anything. Not even pictures. Sue would get home to the remnants of whatever breakfast she had put out and the tea she'd made the night before, then there was the washing and she wouldn't sit down until the girls were in bed. People at work had thought she was snooty because she didn't watch any soaps. But the truth was she didn't have time. She had more time now but she didn't know who any of the characters were. She was drinking too much and put the cup back on the fold-down table without taking any more.

She felt the guilt swell; she should not have put up with it. She never thought to complain. She should've been more Feminist. But all Feminism had done when she was young was sneer at her from a distance. A few fellow students had barked at her at college she supposed. And she had done a bit of reading for that essay Object or Subject, Women in Art in her foundation year. That essay and a few Cosmo quizzes in the '80s were the full extent of her involvement with Feminism. Real women hadn't needed feminism had they. Look at Thatcher. When had she started calling her Thatcher and not Maggie? When had she stopped being staunch? But Steve, she must think about Steve.

Was she already modelling for Steve by the time she wrote that essay? She couldn't remember but she did remember the sneers from some of her fellow students. The women students were worse. Or did she just feel it more from women? Did she care more when women were horrible?

She should've had more confidence. But what did they expect those Feminists? She had the working and the childcare and the cooking and cleaning and to have more confidence on top of all that was just too much.

Yes, she was modelling by then because that was it wasn't it; Object OR Subject. She hadn't understood the question. They decided that she was only an object when she did that modelling for Steve. They had probably already written her off by then. That double sneering. Sneering for aspiring to the discredited 'bourgeois ideals of dead white men'. Just because she wanted to paint well. And sneering because she wasn't bourgeois herself. Was it triple sneering? No bloody wonder she voted Tory. Was that why?

They knew she had a 'good body' even if she hadn't. Why had she cared about their sneers? She could paint. She was good. So what if her work wasn't 'Avant Garde' enough for a bunch of people who threw, literally threw their work together and called it something pretentious. She had never seen or heard of any of them ever again. At least Steve made a living…he hadn't made a living for years though had he.

She had made a living and he had sold the odd picture once in a blue moon. A bit of lecturing, that's how he had met Meggie.

She sighed and swigged before she remembered she should not be drinking so much. She still should have had more confidence in herself. Jo was always saying that. Jo didn't see her at work. That wasn't confidence though. Getting harder and harder until she let bloody Emma walk into that stupid idea. Matching toaster, with a coffee maker, what was she thinking? Perhaps she should've warned her.

Sue looked over the passenger next to her to peer out of the window. Sky. Big blue sky. Sunlight on a little cloud. Moving slowly. Another one of those religious painting skies; shafts of light. Peace. There was sky over Chingford too. She missed her girls. Was Jo's knee healing properly? She realised that she was being slightly hysterical with all these memories and ideas mixing up and needed to slow down. She was full of adrenalin from escaping Albin and Oskar and talking to her girls and it was only natural but it had to stop. She had to slow down and think of Steve.

It had been a messy parting. Oh dear. What had she been thinking with that Alfie? She hadn't had a night like that before. 'What were you thinking?' that's what Jo had said and there hadn't been time to explain before Jan rang from the airport full of fake concern and scaremongering.

What she was thinking was that she was young and beautiful and full of longing and she had missed out on promiscuity the last time. Why couldn't she…you know…if she wanted. Of course, her dedicated counsellor was probably not the best choice but it was still fun. Sort of.

The last morning had been a bit awkward, Alfie had left without so much as a cup of tea and full of embarrassment. Given that it was her first one-night, and then two-nights, stands in… well ever really, she could have done with some feedback.

She felt the warm tide rise in her belly again, it had been fun. Her interest in sex had disappeared into a fog of worthlessness when Steve had 'exchanged her for a newer model'. She was only Forty-five, looked late thirties. But she felt older than she ever got in real time. She had started to feel better about herself after a few years but then the menopause had come. That drained any residual desire out of her.

It was only when it was gone that she realised how much of a sexual person she had been. She had rarely done much about it was true. She and Steve had not done much sex at all, especially after Sam. But sex used to cross her mind a lot more than she realised before it stopped crossing her mind at all. Well not her mind, her belly. Not so much actual sex, just feelings. Like a warm pool ebbing and flowing in her belly. A nice-looking man in a movie, in an ad break, on the train, in her dreams. Not every six seconds, like they said men thought about it, but every day. She hadn't really known that she was doing it. Then it just stopped, dried up and she woke up one morning and noticed.

She hadn't missed it. In fact, it had been a bit of a relief, one less thing to bother her. And quite funny sometimes. When she saw other people flirting it looked so silly. Then it came back. And she was happy. It was the first thing she noticed when she started to rejuvenate. She still had a few welts and blotches on her back. She had discussed it enthusiastically with her dedicated counsellor when he came to see her in the Cambridgeshire Unit. After she had got up off the floor.

She had been trying to get her strength back with some gentle yoga hadn't she. She was in 'Crescent moon pose' and he'd walked in and she'd fallen forward into the splits. And she hadn't done the splits since 1975. He had said something vague and unknowledgeable about hormones. One of many experts to be vague and unknowledgeable. They really didn't know what had happened to her. That's probably why she had fallen for Jan's concern and Oskar's confident spiel.

Then there had been that meeting about types of injunction and it had gone on late and she and Alfie were the only ones left somehow and they had gone for a bite and one thing had led to another and Jo had said, 'what were you thinking?' It was hard for them of course, having a mum who looked younger than them. Well, any change would've been difficult. She saw their brave faces put on in a hurry in the carpark outside the Cambridgeshire unit.

And they had been pleased for her too when she started to get better. After all that was what everyone wanted wasn't it. To look young. Firm smooth skin, supple joints. The girls had found the youth thing much easier to handle than she had really. No not easier. They had been happy for her. A happiness based on an inability to imagine being anything but miserable in an old body.

But they had not been so happy for themselves. Well, Jo hadn't. Sam had taken it all better really, in her stride. Jo was a worrier. Sam was quiet that was all. Was it? Who was it who snuck in so noisily with her late at night and always left before anyone else got up?

She did really need to get home. There was the messy parting and then God knows what Jan had told them when she got that psychiatric report done. They didn't know it was so she and Oskar could lock her up 'for her own safety'.

She had missed her girls so much over the last few weeks but after the phone call this was the first time that she gave any serious thought to how they were feeling. She had needed them to be okay so that is what she had imagined. Just a few worries about the state they were leaving the sink. Not the anxiety of having a mum with possibly unstable genes and probably unstable mind on the run from their Auntie Jan and phoning from God knows where. They must've been pulling their hair out with worry. And the familiar mum guilt wave built up higher than usual and crashed hard and down so she slumped into her seat.

It had not been fair for her to bring Alfie back to the house. Sam and Jo's mum had gone from a reliable Fifty-something and basically sexless woman who moaned about washing and college fees, through a serious illness where no-one not even the doctors knew what was going on or if she would even live to a giggling schoolgirl. Perhaps she had gone a bit mad. Never mind what that NHS psychiatrist had said. Never mind Alfie's 'Don't over generalise, negativise and something else with no 'ise' in it mantra. The girls needed Sue to be her.

She owed it to them to act with some consistency. They would have to work out what that consistency was together. If they could forgive her. They were big girls; they could take it. And it wasn't like the pair of them were nuns either. Who was that on the stairs? She should ring Alfie when she got back. Not for more sex, no. She fancied a bit of variety this time round. No, she just wanted some feedback that's all. The tide swelled up and brimmed into a lovely little memory of Alfie's lovely tummy. All brown and firm and yummy. Sam thought he looked like that footballer. He did look after himself. His thighs were … Oh dear.

But the tide of desire had risen again. She sighed and leaned back in her seat and fancied a change. Who? That singer? That actor? No, that boy she had really liked back in college? The one who did those rubbish things with wire. There was a dark-haired white man on the train with a, what did they call it, well, scruffy look about him? She had seen him get off at Liverpool Street smoking a fag and walking like he had a sack on his back. What had she seen in him? The steward? He had a nice bum. She closed her eyes.

Oh yes, him. Now, where? She couldn't just imagine him in a towel and start fantasising. No, the fantasy had to have some back story. She had seen that space between the trees on the drive down that scary hill in Puerto Rico. It was a vivid memory for such a short glimpse, she must've thought she was going to die. She and he stood there in the tropical clearing, facing each other and clad only in the rapidly rising dew. It was morning and the sunlight was dappling over his face, his cheek. The heavy dew evaporated from his tousled hair. He sighed as the big leaves around him unfolded and lifted towards the sun. He looked at her and smiled. She smiled and they walked towards each other slowly, no quickly, and kissed passionately on the lips. He lapped dew from the dip in her collar-bone as his nimble fingers ran down her smooth back. Why were they naked in a forest? Had they slept there? What about snakes? Sue pouted in real life and decided that they had both slept there after a romantic night at a restaurant with fairy lights on the terrace. He had a great sense of humour and she had laughed freely.

A waterfall, a waterfall would be nice, in the background. The vapour from the rushing water cooled the air as they kissed some more and Sue ran her wet hands down his taught chest and made him shudder with a smile. He kissed her some more and pulled her close with both hands, caressing her pert bum. A heavy scented shrub hung with pinkish Georgia O'Keeffe flowers brushed against her legs, letting their rich sweet smell fill the air around them. Her hips pushed up to his, he kissed her damp neck and … How tall would that make him? Five foot five? That wasn't very tall. The ground was on a slope towards the waterfall. He had his back to the waterfall, that was nice. There was the vapour and the flowers. The rushing water filled their ears and the grass was thick and soft as they lay down somehow and she held his t ...taught-arse! Fuck! Bloody Emma stood in a dark business suit taking notes, taught-faced. Blocking her view of the waterfall and tapping on a fucking tablet. She would have to come back to that one.

It was time to do up seatbelts again. It was time to be Andrea again. Then Sam. For Steve, she wasn't going to think about Steve until she absolutely had to.

The hour she had lost in Houston she had found in New York. So it was Three O'clock.

Family Resemblance

She was low on cash now. Also, a long slog on public transport would help her get into her role. She didn't ring Steve till she got to Penn Station two hours later after a baffling change at Jamaica Station. Suitably jostled in a major conurbation.

A woman answered the phone, she sounded jostled too.

"Hello, is Steve there?"

"…He's busy, can I take a message." It was Meggie and all that warm and open Americaness that had driven Sue to distraction ten years ago was gone. She couldn't sense any searching for a pen. This woman was ice.

"Er…yes, yes. It's Sam… Samantha Duggen…his daughter? I'm in New York and I'm a bit stuck I…is that Meggie?"

"Samantha? Oh! Wow! Samantha…the younger…Wow. How are you? Wait there…" And Sue heard a bit of melting and "Stephen" and the line went quiet. Then it was quiet some more.

"Hello?" It was Steve. Sue gulped.

"Hello Dad?"

"Sam?"

"Yes Dad. Sam…I'm in New York and I'm a bit stuck, …" and she began crying as planned, without much effort. Bastard! Bastard!

"Wh..How are you…where are you?"

"Pennsylvania Avenue Station…I've got no money and he's left me, oh Dad!" And she cried some more.

"Okay okay, it's okay Sam. We'll get you out of this, …" he had learned to deal with crying women, that was interesting.

"I don't know what to do Dad. He just left. He took all the money…oh Dad."

"Ok, I'll come and get you…Go get yourself a coffee, you've got money for a coffee? Great, get a coffee and wait for me. I won't be long. Did he…You okay…okay physically? She assented. "…We'll get you out of this," that was definite burring with a slight American twang, Steve Duggen, Monosyllabic Steve, was burring. He wasn't telling her to stop crying or telling her how she was feeling or should be feeling. Not telling her she was not really upset. Like last time. He was being supportive. Sue was confused.

"Okay, okay, thanks Dad…how long will you be?"

"I'll be there in less than an hour. Don't worry Sam… You on a cell?"

"Yes Dad."

"This is your number?"

"Yes Dad," saying dad was good, she would keep doing that.

"Okay I'll call you when I get to Penn," she assented. "…Don't worry Sam we'll get you out of this." and he hung up. Sue wove and danced around and through the waves and bubbles of people using the station for its intended purpose.

She found a pharmacy and finally bought some deodorant. And deodorant wipes, did they have them in

England? Then she found the loos in the station. She looked sternly in the mirror and asked herself if her ex-husband would recognise her? Well, this new/old face was starting to look a bit more like her now.

Maybe she was just getting used to it again. The smoothness of it. The prettiness. She was also slightly amazed at the resilience of youth. She certainly had the rather too alert stare of someone who had started her very eventful day at midnight on a drug runner's boat in Puerto Rico and had to pretend to be her daughter before she could relax. But her face, her actual face, the physiognomy of it, was as fresh as a daisy. She still couldn't actually remember if she had looked like this in 1979. Only the self-conscious thoughts about her nose being too small and her bottom lip being too big. She still couldn't remember being that pretty. Apart from her bum, the bum she remembered had always been a bit flat. Now, she loved her bum, because it was her same old flat bum. But the important thing now was that she look like Sam.

Sam was also pretty, but in a different way. Sam's lips were more balanced and her nose was more like Auntie Ada's than her Grandma. But would Steve know that? The last time Steve had met up with the girls was in 2010 when Sam was fifteen. Adolescent faces changed almost every day. She was dark haired; Sam was mousy but she dyed blonde like Sue was now. That made a surprisingly big difference. They kept in touch via Facebook though. But Sam was more into Instagram, now wasn't she? Was Steve?

This could only work because Steve would be expecting to see Sam and not a rejuvenated and blonde Sue.

It would work. She brushed her hair so that half of it fell down over her face like Sam's and then brushed it back. Then she brushed it over the other half of her face. It would work. She bundled the wipes and brush back into her hold-all and set off to find a coffee shop where she could gloat for half an hour.

Sue sipped her frothy beverage perched on her stool and prepared for the gloat. Streams, eddies, flows of commuters scurried and rushed and skipped to their platforms. A few odd people were moving across the various currents challenged by going against some pretty determined people. There must've been a thousand people in there at any given moment. Very few were actually present in the station though, their minds would be running ahead to getting to the cashpoint, the grocery store, the childcare, the running or knitting club or home. Planning a presentation or a spreadsheet for tomorrow. Rent or mortgage. Car payments, whatever they were and which featured heavily in American films and telly. Or doctor's bills. They had to pay doctors' bills didn't they. However did they manage that? They paid blood donors by the pint here didn't they? Not with a glass of squash and a biccy and a sense of a public service well done. But cash. And they looked so civilised. No NHS. What if they got something serious?

Or they'd still be running behind. Rehearsing how that meeting or that report had gone, the incident with so and so at the xerox. Their mother's birthday phone call or that rude girl in the store. How many people were wondering about something they had read on the Internet? Ten? Fifty?

Five hundred? Could fifty percent of these people, these ordinary sane looking people, could fifty percent of them really believe in aliens? People in England used to say that a lot, how fifty percent of Americans believed in Aliens. People in England didn't believe in anything though did they.

How many people were actually experiencing that place at that moment? Only the ones who had been doing their particular journey for anything from the first to the fourth time she supposed. After that, you didn't really need to be there. Thinking about your commute was a waste of precious time.

When Sue was younger, Thirty or Forty, the only waking time that had actually been her own was on her commute. While she was going to, being on and leaving a train she was not someone's daughter, someone's wife, someone's mum, someone's boss or someone's employee. Was that why people went on so long about delays, or having to stand up all the way to Bracknell. Did they resent the imposition of having to think during their precious me time in an otherwise selfless day?

She couldn't gloat. That daily commute and all those worries and things to do were much harder than her life now. No time to wonder. Years and years of commuting until you just physically couldn't do it anymore, or you weren't wanted any more. She tried to look for a woman her age, her real age, somewhere in the thousands and thousands of people. Definitely under represented. Why was that? Where were all those Fifty-plus women? Cars...did they all drive to work? Her face was suitably ponderous when Steve arrived.

"Found you!" He said obviously proud of himself for picking out his estranged daughter who was actually his ex-wife in a crowd of thousands. He gave her an enthusiastic hug.

"God! You look so like your mother!" He said his eyes wide and wandering over her face. Of course. He remembered what she looked like.

"People are always saying that. Hello Dad," said Sue, his face was ten years older but he was still handsome. Craggy, with a full head of salt and pepper hair. He had not gone bald. Bastard.

"I've missed you so much," he said with an American twang and she hugged him back awkwardly thinking 'have you now?' and 'bastard'. She felt she needed to look pathetic and cry but she couldn't get one tear out. She was angry, she knew she'd be angry, she had tried to stop herself being angry but it had crept up on her. Bastard. She rubbed her forehead and panicked, keeping her head down. No scar! No chicken pox scar on her forehead from when Sam was four. She pulled her hair down over her face on the side where the scar should be. She looked up. She couldn't see much now because she had already brushed the hair down on the other side in the restroom. Steve smiled a sentimental smile and gently pushed the hair behind her ear, like Sam had worn it when she was young. She burst into tears. Bastard.

"It's alright, it's alright. Let's get you to my place and we can sort out all this mess," said Steve and he guided her through the throng of absent people to the street where a cab was waiting. Steve put his arm around her and she put her head into his chest and cried. Never mind his abandoning her and their children. Never mind all the things he did or didn't do when they were together. He was here now. Here for Sam his youngest daughter, the more sensitive of the two, in her hour of need. She had not felt that safe for days. She cried and cried and cried all the way to Brooklyn.

"Is this a brownstone?" she asked as she stepped out of the cab to face a building she had seen a thousand times in the movies.

"Yes," said Steve puzzled by the switch from deep misery to architectural curiosity.

"I've seen these in the movies," said Sue, somehow breaking the bond that hugging and crying had formed in the cab. Their connection was very fragile. She put her arm through his and smiled up at him. He did that thing with her hair again and she smiled as much like Sam as she could. Once inside, the tenuous feeling of warmth and safety was entirely evaporated in the icy blast of Meggie's gaze. Meggie embraced Sam and looked at her.

"You look so like your mother," she said and smiled. A nice genuine smile. She had aged ten years and then some since the last time Sue had seen her. Sue could not help an internal 'hah!', then she felt guilty.

"Have you had anything to eat?" asked Meggie kindly and Sam shook her head. Apparently, the cold look was directed not at Sam/Sue, but at Steve. If Sue had actually been Sam she would have felt confused and vulnerable. A cuckoo in Meggie's nest. A link with Steve's past that Meggie wanted to skim over. The creator of tension. Luckily, she could see a woman saying 'bastard' with her eyes from twenty paces and wondered who he had been a bastard over this time. She just had to navigate the tension between them and get a plane ticket to England out of him.

"Is pasta okay?" And Sue/Sam nodded and followed Meggie. "…Have you eaten yet Stephen?" She added blankly. Steve/Stephen nodded and followed her. Sue kept her awe at the massive size of their house to herself. You could have played cricket in their hall, or baseball. On the way to the kitchen Sue stopped dead. On a wall in the vault like passage was 'Girl in Lavender'. But Steve had sold that, it had been the making of his reputation. Before his other reputation. The reputation he had been perfectly happy with till Meggie. Had he bought it back? She walked unconsciously up to the large canvass.

"Er… is that Mum?" She asked. Remembering the ache in her neck and the sharpness of the bushes on her legs. As she got closer, she could feel the warmth of the sun and smell the balmy lavender all around her. The light was amazing and he had captured it perfectly.

"No." Said Meggie walking up to her. "…it's a model called…what was her name?" Steve shrugged "…it's called Woman in…" and she sighed "…. Woman in sunlight," and her voice trailed off. The girl looking at the picture looked like the woman in the painting and that was why Stephen had said he didn't want to sell it or put it in the living room. And she wasn't in the least surprised.

Sue went back to looking at the picture and saw that there were subtle differences, the angle of the neck so you couldn't quite see this girl's face, the length of the foreleg. And there she was comparing herself to another woman again. The brush strokes were longer too. But the basic composition; the girl, the lavender, that wonderful French sunlight, the negative space in the centre that brought them into such a harmony, they were all the same. And as for the colouring it was almost identical. Sue laughed a little as she remembered what Steve had said when they were still at Art School. She was complaining about how nobody took figurative art seriously and the hostility that her insistence in painting people and things was receiving. He had said,

"Just do what I do; make your subjects look unhappy or uncomfortable, put a lot of green and mauve in the skin tone, never blend in and everyone will leave you alone." It had worked. For him. When she tried it, her teachers made remarks with 'derivative' in them. Her fellow students just sneered and carried on with barbed comments about 'latent context', whatever that was. Steve made greeny mauveish people look awkward, uncomfortable and/or unhappy in various, usually internal and shabby, spaces and everyone, except a few old fogeys who lapped up everything he did, left him alone.

That was how they had come up with the idea for the lavender field in the first place. The greens and mauves of her never-had-a-foreign-holiday skin were reworked in the plants around her, complementing the pink. She can't have been that pink surely? and her hair, it was years since she'd seen her natural colour. There was her deep brown hair and the soil that they had had to dig up with their fingernails and pour on water every few minutes to keep it a similar shade to her hair. What was missing was the flicker of the sun-bleached blue sky in her eyes. She remembered how flattered she had felt. Jan had cornflower blue eyes and everyone had silently agreed that hers were too light.

They had had to go to France to find a lavender field. And she hadn't been pink or green or mauve after that hot uncomfortable day. She had been black and blue and her neck and back and arms and one inner thigh had been bright red with sunburn. But they had drunk cheap wine and made love in the little Pension and she had forgotten the pain.

The first time she had been out of England. Using all her money from that Saturday job in Boots. Steve was 'old money' which meant he never had any money. Sue sighed one big sigh for all that sunlight in July 1980, their lost love and something else about Steve that she couldn't quite put her finger on. Meggie was already down the massive hall.

"That light is awesome Dad," she said to Steve. Awesome was a good word, she would say awesome some more.

Eating like Sam was great fun, wolfing food and slurping like a pig. Making up a bullshit story about how she had loved Simon and he had taken her away and left her was easy. Everyone there already knew the script. Sue was the mother of two young women. Steve was a lecturer at a graduate school. Meggie was a human female. She added in a bit about a plan to surprise Steve with a portfolio of road trip sketches on the way back so he wouldn't feel hurt. Any awkward details about where or why or how could be covered over by saying she didn't know and/or crying. Stretching out the bits about Simon promising her the road trip of a lifetime was almost pleasurable. She could almost see his leather-clad back sneaking out of a motel room on a dusty highway. But then while her ex-husband was making her a cup of tea Meggie asked,

"Have you called your mom?" And Sue was stumped. That would have been the first thing the real Sam would've done. The silence was long while Sue went through all the reasons why Sam wouldn't call her; away on business wouldn't cut it in a world full of mobile phones, sickness was possible but would require medical details and someone was liable to say 'oh my mum had that' and Sue had always been as fit as a horse; money worries were out because Sue was great with money. She had to say something,

"I can't…Mum is…me and mum don't really get on that well at the moment," lame, lame, lame. Then inspiration struck. The inspiration that had got her out of Zurich, Puerto Rico and Houston. She was very proud of herself,

"Mum doesn't want me to focus on my art…it's too insecure she says…she wants me to do a proper degree," and Steve's arm was round her shoulders again.

"My mother said the same thing," he cooed. Sue knew that and that is why she had said it. Steve's mum had wanted her only son to go into 'something with a suit' like his father.

In fact, Sue was very proud of Sam's ability to draw and paint. There was no such thing as a secure job any more anyway. It was Sam who was reluctant to pursue it, or anything really. She was only at Art School because it was the one thing she enjoyed in a world where everyone had to go to university whether they wanted to or not. "…You know, Art School didn't turn out so well for her and, …" she let the bastard finish that sentence in his head. Meggie was left with an 'and what' face so Steve/Stephen said,

"Sue said Art School was full of reverse snobs." Did she say that? Maybe she had.

"She wanted, wants me to be something in a suit," said the woman who had worn 40 or 50 very nice suits to date and everyone laughed at the very idea. "…Have you got anything with you?" Asked Steve eagerly. Uh-oh. Sue knew he was never without a pad or something. Sam would've taken at least an A4 pad with her if she was going away on a road trip across America.

"I lost all my stuff…my clothes and my camera on the bus…I nearly missed my stop and I left it…on Route Sixty something," said Sue. "…I had a lovely set of brushes," she added for good measure. Steve looked at her quizzically, she remembered that look and answered, "…water colours." He got up and left the kitchen. Sue knew that he was going to get his daughter, The-Artist-Stephen-Duggen's daughter, a set of brushes and some paper.

"I've got plenty of clothes you're welcome to try on." said Meggie who was bigger in the hips than she had been. "…and you've given me an idea…let me talk to Stephen," and Meggie left the room too. Sue slumped over the table with her head in her hands. This was weird.

She was still staring at her empty plate when Meggie and Steve came back into the room. Steve pushed the plate away with an A4 pad, some pencils and a small watercolour box with a few good brushes.

"Wow! Dad! Are you sure?" She said with that flat unenthusiastic tone of youth nowadays. He didn't answer, just put his hand on her shoulder and looked at her. Monosyllabic Steve was back, back with those eyes full of import. Eyes saying, I understand that these items are as vital to you as food and drink. Eyes full of love.

Sue welled up, "…Thank you…Dad." And she wept more with her shoulders than her face. She had loved that man so much. He was supporting his daughter in a way he had never supported her. Bastard! Bastard.

She looked up at her ex-husband standing over her with a look of love and pride in his eyes and wept. Could he see the woman looking back at him was Sue weeping for the loss of just that look? Weeping for the encouragement and pride, not in her and her talent, but for a daughter he didn't even recognise. Weeping for that awful last picture he had painted. That picture of her old and tired and unloved. All those contemptuous oranges and blues. The picture that pushed him into the big league just to rub it in. Steve's eyes moistened and he hugged her again. Hugged Sam. Hugged the girl he had betrayed as much as her.

She stopped crying just as suddenly as she had begun. She sniffed and pulled herself away, almost revolted, still looking up at him. No pretence this time, no betrayed defensiveness like before, no attempt to make him see, really see, what he had done, just Sue looking up at her ex. Steve's face blanched.

"You must be tired," said Meggie, "...we think we've found a way to get you home but Stephen needs to talk to some people at the Academy and you need some sleep...and a shower." Sue sniffed and smiled at Meggie and Steve didn't smile and looked at Meggie.

"Yes," he said emphatically. "...you must be tired," and he walked away into the middle of the enormous kitchen with his back to them both. What had he seen?

"Yes, yes I'm totally exhausted," said Sue confused and trying to sound tired. Meggie appeared used to Steve's back and took her up to the guest room. "...Night Dad," she said and he stayed where he was and said,

"Night Sam." Quietly. Bastard.

When they were alone and had sorted out towels Meggie put her hand on Sue's shoulder and said,

"Your dad is very happy to see you...it's just...you have to understand all this is hard for him too. He hasn't seen you for years...you know your mom wasn't..."

"I'm sorry Meggie I didn't want to bother you; it must be hard for you too..." Meggie smiled dismissively "...but I had nowhere else to go and I..." Meggie shook her head to say there was no need to explain.

"We want you here. It's great to see you whatever the circumstances. Great you still trust Stephen after everything your mom said..." Sue sniffed and looked innocent. Meggie smiled at her loyalty and diplomacy. "...Get some rest...and we'll go out for breakfast tomorrow. Don't worry Sam. Have a good night," and she kissed her on the cheek warmly and left. Sue was still holding the pad and tools to her chest. She put them on the side table in the spare room as big as, bigger than, her master bedroom, and people were always saying she had a big house. Got in before the boom. She liked being round the corner from her mum and the poshness of saying Forest View. He liked the light. He also liked watching her decorate with a scarf tied round her head. No, loved watching her.

Then she got old. Old and tired, tired of him not lifting a bloody finger unless it had a brush in it. A little tiny brush. She had decorated that entire house, not just decorated, renovated. All that dust. This place was nice. She got into a shower at last. It had been a long long day.

Sue had curled into a ball ready for the rest she dearly needed but when it didn't come, she rolled over and felt for the bedside light. It illuminated part of the vast room; the bed, some tasteful antique looking rug and the bedside table with the art stuff on it.

A car swished by; it was wet outside. She looked towards the window. A few streaks of yellow light made it between the curtains onto the carpet, their trembling telling her it was still raining. When she heard the knock on the door, she realised she had the pad open on her lap and a pencil in her hand. She closed the pad quickly and said,

Hello? ...Come in?" The door opened a crack and Steve put his head round the door.

"I saw the light on...you decent?"

"I'm always decent Dad, come in," he stood at the edge of the bed and smiled unsurely. Sue couldn't exactly see Meggie's hand pushing him into the room, but it was there one way or another,

"I just came to say good night…you drawing?" She could see he was eager to see if she had any talent. She opened the pad and turned it round so he could see. Not caring about what he thought, but curious.

He held it under the light and smiled, almost relieved. He moved his eyes to the bedroom floor and back to the pad and kept smiling as he looked at her. He had never looked at any of her work like that before. But she hadn't drawn anything except kettles for years. This was a few lines describing the light on the floor.

"I like it…fluid," he said. He had criticised her in the past for lacking that and she felt pride and resentment in equal measure,

"Thanks Dad," said Sue and she smiled insecurely back at him. He sat down on the edge of the bed still smiling warmly, "…it's good to see you Sammo, "he said. Sammo? "…and Jo-Jo how is she? Is she still at that Design place?" Jo-Jo? He was being warm. Paternal. Kind. Familiar. He used pet names that she had never heard, or didn't remember hearing. His only slip was that he had really tried to say 'design' without contempt but it hadn't worked. Design had kept him in bloody brushes for decades. And he had no right to talk like a father, he had not been a father.

"Y…yes…she's just got some tableware for a chain of cafés. They're beautiful. She's got a lovely eye. I'll send you a, …" but she wasn't going to send him any pictures so she stopped talking, it didn't matter,

"Well, you both have. Always did…have you still got those books?" And he saw her quizzical expression with a little bit of pain but it didn't show when he spoke, "…those books you and Jo-Jo used to draw in when you came home from school...you cost us a fortune in paper, reams and reams," and he laughed. Sue had a vague memory of the girls drawing when they were younger but no more,

"Oh those yes...yes still got them somewhere...Mum keeps everything." Well she thought she did but where had she put those books?

"How is your mum?" He asked reluctantly.

"Oh she's fine...still drawing kettles," and he smiled.

"You know I would have liked to see you more but your mum was...she was quite hostel."

"Hostel...oh hostile! Yes she was...she was very hurt, she felt...betrayed."

"Yes, she was good at that," he said resentfully. Bastard! "...Sorry. She's your mum and...well she's done a great job with you and Jo-Jo and...well I just wish I could have kept closer to you both and..." Closer!? Closer!? Why the fuck did you move three thousand miles away? Thought Sue, "...did you get my last card?" Sue nodded with absolutely no idea of what he was talking about, "...the bouquet?"

"Yes, the bouquet...it's lovely," said Sue.

"I nearly kept it." He smiled, letting her know it was a drawing and that he thought it was so good that he could have sold it. So he had sent Sam a drawing. Last card, he had said. He had sent Sam lots of drawings. Sue was confused and maternal guilt was lapping coldly. Why didn't she know about this? Yes, the post usually came when she was out. Yes, Jo usually put the post on the side table when

99

she came in, which was usually before her. But last card? She should know about this. She sighed confusedly for real and tried to look tired. He leaned forward and pushed her hair back again, this time though he stopped and rubbed her forehead quizzically. "…What happened to your scar? Didn't you have a little scar there?" Sue had already thought of that by now, if it should come up and it had,

"Lasers…mum's treat…I was feeling self-conscious so mum paid for laser treatment." Steve had not been keeping up with the technicalities of beauty treatments either and so he bought it.

"You were so ill…a hundred and five for three solid days…" Sue remembered that. Sam had got the chicken pox with a vengeance. She had been very poorly and Sue had had a presentation on cafetières. They had not gone into cafetières. Sam had got better. Steve had taken care of Sam. "…and the spots! So many spots…all that calamine," and he smiled paternally again "…Oh! how's Jo-Jo's knee? Has she got it done yet? You know the offer still stands…I will pay for her to have it done if the En-Aich-Ess is going to be so…" What offer?

"Yes…yes dad, she's had it done, she's just recovering. It all went well," said Sue utterly baffled. The story of her and Steve had some serious holes.

"That's a relief. Good. Good…" he looked at Sue. Sue looked at him. "…it's late. We can catch up more tomorrow…I have to go to the Academy early tomorrow but we can meet for lunch? I need to see if we can't get you included in the summer residency. It would get you to France and then you could get the Eurostar from Paris. We could just get you a flight but at such short notice... But I won't know till tomorrow, there's been...one of the students has dropped out..." now his face looked like he had a bad knee that was giving him gip. "...we'll have to see if we can't get you to take her place."

"Oh! Okay...That sounds great...I'm so sorry, ..." he shook his head and wrinkled his nose. Sue smiled. "...I am very tired Dad"

"Yes. You've had an eventful few days," he said sounding more English now. He took the pad and put it on the bedside table and tapped it with a 'no more drawing tonight young lady' kind of look. A kind of look that he expected to be understood. A kind of look that exposed a shared past for him and Sam. The story of Steve and Sam. He turned out the light,

"Night Sammo. Sleep well."

"Night Dad.... you too," he crept out and closed the door gently.

Sue lay in the dark as traumatised as when she first metamorphosed. Eyes wide and as big as saucers, stiff as a board. Sam, Sammo and possibly 'Jo-Jo' had been in contact with their dad. They were receiving cards, telling him about knees, what else? Why didn't they warn her? They said on the phone that they hadn't spoken to him? He talked to her/Sam like they had an ongoing relationship? Why hadn't they told her? Sam had never mentioned she was receiving cards from her dad. What else hadn't she told her? Had she been so 'hostel' that Sam had felt she had to keep an ongoing relationship with her dad a secret? What about Jo? How could she, their mum, not have known about all this? They lived in the same house, the same small house. What had she done, what had she said to make them so secretive?

But she knew what she had said, she had said he was a selfish bastard. A selfish, betraying, lying bastard. She had said it over and over again. She had been so upset that she had hidden nothing. She couldn't save all her tears till after they had gone to bed. They had seen her fall apart. Sam was only Nine. And Jo had actually had to support her mum. In her Exam Year. More guilt washed up. She was seventeen and should've been mooning over boys and gossiping. But she had had to sit there passing her mum tissues. Sue should've been passing tissues to Jo. And Sam.

It was Steve's fault of course; he had left her and the girls. He had left suddenly and with an ease that had shocked and hurt them deeply. At the time her mum guilt had become mainly composed of shame at falling apart because they had lost their father and needed one of their parents to be there for them.

She resigned to the guilt reforming into not being there for them now and let it wash over her. She hadn't fallen apart completely of course. She had made it to work and the shops and checked homework. She had managed to clatter and sob supper onto the table every night. But when she wasn't crying she was more or less a zombie. A mum shaped zombie going through the day asking 'how was your day?' with all the enthusiasm and believability of a tele-sales operative.

But that was only a few months. Couldn't they have told her at some time in the last ten years? Or was it just

Sam? Was that why she never left her room except to eat or go to college? Was she in there Facebooking her dad? But he didn't know she drew for fun. He was not that surprised that her scar was 'gone'. He didn't know Jo had had her operation. She knew Jo had had her operation and she was on the run from a drugs conglomerate and British Intelligence or their representatives 'gone rogue'. Maybe he needed a story where he was still involved with his kids even if he wasn't.

Sammo? Jo-Jo? What about the pet names? Had she forgotten? Had she driven the memories deep down into herself because they didn't fit her angry version of events?

She could reason that she often used to leave for work while they were all still in their pyjamas and then get home when they were already in bed. She distinctly remembered her shock at seeing Sam in her secondary school uniform for the first time when she was Fifteen. Sam had been sick at school and Steve was gone so she had to pick her up. But that meant that before he had gone he had picked up Sam when she was sick didn't it? He must've done. She was at work.

But she couldn't imagine Steve getting the pans dirty reheating the food that she had made. She couldn't imagine him insisting they eat their peas. But he must've done. The food had been gone. The pans had been dirty. They got bigger and stronger. Had she been so busy tidying the kitchen, washing plates and pans, loading the washing machine, doing all the things he hadn't done, all the while rehearsing the next day at work, that she hadn't noticed what he had done? Had she noticed him? Was she so busy with

103

kettles, toasters and mergers, so many mergers, that she had neglected her kids? Had she neglected him?

Too many things she didn't know. So many memories she didn't have. Her story of Sue and Steve was not up to the job. She would need a new story. She would need to talk to Jo and Sam and listen to them. Was it safe to call them again? She would need to get home. She picked up the pad and turned on the light.

High Art

Meggie had left Sue/Sam to sleep and it was late in the morning before she walked gingerly down the stairs in a pair of jeans that Meggie thought she should never have bought because they were too young for her. Meggie was standing in the kitchen and on the phone in a pair of culottes,

"I said he's not here! No, no I don't know where he is? Look, if you want to talk to him call his cell!" She hung up the phone and down her head. She muttered something under her breath. Was it 'bastard'? Even with her teenage hearing Sue couldn't make it out.

"Good morning Meggie," Sue said

"Oh! You're up! Good morning, did you sleep well?"

"Yes," said Sue gratefully even though she hadn't. "...it's a beautiful room...did you decorate it?"

"Oh no," said Meggie dismissively "...I've got no 'eye', that's what you Brits say isn't it?"

"Some of us, yes...you write, don't you?" And Meggie smiled appreciatively,

"Yes. Yes, I do. Those jeans look good on you," she smiled and offered Sue a cup of coffee with a gesture. Sue nodded,

"Are you working on anything at the moment?" Asked Sue sounding very grown up. Meggie rose to the attempt from Stephen's daughter to talk to her woman to woman,

"Yes, well I'm just dealing with the fallout from the last piece…let me tell you over breakfast. There's this great diner not far from here. Not many left…it's the real McCoy after all those retro places you're used to in London."

"I'm starving," smiled Sue, they gave up on coffee and walked the half mile or so to the front door and let it hugely clunk shut behind them.

It had stopped raining and the sun was warm enough. There was that wet dust, as clean as a city could get smell. The pavements were still shiny in places. She was glad to be back in a recognisable city; dirty and crowded and everyone speaking English with a variety of accents. These streets were wider and sunnier than London though. And the cabs were yellow and there were hundreds of them. It wasn't London but enough of a city for Sue to feel at home. Then they sat in a diner, in a booth with red leather padded seats, just like home. They ordered large breakfasts neither had any capacity to actually finish. They talked easily, especially Meggie. She tried to talk about their mutual loved one,

"Your dad has missed you," and Sue nodded from a large mouthful of pancakes and sausage and maple syrup. Meggie took another breath to speak and stopped and took a sip of coffee.

"That article?" Asked Sue after swallowing, and Meggie lightened. Meggie was an established art critic now. She had just got a little bit more established. She had written a piece called High Art as Sub-culture. for a magazine that lots of people who liked an argument had read. She talked about big ideas in a relaxed way that Sue could understand. More than that. The lovely thing about Meggie was that when Sue's face went puzzled because she couldn't remember/had never really understood (it was a long time ago) what 'mimetic' meant Meggie didn't use-it somehow.

Back home if someone who knew what 'mimetic' meant was talking to someone who didn't it was almost their duty to use-it. They had to patronisingly explain it badly so that the person still didn't know what mimetic meant or carry on talking with no intention of letting the other person know what mimetic meant. The important thing was to show the other person they knew something the other did not, not to communicate.

All Meggie said was, "...copying...representing something, with the emphasis on the artist trying to represent something more than the object or person...you know like truth or beauty?" And then carried on talking. Sue carried on listening as Meggie talked about mimetics becoming less of a dirty word and more just a niche interest for an unrepresented but wealthy group. Not the art élite but the moneyed élite. Something like that.

Sue was interested but had one internal eye on a memory about the last time someone had said truth or beauty without metaphorical quotation marks around them. It was a very long time ago, but just like in design with 'trim', it appeared that what had gone around was coming around, albeit as 'accent'.

It was her who had said truth and beauty without irony and she had been eighteen and just started the foundation year of her fine art degree. Why had she returned to that time again? Just because she looked eighteen again or because it was important? There was only one way to find out and while Meggie chatted amiably about Andy Warhol actually valuing fine art. Sue's mind wandered back to the late '70s again.

She had been in her first proper life class at a top London Art School. Like her father and possibly her grandfather had wanted to be, could have been if they hadn't had to go to work.

Sue was the first person in her family to go to any kind of further education. They were so proud, so happy. And so was she. She was used to snobby girls sneering at her because she was a clever working-class girl who had gone to the local Good-Comp. Besides she had known that she was good at art. She had learned from her dad and brilliant teacher, Mr Smith, who had indulged himself, not 'like that', by letting her spend hours in the art department.

Her Art School contemporaries had actually been to Amsterdam and Paris and Rome. Walked their streets and felt their particular light on their faces. They had looked up at paintings that she had put a magnifying glass over. Musty-smelling books containing mainly black-and-white photos with fine tissue paper pages over them. She still had them somewhere. Her dad's books. The loft probably. She would get those down.

She didn't feel like the only neatly dressed 'plebby' girl in her year even though she was. She sat in a room full of posh people from South Kensington and Chelsea townhouses all trying to look like New York heroin addicts who lived in doorways. Talking like they came from a 1950s film about the East End. It was painful. The safety pins and carefully torn clothes. And Hugo whatsisface would actually overdose too. They all sneered and snorted and sniggered at her crochet beret and she sat up tall on her stool. A better artist than nearly all of them.

She felt she was sitting with her dad and her grandfather in that first life class, autodidacts the pair of them. Men who had spent their Sunday afternoons traipsing around London looking at beautiful pictures and searching through second-hand books in obscure locations all over the South East. Bored the pants off her mum and her nan with the beauties of Renaissance Florence and Rome. Sent her sister off to sleep at night with eulogies to Donatello. Not her though. She had lapped it up. While Jan had sulked round the National Sue had gazed up at The Judgement of Paris enraptured. Bathed in the beauty in the soft white skin and the love of her dad.

Then, at the life class at least two generations had worked to get her into, a less attractive model had settled into a pose and she had drawn quickly and bold. The teacher had been impressed, other students had leaned back on their stools to look and the teacher had turned her easel round so everyone could see. He asked her what she had been trying to achieve,

"Something beautiful." She had said meekly, a little tired from the intense effort. It felt like the entire room had burst out laughing. Then, what was her name? Pip. Pip had said in her posh East London drawl,

"But wha' is bwooty?" With an intensity as fake as her accent and everyone had burst out laughing again. All

109

that work, not just by her but by her dad as well, to get to a place where she could explore things that were beautiful.

Years of drawing and drawing and drawing, perfecting a skill. Looking and looking and looking to find what made a picture marvellous. Only to find that it was all about 'subjective expression' now. Beauty was subjective, truth was subjective and your judgement was only your perspective.

At the time Sue had thought it was just a convenient theory for a bunch of complacent toffs who didn't want to do their homework. Lazy left-wing intellectuals she had called them at home. With their fake Working-Class accents and their contempt for her, an actual Working-Class person. No wonder she had voted for Norman Tebbit. He was from Ponders End, not far from her and he went to grammar school. Not like that IDS they had in now, public school, he didn't even sound Scottish.

But that wasn't right? She'd already voted Tory by then hadn't she. She was eighteen on the 1st and voted on the 4th of May, but she didn't start college until the October. Had she already made up her mind about Pip and the others?

Anyway, Apparently, judging by what Meggie said, Pip's ideas had taken hold and now,

"...the view the mainstream has of it is derogatory and dismissive...People who participate in high art are largely wealthy but the status of high art itself is no longer unquestioned..." Sue sighed. She thought Meggie was stretching a point to make an article. And people shouldn't quote themselves, that wasn't polite.

She was also deeply resentful. Back in the day when she had tried to explain how she felt to Steve he had been derogatory and dismissive. The son of 'old money' he didn't seem to care about what she had labelled 'standards' like the staunch Thatcherite that she had been.

She suddenly regretted the way she had said 'Well you're old money' so nastily when she had spent, the new and actual, money she had earned on something he thought was 'kitsch' or 'passé' or one of those other snobby words. How had they stayed together so long? He had 'done the tour', albeit in a tent, when he was twelve or thirteen. He and his parents talked about those trips with a kind of nostalgic but dismissive guiltiness just to emphasise their social class in a world that only said that 'classlessness' was good. Snobs to the core.

The snobby Duggens had prints, whole books of prints when those things had been Thirty Pounds, a week's wages. He took it all for granted too. More than that, when Pip et al had sniggered at her he had not defended her.

Now he was married to someone who agreed with Sue but could say it differently. But now she wasn't sure she agreed with that Sue anymore, and she was a Sue underneath the Sam or Andrea or whoever.

Wasn't it good that things had opened up? That people whose skin wasn't white, or sometimes a bit 'olive', were recognised as beautiful? That people who hadn't done the tour could judge beauty for themselves? But then so much of what was art now wasn't beautiful at all? But then, was beauty the be all and end all anyway?

"…I'm boring you," said Meggie.

"Oh no no sorry no I was miles aw...the opposite of bored I was...just thinking about what you said...it's about who decides right? Who decides what's good or not?" Meggie nodded reservedly, "...my mum says she thinks it's supposed to be all about feelings now, not the thing, what the picture or whatever actually looks like, but how everyone...each different person... feels about it?"

"Yes, that's more or less it. But...how is it in London now? I've heard it's pretty bad there? And now Brexit!" asked Meggie in a conspiratorial tone. Sam had voted Remain. Sue pretended she was at work for a moment and ignored the last part,

"Well you know, as long as your subjects look unhappy and stay in shabby rooms...and for people who are supposed to be pushing boundaries and offending the establishment they don't half get offended easily...I... my mum says..."

"But they are the establishment now that's what I've been saying" Meggie was getting passionate now, not aggressive or anything just passionate, "... I mean...they're the ones who decide what's good...wasn't your mum at school with Paul Elder?" Meggie meant college when she said school Sue knew that, but Paul Elder was a mystery.

"Was she? I don't know...Who's Paul Elder"

"Well he's... a...he welds the pipes? She said 'welds' as if just saying the word would get her shirt grimy.

"Oh him...I quite like those pipes, for a bit, Intriguing? For a bit. I think most people don't like them you know, ...cos they're not you know...beautiful... Not like a...I think normal people have got that old sort of taste, really haven't they? We? …did mum go to college with him?" She had no memory, but she had not been into sculpture, and had dropped out.

"Yes, yes, you should ask her… he's a fellow of the Royal Society now," Sue was going to assume Meggie was talking about the Royal Society of Arts not the one for the protection of birds. "…it's come full circle…the lunatics have taken over the asylum. I didn't write that of course, but most people understood what I meant by the 'attempt to democratize art undermined art itself' paragraph." She was quoting herself again. Sue nodded like a teenager who wanted to look like she understood but didn't and said,

"Paul Elder." as if repeating the name so that she wouldn't forget it. "…they did a lovely Rubens exhibition last spring, or the spring before? …oh no that's the Royal Academy. But? The exhibitions that get the crowds, they're all, well mostly, 'high art', in London I mean. There was the Rubens and one on the idea of Greek beauty at the British Museum last year. They're the ones that sell the fridge magnets. My mum's got loads. Most normal people, ordinary people I mean, they love high art…say nasty things about Tracy Emin's bed. She can't draw. Well, in London anyway," this interested Meggie and her eyes lit up with the prospect of a follow-up article,

"I think it's similar here. I had been thinking of the big exhibitions as more part of the tourism industry but…tourists are people too?" The inhabitants of two very different but equally touristy cities laughed conspiratorially, both thinking of their underground rail networks in August. "…Maybe there's another…maybe there are three groups we should be looking at?" She could see that Sue/Sam was struggling to find just one. "I mean, the old élite that is no longer, the new élite that tries so hard not to be elitist but is, and the…" and Sue/Sam interrupted because she just knew that Meggie, whose Facebook post about the clothes of the people in the queues at the Louvre had been a thinly disguised anti-pleb rant, would struggle to find a nice word for the rest of us,

"Normal people," she said emphatically and they laughed again for different reasons.

"…But that's a bit neat. Life isn't that neat and…but isn't the place Dad works…isn't that all about…realism…and skill…isn't skill important for Dad?" She had been so very angry when he left that she hadn't really taken in his excuse for leaving.

"The Academy. Yes. The Academy does maintain high standards in representing...particularly the figure but…"

"…and didn't Andy Warhol help set it up or something…wasn't he anti-establishment er new establishment back in the day, Andy Warhol?"

"Yes… But the point is it's about whose judgement of what art is has influence now and the status of high art within a new paradigm."

"Is Dad not selling so well nowadays?"

"Yes, yes, he's selling pretty well…but it's not about the money so much…there's a lot of money to go around…it's about the status of high art. It's not perceived as the best any more, merely another niche interest at best and sometimes just a foil for the new élite to rail against.

They cannot stand the idea of their being the establishment and, well, Stephen doesn't command the sort of fees that say a Koons can …. he did the giant puppy covered in flowers?" Sue had seen a picture of it somewhere a long time ago and nodded at the now very passionate American lady.

"That might be fashion?" She said tentatively. Meggie's face looked bored, just for a moment "…And well, some of the new stuff is good isn't it? Well I like some modern art. Can't you just love both, you know have your own individual tastes? That you build up over your life?" but Meggie wasn't sure, she nodded a 'sort of' nod, "…I can sort of see what you're saying. I…my mum says…she works in design... that some people coming in now with good degrees from good colleges can't really draw, Standards…is that what you're saying?"

"That's part of it…yes…it's more about the dominant ideology that imposes…" and Meggie looked at her watch and looked regretful. Really. "…I'm sorry I've been raving and now it's almost Eleven-thirty. "…I actually have a meeting in less than half an hour. Let's talk more later if you want? That idea about tourists being people too is worth thinking about..." Sue nodded enthusiastically thinking Meggie did indeed need to get out more, "…What do you want to do? You could go back to the house or…?" Sue didn't think she wanted to sit about.

"I think I'll go for a wander. I've always wanted to…I love New York," and she smiled unable to remember where yesterday's story of young love and betrayal had started or gone. Meggie gave her a key and pointed her in the direction of Central Park.

Once she had started walking and didn't have to pretend to be nineteen or was it twenty for a while, Sue realised how tired she was. She walked another block and found a Starbucks. A familiar place where she knew the coffee would be good enough. It wasn't busy and she got a comfy chair. There she was in New York for the first time with the museums and the skyscrapers and yellow taxis. The list of paintings she liked that were in New York was as long as her arm.

She had always wanted to go to New York and look at the art and eat a hotdog in central Park. Julie had been and bought another suitcase to bring back all the toys and clothes that cost as many dollars as they would in pounds back home. Or a 'thrift store', she could be in one of those picking up something interesting for one of her girls so they could say 'my mum picked it up in a New York thrift store'. Or Grand Central Station, she had seen that beautiful place in a dozen films. She had time to go up the Statue of Liberty or the Rockefeller or the Empire State Building and take in the magisterial views in the land of the free.

But no. She was on the ground staring blankly at a wall in Starbucks. Not that she could tell you what colour it was or anything. Over the last how-many months she had done or had done to her a lot of things that were worth thinking about. But she wasn't thinking about any of those.

She wasn't thinking about anything. Her wondering had dried up. She was staring blankly at a wall without looking. Vacant. Not even trying to focus on anything. She wasn't feeling anything either. Not that she thought about it. She let out a slow sigh and stared towards the wall some more. Just like when the kids were small. Time passed with the only event being that her coffee got cold.

She was still staring at the wall when her phone rang. It was Steve,

"Hi Sammo it's Dad. We've got you a flight on our residency scheme. The only problem is that you'll have to leave this afternoon. Can you get here in half an hour...I'll stand you a cab...There's some admin. Nothing heavy."

"Okay...Dad.... where are you." Time to reboot.

Steve was on the phone again when she arrived at the refurbished warehouse of the type that most of the London offices had been based on since 1984. Some exposed brickwork, a metal pillar, a sample-book patchwork of different sorts of uneven flooring. Or it could have been a coffee shop from anywhere in Europe with better pictures on the wall, this Academy.

Was this place, the real deal as it was, somehow more authentic because it was the first to pretend no effort had been made? Or less? Steve put his hand over the microphone on a cell phone and pointed to a sophisticated-looking woman about her age saying,

"This is Aggie, she'll do the admin..." before turning away and walking into an office and going back to a placatory tone, "...Mr Pointer I'm sure no... I know your daughter... yes she has a name... very upset but the Academy cannot be held resp....Yes, yes, I am responsible but it is a personal matter between myself and...No, no, I know how old she is but she is an adul..." and the door swung shut.

Sophisticated Aggie had been watching him go. She sighed and stopped herself from making an unsophisticated face out of respect for his daughter.

"Hello, it's Samantha isn't it?" She said with pleasant efficiency. Sue/Samantha's face froze. What was the name on the passport? How was she going to manage this one? Ah yes, that was easy. The key would be to follow the fashion of the day and give Aggie Too Much Information.

"Yes, that's what my dad calls me," she smiled and puffed out a little 'let me explain' huff. Aggie sighed with resignation and led her into the office at the back of the foyer.

"You see after the divorce I, my mum told me what my dad had done, you know, and I..." But Aggie stopped her with a raised eyebrow. This woman wasn't going to chat amicably and tell her how she did her commute. Samantha/Sue reached into her bag and quickly looked into her passport to see what her name was (Andrea McCauley, 1st of May 1994. She was twenty-three) before passing it over.

"My step-father is American...my middle name...everyone except dad calls me...Andy." The name made her flinch. Aggie didn't flinch or look up from her screen, she was an administrator in a top post-graduate Academy, half of the students and most of the staff's names changed at least every few semesters. She just kept typing. She stood up and photocopied the passport and came back to her small neat desk where her boss's sudden daughter who was cadging a flight to Monet's garden with her Unit Fours was now sitting docile.

"Okay Andy, I'm going to give you a ticket on United two-one-three, check-in at Three from Jay-Eff-Kay, Gate Five." And the printer began to whirr. "…You'll get to Paris at around Nine in the morning, where the other students will catch a train. You, presumably, will not want a trip to Giverny?" Sue/Samantha/Andrea/Andy shook her head. "…so, you'll need a Eurostar to London? You can find a hotel in central Paris on your own?" And she typed and swished on her tablet without waiting for answers, "…For which your father will pay," she added with some relish, "…The only available train is at Seven-Thirty the following evening. You will get a day in Paris. Will you be making your own way to the airport?" she asked in the tone of someone with a lot to do and who expected an affirmative answer. Sue nodded obediently. Aggie leaned back to the printer, pulled the ticket confirmation from the tray and handed it to Sue.

"All done?"

"All done," and Aggie smiled and added, "…nice to meet you Andy." Which made Andy get up and say,

"Thank you, Aggie, nice to meet you," and go away.

Sue had her ticket home now and the feeling of relief was exhilarating. She texted Steve from a cab to say she couldn't find him and she had to go back and pick up her stuff and get to the airport. She sat spread out in the seat and realised that she was leaving Steve suddenly and without a proper acknowledgement of what he had done for her. Her eyes twinkled as she looked out of the window at all the New York-New Yorkishness going by.

She gasped, time for another revelation. She was in New York. The New York. The New York of *Wolf and Fox Hunt, Peter Paul Rubens, ca 1615-21, Oil on canvas; 96 5/8 x 148 1/8 in, Metropolitan Museum of Art, John Stewart Kennedy Fund, 1910*. From Mr Smith's art room wall in Chingford. She reached into her pocket to check the time on her phone. She looked into her purse to see how many dollars she had left,

"Excuse me driver?" She said in her own voice. "…could you drop me off at the Metropolitan Museum?" She was feeling insecure so she was already carrying most of her, and Albin's, possessions with her. She could get a new toothbrush and some more deodorant at the airport. She only had about forty minutes so she would have to be selective, very selective.

Sue almost ran to the second floor of the absolutely massive building that made the UK's National Gallery look like a measly but contractually unavoidable bequeathed Town-Hall annex in a small provincial town. She asked the man in the corner and walked briskly in the directions she had been given. There it was.

What would she see this time? Would she get that feeling? That lost-it-doesn't-matter feeling? She did in Rennes when she saw The Tiger Hunt (Funny place for a German domestic electricals merger jolly up, but there you go). Not a curly edged poster in a Chingford Good-comp school's art room. Not a too glossy reproduction in a yellowing book in her attic, also in Chingford. The actual thing. The actual *Wolf and Fox Hunt, Peter Paul Rubens, ca 1615-21, Oil on canvas; 96 5/8 x 148 1/8 in, Metropolitan Museum of Art, John Stewart Kennedy Fund, 1910.*

The desperate and wild-eyed wolves, that horse that wasn't quite as frightened as he was in *Tiger Hunt, Peter Paul Rubens, 1615-1616, oil on canvas, 101 x 128 in, Musée des Beaux Arts de Rennes*, and not as beautiful as he was in the little drawing in the National Gallery, that horse had been through a lot.

And that horrible woman just looking on at all that pain. Amused. Thank you, Dad, thank you Mr Smith.

But hang on, that calf on the red-coated hunter with the spear? Come to think of it, the coat as well? Not up to Peter Paul's usual standards. She refocused on the poor animals in the centre. They were brilliant. Fighting for their lives. The fox sneaking off, would he make it out alive? The other one under the horse's hooves. And that bloody woman entertained by it all.

But then all of a sudden Sue was looking hard at the posh woman's companion. Wasn't he enjoying it too? Why had she never thought about that in all the years she had been coming back to Mr Smith's posters illustrating the same horse in three different masterpieces? She sighed and looked. His eyes were fixed on one of the wolves. The wolf had seen him and stared back as two dogs bit into him and the man was drawing his sword. Where was the sport in that? The wolf was done very well, you could see he was fighting for his life and knew where the next blows would be coming from.

But the man, smug enough, but his face just wasn't up to Ruben's par. She had got fussy over the years.

Okay it had to happen sometime and now was the time; Sue Duggen did not like a Rubens.

Given that she had not exactly made a special trip to see the painting she was not that put out. A bit shocked maybe, but not unhappy. She would get on the plane, see her girls and then go to the National and look at the drawing of the horse for the Tiger Hunt and be happy.

And the Judgement of Paris of course, that painting had been her companion since she was a little girl and she missed it dreadfully. There had been times, long times when she hadn't gone to see it for over a year but she always came back to the soft skin and lush woodland. She would get on the plane, see her girls and go to the National.

She needed to catch up with Julie too, how was her mum? The plane! What time was it? Time to go. She had spent twenty minutes looking at some art and then the same amount of time in the shop picking up some presents for the girls, her best friend and bloody Emma for some reason. She bought things with images of work she hadn't had time to see. In the queue in the gift shop her phone rang. It was Steve. She pressed 'reject call' and twinkled all over again.

Luckily, Aggie had lied about the check in time. Sue was glad she was a bit late so that she could spend as little time as possible in the airport. She now associated airports with being accosted by fat Swiss human vivisectionists. She kept her eyes open but there was no sign of him. He had probably lost her trail. Once on the plane Sue was greeted by a genuine post-graduate student of fine art,

"Hi, you must be Samantha Duggen," smiled a beautiful and beautifully dressed young American with large white teeth. Sue told the truth,

"Sorry, no," she smiled emphatically with her little yellow gnashers. But that was too antisocial and the group to which the woman belonged looked friendly enough. It was just she was fed up with pretending to be someone else. She realised she had ten hours sitting next to these people so she added, "…I'm Sue…Sue Jolly (her maiden name) …do people think I'm Steve's daughter?" The beautiful American laughed an embarrassed yes. "…I'm his ex…an ex-partner…I get on with his daughters though," she said and the thrill of the possibility of a nice long gossip ran through the group.

Given that the ten young people were spaced out along a window and centre aisle and into the next row, some people spent most of the first hour of the flight simply passing juicy bits back and forth. The remaining seat in the second centre aisle was occupied by a mechanical engineer from Stroud on his way back from visiting his mum. He was fascinated.

Sue was vague about time frames, going for the 'on and off' explanation to explain how she knew him, his current wife, his daughters and his ex-wife while ostensibly being only in her early twenties. She did not cast Steve in a very good light. In return she found out that apparently, Steve had a thing for post-graduate young women and was currently in the middle of a scandal with one Delilah Pointer who was supposed to come to Giverny but had dropped out at the last minute. Sue had her seat.

Delilah, being a native New Yorker who already had friends in the city, had not socialized much with her fellow students. The beautiful young man next to the beautiful young woman (Josh and Ellen respectively) had been the closest to Delilah through a shared interest early Italian Renaissance painting and Northern Italian food. For an indigenous she had not been that savvy and according to Josh had 'daddy issues. Josh was very keen on finding out how Meggie felt but Sue could only share her suspicion that things were 'icy' between them.

It was, according to everyone including the mechanical engineer, a great shame because Delilah was so talented, or more accurately, sooO talented. Josh had some photos on his phone and everyone was right. Delilah's drawings were delicate without being prissy. They appeared to catch characters pretty well if her sketches of Steve were anything to go by.

At one point, a woman called Sarah, who had taken advantage of the stewardess service quite a lot, broke into a passable rendition of 'My My My Delilah' by Tom Jones, which made Sue smile because she used to sing that with her Mum when it first came out. And Jan, or Janet as she was then. And Dad trying to look disgruntled while he read the paper.

Prancing around the tiny flat with wooden spoons. The music wafting from the radio in the kitchenette, through the hatch and to the sitting room, as they, all three of them, swirled in and out singing, "My my, my Delilah, Why why, why Delilah," all three of them, her and Mum and Janet. Singing about a man explaining what he'd done to his girlfriend. He hadn't called her a 'bitch' or a 'ho', just stabbed her to death.

Janet must only have been Five or Six then. She must have been what? Ten? That made Sue feel a bit old then. Thinking about the 'gramophone' that looked like a cupboard and the thinning lino and the orange splodgey wallpaper. Thinking about her Mum long gone now. Massive stroke when the girls were so small. Then her dad not long after. Cancer. The knowledge that he might have got Alzheimer's if he had lived was no consolation.

Much as she was enjoying the company of these youngsters, with all their enthusiasm and carefree charm, she liked feeling a bit old. Liked all the memories. Even the painful ones. 'Experience...' she thought before saying slightly out of the blue,

"Delilah will be fine, she's young," that seemed to be the end of the Stephen Duggen and his peccadillos part of the conversation and the group broke into smaller chats that better suited the seating plan.

Sue listened politely to Ellen's East Coast oh so enthusiastic babbling for long enough to be polite. Then she closed her eyes and pretended to sleep. Jan had been such a pretty child, classic. A lovely round face, likened to the ultimate back then, Twiggy. blonde hair, blue eyes, when blonde hair and blue eyes was unequivocally the best. The ideal.

There had been three TV channels and about the same number of ways of being beautiful. There was 'dark and lovely', not actually black just a bit olive-skinned. Sue had been in her twenties when she first heard the phrase 'black is beautiful'. There was …no there were only two ways to be beautiful back then. And blonde was definitely the best.

Jan had won the DNA lottery. No-one had really expected Jan to achieve anything at school. She didn't even need a personality really. All she had to do was carry on looking pretty, have good manners and land herself a nice man. So while Sue slogged away at O and then A levels, Jan read Jackie magazine and prattled on with mum in the kitchen. And dad shouted 'Get off that phone' as she sat on the telephone table by the front door and chatted with not quite as pretty Mandy after tea.

"I was never allowed seconds." That's what Jan had said so many years later, before the hospital door was locked in Zurich. Sue hadn't known what she meant, thought Jan was deranged. Intoxicated by the desperation to have a young body again. But now she remembered. Jan was never allowed another helping of dinner. Mum was harder on Jan. Sue always sort of knew that. But now she remembered. Jan had to keep looking pretty. Sue was dark-haired and, at least when she was young, quite plain.

Plain. That was a word she had truly hated. Heard through the hatch or walking down the corridor. Then when she was in the room it was all about how bright she was. And the word 'intelligent' always used with that tone of mistrust. Intelligence was second prize for girls back then. If being blonde and blue eyed was the bottle of champagne, then intelligence was a box of liqueur chocolates. Turned to only in desperation.

Yes, her mum and dad were truly proud of her when she passed the eleven-plus exam and got into the Good-comp, then college. But they were also relieved. If she couldn't be beautiful...

Of course, by the time she realised that she wasn't actually that intelligent she'd already established herself in Design. But that was much later, perhaps thirty years. And she only really understood that Jan was actually quite intelligent a month ago. But when she was seventeen Sue would sit in the National Gallery unconsoled by being intelligent and stare bitterly at golden haired Venus just taking the apple from Paris, not even bothering to smile in gratitude and not at all surprised. Juno was right to be angry. And Venus had fat thighs. Great big fat thighs.

They were both slim but Jan was the pretty one, everyone said it, and pretty mattered so much more back then. Maybe things had been changing in other places but not Chingford. So, Jan didn't have to work for anything. She just had to be. She had got a few CSEs and a job as a pretty secretary in some company's West End office where she matched the décor in the foyer. Then she married an exec.

Sue worked and slogged her way up the increasingly greasy pole. Got called hard, unfeminine, heard people say they couldn't believe she had a husband, and 'her poor kids'. Jan just sat in her big house in Switzerland and looked pretty.

Jo and Sam of course had to be both bright and pretty. But it wasn't the same for them. They were expected to work, achieve something. Be something. Not just pretty. They could have any colour hair they wanted, wear anything and it was okay. All Jan had was 'pretty' and 'natural blonde'. All she ever had.

She had been schooled in how to be the ideal woman. By everyone. She had the requisite physical characteristics; blonde, slim, peaches-and-cream skin. Rubens would have died for that skin. But the, what would you call it; 'manner'? Her manner had to be learned. Learned from dad and mum and school and the telly. Everyone.

Sue had good skin too, Steve had seen that, painted it. But Jan was truly radiant just doing the drying up. Sue couldn't remember washing up, she was busy doing her homework or watching the news with dad. Had they just pretended she was a boy? They never got a son and back then when their mum showed off her second daughter down the shops people would say things like 'better luck next time' or 'still, she's very pretty' into the pram. Was Sue the boy and Janet the girl?

There was that settee, two seats; one for mum and one for dad. And Sue had the easy chair when she came into the sitting room from doing her homework. Dad would lean over and tap Jan on the shoulder and Jan would get out of the easy chair and go to the leatherette pouffe without a word. And they would watch the news, Sue and her dad, and it was all strikes and stoppages and balance of payments and dad and Sue would argue.

They were both Labour to begin with but they were always anti-strike together. They'd agree on 'holding the country to ransom' with their blood up in the sitting room. She had felt so grown up and a part of something.

Sue heard herself, the first time she was Eighteen and about to vote, all impassioned and shrill, '…held to ransom by the trade unions…state monopolies. She couldn't remember or even imagine who that person was who voted for Norman Tebbit. That shrivelled-up old politician who had once said 'on your bike'. She could see Jan rolling her eyes and waiting for the next programme. She could see her flicked blonde hair like Farah Fawcett, remembered that skirt she had with the pleats.

But she couldn't remember what Jan actually thought about anything. Or her mum. She saw Jan drying the dishes with mum in the kitchen through the hatch. She could still just feel that sort of jealous feeling that she was not included. She heard Jan call through,

"But won't we just get more inflation again?" Her dad heard too and said,

"Any tea going?" Saw the way he raised his eyebrows as he turned his head and looked at her before turning back to the news. And she had raised her eyebrows too hadn't she. Said something about private investment and Whitehall bureaucrats. She had held Jan back too. Had she?

Jan would sit on the pouffe and turn and smile and beg to watch Top of the Pops and dad would lean forward and tousle her hair and let her watch. He never bothered to argue with Jan. Except about that wedding. Dad had thought that wedding was 'too fancy…a waste of money.' But Oskar had lots of money so it didn't matter.

Mum and dad had loved Jan's wedding, not Sue and starving artist Steve's wedding, making his wife go out and work, not a proper one. It had sounded lovely; Steve's family church in Shropshire. Dingy little chapel. Rain dripping in from a leaky roof while the vicar droned on and half her friends lost on the A-roads. Dull reception at Steve's snobby Mum's. No beer for her dad.

Jan's wedding was planned and dreamed of and everyone got new clothes. Copies of Pronuptia all over the place whenever Sue came home. But she was busy with her padded shoulders and Tongs herself wasn't she. Her dad and mum had gone out and bought a whole set of kitchen equipment that Sue had designed as a wedding present.

And that dress! Her dad made a remark about meringues and muttered something about Princess Di being jealous under his breath. Big Church in the West End. And all that talk about her kitchen in Zurich when Oskar got promoted. Jan had remodelled it to match the coffeemaker. She had been proud of her big sister once. And her lovely clothes. She shopped and entertained. And picked up French for Oskar and German for everyone else in a month. But Oskar didn't marry her for that so she shopped and entertained and moaned about the help. She took up aerobics and jogging and then Pilates and then something else.

And bit by bit, she started to look down on Sue as Sue slogged away and got as high up in domestic electrical design as it was possible to get, which wasn't high enough for Jan. Oskar worked in pharmaceuticals and got richer and richer and richer. And Jan kept jogging and going to the hairdressers and was trim and peachy and beautiful.

No kids, they weren't that fertile either of them. Look how long it took Sue to have her first. But Jan wasn't that interested in kids, forgot Sam and Jo's birthdays. Kept her figure. Did everything she was supposed to year on year, from the shifting shades of ash highlights in her hair right down to the perfect shade of polish on her pinkie toenails. Laughed and flirted with his friends, had lunch with their wives. The ideal woman. Then she got old. Not even old, just not young any more.

Sue felt a burst of guilt for hitting Jan so hard on the head with that jug in the hospital. It was difficult this revelation, Jan couldn't help being pretty, Sue couldn't help being bright. Neither of them asked for things to be that way. Unless being one of the best domestic appliance designers in Europe counted then neither of them had done much to change things for the better. Sue felt a nudge and warm breath on her cheek, her cheeks were wet.

"You okay Sue?" Asked the beautiful American with the white teeth. She had been crying in her 'sleep'.

"I was just thinking about my sister," she said and sniffed. "…sorry." But she didn't want to talk really. What could a twenty-year-old American know about prancing about on lino in 1969. She'd have to explain what a hatch was. Probably end up defending the En-Aich-of-Ess too.

"I've got a sister," said the beautiful American and she put her arm around Sue and squeezed gently. They took each other's hands and sat. Sue saw that Ellen wasn't going to ask her to talk about it and she was going to sit and hold hands.

Ellen dozed off and moved her hand away to get comfy. Sue couldn't sleep straight away. She was nearly home and if Oskar or Albin hadn't got free or hadn't picked up her trail, she would be home perhaps by tomorrow afternoon. She would stay out in public places so that if Albin or Oskar tried to grab her, she could make public exhibition of herself again. She would see her girls and they could stop worrying. They could see she wasn't mad. She was still their mum. And Jo's knee was fixed. And she could pop round to Julie's for a coffee and a chat. She could get her something nice from Paris. Maybe call Alfie. Oh dear.

Nearly home. She needed to sort out her bag and reduce the people she was to a manageable number before she could be just her again. Not in front of this lot. She'd have time in Paris. And she fell asleep too.

What's it all About Alfie?

Albin and Oskar were looking for a shampoo-advert girl with long blonde hair and great boots on the concourse of the Gare du Nord. So they didn't notice the brown-bobbed sophisticate in a lovely and very expensive suit purchased via her very own personal shopper on a Visa courtesy of Albin Johnson on the Champs Eliseé. Sue had found the card in Albin's wallet when she was finally clearing out her bag at a café in Paris.

At first she had been quite cross. Had she known about the credit card she might've avoided having to see Steve again. She could've gone straight from Houston to London if she had found a way to deal with her passport name and her credit card name being different. But if she had used the card Albin might have been able to track her. At least now she was nearly home. She could get a personalised Paris makeover and get some clothes that she felt more like herself in. Tailored. Smart. Shoes that didn't weigh a ton.

Sue had enjoyed the company of the twenty-somethings babbling and bubbling along; experiencing for the first-time things that she had been and done years ago. Amazed at the ordinary. Deaf, dumb and blind to lots of things yet. Completely oblivious to their own uniqueness and trying so hard to make themselves appear interesting. Unaware that they didn't have to try. So fresh and new. Her own kids seemed savvier somehow? Not as gushing. Maybe they gushed more with people their own age?

Sue wasn't really gushy at all, never had been, and found it quite tiring. And she wanted to look older and wiser because she was. And she was nearly home. She could wear the suit to meetings. Or not, she didn't care. The great boots were in her newly purchased black wheeled suitcase, they would look great on Sam. Her suéded toes virtually floated over the concourse. She was nearly home. Nearly with Sam and Jo, a proper cup of tea and a trip to the National with Julie. Julie needed to get out and they could have tea and cake in the café afterwards. She was getting a bit obsessed with that trip to the National. Why was that so important?

First class is lovely. She could stretch out and smile at the businessman in her carriage and try and read a French paper. They were just over half-way into the tunnel when the train just stopped. The tannoy explained that blah de blah. She and another British person laughed out loud. Nearly home. She slept like a baby.

She didn't notice Albin and Oskar either. Not until they were all getting off the train at Saint Pancras. They'd gone first class too and they were a few paces in front of her looking around keenly. She quickly got out her phone and looked down at it as she walked slowly. Her bob obscured her face, her ankle turned, she kept walking, stayed in the crowd. She controlled her breathing, she suppressed wondering how or if they knew she was there, she looked at her phone. She followed an American family so she'd end up in the right passport queue without having to look up. All the while trying to find the camera so she could take incriminating photos. She dropped her phone. A hand, a man's hand picked it up. Of course they knew she was there.

"Hello Sue," said Albin cheerfully as he interlocked his arm with hers and deftly pushed her wrist downwards with her phone. It would hurt if she struggled. She rolled her eyes and looked towards the Customs barrier. Both the guards were already looking at her.

"You can't do this!" She yelled. "...I'm a British subject, this is kidnapping!" People looked round, Albin didn't care and he purred quietly,

"It's Prevention of Terrorism," and raised his eyebrows. Sue burst into tears,

"You can't do this," she wept and Albin squashed his mouth into an oh-yes-I-can as he pulled her along with no pretence of gentleness. "...This is wrong...I haven't done..." but she couldn't finish. There wasn't much about the Prevention of Terrorism Act in the Metro as a rule but if local councils could use it catch people who weren't recycling properly it was probably pretty comprehensive when it came to false passports, theft, assaulting MI5 or 6 officers and so forth. She didn't know what to do. But what was this? "...My name is..." Albin got his free hand over her mouth, smacking her in the teeth with her phone. The American family looked round. She managed to turn her head enough to bite into his wrist hard and wriggled and wrestled wildly and shouted. "...please..." Albin grabbed her hair but she pulled back, losing a clump to his fist. She didn't feel it. "... Albin...someone...this man has..." Albin grabbed her face so she stamped on his foot as hard as she could and writhed," ... I'm not a terrorist! I'm Church of

135

England." She could see a few people looking at her suspiciously as she struggled as best she could. Albin was red-eyed, he huffed and heaved her along with a weary expression on his face for the crowd. She wouldn't get away this time. He reached into his pocket and produced an ID of some kind and the guards let them through onto the shopping mall. He had a smug professional look on his face. She screamed through his hand but hardly any sound came out. As he dragged her on her heels she lost a lovely new suède shoe. A wall of police appeared from nowhere like a storm-tossed hull and one of them held on to her. "…this is wrong!" she pleaded, looking straight into the young officer's face,

"It's all right Miss…Madam," he said "…we know… we've got you now." She heard a not so loud but ear piercingly posh,

"What!" From behind her. Another two policemen were holding onto Albin. He was trying to wave his ID but his hands were put behind his back.

"All right madam come with me, we'll get you somewhere safe," said the policeman. She let him lead her away, dazed, as someone else slipped on her shoe. Outside, her dedicated counsellor, Alfie, appeared from a bank of police cars.

"Sue, Sue, you okay?" Sue didn't understand the question and stared at him. "…It's okay Sue you're safe now, you'll be home soon." And he smiled and took her hands in his. "…you've been gone a while. How are you feeling?" Sue didn't understand that question either. Alfie smiled and looked into her eyes. "…Physically, how you feeling physically?"

"Okay? Yes, yes, I'm fine thank you how are you?" Said Sue mechanically,

"Oh I'm fine too," He smiled, "…We've all missed you, the girls are fine, Julie is okay and we'll get you back home as soon as... is it okay if a doctor looks you over?"

"Is it Angela?"

"No unfortunately, sorry she's already at the Ministry, Department of Health, she's been working tirelessly and you can see her very soon…if you don't mind…it's a Dr Singh, just to make sure you're okay…you know…" And he let the Big C shadow finish his sentence. She had been successfully avoiding that shadow and had to resign herself again. Alfie had counselled it. She must not, Over-generalise, Personalise, Negativise or something else without 'ise' at the end. Even if she had been told she could develop any type, anywhere in or on her body, at any time, she was the only person in the world ever to be in that situation and no-one knew what had happened or would happen to her body. She made a mental image of the Big C shadow and shrank it with a not so revolutionary nor new dose of denial. She could get run over by a bus tomorrow.

She realised that they had walked across the incongruously empty road to a big half-finished building where two policemen were holding open a shiny glass door that still had its plastic on. Sue looked at Alfie confused some more and he explained,

"It's a new research institute, they're letting us use a room."

"But isn't You-Cee-Aich just down the road, I've been to You-Cee-Aich…Dr Singh did some…Dr Singh only works down the road?"

"Oh good, you remember him, there's been so many doctors, I didn't know…are you okay with him?" Sue nodded,

"He's very nice. To the point. But why don't we just go down the road?"

"You-Cee-Aich is crawling with journalists…there's been a leak…it's very hard to keep them out of a public building and everyone's got a cam…well…it's being looked into but this place will give you a bit more privacy and if there's anything immediately to worry about you can go in an ambulance to the hospital, is that okay?" Sue didn't say anything. "…Okay. And we can talk if you want?" Said Alfie in his dedicated counsellor's voice,

"Okay. I need to talk to the girls."

"Yes, yes of course, do you want to do that now? You can use my phone," and Alfie stopped walking up the shiny new stairs they were on and reached for his mobile before Sue shook her head and reached for hers, "…I should warn you, you'll need to do a preliminary debriefing with some people from the Department of Health and some security types, like a police statement, if you're up to it? But you should be home by teatime, I mean if you don't mind, it's just a lot of people have been very worried and…but there's plenty of time if you just want to…do you want a cup of tea?" Sue shook her head,

"No thanks I'm fine…hello Sam, Sam is that you?"

"Mum! Jo! Its Mum!" And the extension clicked straight away,

"Hello girls, I'm home…in London."

"Oh Mum, Mum! Yes! Oh Mum…where are you? What's happening, there's been all sorts of people…oh Mum, you okay?" Came the garbled responses of two very happy young women. Sue heard their joy and caught it immediately.

"I'm fine, I'm fine, I'll be home by teatime…ignore all that…are you okay? Jo how's your knee?"

"My knee's fine Mum. How are you? Where are you, whose…"

"I'm fine the police have arrested the man who tried to…I'm safe, I'm with Alfie, you remember Alfie don't you?" It wasn't a long silence but it was enough to say they remembered all right. "…I'm going to have a quick check-up just to make sure and then I have to give a statement and then I'll be home."

"What man? How did you? Dad rang he said I'd been to New York?"

"It's pretty complicated, well, not complicated, convoluted, it's a convoluted story and I'll tell you all about it when I get home…" Alfie touched Sue's arm to indicate that there were three well-dressed people at the top of the stairs making faces at him. She turned her back, "…I just wanted to call to say I'm home and I won't be long. I've missed you so much girls," and all three chorused a kind of sob and there were some more 'oh Mum's. The three well-dressed people were smiling and walking down the stairs now, "…look, look, you get off to college Sam, Jo put your feet up and I'll be home in a few hours, okay?"

"Okay Mum, Mum we missed you sooo much…do you want anything from the sh…shall I cook?"

"No, no, I think we deserve a take-away don't you. Oh Jo! Could you ring my bank and say you're me, my password is my birthday; tell them I need to move £5, 000 into my current account, I went on holiday and had a bit of a splurge, the security question is Jolly" And all three sobbed again at the ordinariness, the wonderful ordinariness of a take-away and pretending to be each other on the phone. The well-dressed people were not so impressed, one of them said,

"Sue? I'm sorry to interrupt…" but she obviously wasn't so Sue smiled sweetly at her and turned her back some more. Alfie stepped to the side to block any further interruptions and whispered something placatory,

"Could you do me another favour Jo? …Could you give Julie a ring and tell her I'm okay, say I'll ring her tonight at the latest."

"Yes Mum, ASAP, she has been calling, just to you know…yesterday was the last time…oh Mum, what time are you back?"

"Five at the very latest, it's best to get it over with…you know what these people are like, they won't leave us alone 'till we've given them a statement and a sample," and they laughed,

"Alright Mum. Five, right?"

"Five…I love you girls," she got two 'I love you's back.

"And keep that knee up…and get to college…and, and I love you and I'll see you at Five."

"Five Mum. Five," and Alfie put his hand on Sue's arm again.

"Okay, I love you, bye, bye, bye, I love you, bye." She couldn't hang up.

"We love you Mum, oh Mum." The line went dead and the well-dressed woman took in a breath, Alfie spoke, slightly irritated,

"Sue, this is er Anabelle Miller from the Minister's office, and Adam Smith from the Dee-Bee-Eye-Ess? Is that it, yes, and Abigail McCallum from…?" Abigail McCallum leaned through the other two and shook Sue's hand,

"Abigail McCallum from the Security Services, pleased to meet you. I am really very sorry you have…" she looked a bit like bloody Emma from work, she had let the 'I am really very sorry you' bit blend into one meaningless word,

"Do you work with Albin?" Asked Sue sharply, Abigail looked quizzical, "…that man who tried to grab me."

"I have worked with him, yes. But…Albin…was not working with British Government authority…"

"Yes, and we have all been briefed by Doctor Carter and understand that you need some time and space for a medical check and to adjust to the situation, there will plenty of time for detail…" Interjected Alfie and he left a pause where possibly 'back off' ought to be, possibly something stronger. They did actually back off, a bit, "…Mrs Duggen is going to receive some counselling and then see her medical doctor now, she will then attend the debriefing," said Alfie all authoritative. And they backed off some more and said nice-to-meet-you type things while Sue and Alfie walked up the stairs. She squeezed his arm in thanks and then stopped squeezing. Oh dear.

"About the other night?" she said with only a lifetime of rom-coms to guide her. Alfie didn't watch that stuff and looked even more uncomfortable. But he stopped walking and looked at her, "...Well, I had a lovely time and but...it was fun and...but...I don't think it...well it was a wise thing to do we are both grown-ups and but...I don't think I'm ready for a...thing and...?" Alfie smiled and squeezed her hand now. Luckily, he had prepared something,

"No, I agree. It was a very special night that I do not regret. Except for having to rush off, it was a..." and he decided to go off script, "...my Aunt, My mum's sister had an accident, turned out not too serious but we're a close family and I'm the medical one, but I wanted to stay and...well I was a bit worried you know and maybe... I'm supposed to... " and he went back into his prepared speech, "It was very unprofessional of me. I only hope we can rebuild..."

"Or even build on...you know...it was a new situation for all of us and...we're friends now right? Finally, one of them had said the right thing and they both smiled,

"Friends," said Alfie and they walked upstairs into a rather Spartan room containing no-they-don't-go-with anything beige blinds, a couple of sorry-you-have misunderstood-the-word-neutral green institutional soft chairs and a low pale wooden table.

"So, how are you?" Asked Alfie sitting down and getting out his old A4 notebook, Sue sat down too,

"Glad to be home," she sighed, "…and to have our little chats again." and she looked round the sterile off-white painted room some more. She had seen so many over the last few months. It looked like someone had very recently removed that fine layer of dust that new buildings have. The room looked clean and bright but it smelled of powdered concrete.

"Good. And I'm not here to interrogate you about where you've been or what you've been up to. Just to find out how you feel now and support you in whatever decisions you want to make right now." Sue assented with a smile.

"I just want to go home really." she said.

"Of course, and so you will…I just want to help you…Have you had any worries I need to know about. You know the Cancer worries we talked about?"

"To be honest I haven't really thought about Cancer at all over the last couple of months…" Alfie nodded approvingly, "…Maybe I'm in denial?" Alfie cocked his head, "…I know I have to not over generalise or negativise…or personalise or…?"

"Good, good. And you just want to get home to your girls?" He smiled,

"Yes. I…"

"You just want what's best for them? Help them to a secure future?" He was rushed and flushed and speaking for her; the Minister must be waiting.

"Well, yes. But to be honest I just want to see them smile,"

"Of course? No change there then….and have your views changed on anything else? You know the 'values' we talked about? Wanting to give something back to the 'Good-Ole-En-Aich-of-Ess', make sure what happened to you is used for the public good and everything? 'Shared' that's what you said."

"Oh? No, no change there…that Fielding and Hardy need to share whatever it is they've got for the good of everyone. You know as much as possible, you have to be realistic. But you know about Heather, my friend Julie's mum. If I could help to stop any other person from having to go through that…well there is that hope isn't there?"

"Realistic. Yes. Yes, there is that hope. And you can help a lot of people. And your girls as well. But what about your sister and brother in law? At Zabtrex? How do you feel about them?" Sue had to pause; how did she feel about Jan now?

"Well I'm very angry. She locked me up you know? Had me locked in a room with no-one to talk to. I talked to myself just to keep myself going sometimes." Alfie looked sympathetic, and pained. He wrote something down,

"What did you tell yourself?"

"Oh, you know stupid stuff. I was going to strangle her and…I cried a lot. A lot," a tear fell off her cheek as she thought about what Jan did, "…my own sister." Alfie leaned over and passed her a tissue. He didn't say anything but looked deep into her eyes. She was reassured, "…And she is my sister, she was…well desperate and…being young-looking was so important for her…in her position she…"

"But what she did was wrong Sue. You know that don't you."

"Oh yes I know that I haven't got…. that syndrome for when you've been kidnapped or anything but she is my sister." Alfie put his hand on her shoulder,

"Yes, yes of course. But your priority is your girls isn't it. They are the ones that matter aren't they. A secure future for them." He was still looking into her eyes and she answered,

"Yes. My girls and their… Our future."

"Well done Sue. Now I have to ask…when you left England you were…how were you feeling then Sue?" There was the tiniest plaintive twang in his tone. He was sweating a bit.

"Well Jan said they could, Oskar could find out what happened to me. They had better facilities."

"Better than ours?" Asked Alfie, shocked.

"Oh, I know we've got the facilities Alfie but, well, it was all getting so complicated and… I could smell the greed? No, not just that? The career plans. I could actually see the career plans while they were talking to me, the grants, the positions they could all get out of me. And there were so many of them, Doctors, researchers, honchos, all coming and looking at me with greedy career plans in their eyes and…vultures they were like vultures and it didn't matter if I lived or died, I was just a lab rat to them. Worse, something in a petri dish swimming around. No-one cared about me and what I was going through, except you Alfie,

145

you were there for me but…and Angela. But I was just a cash cow to the rest of them. And Jo just waiting and waiting for her knee operation. And Heather dribbling. I just wanted to get away from them. Go somewhere where they would just look after me and help me."

"I see," said Alfie still sweating.

"Are you hot Alfie, shall I open a window?" And Sue made to get up,

"No, no, I…was just running earlier I'll be fine. We have to think about you…" So Sue sat down and leaned forward,

"I know I made a mistake Alfie, but…if it wasn't for the girls, I don't think I would have come back. I still don't trust a lot of people, there's a lot of money in me and that's all they care about…but I'm back now, facing the music…and I probably got you into a lot of trouble but I'm back now and if there's anything I can do to make it…"

"You didn't get me into trouble Sue, it's all fine. I'm fine and you are back…You chose to come back."

"Yes. I've got to face the music. But I'm not going to let people just come and 'examine' me any old time, just when they feel like it. They're just the devils I know that's all and…It was just luck, a lottery, that all this happened to me and not my fault and I want to be treated properly. I only want doctors to look at me for my health and if any research will help people. For Alzheimer's you know. Nothing else. I want to get my normal boring life back, that's all." And she sat back having surprised herself.

"That's very clear Sue, thank you. And you sound like you have thought about this a lot." She hadn't really thought about it much at all but she didn't say anything, "…So you'd be happy for the Good-Ole-En-Aich-of-Ess to work on helping other people. Like before, when we talked before?"

"Only for proper medical things. Not for cosmetic stuff. I mean I know the gene genie's out of the bottle and, and people can be very very frightened of looking old and very very greedy, just look at Jan. My own sister. But I don't have to help with that if I don't want to do I?"

"But," Alfie didn't often contradict her and she listened carefully, "…Well, If the gene genie's out of the bottle already, that's very good; 'gene genie', and well…if money is going to be made, shouldn't that money go to help…for the public good? You talked about that before do you remember? You said the En-Aich-of-Ess could do with some funding, you know cuts and everything. You still feel the same way about that don't you?"

"Oh that? Well I just said that to…? But all this cosmetic stuff, well, it is just cosmetic isn't it. I know better than most, it doesn't actually matter really. Does it? You think everything would be better if you just lost half a stone or had a nose job or just looked younger. But it doesn't change anything really does it? I mean people are nicer to you if you look nice, but you've still got to get out of bed in the morning and stay in the game." Alfie wasn't going to answer, "…But all that can wait I s'pose can't it? How did we get onto that again?"

"You can talk about anything with me Sue. You know that." Was this the time to ask for feedback? Probably not. "…I just wanted to understand a little about why you left and how you feel about things now that's all. To see if your feelings or wishes had changed significantly. We've been worried, I was just concerned that you might have suffered a change…in your feelings or wishes…"

"My feelings are the same, more or less I think Alfie. I just want to go home. A lot of things have been happening lately and I just want my girls,"

"Exactly. Well done Sue. And the sooner I stop bothering you with all these questions the sooner you can get to see them," and he leaned back and scribbled a bit more while he asked, "…Is there anything else? Anything that can't wait till after you've seen the girls."

"Not really," said Sue, "…I mean a lot's happened and I've done some stuff Alfie. You wouldn't believe what I did in Puerto Rico. I…"

"You've been brilliant Sue. Truly brilliant. But let's get you to the doctor now, put your, and everyone's, mind at rest, and then a quick statement and then home." And he smiled and stood up and led her to good old Dr Singh.

"Oh. Is that it? Okay…I like Dr Singh," said Sue who could repeat herself to a friend, "…he doesn't guff and when you ask what caused something, he doesn't just describe it again but with bigger words. If he doesn't know something, he says so and he says when he knows and what should happen because he's an expert. A proper Doctor."

"I'll wait here," said Alfie and Sue went into a makeshift doctor's room to nice Dr Singh in it.

But Alfie did not wait there. When she came out from a very thorough medical examination and a lovely long and reassuring conversation with a little bit of cotton wool stuck on the crook of her forearm, the well-dressed Abigail McCallum who looked like bloody Emma was the only person there,

"Where's Alfie?"

"Hello Sue, may I call you Sue? Alfie has had to go I will escort you until he comes back," she had not paused sufficiently long after 'may I call you Sue' and Sue's back was now up. She didn't say anything but let herself be led down the stairs. Abigail must've worked with Albin because she wasn't very chatty either. She walked behind Sue just a little too close as well,

"Alfie is my dedicated counsellor, he's supposed to…" but Abigail interrupted her. Sue was annoyed more than worried,

"He's been called away…You're a very special person Sue, you are going to meet the Minister…" Sue could hear there would be no proper explanation from Abigail,

"Alright, alright. Yes, yes. More meetings, I know the drill…. I like your suit," said Sue "…a colleague of mine has one like it." Abigail sort of smiled. "…So did Albin go rogue then?" Asked Sue knowing she was being optimistic about getting an answer,

"Well that's one way of putting it," said Abigail flatly,

"But he was authorised to come and get me?"

"Yes." Was all she got, all she was going to get that was clear,

"And Oskar…Oskar Blutegel from Zabtrex, my brother in law, have you got him…he was there, he was there too you know…"

"Yes, we know, he won't get far," said bloody Abigail confidently,

"He got away? You let him get away? There were hundreds of police there…"

"Be assured Sue, we'll get him. The Swiss Government want him too," said bloody Abigail bloody confidently. Abigail opened the back door of a police car for Sue and went to sit in the front. In the police car, Sue asked the police woman sitting next to her, who called herself Amy, what was going on. Amy, whose ponytail made her look no more than twenty-two, shrugged sweetly making her flak jacket lift up more than her shoulders.

"Well where are we going?"

"Whitehall," said Amy. "…you've got friends in high places." No she didn't.

"Whitehall?"

"Whitehall, Department of Health, the Minister is waiting," said Abigail turning round in her seat before rapidly turning round to answer her phone,

"Minister!?... Who is the Minister of Health at the moment?" Amy shrugged again.

"Why are there two police in this car?" Asked Sue,

"Oh, you're under police protection," said Amy cheerfully,

"Stop the car," said Sue,

"Excuse me?" Asked Amy, Abigail turned round again, then turned back.

"Stop the car. I don't want to see the Minister yet…if at all. I don't want police protection. I want to see my girls."

"Sorry?" Asked Amy

"Stop the car. I want to get out."

"But the Minister is waiting," said Amy,

"So are my daughters. STOP THE CAR." She wasn't angry, just very insistent.

"But you are under our protection Sue. You are aware of only one of the attempts that have been made to steal...kidnap you. There are interested parties all over the..." said Abigail turning round a little irritated,

"Mrs Duggen to you, young lady. now STOP THE CAR...or arrest me." The car stopped at some lights and Sue began to shake the door handle but it was locked. "...false imprisonment," she said looking sharply at Amy and then Abigail and the policeman driving the car. "...open this door." The policeman at the front, who was less concerned with a civil action than hearing his mum in Sue's voice, pressed the door unlocked from the front. Sue opened the door and dashed onto the pavement before the lights changed.

"Sue.... Mrs Duggen. Stop!" Called Amy trying to sound like an officer of the law.

"Thank you very much Amy, thank you for helping me at the station but I need to go home now and.... where's my suitcase?" No officers present at the scene were able to answer this question.

"But S... Mrs Duggen, the Minister is waiting...we need to debrief you fully and ensure your security and there are Doctors there to monitor your health. You are aware of the question marks over your health...There are people who would do you harm, we have to protect our inter...your interests. You are a subject of..." said Abigail with a calm voice used to being listened to while scrambling in a less assured manner into moving traffic on the Euston Road,

"Yes. Yes, and I will be happy to make a statement at my earliest convenience but I have to get home now. Presumably you've got my details? I'll need that suitcase." Amy, who was now standing in heavy traffic a little wild-eyed, nodded, Abigail put her hand up to stop a Toyota before she could turn to say,

"But you are…the national interest! Mrs Duggen could we please…"

"Okay then, thanks again," said Sue and she stuck out her hand and hailed a black cab. Leaving Amy to start talking into her radio without getting run over and Abigail to get back into the car to use her mobile. Fortunately, Sue had changed her euros at Gare du Nord, after she had got her fridge magnets.

Smoking Indoors

Mercifully, the cab driver, resigned to a long and therefore less lucrative fare, turned up his talk radio station and let a plaintive 'but I really thought voting meant they had to do what we said...?' seep into the back before shutting the internal window. Sue, who could be run over by a bus tomorrow, spread out on the back seat in peace. She must not, Generalise, Personalise, Negativise or something else that did not end in 'ise' after all.

She got out her phone and saw that it was 10.45 in the morning. She texted 'Put the kettle on' and stared at the phone. 'Put the kettle on' was what she always texted when she was coming back from a business trip. Jo texted what she always texted, 'we need milk.' Sue smiled and looked out of the window.

God London is dirty. The grubby cracked streets trundled by. Nearly home.

She got out at the posh deli and walked down her road with the milk and some pastries. Cars were parked chock-a-block on the edge of the green as usual. The bushes and the dog walkers were all familiar but she saw them with fresh eyes. And everything smelling damp and green.

It was no more than scrub really. The patchy grass was short and yellowing on ground hardened by so many people getting in and out of their cars. A far cry from Puerto Rico. One of the neighbours was blowing leaves but she could hear a blackbird singing and there were still plenty of leaves rustling on branches in a strong breeze. She looked out to the trees ahead of her and sighed. A faint scent of the sweet decay of autumn was just discernible in the bluster. She'd missed the whole summer. She shook the hair that was in her eyes out of the way.

A different view every morning for thirty-five years, thanks to those trees. 'Forest View'. Majestic. And, as it turned out, paparazzi proof; big trees back and front to stop people looking into the living room, and a strong front gate.

No wonder the girls didn't move out. She really should downsize and give the girls some money for places of their own. It must be worth a million by now surely. She'd done, or had done, a lot of work on that house over the last thirty-years. She'd had to re-mortgage a bit for the college fees but that was ten years to go. Thinking that still gave her a thrill. No mortgage. Soon.

Ahead of her, another taxi slowed and then stopped just outside her house. She slowed down to see who was getting out. That bloody Abigail didn't look the sort who'd take the opportunity that a cancelled meeting afforded to go shoe shopping. And she was Security Services so she'd have their address, that'd be lesson two probably. But it wasn't Abigail,

"Sam! Sam!" And she began to run. The woman she called turned round startled and looked worried,

"Mum?" She realised she'd had her hair done so Sue stopped running so as not to frighten Sam but kept walking fast towards her daughter, "…Mum!" And Sam ran, hugged her mum and her mum hugged her back. And kept hugging.

When they finally unclenched, both their faces were wet and beaming. Sam's welled up eyes were sparkling in the sunlight, like Jan's. She'd never noticed that before. She seemed to have forgiven her sister. The cabby coughed loudly and Sam looked sheepish. Sue got out her purse,

"Not enough for a tip, sorry." The cabby sighed and drove off.

"I was on the way to college…Jo phoned…did you get milk?" Bubbled Sam as she leaned her head on her mum's and reached for her keys. Sam waved cheerfully at a man sitting in a parked car opposite, "…police…Aaron." Sue smiled and nodded towards the young man who was now talking into a radio, and they walked up the path to their front door. They kicked their shoes into a heap and shuffled on their slippers and Sue's eyes were wet,

"…Jo! Jo it's Mum! Mum's home!" Yelled Sam and Jo hobbled fast from the kitchen into the hall and hugged her mum, and her mum hugged her back. Jo began rocking from side to side as she always did in a long hug,

"Watch that knee," said Sue and hugged her Jo some more taking her weight.

"Kettle's boiled…did you get milk?" Sobbed Jo happily and she leaned on her mum and her sister and they bundled into the kitchen,

"Yes…and pastries."

"From Marco's?"

"From Marcos." And she burst into tears. Sam burst into tears. Jo burst into tears.

"Mum…Mum." They sobbed and leaned on her.

"Girls…my girls," she sobbed and leaned on them. It had been nine months and felt much longer. They held each other until their tears had turned to smiles. Then they held each other a bit more. Then, because she was the Mum, she sniffed first and said,

"I am dying for a proper cup of tea," and she helped her Jo into a kitchen chair, who sat face shining looking at her mum.

"Not coffee? It goes better with the pastries?" Asked her Sam, now and forever practical, and Sue nodded in an outnumbered way and her Sam got on with coffee, looking back at her mum at the kitchen table and blinking every so often. And Sue sat shocked at how beautiful her girls were, and how Sam was making coffee. She had moved the cups into the cupboard over the sink and it worked.

"So, what happened Mum?" Asked Jo, "…. where have you been?"

"God, all over girls, all over…. where do I start?"

"With that suit. That's a great suit Mum, where'd you get it?" Said Sam and they all laughed. Jo stopped first and her lips trembled. She didn't want to say it so Sue did,

"You've been very worried, it's been awful…and I have had a terrible time of it but I'm alright and I'm home now and you're alright and and…" But Sam piped up again, that was new,

"But where have you been? Why did you run away from Auntie Jan? Why did dad ring saying I was in New York?"

"What did you tell him? Oh never mind? ..." And she took a deep breath, "...Auntie Jan...and Oskar wanted to find out what had happened to me..."

"Yes, isn't that why you went though Mum?"

"Yes, yes, I went for help but they wanted to replicate it, the youth thing, so they could sell it...and Jan wanted it for herself...to look young again? So they started with some experiments but I didn't want..."

"Experiments?!...what did they do to you Mum?"

"Nasty things and...nothing permanent. They tried to give me shingles again...but I found out, well I kind of knew...she is my sister...that they weren't trying to help...they just wanted my Dee-En-Ay, they took my eggs, the only part of me that's still the same you know...They tried to make me sign things you know... patent documents?"

"Your eggs? What did they want with them? ...But didn't Angela already patent your Dee-En-Ay?" Asked Sam,

"Did she?" Chorused Jo and Sue.

"Yes, yes, you remember Jo when mum was getting better and we saw those patches of new skin on her face and arm? And Angela said it was more than rested?" Jo's face lit up,

"Oh yes... 'more than rested'...I remember...so you signed that thing ...?"

"Oh that! I thought that was so the En-Aich-Ess could get some money back off Fielding and Hardy for the cost of my treatment... and compensation?"

"Yes, yes that, and, but we also did the patent thing for you because of the left and right-handed Octopus thing?" Said Sam. "...That's what she said wasn't it? Dr Carter. Remember?"

"Oh yes, she went on about that Hospital Trust she used to work for," said Sue and she carried on looking confused, "...I'll have to check that, I had a lot on my mind...you said she called, Angela, when I was in Houston that..."

"Houston," said Sam.

"What were you doing in Houston?" Said Jo

"I was using the tickets I... got from Albin..."

"Albin?" Asked Jo,

"Angela called after that didn't she though," said Sam "...that's when we told her about Dad and..." Sue was confused some more,

"Okay okay let's do all this in date order, when did Angela call last?"

"Two days ago...but Mum can we do what happened to you, that was first?"

"Okay, okay. Well Jan and Oskar took me to the posh private hospital in Zurich, private room..."

"Not their house? Jan said you were in her house till you went...Did you hit her Mum?"

"Once, well once so it hurt...it was self-defence. No. They took me straight to the hospital...and it was okay I thought but then... and they took to locking the door. They locked me in."

"Why...would they do that...were you...you know...psychotic?"

"No, not then…I did go psychotic but that was later and anyway it was only…that was perfectly understandable…the only rational response really…I only hit her because she was trying to handcuff me to a bed, I think that's fair? But date order, date order…They took to locking the door because Oskar had not informed his company. He said I was to keep a low profile so that he could claim the treatment on his family insurance but he was actually trying to get…develop a new drug on the sly…for money…I found out because him and Jan had a bust-up one night when they visited me…all in Swissy French I couldn't follow it all, and all the scientific stuff in another language, but I got she wasn't happy about the sorts of Dee-En-Aye he was looking at and…all the 'treatment' was at night…only Oskar came and a Security Man…no Doctors or Nurses or anything… And when he, at first, when I got there to start with, he asked me all sorts of questions that didn't feel right, I should've known then but…. anyway. There's an awful lot of people would pay a lot of money for a real anti-aging treatment." The girls gave her a 'bleeding obvious' face.

"…and Jan, Jan was very keen, kept going on about our shared Dee-En-Ay and eyeing where my crow's feet used to be…and my chest…it was weird," The girls' faces both went disgusted and hardened, Sue saw and shook her head "…you have to see…Jan is from…we're from a different time, she never had the chances you…we had…I know we're sisters but it wasn't that simple, Mum and Dad treated us differently, she wasn't encouraged to be anything except beautiful…Dad and Mum never encouraged her in anything…Mum never let her have seconds…and the school she went to didn't help, churned out secretaries." The girls looked confused. "...the world needed a lot of secretaries before computers. But Jan was so beautiful, you should've seen her. If she'd've been taller, she could've been a model...no-one expected anything of her, ever. You can't imagine that can you?" and she wanted to say it was a different time again but then her girls would think something nasty had happened when they were children.

. "...she was like a toy, she was treated like a doll...not just for a selfie, all the time, or by one stupid boyfriend, everyone; Mum...Nanny, Grandad, me, teachers, strangers, everyone. Everyone treated her like a pretty little doll. She didn't know anything else." Jo was the oldest so she made a 'we can understand this' and then a 'but get on with it' face. Sam took a moment and then started listening again.

While Sue waited the moment or two it would take for Sam to 'come back' she sighed and realised how like her Dad Sam could be, in a good way. Had she forgiven him too? "...She was objectified that's it. Not like now, now it's all about what you look like...but you still have to go to college and work. Before, when we were young, it went all the way through." This was important to Sue, that the girls understand what it was like for Jan, and her too. She racked her brains. "...She was like a collectable. Being objectified does things to you, girls. And then she got old and she panicked. Panicked for years and years." The girls who were actually women didn't care about Jan as much as they did their mum,

"...So. I was suspicious, well naturally very suspicious, and during the day I started going to the cashpoint down the hill I still don't really know why just in case and, maybe it was the way Oskar was? Anyway, one day Jan saw me walking back and shouted and I shouted and that's when they started locking the door...took away my clothes...But Yusef...I made friends with this Security Guard...Yusef...he had a cousin...any way...I was stashing money away...they had my passport, my keys everything except my card. I keep my card in my wash kit, I've told you how to do that haven't I?" The women nodded. "...But Yusef...lonely it was very lonely...my phone went missing on the second day...had already gone... and Oskar said he'd look into it, then he'd get me another one but of course...Any way..." and she took a swig of coffee while the girls chomped on posh pastries with big beautiful eyes open wide. They both had Jan's eyes. "...So...my phone went missing and I got suspicious and I started hoarding cash and then they started locking me in and..."

"Why didn't you find a phone box or something, why didn't you call?" Sue smiled; how many times had she said that to both of them at different times. Then she looked sheepish.

" I was afraid Jo, and maybe a bit paranoid...I thought they'd tapped the phone or something, then Albin told me not to...God! No wonder he said that, I thought it was odd.... but he was my only hope then and...but...He made me paranoid, he kept talking about corporate espionage and..."

"What about the police, couldn't you call the police…in French."

"I did! that's how I got in touch with Albin…they, well Angela then the police, called in the intelligence services, he's in Em-Eye-Five or Six? But that was Yusef, he called the police, well after he…I called the police in the…in the lobby, the hospital lobby… but they were German speaking I couldn't and Yusef…he felt bad about it afterwards when I explained…but he dragged me off locked me up again…then he started helping me…he's got a sister and she…well any way"

"Why didn't Yusef call the police then?" Sam wasn't keeping up and sounded indignant.

"He did…and got me a phone…and eventually…well this man…Albin…he rang back said he was from British Intelligence…well I think he was…he said I'd been passed on to him and my Government was aware and I was to 'sit tight'….it was diplomatically sensitive because Zabtrex had a big contract with the Government for some classified something…and my Dee-En-Ay was a trade secret and Zabtrex were claiming no formal knowledge…he was lying, well some of it was probably lies and some true…maybe they do have a contract but they didn't know I was there, well that's what bloody Abigail said. If anyone called Abigail Mc, something beginning with Mc? If she calls don't say anything…. Any way he's got away…Oskar has.

…Albin went freelance, didn't he, started working for Oskar…but I didn't know that…then he said to meet him at the service entrance…but he wasn't there and… that was later.... first I went psychotic. Hit Jan." She took another swig and looked at her untouched pastry hungrily. But she had to explain to her girls, "...Oskar gave up trying to lie to me, just stopped answering my questions...sent Jan to tell me a pack of lies and start saying things about stress...the injections weren't doing what he wanted I think no symptoms, nothing...as far as I know...and the eggs he took, well I don't know what he did with those? Stressed! Huh. Stressed and then 'volatile' and then 'psychotic' then they got this psychiatrist to look at me, call me mad, so no-one would believe me. I mean I don't look like what I am so when I said what I am the psychiatrist thought I was mad...who would fantasise that they were a Fifty-eight-year-old domestic appliance designer from Chingford? I mean."

"That's what Jan said...not the Fifty-eight bit, said you were traumatised...we kept phoning and she kept saying you were in the shower and at the shops and blah blah. Then she said you'd gone mad and we booked a flight...but then Jo's op' came up but she was all about to cancel when Jan phoned and asked if we'd seen you. We all thought you would come straight home. We didn't know where you were," said Sam quickly before fizzling out. Sue smiled and took their hands for a moment before nodding to them to keep eating,

"Any way...Yusef's cousin's mother-in-law needed this drug for her feet." The girls stopped chewing. "...Yusef, the security guard, his cousin Yunis wanted him to get some of these drugs for his mother-in-law's feet...circulation or inflammation something... his English was quite patchy and

I don't speak Somali, although his German was fine? But I don't speak German... and his French accent was...well I couldn't understand him properly...but he wanted to get the drugs for his cousin Yunis who had helped him get into Europe...had a boat...So when Albin didn't show up it was the same night as he was going to take these drugs, expensive top-notch drugs that her Doctor...Yunis's mother-in-law...I must tell you about him he was a lovely man, anyway...Her health insurance, American, didn't cover them, they were very expensive so...We took the drugs to the service entrance... to the service entrance for Yunis, his cousin. And I took the drugs and some other random ones so he wouldn't lose his job and the alarm had gone off and I'd hit Jan. She'd turned up and Yusef was going to come soon and she started shouting about seconds again and and I hit her and she was lying there I thought she was...so I asked for a lift. I didn't want to go back in that room and all I had was a hospital gown and eight-thousand Euros and no Albin."

"Oh Mum, you poor...oh Mum." said Jo and both girls reached out and held a shoulder each. Sue let herself sag into their support and they sat a moment. All that could be heard was the swish of the washing machine. Sue looked round and saw an A4 piece of paper taped to the machine's door, 'Jo do not touch!' it said in Sam's handwriting,

"Did you put a load of washing on with that knee?" Sue asked inquisitorially,

"It's getting better Mum...I must keep it moving a bit...the doctor said," Sam nodded,

"That's an old sign Mum, she's getting much better."

"Okay…. Okay. So Yunis…I gave Yusef some money and most of the rest to Yunis and he let…" she saw her daughter's dubious faces, "…I'm an experienced woman, I could tell Yunis was nice…he let me go in the back of his van and we drove to Genova…it's in Italy, a big port. Well we stopped off in Milan…I've got some great boots, they'll look great on you Sam…" Sam raised an eyebrow in thanks, "…He was going to drop me off at…no before that Albin rang Yusef, he got a new phone after that but anyway Albin gave Yusef a number and I rang from Genova and then off the Canary Islands…there was no question about dropping me off closer to home I don't know why…and it suited me really you know, to keep the other 'interested parties' 'off my tail'. Maybe I knew that? Any way we couldn't stop at the Canary Islands because of the storms…terrible storms," and she sighed, "…When we got to Puerto Rico…" Jo sighed then and slumped back in her chair. It was a lot to take in, "…it's a lot to take in I know, I'm getting dizzy just saying it…but…well it's nice to get it off my chest you know…so much has happened and well, do you know how the Minister for Health, and the police come to think of? Do you know how they knew I was on the Eurostar?"

"Yes. When Dad rang because I hadn't rung him back in New York even though I was in London…he rang the Embassy and we worked out it was you, and they, the, someone from the Department of Health rang and said… said you were on your way home…But Mum you must've been so frightened." Sue turned her head to one side. Had she been frightened?

"I think I was too busy to be frightened, and angry. Very angry."

"You worked it out Sam, about Dad, I was clueless," said Jo, "...any way we told Angela when she rang because...she was very concerned Mum. We talked a long time...well we all like Angela don't we..." Everyone nodded enthusiastically, "...Well, Angela phoned her boss and the Health and Social Care Information Centre and they phoned all sorts of people and the Minister, well he knew about you already from the trials any way but he wanted to make a point of saying this wasn't to do with public private stuff or something? The inquiry is due soon..." She looked quizzical, "...was Albin the 'Em-Eye-Six' operative'?... that Angela said had said was working 'off piste' or something?"

"Must be," said Sue with a mouth full of very tasty pastry at last. "...But that doesn't, how did they know I'd be on that train?" no-one knew.

"Did Dad say something? They rang him too, then he rang us again...someone had gone round to his work didn't he say?" And Sam looked to Jo who nodded,

"Looked like a minor character out a John Le Carre, he said, I had to Google it," said Jo,

"Maybe? Yes, probably...And then I bought the suit...so he could track me...I used his card...I took it when I taped him up." And back in her normal kitchen with her normal daughters Sue's eyes widened at what she'd done, "...Oh I've done some stuff girls." And Sue took a deep breath, "...Where were we up to? Oh yes Puerto Rico...I'd agreed to meet Albin in Puerto Rico where Yunis's mother-in-law lived. His wife and son had taken a plane but he had the drugs…and me… and his paperwork was a bit patchy and he is Moslem, and black, so he you know, would probably get stopped just for that," Sam and Jo's face's went neutral in a way that she had seen before when she had brought up immigration. It was safe to say that she had not been entirely pro-immigration. Now, she smiled, "…Yes, I know, but I was an illegal immigrant myself for a bit and, well I suppose I can see more of the benefits, I s'pose," her daughters were grinning from ear to ear, Sue did know how to back down, but it didn't happen often."…Anyway," and Sam and Jo grinned some more,

"But Albin was a bad man?" Asked Sam,

"Yes, but I didn't know that. He was with British Intelligence and he said I would get me home without a fuss and…God! Is Jan alright? …I hit Jan on the head that night…with a jug…is she actually okay?" The girls looked confused, again.

"No-one's said anything…she rang us about two weeks ago…when you escaped from the hospital didn't she?" Said Sam and Jo nodded. Sue sighed.

"Yes, yes, sorry it's, he was such a liar, told me she was okay but…I didn't trust him the moment I met him…that's why I never told him about the W…oozy. Thank goodness."

"Uzi! You had an Uzi mum!?" Said Sam and Jo,

"Yes, just a small one, still pretty heavy though…Yunis gave it to me. He didn't like the idea of me wandering around on my own without a gun…such a nice man."

"And what was he doing with an Uzi mum?" asked Jo with a slightly moralistic tone and a raised eyebrow.

"Well he didn't have a Glock did he, that's much better for women apparently, Maria's got a pink one…. He did used to be a people-trafficker Jo. And Well, he ferried people across the Mediterranean really…that's how he met his wife, Maria, she was running a little tour boat business in Southern Spain with her dad, and so was he in a manner of speaking. And both their dads used to be fishermen. They met when their anchors got twisted together…love at first sight he said…gave up after the boy was born…went into conventional tourism…but he still had the oozy and then his mother-in-law got this problem with her feet. He's much older of course, but it seems to work." Jo looked very sceptical; Sam's head was cocked to one side,

"Are you sure they were foot drugs Mum?" Asked Jo,

"Why would he lie? It didn't matter to me what he was doing did it? I was desperate…he had been desperate once but now he was okay…and I gave him a lot of money for a trip he was making any way. And I made myself useful on the boat. We were in a storm in the middle of the Atlantic for three solid days and nights and we got to know each other pretty well. He was a good man girls. They do exist. Apart from, well, he was a bit sorry for me only having daughters but…He was, is, a very nice man and I hope his mother-in-law gets better and I won't have a word said against him. Not like that Albin. Is there any more coffee Sam?"

And to Sue saying that last sentence was more shocking than relating her piratical exploits on the high seas to two well-brought-up young women from Chingford. She had lived it, and it felt perfectly normal at the time. What was amazing was that her youngest daughter was moving around the kitchen making coffee. Then Sam wiped a spill up and she was aghast,

"Well I must say all this, me being away and Jo's knee seems to have done you both a bit of good…I mean not the worry that was terrible but you have managed perfectly well without me haven't you."

"I don't know about managed Mum. Coped is more like it. We survived Mum," said Sam as she put the refills down on the table slightly irritated. Jo was itching to say something. Sue looked at Jo with a 'go on then' face, Jo looked at Sam and said,

"If you want one just have one," Sam raised an eyebrow and leaned sideways and back to reach into a drawer. She took out a packet of cigarettes and a lighter sitting in an ashtray.

Sue raised an eyebrow, said, "Oh Sam." In a very disappointed tone and then helped herself to a cigarette,

"Mum!?" Both girls chorused, they had never seen her smoke. Largely because prior to being labelled mentally ill she had not smoked,

"I've been under a lot of stress…and everyone in that van and on that boat smoked like chimneys. The only way I could stop feeling sick was to join in too…. Do you smoke in your bedroom Sam?" Sam nodded a guilty sort of nod,

"Well, that has got to stop. If you want to smoke you can do it in the garden like everyone else," said Sue in emphatic maternal tone before taking a drag. "…after today. Today is special." She added. Jo sat back and folded her arms and looked at both of them, very disappointed indeed. It was the same face she had used when Sue had brought Alfie home that night. Sue began to speak but the difference between carcinogenic habits and a bit of hanky-panky could wait. She was home now. And sort of relieved that the reason Sam stayed in her room so much was only to have a quiet smoke. Hopefully. "…Where were we?"

"Puerto Rico with Albin," said Sam.

"Yes, Puerto Rico. Well Albin took me to a safe house and I think he drugged me, anyway I had a very strange dream or something, I think he did drug me. He took my blood. He asked me a lot of questions about the trials and Dee-En-Aye and I didn't trust him…quite rightly as it turned out so I taped him up and took the tickets and the new fake passports and his wallet and I got on a plane to…"

"You taped him up?!" Asked Sam,

"Yes, well I had the oozy didn't I. I still had to be sneaky though…domestic electrical design teaches you a lot about how to be sneaky…Wait 'til you start working Sam. Doing a good job is only half the story….It used to be a load of old men at the top telling you that you were a stupid woman to your face, now it's a bunch of young men, and women, all sneaking around 'networking' and trying to 'co-operate' you out of a meeting while the top's sitting in, is it Germany or France now? I can't keep up with all the mergers…the top's somewhere far away and waffling on

170

about 'responsibility' and totally oblivious to who actually does a good job or not. You need the wits of a ninja to 'stay in the game' at my age. You wait Sam…Then you'll be wishing for an oozy." Jo nodded; it was the same in ceramic design. "… Phew! Where did that come from? Sorry…but it's true. Anyway. Where was I? Oh yes, I got a plane to Houston. Albin said there were no direct flights and those were the tickets I took. That's where I was when I rang you."

"And we gave you Dad's Number," said Jo,

"Yes. Then Oskar turned up and tried to grab me… in a very amateur way but I think he was going to meet Albin in Houston and just made a grab for me…He'd brought Yusef as his muscle but Yusef didn't want to be muscle anymore and went off, I think to Florida, but I made a fuss and cried and normal people helped me and I got on a plane to New York. Then, because I knew your dad wouldn't understand it was me because I look young and I didn't want to deal with all that has happened between us…" And she took a breath, "…I pretended to be Sam…oh my hair was long and blonde then, I did that in our stopover in Milan as a disguise you know." Both girls shrugged a but-of-course type of shrug. The woman smoked, for God's sake. "…Well your dad is well and so is Meggie and they were very nice to you Sam…maybe you could go over for a visit, I mean really you, both of you?" The girls didn't rule it out." …well anyway they were very nice, lovely house the size of St Paul's Cathedral, they put me on a flight to Paris and then I got a Paris makeover and got on a train. Albin and Oskar were also on the train but they didn't see me. I didn't see them till I got off the train. Then Albin, amateurishly but successfully because he had the Prevention of Terrorism Act - I lost a shoe but a nice American lady found it for me- he got me in this hold I thought he was going to break my arm...so I bit him..."

"...as you do," said Jo and Sam smiled, then Sue smiled.

"...and shouted out a lot. Then, about a hundred police turned up and took him... they gave me a check-up and put me in a car to see the Minister of Health but I wanted to come home so they let me out...and lost my suitcase! ... and I got a cab and here I am." and she sat back really quite exhausted.

"What sort of check-up mum, you okay?" Asked Jo.

"Oh yes I'm fine, that nice Dr Singh gave me a onceover...said I look okay, nothing obvious but the tests'll be ready next week sometime. Then it's back to You-Cee-Aich." And the big C shadow filled up the empty space where knowledge ought to be. No-one knew what had happened or what would happen to Sue, "...unless I get run over by a bus tomorrow." Sue joked and her girls smiled obediently.

"What happened to Oskar? Did they get him too?"

"No, they bloody didn't. But don't worry he's a big fat coward. He won't try anything without backup...probably...and they'll get him soon." The girls looked worried, "...the back door's locked isn't it." Jo nodded,

"And there's been a policeman outside since you left Mum...oh does Aaron want his refill yet?" Sam looked at the clock and shook her head.

They all sat for a moment looking at their cups. Sam spoke first,

"I don't understand why Jan would do that to you? Never mind objectified. She's your sister?"

"I know Sam. But she only had that one thing and it was draining away. And the pressure to look young, well you know all the magazines and…I felt it too, and I had you and friends and a job I liked, mostly, and art to think about and the garden and I was never that pretty so I didn't miss it. All Jan had was Oskar and, well you know what some men are like, that generation…there're just different…they've got this sense that what they think counts more than…I don't think they even think we think properly sometimes, women I mean. Well, they've changed a lot of them, learned I mean…you know they need reminding but…but some are just stuck somehow? Oskar was always creepy. He'd 'trade up' as soon as look at you…and if he does come knocking the three of us could knock him over easy…he's a big fat pig."

"But Jan Mum. Your own sister?" said Jo,

"I know, my own sister and all those years growing up in that little flat together. But all those things she was losing; Oskar and her skin…? She was so afraid, afraid and desperate, poor woman."

"Poor woman! Poor woman. So what if she was getting saggy, so what if Oskar left her just for getting old? So what Mum. She tried to handcuff you to a bed Mum and let Oskar stick needles in you, who does that?!" Said Jo,

"Who does that Mum?!" reiterated the younger sister in the room "…and Mum, the money, don't forget she was after lots and lots of money. She treated you like a lab rat for vanity and money."

"Yes, vanity and money. I'm not condoning it girls, of course I'm not. She betrayed me and abused me and I'm not condoning it but I've got to try and understand it girls. She's my sister…and understanding isn't the same as agreeing with it, is it?" And she rubbed her forehead, "…like people trafficking or vegetarians or whatever," and she kept rubbing her forehead till Sam took her other hand and Jo took Sam's other hand and they sat for a bit. Some sighing went on.

"Well, the Minister rang," said Jo nonchalantly. Nobody moved. Sam and Sue puffed on their fags.

"Who is the Minister for Health at the moment?" Asked Sam. Jo tried to remember.

"He did say…? And something about your physical and mental health being a priority." she said vaguely.

"Does anyone want any more coffee?" Asked Sam. No-one did. Sue put out her cigarette, took both her girl's hands again and kissed them. And they sat holding hands across the table for a minute more.

"So how did the op' go?" Asked Sue. Jo sat up to tell her mum about her operation on her knee and Sam got up to put the cups in the dishwasher. "…was it the Whittington?"

"No, a private place in Stratford, very nice, very clean," said Jo "…it was very quick after all that time…I was home by Four o'clock." Her mum smiled appreciatively, "…and it's healing up nicely, thanks to Sam, she makes a mean Spag'-Bol' mum…better than yours!"

"Impossible," said Sue and Sam looked round to say,

"Well…"

"You going to try to get back to College today Sam?"

"No, it was silly to try…but you did say…and well, well my tutor says…"

"Are you behind with your coursework?"

"No Mum I'm not behind with my coursework…in fact my tutor says I should get a lot of attention at the End of Year Show." Sue beamed.

"She's done some beautiful work Mum; you should see it."

"Can I?"

"What now?" said Sam,

"Don't see why not…I mean no time like the present is there," said Sue. Sam obediently led her upstairs to her room.

Jo stood up and limped carefully to the phone and put it back on the hook. It rang immediately.

"…She's busy at the moment, can I take a message…. okay hold on…MU-UM it's the Minister's Office." Sue shouted back down the stairs,

"Can you take a number?"

"She really is very busy…I've got your number already…yes, yes I'll tell her…. b…I'm trying…Oh can't you take a hint," and she hung up. The phone rang. Jo sighed; it had been like this for days. The notepad next to her laptop on the side table was covered in the messages and notes she'd been writing down. Relatives, friends, the police, 'Intelligence', journalists, despite the Court Order, The Head of this, the CEO of that. She pondered whether all the rejuvenation business had made this part easier. She hadn't wanted her mum to do the trial and then she had nearly died. Nearly died. Then she was skipping about, touching her toes, dancing and prancing around with her soft pert body. And then behaving disgracefully. Absolutely disgracefully, with that horrible smarmy counsellor man. Yes, it had softened her up for all the phone calls.

And the sitting about not knowing anything. And journalists; journalists claiming to be from broadsheets and talking about public interest, journalists claiming to be from red tops offering exclusives and money, journalists pretending to be Heads or CEOs of something, Journalists pretending to be tourists, journalists pretending to be from British Gas. Well not pretending, alluding. How did they do that? And all like there was no injunction anyway.

She sighed a big sigh and let the phone ring some more. They had successfully kept mum's new face out of the paper all this time. They couldn't stop the 'Secret of Eternal Youth' stories from happening on the 'Net and abroad but at least mum could walk down the street without being accosted or stared at like an A-lister. Now her new photo from the station was probably going viral as she sat there. She'd have to dye her hair again.

And she hadn't written it down but Jacob had rung and almost apologised and almost said he was going to pay her back for the furniture. Just so he could ask her about her mum and 'this secret to eternal youth thing'. And he'd be ringing again just to be nosy. She sighed again.

An hour ago she had been anxious and efficient. Writing down messages because there was nothing else she could do. Saying variations of 'I don't know anything' to all and sundry. She'd even changed the answerphone message. Now, she just sat with her leg up and leaned back listening to the phone ring and click onto message. Mum was home. Her gun-toting, cigarette-smoking, not at all psychotic mum. She leaned over and picked up the phone,

"Duggen residence." She said in a hoity-toity tone and sighed, bracing herself, what now?

Peer Review

Sue had not been in Sam's room for Five Years and neither had the cleaner. Not after The Pizza and the Rodent Incident. After that they had all agreed that, If Sam wanted to live like that then she could as long as there were no more rats. They were still in dispute as to whether it had been a mouse or a rat that had caused Flora, a very nice woman who didn't deserve it, to nearly resign. Five Years ago, the smell and the clothes piled, no piled was too neat, strewn on the floor with the dirty mugs and plates and crumbs and stains was more than she could bear. Then there was the chance she might catch something, but she never did.

Enough washing made its way to the laundry basket to show that she was safe if ever she got run over. And while her hair may have got a bit lank from time to time, she was never actually dirty when she came out. Sue tried to sound nonchalant as she said,

"Oh, you've redecorated," and scanned a not exactly neat but certainly clean and stink-free bedroom. The purple walls were still purple but the woodwork was now a complimentary shade of green and the same fuchsia-pink satin curtains she'd had since she was little were open. The rows they had had about those curtains, Sue had used the word 'common' but Steve had insisted that Sam had to make her own mistakes. He was right of course. Really, the only colours that could forgive that fuchsia were green and purple. There were a lot of clothes piled up on one chair but the floor was clear.

"You've had those curtains a long time. Would you like some new ones?" Sam shrugged a maybe and pulled a large portfolio onto the big work table under the window. Sue pushed an ash tray and pot of pencils out of the way.

With restraint, Sue loitered to let Sam choose what she wanted to show her. Sam stood back to let her mum see anything she wanted. Sue leafed through smiling appreciatively at pencil drawings, chalks, the obligatory collages and some acrylics till she found the new stuff. Sam, smoking again, said,

"What do you think?" Which was an all-time first in itself. Sue took her daughter's cigarette and dragged on it, she put her head to one side,

"They're amazing," she said matter of factly, "...the colours...they're bright...brave...but they don't attack you and the...this one of Jo, it's her...it's just her...oh Sam..." And there were tears in her eyes. But not too many. She pushed down the urge to photograph everything and put them all on Facebook but she was definitely going to change her profile picture.

"You should show your dad. He'd be very proud," she said and Sam looked at her for a bit then smiled,

"Maybe," she said "...he sends me the odd one of his now and again...out of the blue. But, well he's a Facebook friend really isn't he."

"He's still your father and he loves you in a way. I saw that the other day when I was you."

"And he didn't guess? No, why would he…. Anyway…There's this one…where is it…I did it from a photo…of Auntie Julie's…while you were away…" And Sam flicked through her work, "…Oh no, it's still in the book…" And she found a large A3 sketchpad," …it's not finished…" She added and let her mum look. In the corner was a photo Julie had taken of all three of them the Christmas before last. They were all squashed onto Julie's two-seater sofa and although you couldn't see it in the photo Jo was in the process of spilling a glass of wine down Sam's top because her mum had just tickled them both in the ribs.

They were all laughing. Sam's drawing focused on their faces and she had only started on Sue's in any detail. It was her old face. The one with the lines and the droopy eyelids. Sue looked at it a long time. She missed her old face, or was it just the old her?

"It's very good, great movement…and definitely us…Do you miss my old face?" She asked

"A bit," said Sam, "…but this is your face too." And she kissed it on the cheek. Sue smiled and lowered her head and handed the cigarette back,

"Last day indoors." She warned,

"Yes, mum," said Sam and let her mum keep looking at her work, with a,

"Who's this?" and a, "…Is there a reason why you made this shape so bold…oh yes…" And a "…your sense of colour…that line there really brings out the shape of that…" Then Sue looked up at her daughter and they smiled. "…I know I don't need to say it Sam but these are excellent." Sam put her head on her mum's shoulder and closed her sketchbook.

"Thanks mum." Actually, she did need to say it. Her mum helped her tidy up her portfolio.

"I've done a few sketches...do you want to see?" said Sue and they went downstairs.

With the phone back off the hook the three of them looked at Sue's pictures on her A4 pad. There was the one she had drawn of the rainy-window shadows on the rug, one of Steve and Meggie, well their backs, and a sketch of Meggie's face in the diner. They were all curves and sweeps giving the impression of shadows and people. She felt she had got Steve's turn of head just right but she wasn't sure about Meggie.

The next three were done on the train, some Plane trees and a huge ploughed field whizzing by, a sleeping crumpled-up business man and a self-portrait as reflected in the train window in the tunnel. Sam and Jo both saw the rather wary alert eyes staring at the black. But they said nothing because mum was home now and they could squeeze her hand instead. The last three were much more jagged and angular and the difference in styles was the first thing Jo picked up on out loud. Sue thought for a moment,

"These first three are haunted by kettles, some of the lines are longer that's all...and these three are very much anti-kettle." And they laughed,

"You going back to work Mum?" Asked Jo, "...not now I mean but sometime?"

"I don't know...I was just assuming I'd go back again but...do something design-related...I am down for early retirement," and they giggled, "…and this place…you need places of your own girls." But the girls didn't want to hear about that now and both writhed, "…Yes, yes, it's all been a bit much…. there's plenty of time to sort all that out…" And she hugged her girls and sighed and smiled. Then, once she had leaned back and they were comfy on her shoulders, she sighed and smiled again. Her arms around them both. On their big comfy sofa with a blackbird singing in the front garden. Home. It was a shame they had to keep the curtains shut, but apart from that it was perfect.

"Dad was pretty angry when he found out," smiled Sam eyeing the sketch on the coffee table, Jo smirked a little bit. Now she was back being Mum Sue didn't twinkle,

"Yes, I feel a bit bad about that…I just couldn't face explaining all the rejuvenating and Jan business…and we weren't on good terms when he left, would he even have helped me?... I just wanted to get home."

"Oh, he would have Mum, I'm sure he would…so he didn't recognise you, me?"

"He thought he did…recognise you I mean…and I looked more like you when I was blonde. He was very pleased to see you and he talked a lot about you both…he asked after your knee," said Sue squeezing each girl's shoulder in turn. "…and it made me think as well, he looked after you a lot when you were small, took you to school, made your tea every night and when you had chicken pox…"

"We know that Mum, that's obvious," said Jo and Sam lifted her head to look at her mum,

"Yes, yes, but I'd blocked it out some somehow…I had this idea in my head that…the place was always such a mess when I got home and…it doesn't matter. He was a good dad when you were small…and I think I was jealous. Always working." And Sam put her head back on her mum's shoulder.

"Don't be silly mum," she said "…you were great when we were small…and we were proud of you…are proud of you…and well look what you've done Mum, you've escaped and got home and used a gun and…well you paid for this house and college, had a career before all that as well."

"I didn't use it, the gun. But I did point it at someone…with the safety catch off…" And her brow furrowed. Now she was home with her girls it felt like someone else's memory in her head. Until she remembered Albin's smug face then the anger was fresh and it all made sense, "…at the time it was right thing to do." She reasoned and now Jo and Sam squeezed her.

"God Mum," said Jo "…you've been awesome."

"I have a bit haven't I…and you…you must have been in bits…I'm so sorry I left you, I thought it'd be a month or two at most and…"

"We're big girls Mum and, well we were worried when we didn't know what was happening and all these people phoning up or coming round when Jo was supposed to keep her knee up. But we coped Mum, we coped," said Sam, "…and now we've got to cope with all the fuss." and they all sighed and Jo got up and got the pad and the lap-top and took a deep breath,

"We have got…Department of Health, En-Aich-Ess England, En-Aich-Ess Trust, En-Aich-Ess Research, Cee-Aye-Gee, Eye-Pee-Aich, Police, Security, the Department for Business, Innovation and Skills, Alzheimer's Research, Aich-Tee-Aye, health insurance, you with Zurich? them, don't know, don't know, Em-Ar-Cee, tourists, lots of tourists, Fielding and Hardy, Dee-Pee-Aich-Cee, Aich-Ess-Cee-Eye-Cee, Angela, Cee-Aich-Eye-Aye-Gee, Cee-Tee-Ess, Genewatch again, Aich-Ar-Aye, police, police, Dad, Julie, don't know…the Ee-Eye-Ee-Eye…that can't be right:?" They giggled again.

"Right, let's start at the top," said Sue and she picked up the phone,

"Hello Julie? Yes it's me…yes, yes I'm fine…I'm home…yes, yes, no…no! What? Check the curtains girls the media are on their way." Sam got up and checked that the curtains were completely shut, the doorbell rang, "…Don't answer it! No, wait, see who it is…How are you Julie?" And Julie didn't have to say anything because Sue could tell from the pause. "…What is it Julie, is it Heather?" And Julie sighed and Sue knew, "…Oh Julie I'm so sorry, your poor mum," And she sighed again and listened,

"She was very peaceful at the end. Just a shell. So small," said Julie and tears filled up in Sue's eyes. She looked up at Jo and Sam and their faces fell. Then Sue saw that Sam had let the person who had rung the doorbell inside and it was okay because it was a stylishly dressed woman about her age carrying her massive handbag as usual, it was Angela.

Sam whispered something to her and they walked into the kitchen.

Sue was still on the phone with Julie when Sam came in with a cup of tea and something she wanted to say,

"One second Julie," said Sue gently and she put her hand over the mike,

"Mum, Angela's written a report she wants us all to have a look at, I think it's quite important." Whispered Sam,

"Okay love, you go ahead and I'll be in in a while, sorry Julie more stuff…no, no. It can wait half an hour… so they put her on the new trial, yes, yes, I'll thank Angela, she took a risk there I know, so why didn't it work?"

"It was too late, they did warn us but you know…we wanted to try…and there was some improvement, well I thought so. She seemed to recognise me, in her eyes…."

Sam went back into the kitchen and said,

"She says it's okay for us to read it while she talks to Julie." Angela took a fat pile of typed A4 out of her bag and paused,

"Before we start Jo, Sam, how are you two feeling?"

"Oh? We're okay, aren't we Sam?" Said Jo, and Sam nodded.

"Yes? … And your thoughts about your mother, how she should live her life, as we discussed over the phone the other day, your wishes for her future?"

"… Our wishes are the same as hers, she just wants a normal life?" Said Sam,

"And to help? Do you remember our conversations about how your mother wants to help, help the researchers find treatments for age related issues?" Asked Angela,

"Yes?" chorused Sam and Jo,

"Do you still feel the same way?"

"Yes?" Said the girls again and Angela handed over the file as she said,

"Good. Great. So often the wishes and feelings of a subject's loved ones are not addressed. I feel I have a responsibility to consider your wishes and feelings too."

"Oh we're tough old birds … thank you Angela," said Jo. She was the oldest so she read a page first and handed it to Sam. Angela got out a hard-backed book and opened it at her book-mark, "…Should we be reading this Angela?" Asked Jo,

"Of course, you should. You are Sue's family; your views are vital to my assessment. Any questions, just say," she said and all three started reading. [The Science Part]

'Draft Report for the Parliamentary Health Committee into Post Genomic Clinical Pharmacogenetic Trial January 3rd 2017 to July 5th 2018 Conducted by Fielding Hardy Incorporated (FHI) in partnership with the UK Department for Population Health at Cambridge and the Health and Social Care Information Centre conducted by DR Angela Carter MD, PhD, PMT, PTA, RSPB, BLT, FAB, Senior Advisor for the Medicines and Healthcare Regulatory Authority'…. Both girls took turns to sigh as they read on.

'…Some concern has been raised in the Media as to the professionalism of the Counsellor assigned to subject 33…Mr Alfie Bester, with reports of an inappropriate relationship…It was alleged…. This enquiry could find no substantiation to these rumours.'

186

"Yes, well, you didn't ask did you Angela? About Alfie…I could have told you a thing or two" Muttered Jo. Angela continued to read her book, which was apparently completely fascinating.

'…*Preliminary tests carried out at the beginning of the trial showed that subject 33's alcohol and blood sugar levels were abnormally high…*' Jo nudged her sister and showed her the last sentence,

"Well, it was Julie's birthday the night before wasn't it," said Sam. Jo read on,

'….*and her hormone levels were slightly below average…*'

Sam's brow furrowed, she paused and reread a paragraph, then she sighed and carried on,

'…*The patent for the modified genes of subject 33 belong to subject 33…legal disputes with the Swiss Government, Zabtrex Incorporated, the European Inspectorate for Ethics in Industry and the legal representatives of subject 33…*'

"Mum hasn't got any legal representatives?" Said Jo, "…it says here she's got legal representatives?!"

"Oh, we…the Ministry of Health appointed someone do you remember? I told you last…a couple of weeks ago?" Jo tried to think back, so many phone calls. "…You know when we talked about her wishes and feelings, and Alfie?" It came back to Jo then, vaguely," ….to represent her while her behaviour, her mental state was so…under question. It's nothing to worry about, it's to protect her rights," said Angela without looking up from her compelling read.

187

'...Concerted attempts are being made to locate the subject and persuade her to return to assess her condition.

Given the unprecedented nature of the case it is difficult to state a definitive medical prognosis at this stage. Test results over such a short time period cannot indicate whether the subject's metabolism will begin to age again or remain in its current state. There is concern over the stability of the gene modification and the subject should be monitored carefully for the foreseeable future. However, the primary concern is that rapid cell division of the kind experienced by the subject indicates a severe risk of the development of several types of cancer.'

Jo and then Sam sighed one last time. Angela saw that Jo had finished reading and Sam was on the second to last page.

"Can I make anyone a cup of tea?" She asked and both women nodded, Jo kind of exhausted and Sam still intent. She was filling the kettle when Sam realised what had happened. Before her mum had gone away Angela had been what all three of the Duggens present had taken to calling 'diplomatic' or 'professional'. She had been kind and supportive and explained complicated things about Dee-En-Aye but she had not really said anything. Not about what she thought about anything. Sam decided to push things and said,

"It doesn't say it was you who looked after mum…or got us to do the patent thing?" Angela turned off the tap and replied,

"No, nor is it going to Sam…I did not advise you to take out any patent I merely informed you that Fielding and

Hardy had not…and told you where the patent office was located… As I said at the time, I'd prefer it if my input in that regard wasn't widely discussed." Jo put her head to one side and looked at Angela,

"We couldn't have, wouldn't have thought to…Why did you do that Angela?" Angela looked up at the ceiling where the answer appeared to be written,

"Well, it was clear to me that your mother, and you, are sceptical about privately dominated medical care and research." The girls nodded vigorously, "…And Sue found all those groups on the first page, most of which sent representatives to the hospital to see her in those first few weeks, you remember." Jo remembered making a lot of tea, "… well, as I discussed with your mother, they're like an Octopus with lots of left hands and right hands and only one or two of them know what the others are doing. So, the details did not concern her, I didn't want to burden her with unnecessary detail, particularly at a time of political uncertainty; the European Union is involved in a number of medical research partnerships which could be undermined, if the British do decide to leave. And the difficulty faced by the Dee Bee Eye Ess in their negotiations with the You-Ess, Feilding and Hardy is run from the You-Ess, you know that?" The girls now shook their heads slowly, "…Their attempts to negotiate new trade agreements with the You-Ess have been affected by what happened to your mother. It is her Dee-En-Aye, and she is reliable as far as research…I thought that it would be simpler, and ethically sound to…"

"Add another hand?" Asked Sam,

"Well no, your mum is another thing entirely, she's the subject, it's her Dee-En-Aye after all, and was, is reliable …a decent sort, aware of the benefits of co-operation with our European partners, sceptical of You-Ess involvement in the Enn Aich Ess, so…"

"So, Mum's got power over all that research, that can't be right," said Jo,

"Why not?" Asked Sam, "It's her Dee-En-Aye and it says there that Fielding and Hardy can still do the Alzheimer's research, doesn't it?" And she looked to Angela who nodded a 'sort of' nod and added,

"In partnership with the appropriate regulatory and independent British and European bodies, subject to legal clarification on patent issues. You see the bit in the report about the contracts? They…the You-Kay-Aich-Cee or more properly, the Aich-Ess-Cee-Eye-Cee might have been wiser to consider tighter provisions to ensure that the Ee-you, the You-Kay benefited more directly from any resultant treatments or therapies, you know economically. That's one of my recommendations…er…I haven't written those up yet, that's why they aren't there. They won't be making that mistake again, not with this, probably won't…"

"Yes, but what if she just sells her genes to some big conglomerate or something. What if loads of rich old octogenarians all get their hands on some youth drug or something?" Said Jo,

"What Mum? Our…Your Mum Jo? You've been reading the Mail Online again haven't you." said Sam,

"No! no, I haven't!" Said Jo indignant, "…Well just for the fashion…and they do a lot on Alzheimer's…Any way don't just dismiss what I said with some nasty comment Sam. She could get greedy, even nice people get greedy Sam. And look at Auntie Jan. She could sell her genes to the highest bidder and fill the world up with old people couldn't she, well old people rich enough to pay for it."

"Well they wouldn't be old then would they, they'd be young and healthy and could go to work or look after the great-grandkids or...So what if they all went out and bought a motorbike and took up drinking in the afternoons anyway? They'd be spending all the money they couldn't take with them anyway. Or is that what you're...No! Sorry Jo. So sorry, you wouldn't." And Sam's hands were over her mouth, it was getting heated. And repetitive. Sam and Jo had talked about this a great deal over the last few months, to no avail. Jo forgave her sister,

"No, I know Sam it's okay...Don't worry I don't think you think...We...But Sam, think about it...if no-one ever died...this planet can't sustain that many people, it's just not (she couldn't say natural, her mum wasn't natural and she loved her mum) ...right."

"Let's not get ahead of ourselves," said Angela in that calm and not aggravating way she had. "...We don't know what the long-term effects of the trials have had on your mum, we don't know what's going to happen..." And she paused the let the Big C shadows linger, "...None of the experts involved understand fully what happened to her yet, she could be completely unique or there could be a regenerative treatment for heart disease just around the corner..." Jo tried to interject but Angela talked over her in an uncharacteristic and therefore it must be important way,

"…All we do know is that we, the You-Kay together with our European partners, are ahead in finding an effective treatment, even a cure for Alzheimer's…." And she paused to let the A shadow cast in from the living room where Sue was on the phone to Julie, Jo did not try to interrupt." …All this 'fountain of eternal youth' nonsense that the media is so full of is just that, nonsense. Probably. And the regulations and restrictions on any further research are comprehensive to say the least and…"

"Here they are, maybe, what about America? Or China? All someone has to do is sneak up behind our mum, snip off a bit of her hair or nick her cup in Starbucks then nip off to China or India or somewhere and bingo; the rich don't die," said Jo. Angela sighed. Sam sighed. Jo sighed.

"I'm more worried about the Dee-Bee-Eye-Ess," said Sam and Angela raised her eyebrows, in, was it, acknowledgement? And Jo furrowed hers in confusion, "…the Department for Business Innovation and Skills…they've rung up a lot, haven't they? And it was them, that man Adrian something? that called her an 'asset' a 'national asset'. This could all be worth millions couldn't it. Billions even. And the deficit and everything. They could just take her patent and tear it up, couldn't they? Or take her away to some lab. How long is Aaron going to be sitting outside our door? Forever?"

"I doubt that Sam. Well, not tear it up. No Government, not even this…it would be a very stupid Government that undermined patent law. Patent and copyright underpin all trade and industry…"

"A stupid Government…" Was all Jo had to say at that point with her eyebrows very much up this time, Angela went back to her work voice,

"It is possible that your mother could… it might not necessarily need to be the Dee-Bee-Eye-Ess, although they have shown a keen interest, but there are some individuals within some Government… Health Agencies, that could under some circumstances…it need not be a negative outcome. Your mum can be pers…" But she was interrupted because the subject had walked into the kitchen sniffing.

A Fuck-Off Lawyer

"I've had to tell her I can't get over there till tonight…and she was straight over when it was my mum." And the tears overflowed as she stood in the doorway. everyone stood up and Sam and Jo went to cuddle her mum and sit her down. "…She didn't know her at the end at all, not for months, her own daughter." And she looked at her girls and cried a little bit more. "…she wasn't her any more…just a…and when my mum died Julie was over like a shot and…she's so tired just so tired, it's been a living hell…she won't say so but…she's so tired." but she'd run out of words. no-one knew what to say.

Angela re-boiled the kettle. She put a fresh cup of tea in front of Sue and sat down. After a long time, Sue took a sip of tea.

"…I'll get over there tonight, there's nothing I can…We've got to get this sorted out. Why are you…It's great to see you Angela…"

"I'm sorry to intrude yet again Sue. I'm very happy to see you, and looking so well…"

"No, no it's lovely to see you again and thank you, you've been so helpful, and I'm sorry I left I was just so sceptical…Julie said you got her mum on the trial but it was too late…just too far gone…they did say, said it was too late, well you said that…" And she trailed off,

"I'm so sorry Sue," said Angela and put her hand on her arm.

"Thank you, thank you Angela, it's very good of you. Again." And she smiled a weak smile. "…but you're a very busy woman and I'm wasting your time…"

"Not at all," said Angela and she smiled. Sue looked at this woman about her age who had done so much for her so far. Beyond the call of duty. A real public servant. Like her mum.

Angela had told her all about her mum coming over in the '50s. She'd been a nurse and worked nights for twenty years. Coming home from the hospital before Angela got up to make porridge and help her with her homework before finally going to bed. Dreamed of back home and green bananas that didn't cost an arm and a leg. Never did get back home. Died of a heart attack the same year as Sue's mum. The En-Aich-Ess had a lot to answer for there. Never mind Bevan, Angela's mum had built the En-Aich-of-Ess really.

But Angela was a doctor, not just of medicine, she was a bigwig. Angela did ethics for the Government. That must be very hard to do. But Angela didn't show it.

"I'm sorry Angela but did you get me to sign something about patents?"

"Well yes, I'm sorry I thought I'd explained but…well it was a busy time…didn't you agree it might manage the risk of abuse of the results of the research…They are your genes."

"Well yes, and it's probably for the best, and you took a risk yourself there and…don't worry we won't say anything. Will we girls." And her daughters shook their heads.

"It's probably best," said Jo "…Thank you Angela."

"No need for that, I haven't done anything without the full knowledge of the Em-Ar-Aich-Cee, and any way…well Sue. Given the number of interested parties, we talked about that before you left?

"Yes. The Octopus situation," smiled Sue,

"Well the Octopus has a grown a few more tentacles since you left so, given our previous relationship I have been nominated as your Primary Contact Person, if you agree. My job would be to act as a sort of conduit so that you only have to deal with one person in the Partnership…"

"Wasn't that Alfie?" But…you know I'm a grown woman don't you and he's a grown man…"

"Yes, Sue I do, and he is still your advocate… your liaison with Alfie is not the primary reason why I have been designated. I am slightly higher up the food chain in all this and so I can talk to people, and people are more likely to listen. This situation is very new to everyone and some people are concerned you might go walk-about again if you felt…overwhelmed again. So, the Minister thought it would be better if just one expert who was also a familiar face liaised with you. You might still be asked to meet with various other interested people but your physical and mental health will always be our priority. Is that acceptable to you?"

"I suppose so, well if I have to have a Primary Contact Person, Yes Angela, thank you."

"Good. Well cracking on. You remember about the Select Committees?"

"Yes, there were three weren't there, are they still going? Of course they are. So much has happened. When can I see the other reports?"

"Yes, and I'm sorry to burden you when you have only just got home, but there are pressures, time pressures. The Dee-Bee-Eye-Ess is keen to clarify the issues going forward and well the Prince of Wales has expressed his interest..." Sue was excited, a member of the royal family, heir to the throne, interested in her. She beamed,

"Stuck his oar in you mean...I saw that thing on YouTube, his speech at that Mutton Club. Bloody cheek!" Said Sam and Sue's face fell. Sue was a staunch royalist, the Olympic opening ceremony in 2012 had sent her into fits. The Queen of England, her queen, the Head of the Church of England, her church, made out to show her knickers and everyone cheering. It was disrespectful. And she loved her Duchy Originals. Jo backed her sister up,

"Wait till you see it Mum." And Sue was outnumbered, that's the price one pays for democracy.

"Some of his comments have been seen as somewhat controversial and what is needed is clarity going forward so the Minister, My Minister, for Health, wants a..."

"Who is the Minister at the moment?" Asked Sam

"Anthea Andrews," said Angela. "...She's very keen to meet you, but well it's lucky you came home when you did, it gives you a chance to get up to speed with developments." And she handed Sue the report. "...I'm sorry this is such a bad time but it might be wise to make you aware of what is happening...It's only a draft and I'd like to make sure that you fully understand as much as possible, add your input if I can. I want to take your wishes and feelings into account, make sure that I can support any future decisions, now you're back?"

"Yes, yes, you're right as usual Angela," and Sue took a deep breath and Sue began to read. Jo looked angry,

"Could you just leave it here and we'll give it back next time we see you? Mum's very tired she's just got back and her friend's mum has just died," said Jo, unable to keep the emotion out of her voice. Angela sighed,

"I'm afraid I can't do that, the Minister."

"No. No it's okay Angela. Thank you. Don't worry Jo I'm a tough old bird." And she nudged her daughter affectionately. She put her head down and tried to read as quickly as possible. Angela whispered to Jo and Sam,

"You have kept all the paperwork haven't you, and the discs, the patent and the reports, letters, haven't you." Jo nodded vaguely, "Can you remember if they're in a secure loca...place?" Jo interrupted her with another, more authorative nod. For some reason she couldn't put a finger on, she did not want Angela to know where her mum's papers were kept. Her eyes fell towards the kitchen-table drawer. Then she looked up at the clock,

"It's lunch time, does anyone want a sandwich?" Everyone shook their heads and Sue said without looking up,

"Some of that coffee would be nice, Jo? Angela? Coffee?" and her daughters and Angela caught a little glimpse of work-Sue, the Sue who asked for coffee not the Sue who made it. And Sam got a glimpse of what work Sam would be doing when she finished college unless her mum sold her genes to a conglomerate; Sam went to put the kettle on.

"Ooh Aaron's Elevenses! and it's past Twelve!" Exclaimed Jo and she went to find come biscuits, "…I'll make it, then I can do Aaron's Elevenses."

"Who's Aaron?" Asked Angela.

"He's our Policeman in the car outside," said Jo and she made his tea while she did the coffee.

Oh? How are you Sue?" Asked Angela,

"Well, how do you think?" Said Sue, "…Sorry Angela, how are you?"

"Oh, I am very well, thank you Sue, rather busy," and she looked down at the report. Sue leaned forward to pick it up but Angela put her hand on Sue's outstretched hand, "… how are you?"

"I'm doing okay, thanks Angela," said Sue and she smiled appreciatively. Angela smiled too, "That's good Sue, you have great strength, great devotion to your friend and your daughters … and your principles."

"Oh, I can't afford principles at the moment Angela, I've done some things," said Sue with a dry laugh.

"Oh, you don't believe that," laughed Angela with some relish. "…You're still the same old Sue underneath after all," she said reminding Sue of conversations they had shared before Sue went away with Janet, and Sue smiled.

They had spent hours talking, Angela had helped her come to terms with the strangest thing that had ever happened to her. Sue reciprocated, in gratitude almost, by echoing from those long sessions,

"Yes Angela, I s'pose I am adjusted, thanks to you." And she turned to the report feeling a little bit devoted to Angela. While her mum read, Sam went out of the room watching Angela, who looked at the kitchen drawer, then her phone rang.

"Angela Carter! Hello Anthea, yes, yes, yes. No?" She got up and went into the living room to talk for a long time. To the Minister. When she came back Jo was drawing, Sam had disappeared and Sue was on the phone,

"I've got to go Linda, Yes thanks. It's very reassuring, as long as she's well you know…Thanks Linda…about Six? Ok bye. Sorry Angela, my friend. I've read it all. And well, apart from the patent thing, I sort of knew it all already, you know being there and everything. It's a good report. Thank you. What about the other reports, could I see those at some point…"? And Angela nearly laughed out loud, and not in a good way,

"Some of the draft conclusions may have been superseded. There has been a development." She said. She did not sit down.

"Good news?" Asked Sue more hopefully than she had a right to, given Angela's face.

"It seems that there's an injunction."

"Yes, I know. That happened before Jan took me, remember. And now Fielding and Hardy's,"

"There's been another injunction and this one, well…" And Angela decided it might be best to sit down after all. "Well, the original injunction has been overturned."

"Overturned? But I don't want the media all over me! You know that more than anyone!" There was panic in Sue's voice,

"No, don't worry about that Sue there won't be any paparazzi on your doorstep, the new injunction covers that as well. Comprehensively" And Sue realised she had been so happy to be home and with her girls and in her kitchen, normal, that she hadn't noticed just how normal it had been. Apparently though it wasn't normal.

Angela put her hand on her forehead, "… I'm sorry Sue. The injunction we, the Em-Ar-Aich-Cee, with the Ministry of Health's blessing, we took out, on your behalf, was a simple breach of confidence injunction, just to stop the media and anybody else, you know those people from that American Company that visited you, and there were others, to stop them from bugging you. It was, is, a matter of confidential medical treatment as far as we're concerned and the Minister, my old Minister, at the time and this Minister, Anthea agreed." And she sighed and rubbed her forehead again. Sue had never seen her rub her forehead before,

"Well, I bet she's got a hospital in her constituency and she had to be seen to be putting patients first didn't she," said Sam. She might not have known her name but she had Anthea Andrews pegged,

"There was the consensus in the Ministry, to proceed ethically, and she was persuaded that your needs as a patient had to appea…were the priority."

"So, things are not proceeding ethically now?" Asked Sue very worried indeed. She had known that Angela had done the persuading and she knew that the only thing that was helping her persuade some very greedy people was looking like they were ethical. Angela was the only person with any clout who she could trust to do the right thing for the right reasons and Angela was rubbing her forehead.

"Your privacy is still the priority. We were all set to get the Fielding and Hardy injunction overturned on your return. The judge had made it part of his ruling," said Angela but she sounded like she was mouthing someone else's words, another first. "...the new injunction is a little more comprehensive."

"Is it a super injunction?" Asked Jo, remembering some news from a few years back, she had googled 'married actor' like everyone else,

"No, not a super injunction, it's...sort of...Well, there was talk about doing it a month ago, the Dee-Bee-Eye-Es put forward the idea but it was a Health matter and it was rejected. There wasn't the evidence, you, needless to say, are the evidence, well your Mental Capacity is." And she sighed again.

She seemed to be hoping for someone to interject but they didn't, "...When you... went away with your sister, you were, in effect, refusing medical treatment and so, given the serious medical risks you were facing, it could be interpreted as irrational, so...then you came back and there was the kerfuffle at the station and, and you got out of a car in moving traffic? Yes, I know about it, I was at the Ministry waiting for you... So together with the injunction, Anthea was unclear as to which Department initiated...In addition to the new injunction the Court has made you a Protected

Party, the Order, under the Mental Capacity Act, says that you lack the Mental Capacity to consent to tests unaided and therefore an application was made to The Court and then your advocate applied in your name to the Civil Court for a contra mundum mandatory injunction on grounds of both your privacy under European legislation and a potential or actual disclosure of patent, confidential information, and trespass to goods...probably with a nod from the Pee-Em...which was granted. No mention of breach of confidence. It applies generally to the whole world and directly to Fielding and Hardy and Zabtrex, and you."

"What!? This morning! That was an hour ago, this morning! They can't...trespass to goods, what goods."

"You Sue. You're the goods, the goods, the genes are yours and Fielding and Hardy's. Well, it's a moot point legally, but your genes, your genes are the goods. Heavy-handed I know but the potential economic benefits to the You-Kay and her Partners..." and dried up again.

"I'm the goods and my goods are mine and Fielding and Hardy's? Bloody Shylocks. But I've got patent, but, Protected Party? I'm Fifty-Eight years old! Mental Capacity?! I had the Mental Capacity to get back here didn't I...oh I was confused, overwhelmed, yes, but...I did consent to tests, in Switzerland, then I didn't but they weren't tests they were vivisection! They can't do that! I'm a tax payer! I'm a British subject! They can't just make me a Protected Party because I wanted to go to my sister's, or back home! Wouldn't anybody. They're my genes I can't help that!... What about the Human Rights Act?"

"That's what they've used to protect your privacy, Section Eight; right to privacy and family life, not breach of confidence, which is based on old-fashioned British case law and acknowledges…"

"Hang, doesn't the case law say I'm a patient, isn't it better to keep being a patient, and protect my privacy, my medical records that way?"

"The implications…there are a great many implications. I'm going to have to ask you to sit tight for a while, I have to get to the Ministry."

"But Mental Capacity? Privacy? Human Rights? That's what I was doing; getting to my privacy and family life by myself I don't need...This is why I left, all this is bloody rubbish," said Sue,

"Yes, well, you didn't think 'all this' would all just stop because of that did you?" Said Angela starting to sound annoyed,

Sam was standing in the doorway with Aaron's dirty cup. She had heard it all,

"But Angela, you said…you said, your report said, she's the subject. My mum's the subject. They can't do that. You said." and Angela cooled down to her sympathetic self again,

"Yes Sam, I did say, but events have moved on and she is also a subject of the Crown and an asset to the You-Kay economy and her Partners. You may have been right about the Dee-Be-Eye-Es Sam…Look, you have been made a Protected Party so that your legal and welfare decisions are to be considered by someone who has been appointed by the Court, that person will have to be independent of the other interests, I, your advocate will be on your side. There is also an injunction where your genes, and by implication you, cannot be discussed publicly by any one. That is useful and can protect your privacy, this may not be as negative as it appears…I'm sorry, I need to get back to the Ministry." And Angela picked up the draft report and shoved it in her bag, "…I'm sorry, I will try and represent your interests, get your rights, rights represented ethically, the Protected Party aspect may actually be useful, I will do my best. There are several interests within the first, second and third sectors and it is important to maintain your interests, as a patient, paramount." Sue touched her arm; she knew that Angela would try her best. "…I wish I could stay and talk…just sit tight I'll ring as soon as I know more."

And Angela left.

There was a lot to take in. There was a silence. Sue spoke into it.

"The subject? A subject? Subject or object?" Letting words and memories elide and doing nothing to comfort the two young women whose mother's Mental Capacity had been taken away by the Department for Business Innovation and Skills. The silence resumed. Sue nicked one of Sam's cigarettes without asking. Sam didn't care. She was looking at her older sister. Jo spoke,

"Don't start Sam."

"Start what?" Asked Sue,

"Oh, nothing Mum," said Sam, not starting, honest.

"What is it? Out with it. Come on, I don't need any more things I don't know girls, what is it?" So, Jo started,

"Sam's got a conspiracy theory." She said,

"But it's not a theory is it, not now. Now it's happening," said Sam

"What's happening?"

"Sam thinks we should be very wary of the Government, even Angela."

"Even Angela?" Asked Sue looking at Sam, but Sam wasn't starting so Jo answered her any way,

"Angela's not the Government, she's the Medical Research and…? … Health Ethics Authority, that's independent. And look what happened last time Mum stopped trusting Angela, she got kidnapped. By a multinational Corporation. That's what happened isn't it Mum, I know he's our uncle but he just used that to get an edge on the competition didn't he. She's, Angela's, the only one who's looked out for Mum, us, this whole time." Sue really did want someone she could trust, but the girls were talking it out. Well, she hoped they were talking it out, the way Jo had said multinational corporation sounded like she had said it before, lots of times.

"But she's a small cog in a big machine…and who's paying her, her mortgage? The Government. They're all Government funded. How independent can she really be?" Sam had said all this before too,

"Okay, girls let's just look at it carefully, rationally, it's important not to over generalise, personalise or neg…"

"I am looking at it carefully," said Sam, "I said that the Dee-Be-Eye-Es wanted your genes and now they've got them, they've made you a Protected Party and slapped an injunction on your genes. Your genes of which you are made, that's you. Now they can do what they like. With you."

"No, they can't Sam," said Jo, "…it's not like they've locked her up in a room. Like uncle Oskar did…they're just one tentacle of the Octopus, and Angela's another one but she's a good person and she's going to try and sort it out. You heard her."

"Yeah we're just feeding snacks to our twenty-four-hour surveillance! Just cos we know how Aaron likes his tea doesn't make him our friend. And if someone from the nearly-Government is deciding what is good for her, Mum, then Aaron will do what that person says, not Mum. Anyway. How?" Said Sam, "…. How exactly is a medical research ethics expert going to take on the Department for Business, Innovation and Skills Jo? How does that work?" Sue wasn't taking sides, but it was an excellent question. She looked to Jo for the answer,

"Aaron is there to protect us that's all, stop the paparazzi, our privacy, he…"

"Protect us, or the Department's assets? Privacy, or…copyright?"

"But Angela…She's talking to the Minister, for Health, she's calling her Anthea, you heard her, she's going to talk to the Minister and overturn the injunction and get mum's Mental Capacity back. This is a glitch…and then mum can decide what to do next, she's the subject. It's a health matter, nothing else. Angela knows that, can use that. Mum's got patent of most of the genes and this is just a panicky thing the Department for Business has done to, because mum went off and then came home instead of going to the Ministry."

"Panicky thing? They were waiting for an excuse that's all. Yes, Angela knows that and they know that and they don't want an ordinary citizen walking around with a potentially not very secret to eternal life in her spit do they?"

"They only want to stop Zabtrex or Fielding and Hardy from ripping us off or the Government. Protecting her, her interests as well as this country's. What they need and what Mum needs are the same thing. Health and using her genes for curing Alzheimer's and heart disease. Zabtrex…did kidnap her…"

"Well it was your Auntie Jan," said Sue in an FYI type way,

"Yes, Auntie Jan whose husband works for the biggest pharmaceutical company in Europe, it's the pharmaceutical companies we have to watch. Mum is a You-Kay citizen and the Dee-Be-Eye-Es is probably just trying to protect her. They've been heavy-handed, and wrong I know that but…they've misinterpreted some of her actions and Angela will talk to them and sort it out. It's not like she's locked up or anything and…"

"I'm not a citizen, none of us are, this is the United Kingdom, we are all subjects of Her Majesty the Queen of England, Wales, Scotland and Northern Ireland." Both her daughters rolled their eyes out of habit, their mum was quite proud of being a subject not a citizen. She carried on thinking aloud "…And well, being locked up or even watched around the clock isn't the only way a person can lose their ability to decide things for themselves. I don't like this Protected Party thing one bit...someone else is deciding for me and that's wrong....and... I didn't vote Brexit just to have my own Government take away my, my, rights and, but... didn't, Angela said something about a nod from the Pee-Em? The Dee-Bee-Eye-Ess wouldn't, couldn't go over the En-Aich-Es without a nod from the Pee-Em, could they? But any way Angela is going to do her best but...she is an ethicist... The odds are not good. We might as well face up to it... I think I need a lawyer, a big wigged-up excuse my French fuck-off lawyer, preferably called Khan or Erskine, those are good names for lawyers; professional...Why didn't Angela say that? All this time and no mention of a lawyer?"

"You've got a lawyer Mum. It's in the report didn't you read that bit Mum?... in Angela's report," said Jo trailing off and accepting a look from Sam.

"Have I? No, well I was skimming really...It's a chaotic situation. But...I want one working for me and me alone. No offence to Angela. Didn't that human-rights lawyer, or did that beardy man from Genewatch say something about a big human-rights lawyer?"

The women were quiet for a moment as they looked at each other, accepting that Jo had been right, that they should have had a lawyer from the outset. Sue hadn't wanted to sue anyone so she didn't think she needed one. She had also been frightened of the cost. And they had Angela.

Sam picked up the key from the kitchen table, Jo flicked back through the notebook "...I should've listened to you Jo, back in the unit, you said I needed a lawyer, didn't you?"

"Yeah, but then you persuaded me we didn't Mum; the cost and not wanting to sue any one," replied Jo honestly. Her mum said sorry with a regretful smile and said,

"I'm sorry…We're all a bit fractious, we have missed lunch. I'm going to make some pasta…" And she called out the rest of what she had to say so that Sam could hear her by the dresser, "…And it's not either/or is it girls, not a multi-conglomerate conspiracy, or a Government conspiracy, it's both, or neither? Its public-private partnership all the way down and total chaos. Thinking there's a conspiracy makes it look like someone knows what they're doing. Look at what happened to me in the Unit. Before I went into the coma, there were doctors and experts and advisors from here, there and everywhere and it was chaos. None of them knew what they were doing. It's like that. This is a chaotic situation!"

After opening three different cupboards she relocated her pasta pan and began filling it up, "…I'm only doing pesto." She warned. "…It's not liked the films, in films they have a plan, know what they're doing, real life is a free for all and people need to eat now and again…That Angela is a lovely woman but sit tight? What was that about? She's got a lot on her mind, I mustn't get paranoid again, that was not helpful. We should've got a lawyer from the start, I think now that they all thought it was a weakness, not getting a lawyer."

"Found it!" Shouted Sam, who brought in a little embossed, reassuringly expensive, card, "…it was that beardy man who gave it to us."

"Is he called Khan or Erskine?"

"She. Yes. Hilary Bailey-Erskine"

"She's hired…I'll just give her office a ring while the water boils, then we can have a bit of lunch before she calls us back all excited about my case. Hopefully. Protected Party my eye." And that is nearly what happened.

I Love Russets

Sue had to ring the beardy man from Genewatch to get a solicitor to ring the barrister and had not finished her lunch when Ms Bailey-Erskine called back on her way from the Old Bailey in a cab with her Junior. But the kettle was on by the time she rang the doorbell alone. Sue opened the door and forgot her manners. She was a lawyer, tall and angular, with a gown over her arm and a wig sticking out of her case, which presumably also contained briefs,

"I haven't got any money," Sue said instead of 'hello come in'.

"Mrs Duggen? Hilary Bailey-Erskine" Said Ms Bailey-Erskine and she put out a long hand that went with her body. That was some nose; also long. Sue shook the hand and stared at the nose. "…this is strictly pro bono Mrs Duggen rest assured, yours is a very important case." And she was in. Then she politely accepted a bowl of pasta and pesto, which she wolfed down, politely asked absolutely all the right questions, took lots of notes, politely said that her Clerk would telephone tomorrow morning about their own independent psychiatric assessment and she was getting up and going, all within forty minutes because she had to be back in Court after lunch even though it was already nearly two o'clock. As she was walking down the hall, she said,

"You might want to reconsider a suit or two, not for private gain but to show that you mean business."

"Thank you, Ms Bailey-Erskine," she loved saying that, her lawyer was an Erskine and had a wig. Deep in her bones she knew somehow that Erskine was a good name for a lawyer; class, quality. "…I'd rather not if you don't mind," she said in her posh voice that she had been using since she arrived, "…you see I regard this matter as a sort of lottery and it would be…disingenuous of me to pursue that course."

"Well, think about it would you Mrs Duggen, it would hit them where it hurts, in the pocket." And she arched her eyebrows in a shared understanding, but,

"Yes, well it's my pocket isn't it, as a tax payer. And I don't want to make more waves than I have to."

"Don't worry about the conflictual nature of some of the relationships involved Mrs Duggen, conflict is our friend." She said and got into the taxi which had been waiting all the time. Sue shuffled back into the house in her comfy slippers,

"I think I'll go and sit in the garden for ten minutes," she said in her normal voice again. Sam and Jo knew that meant she needed some alone time.

She went and sat on the little bench by the back door and had a look at her garden looking lovely in the sun and then in the shadow of an empty raincloud. Then the sun again. There were still a few droopy blooms on the rose and the grass was damp and lush. Home.

And back to talking, talking all the time. There were days when she was locked up and on the run, when she hadn't spoken a word with anyone. Days and days of no talking. Now she was where she wanted to be and back to constant chatter. She sat in the quiet of the garden, just for ten minutes. A gentle gust rustled the leaves and she looked towards the sound. She hadn't missed them till she saw them again, those old trees. Her old trees. And just what she needed.

The fuss she'd made about having those trees. Insisted. Obsessed. Cried till three in the morning. She could be a real pain sometimes. If anyone had been questioning her Mental Capacity back then…No wonder he'd left. And she smiled, poor Steve. Steve would have nothing to do with them. Said they wouldn't fruit. Then when they did in the year of Jo's birth, he said there was too much. She had had a good-comp education and had quoted a poem from her school days,

> "*Eat it, and you will taste more than the fruit:*
> *The blossom, too,*
> *The sun, the air, the darkness at the root,*
> *The rain, the dew,*" and he had, and he did. They

were great, not too sweet, not too tart.

She'd been brought up in a council flat so she hadn't really known what she was doing. Scared of pruning too much she hadn't pruned enough in the first few years. So, while one merely grew at a slightly wobbly angle the other one had three trunks that now grew out of the ground at angles. The sapling bark had been green and silky and almost as russet as the fruit in some places.

Now it was nobbled and brown and black and gnarled but still shimmered when the sun came out. And she had got better at cutting back, shaping the branches so that they didn't stretch too far out or over the neighbour's fence.

In the winter they were like a bit of frayed hem on a giant's reliable jacket cuff. Some threads thicker and more twisted. Some almost fluff. And the garden behind and the sky, like wearing a different shirt every day. A fresh green chiffon almost obscured the black this afternoon. And specks of yellow, the apples were ripe.

Russets, almost impossible to buy when she planted it before Jo was born. And the dancing! Jo and Sam dancing in the blizzard of tiny petals. How old were they then, nine or ten and five or six? Laughter like a thousand little bells in the spring breeze. And her and Steve sitting on the bench absorbing the fertile scent with the sound. And watching. Together.

And he'd given her 'Apple Blossoms' hadn't he. Well he hadn't taken it with him. It was a huge canvas. She should take it out of the spare room. Hang it somewhere prominent. Mind you, you could hardly see the girls. By anyone else it would have been a bit twee. Maybe it was a bit twee, but she liked it. She could hear that laughter when she looked at it.

She could hear the women they had become indoors, not exactly bickering again. Sue sighed, what now? But when she stood up, she didn't go inside. She left her slippers on the patio and let her tights get damp. Walked up to the tree and stood on tiptoes to see if any were really ripe. Saw the first perfect little tawny ball hiding just within reach. Heard the first whispered pluck of this season's crop and then the crisp burst as she bit through the skin.

Some people didn't like that dry nuttiness that was starting to come through but she loved it. So did Julie. Julie could do all sorts with a russet. The dry tangy taste of Julie's homemade cider washed over her tongue as it remembered. She took a little sip of her apple brandy too. Powerful stuff.

With the fruit firm between her teeth she collected a pound or three in the stylish skirt her personal shopper had picked out on the Champs Elyseé. She looked down at them and said to herself,

"*And every fleck of russet showing clear.*" It was a good year for her apples and she smiled again. What did she care about Paris and his golden apple in that Rubens picture? She had bushels full of her own. For years. And you could eat these. She bit again into the crumbly wet flesh and caught it before it fell out of her mouth. Just what she needed. Maybe Julie would like to go to the National, they could have tea in the café afterwards, take her mind off her mum?

Cheeks still bulging she slid her slippers back on and shuffled with her bundled skirt back into the house. The girls had gone quiet now. Hopefully they had sorted whatever it was out. She sighed through teeth gritted on her produce,

"Hello again Abigail. Have you brought my suitcase?" She asked the woman who looked so like bloody Emma from work it was kind of weird. She had taken off her shoes. Abigail smiled and looked at her roll the fruit out of her skirt onto the kitchen table.

"Hello Mrs Duggen. Yes, I have." And she nodded to the wheeled suitcase in the corner behind her, "… Have you just picked those? Are they russets? I love russets. They grow here?" Sue did not offer her an apple.

"Well it's the South East isn't it," said Jo, "…what's in the case mum?" Sue looked at Abigail the Intelligence Officer as if to say, 'why don't you tell her.' But Abigail smiled on benignly. She walked slowly to the case and said,

"Pressies." She was sort of waiting for Abigail to say something about sorry about interrupting but Abigail was still looking at her and smiling. She didn't feel like giving Jo and Sam their pressies with her watching so she stopped opening it up and said,

"Is there anything else Abigail?"

"Well if you have a few minutes?" Sue opened a few cupboards till she found her colander and started putting apples in it. "…I was wondering if now that you have seen your family you might like to spare some time to fill me in on where you've been and what you've been doing over the last few months?"

"I'm very busy at the moment I'm afraid," said Sue in a distinct 'make me' tone. She ran the apples under the tap,

"Well, it's just it would really help with our investigation if you were to tell us what you know as soon as possible. Not a formal interview or anything, your daughter or daughters can stay if you wish." She knew Sue had no choice but she was being nice,

"We might as well get it over with I suppose. It's got to happen sometime. Apple?" Offered Sue and she settled down to tell Abigail whatever she wanted to know.

What Abigail wanted to know was what Sue had told Jo and Sam. What Sue told her was what she had told Jo and

Sam but more ordered and with less information about Yusef and Yunis.

While Abigail was finishing off her notes, and another apple, Sue watched the droplets of water shining on the rough skin of her fruit in Abigail's hand. Then she had a little wonder about why she was so protective of Yusef and Yunis and smoked another cigarette. They were illegal immigrants and Sue, now she was back in her kitchen, was supposed to be anti-illegal, and quite a lot of legal, immigrants. Her girls went quiet when she started on that. That was one subject she and Andy, Julie's husband and her betrayer, agreed about. It was the one thing she and Jan had agreed on in Switzerland, they were swamped too apparently. But she didn't want anyone to interfere with Yusef or Yunis, they were nice people, very nice. Just working as best they could to build a good life.

But they had broken laws. And they were Illegal immigrants, the ones she and the Metro agreed should have no rights. That was as far as she got before Abigail said,

"I should tell you Mrs Duggen, we caught him." Sue was worried, "…Oskar Blutegel, he was still at the station apparently."

"Oh, oh good…and my sister?"

"Well, we hadn't fully realised the extent of her involvement but after what you have told me we will…is your sister still a British national?"

"I don't know," said Sue,

"Never mind, the Swiss are being very co-operative." Sue sighed, Jan was probably going to be arrested and she didn't know how she felt about it. Maybe go to prison. Her own sister. Abigail was closing up her notebook,

"Well, thank you very much Mrs Duggen you have been very helpful. And I am sorry to have intruded. You must be very…well I don't know how you must be… You have been very resourceful I must say," said Abigail with what passed for genuine admiration. And Sue looked at Abigail and did not say anything.

"Are you going to tell your boss she's not mentally incapacitated?" Asked Jo all hostile, as was her right.

"Oh that, you've heard, Dr Carter told you?" There was no reply "…well I have very little influence over…"

"But you can still say something can't you."

"You have my assurance that I will report your mother's competence and resourcefulness in getting out of Switzerland and returning home. That's all I can say I'm afraid," said Abigail. Sue's head was in her hands, "…you have had an exhausting few weeks Mrs Duggen. I should go and let you…Thanks again for your time." Sue did not get up but did straighten to say,

"And Abigail I know I had to give a statement but from now on if you want to talk to me you should talk to my lawyer first." Abigail raised an eyebrow and took the card that Sam was pushing across the table,

"Yes, yes of course…but I don't think we will need to bother you again…well, goodbye…Ladies…oh and S…Mrs Duggen, it might be best to keep a low profile for the next few days, you know just get your bearings…at home." And she nodded to Sam and Jo and Sam made sure she left.

"Well thank God that's over...say what you like about spies, at least you know what you're dealing with...should I have...? Was she telling me not to go out just then?" Said Sue, before Jo reached to her phone and pressed some buttons, *"... I love russets,"* it said in Abigail's voice.

"...Ooh you clever girl."

"Did you get it? You said to be sneaky mum." Said Sam as she came back in.

"Yup," said Jo. "...Can you check I got all of it Sam?" And Sam who was better at technology pressed some buttons and listened. "...my turn to make tea I think...you look tired Mum; do you want to lie down?" Sue smiled and asked,

"What time is it?

"Nearly Four," said Sam, "...God...what a day."

"I think I will have a lie down...is there anything we should be doing? I should phone Julie."

"Julie can wait an hour Mum, the boys will be with her anyway, you go and have a lie down, you look washed out," said Jo, and Sam nodded with her ear to the phone,

"Your knee Jo, sit down," said her mum,

"It's alright Mum, she needs to increase her activity...go and have a quick rest," said Sam and outnumbered Sue bent her head,

"I'll take a cup of tea up with me," she said realising that she might have had three of four cups by now but she hadn't had a proper one yet. ". ...and have a shower. I might as well dye my hair now as well. Are the packs still in the bathroom cupboard?" Jo nodded,

"There's copper, light brown and blonde," said Sam.

"Copper I think this time," said Sue wearily. She made herself her own tea, picked up a newspaper that was on the side and went slowly upstairs. "…Could you wake me up in an hour?" She said vaguely. It had been so much easier when she was on the run.

Her hair was like straw after all the dyeing and her room was stuffy and too shiny. She opened the window and sneered resentfully at the gloss white built-in cupboards. Now that she had forgiven Steve, she agreed with him about those built-in cupboards, especially gloss white ones. Waste of space. Unbalance the room.

She was relieved when she sat on her bed and found that she had been right about a firmer mattress and lots of pillows. But the coverlet was too shiny too. And rough. Her proper cup of tea swished down her throat leaving that fresh feeling in her mouth. Lovely. She wasn't that tired but didn't fancy reading the paper.

She had some wondering time. She lay back on her pillows which were also too shiny but very soft and pushed out a boring idea about taking out the cupboards.

The words 'subject, object, subject or object' repeated in her head in different people's voices; Steve's new Yankee burr, then Jo's and Sam's worried and questioning but it was all right because they were both just downstairs now, Angela all matter of fact, Alfie slow and thoughtful, Abigail not giving a damn, bloody Emma's snidey twang, fearful Jan, 'subject, object, subject or object'

When it was Julie's turn, she sighed to let the wave of guilt for not being there for her lap coldly at her sides and closed her eyes.

Various images of her apple trees made a power-point presentation in her eyelids using the fade button. Not in any particular order; how it was now, the little saplings from years ago, the blacky green shine of her favourite branch in sunlight, Sam sitting in the crook reading a book and that afternoon when they laughed like bells in the petals. She, aged 35, turned to a 38-year-old Steve and smiled. He kissed her with the awe of his beautiful daughters still in his eyes and then she was asleep. A calm and restful nourishing sleep.

The Elizabeth

The gentle knock on the door was welcome. It was Sam,

"Mum, you awake?" She was now,

"Just waking up, best sleep I've had in ages. You okay?" And Sam walked into the room and sat on the bed smiling. "…What time is it?"

"About Six," said Sam "…you said to wake you up." Sue smiled, "…Julie rang. They're going to the Elizabeth for dinner?"

"That's a good idea. Do you fancy going? Oh, Jo's knee? We could drive."

"It's okay, the walk, slowly, 'll do her good. It's not far." And they chorused,

"It couldn't be flatter." A joke from when Sam was fourteen and they laughed. Sue put her arms round Sam for a hug and got up to brush her hair and wipe away her panda eyes. Sam lay back on the bed and Jo wandered in and joined her sister.

"That's very dark for copper? I like it…We going to the Elizabeth then?" She asked hungrily.

"Yup," said Sam. Sue didn't have a jacket that went with her suit. She took off the top half and put on a cardigan. It wasn't that cold.

With Sue's copper hair still a bit too shiny. they walked slowly away from the roads across the summer worn grass of the common. Then really fast, then slow, then really fast again, so that Adrian, Aaron's replacement for the night shift, had to keep up, then hang back again. Jo's knee appeared to be almost better. They stayed arm in arm with Jo in the middle. Then they found something else stupid to laugh about. A fat strutting man walking a reluctant fat strutting dog.

Through the scrubby wood with enough sunlight to keep the chill off, on the road for Jo's knee. Chatting quietly about Sam's show, which wasn't for months as Sam kept saying before she went on about it some more. And some sort of holiday, they agreed they needed one but Jo had already had two weeks off for her knee and Sam had college. They had got as far as talking about a break somewhere hot at Christmas when they got to the Elizabeth, a great big pub that was built in the early years of the Second Elizabeth's reign in a very loose approximation of the First's; Tudor-style. It was part of a Carvery Chain now.

They looked around to find where Julie, Andy and the 'boys' and Linda and Eddie had already put two tables together in the conservatory bit. Julie stood up and walked quickly towards her friend and they grasped each other and squeezed. Sue did not let go but leaned back to look at Julie's face and Julie did her brave face and Sue's eyes filled up. Julie got a tear in her eye too until they did their 'we're not going to cry' huff together and hugged again, softer this time. Julie let go first and Sue said,

"You don't look as tired as I thought you would." And Julie sighed to say she was tired inside and said,

"Neither do you." They walked to the table for Sue to hug Andy as best she could, then Linda and Eddie while Julie hugged the girls. Sue kissed 'the boys', and said she was sorry about their grandma. James said,

"It was for the best," to Sue because he couldn't say that to his mum yet. But neither of them seemed to want to talk about it, probably talked out by now, so Sue asked after Chris's baby Jacob; sitting up now.

"And Aleska how is she?" She asked Chris,

"Yeah, she's really well." He said and added "…back at work now." Because he knew Sue's old views on Eastern Europeans. And Sue nodded approvingly because she was going to nod approvingly at whatever he said about Aleska to show him he needn't worry about her views on Eastern Europeans. She was family now.

"That Eye-Tee place? They treating her alright?"

"Yes, well they can't do without her knowhow can they," said Chris. Andy came up behind her and put his arms round her rocking her from side to side. Like he always had but now of course it was extremely creepy. Like having one of those uncles.

"Fancy a drink?" He asked and kissed her on the cheek and she smiled as sweetly as ever for Julie's sake and went to sit between Julie and Linda since Eddie had already moved up. They sat a moment; the friends since school. Then Julie said,

"Jo told us what happened…with Jan… and the Government?"

"Yes, not her finest hour," said Sue and they shared a look because Jan had not had too many fine hours at all as

225

far as they were concerned. "…Still I'm back now and once I get my Mental Capacity back off the Department of Business, Innovation and Skills…I have got no idea what I'm going to do really?"

"That's what Julie was saying just now wasn't it Julie," said Linda, and Sue realised Linda was a bit tipsy,

"Yes, now Mum's gone," said Julie and trailed off, and Sue realised Julie was a bit tipsy too, she would have to catch up,

"Well you need a rest girl, that's the first thing." She said,

"Well not really, it got a lot easier once they moved her and I could pop over and…," And Julie trailed off again,

"Yes, but mentally," said Linda "…mentally you need a rest." And Julie showed that that was true by not being able to answer and sitting all saggy in her chair. Andy had got Sue a double, Gin and Tonic as always, and she took a big gulp in appreciation. She took Julie's hand under the table and leaned across her to listen to Linda,

"Julie needs to eat, she hasn't had a thing all day," she said just as Eddie handed them all a menu, this was Sue's cue,

"Well I'm starving I haven't had a proper meal in…? Three weeks?" And before anyone could be sympathetic when it was definitely Julie's turn she added, "…did you know you can get a really good three-course-meal with all the trimmings in Italian Service stations, Autogrills they're called…I didn't have one but I went to the little supermarket thing for snacks and stuff when I was…I was…travelling…with…some…people…lovely loos too. Clean."

"Yeah Andy," Laughed Sam from her lager "…do you know you're sitting with an illegal immigrant." Andy, the policeman, smiled,

"I think Italy's a bit out of my jurisdiction. So we having starters?" He added to stop Sue glaring at her daughter and remember that if she ate a lot the chances were that Julie would eat a lot and Julie needed to eat.

"Yes," said Sue, "I'm having the works; prawn cocktail, steak and chips and chocolate fudge cake with vanilla ice cream." And she put her menu down.

There had been a good decade when you could not get a prawn cocktail anywhere for love nor money. Well, except for at the restaurant at Walthamstow dog track and that was not the sort of place that they would be seen dead in, and it shut down in the '90s. But then the Elizabeth, which had got so shabby they had stopped going, got taken over just after the millennium. It got a corporate 'Premier Inn- type make over complete with a cafeteria-style carvery.

It also had a 'traditional pub food' menu. The fact that the authentic traditional pub food was actually a packet of crisps or a ploughman's if you were lucky did not matter.

Prawn cocktail had been the pinnacle of sophisticated dining back in the day. Shredded iceberg lettuce, some little pink prawns, a dollop of Thousand Island dressing and a very important wedge of lemon. When they finally got another one, they did know it was not at all sophisticated but as long as no-one from work found out they were still going to have one or two. They might go out of style again, then where would they be.

"Me too," said Julie and Linda in unison, "...although I might have the chicken," said Linda,

"Yeah, I might have the soup...no the chicken skewers...no the soup," said Julie and Andy smiled,

"You know you're going to have the prawn cocktail, we all know you're going to have the prawn cocktail, why not just have the prawn cocktail," he said, and the boys nodded and smiled indulgently at their predictable mum,

"I might have something different for a change," she said with a nod to Sue who nodded back." ...What's that one you had the other day Jo, that time, your mum's birthday? Before she..."

"Four cheese ravioli," said Jo,

"Yes, I'm having that," and she did.

Andy kept the drinks flowing and 'the oldies' soaked them up. They were still coming to terms with being 'the oldies' after all. Only Eddie's mum was still alive, with all her marbles thankfully. They talked about Heather, Julie's mum, with an affection it had actually been quite hard to show when she was alive and well. No-one who met Julie first could ever believe that they were related.

"Hard as nails that one," said Sue, "...but kind."

"Mmm," said Julie, "...Hard as nails, you couldn't get much past her could you...when she had her marbles." And her eyes swivelled back to the hospice and the little lolling head on a limp little body she'd visited two days before. "...not even Seventy-Seven. Like a rag doll." And her gaze wandered further, "…but when she was in her prime! What a woman."

"To Heather," said Andy,

"To Heather," everyone chorused and they chinked their glassed and swigged,

"Hard as nails," said Chris,

"Hard as nails…till her hip went, that was the start of it wasn't it…Before that, you took your life in your hands if you crossed her, aye Julie…And she didn't stand on ceremony did she," said Linda,

"That's one way of putting it," said Julie," …but she was always there…and honest. You knew where you stood with my mum, even if you didn't like where it was. And…well she gave you a hard time sometimes didn't she Andy." Andy nodded a small nod and looked into his pint.

"She gave everyone a hard time…that time when she was aiming at you and hit me straight in the face with that wooden spoon." Laughed Linda, who had known Julie even longer than Sue. "…How old were we then, Ten?"

"Ten." Affirmed Julie and she smiled, "…Mind you your mum, well all our mums were handy with a spoon."

"Do you remember, did you ever sing into those spoons, you know like they were microphones?" Sue asked, and Linda and Julie's eyes lit up in recognition. Discovering something new that they had in common after the best part of 50 years was very satisfying.

"There was the brushes, we did that together didn't we…but with Mum it was always a spoon," said Julie delighted to remember something nice about her mum at last. Sue began a chorus of 'My, My Delilah' and all the

229

'oldies' joined in. Andy was the loudest and he knew all the words, not just the chorus and the bit about the knife. Linda did the trumpets bit and the others hit the tables to do the drums. Their offspring looked on and smiled and carried on their quiet and vaguely conspiratorial conversations about their mums' mental capacities, 'The oldies' looked back as they sang at them. They had smiled and conspired themselves just a few short decades ago. The singing stopped with a rebellious repetition of,

'Forgive me Delilah I just couldn't take any more' crescendo-ing far too high into the faces of their offspring. Julie had definitely perked up now she had eaten and sung. She listened attentively to Andy get a different answer to a question he had been asking Sue for months,

"Yes, Andy. I have got a lawyer; you were right I needed one all along and now I definitely need one. Her name's Hilary Bailey-Erskine." She said proudly through the G&T. Everyone else also knew somehow that Erskine was a good name for a lawyer. "…her Clerk is ringing me in the morning for an independent psychological assessment to get my Mental Capacity back. And, it won't cost me a penny. Precedents or something?"

"Can he get me mine as well," said Julie and they laughed, "…When did Andy tell you to get a lawyer?" And Sue said quickly,

"Well haven't you all at some point…. Do you fancy a trip into town, if you're not too busy?"

"Yes. I would like that. I'd like that a lot. After the funeral. You could show me some pictures."

"I've been showing you some pictures since Nineteen-Seventy-Six, you know more about them than me," said Sue, "We could go on…are you going to stay part-time?"

"Condensed day. Not much choice. They don't want me there at all really," said Julie demoralised. She had been working at the clothing retailer NEXT since it started and worked her way up to middle management in the Finance Department of the London Regional Office.

"They're all Fourteen at NEXT," said Linda, and all three of them sighed even though Sue could pass for 14 if she dressed like a prostitute.

Then it was time to pay the bill and Linda and Julie got out their Diamond Club membership cards and smiled smugly at Sue. A newish running joke. They all had Diamond Club membership cards but Sue, counselled by Alfie to protect her privacy, had had to stop using hers. It was a reward card for over-50s. Linda and Julie gloated just a little bit more but Andy had already paid.

It was dark but not that nippy. Sue got a tray with bottles of wine, lager and gin and wobbled it into the garden so that Andy, and she and Jo, could smoke and everyone could start talking a load of drunken rubbish.

"You had a gun!?" Said a startled Linda who had overheard Jo talking to Chris and James. Sue was startled too and her eyes darted towards Andy who looked very uncomfortable trying to push a Mandatory Five Years under the cushion of his garden chair.

"In America, they're allowed in America." Sam said quickly trying to be helpful, "…and she was in a lot of danger, she was travelling with Somali people-traffickers and an Em-Eye-Five or Six Agent was after her." She added failing to be helpful. Everyone was looking at Sue,

"I didn't use it…I…it was a good idea at the time…I…" Under the fairy lights of the pub garden in Chingford it was hard to remember the person who had been more prepared to shoot another person than she liked to admit. Andy, so tired of being the rock for Julie for nearly two years, and 'dealing with' her mad friend and bleary from engaging in the culturally specific post-traumatic-shock therapy commonly known as getting bladdered, managed to say,

"People-traffickers? What was that like?" to his, it felt like, one remaining ally when it came to immigration,

"Oh, they were lovely!" Said Sue, both animated from the drink and up for challenging the man she knew had sold her best friend's photos to an Italian magazine. "…if it wasn't for them I'd still be in Switzerland!" Andy was befuddled,

"Sue," he said in his best police officer's let's-all-be-reasonable voice, "…what about, you know…?"

"What?" Asked Sue. The rest of the table had gone a bit quiet, "…oh my travels have…? I think immigration is a good thing. Not just something you have to put up with but an actual good thing. When I was stuck in the back of that van I couldn't see where I was going you know? I…so I had this mental picture in my mind; all the roads and tunnels of Europe spread out like veins and arteries. Well I've been shown a lot of diagrams lately and they sort of mixed in my mind with Biology 'O' Level, And me and…the chaps, we were the cells, like blood you know, flowing across Europe down all the roads, bringing cheap handbags and medicines and ways of going about things all over the continent. New blood you know." Everyone, including Andy, was gob smacked, "…I've changed my mind, that's all." She explained, and she added just so Andy would know he wouldn't be able to sell any more photos behind his wife's back, "…I've changed my mind about a lot of things really." And she took a dainty sip of gin and smiled into her glass mischievously. And Chris, who had had the odd run in with his dad over the same issue, and was married to a Pole, raised his glass,

"To immigration." He toasted and nearly everyone joined in. Andy, who had already expressed a clear view that his daughter-in-law was an exception to a very strict rule on several occasions, said,

"Well, let's see how you feel in five years' time, but not very loudly and took another, it must be nearly closing time surely, swig of lager.

"Mum explained it all in her statement to the Security Services. She's home now," said Jo, who still felt like she needed to dig at that hole. Sue looked at Julie, who was looking worried. Chris asked,

"So, you won't be voting for the Brexit Party any more then Sue?"

"Brexit Party? There's a Brexit Party?" She had been away since March.

"Oh yes!" piped up Andy, "…Nigel Farage set up another…"

"Nigel Farage!" squeamed Sue, "…That, that, that…"

"Politician," said Julie,

"Yes, politician. What do we need a Brexit Party for?" No-one said anything as they realised, she didn't know about the delays, "…So how did it go? Leaving? At the end of March? I missed it."

"We all missed it Sue," said Linda, "…We're going on the Thirty-First now, this Thursday, maybe."

"What? What is Theresa May up to?"

"Who knows, she went months ago, its Bo-Jo now," said Sam, her mother looked confused, "…Boris Johnson, he's the Pee-Em now." Sue was silent, they were all silent. Sue took a large swig of Gin, they all did. Boris Johnson had been Mayor of London. Chingford was in London, Everyone took another mouthful of booze. "…So Boris Johnson is in Number Ten and, is Trump still in the Whitehouse?" There were lots of nods, followed by more deep slurps. Sue let out a little drunken giggle, then Julie laughed and hers spread round the table in a wave. Still smiling Andy said,

"You've got to laugh," and they'd had a drink so they could.

Linda sighed and Sue said,

"I wasn't away that long? I think I had better catch up a bit. He better bloody get us out,"

"But I thought you liked immigrants now," said Chris,

"I do, and I don't just want white ones either. My friend Yunis told me how British people can't get their families into Britain and the Ee-You pays to keep black ones in camps in Africa to stop them coming! He better get us bloody out...Bo-Jo? Boris Johnson is the Prime-Minister?" They drank again, until their glasses were empty. Chris went to the bar to get another round in.

Andy spoke into the silence,

"So you've given your statement Sue," everyone was mightily relieved,

"Yes. I've given my statement to...the apples! I've left them at the table!" And Sue got up quickly and rushed into the pub. When she came back, she sat gently next to Julie with a carrier bag full of apples for her friend.

"Already?" Said Julie smiling,

"Yes, it must've been a good summer," said Sue smiling back. "...neither of us had much of a summer did we...me and the girls were talking about a holiday...later in the year. You and Andy could do with a holiday."

"Yes," said Julie vaguely, "...after the funeral." Squiffy Sue finally saw that Julie wasn't in the mood to think about anything until after the funeral. They looked into each other's eyes and Sue thought she saw Julie wondering which one of them would die first too. They looked away.

It wasn't closing time but it had gone quiet and Andy was mustering, he raised his glass,

"To Heather," he said,

"To Heather," said everyone else and they all drank to Julie's mum. Andy had some beer left in the bottom of his glass, he raised it again,

"Hard as nails."

"Hard as nails." Came the chorus. There was a silence and then Julie followed her husband's cue,

"Time to go." She said and so they did.

As they were walking out Linda brought up the subject of the wake, which she fully expected to help cater. Julie did the food for a lot of dos. Sue already knew the plans that Julie outlined,

"Well, I thought we'd have it at the County Hotel, it's where Carol's daughter had her reception...it's been done up since then and we thought we'd give her a good send off."

"And it's not too far from the cemetery." Added Sue. She stood and watched Linda and Julie hug as Andy came up behind her and hugged her again. She leaned back into him and asked cautiously,

"You alright Andy?"

"Yeah I'm alright. I'll have to give them some more though now. You know that? I've got no choice." He said right into her ear so no-one else could see anything other than two old friends flirting sociably to make-up after their little spat. He hugged her some more. She stiffened and whispered in the wrong tone for the words, for Julie's sake,

"Of course you've got a choice. Even a policeman in the Met has a..."

"That's the way London is Sue, it's expected, the domestic market is nothing, I'll just feed them something small, like the gun? We should work together...decide what we want to tell them. I'd feel better if we worked together, managed the..."

"Sometimes feeling better about something is not a good idea Andy. You don't have to talk to journalists at all, you could..."

"Get real Sue." he said harshly, like a policeman, then he softened, "...that's how it works in London Sue. If it wasn't me it'd be someone else. The Media..." But Sue put and her arm over Andy's with as much affection as she could act and said,

"Never mind the Media they're just jackals. I'm a tax-payer, I pay your wages, you're supposed to uphold the..." but Julie was walking over with an,

"Okay, okay, break it up." And a smile on her face for the first time in ages. Sue sighed deeply and slid Andy's corruption, back into its little box, wrapped the blue and white checked ribbon back around it and stacked it in the denial pile in her head. She was good at denial. Well she had to be. It was his jurisdiction.

She said in a different, perhaps too sweet, a tone, "...it's only a few hundred pounds darling, nothing for such an old friend," and she turned so that she and Julie could hug, soft and gentle, Julie whispered,

"You're not offering us money again are you Sue? You know Mum was with the Co-op and everything's paid for." Sue came out of their embrace with a,

"Well you know I had to ask Jules, after all, what are friends for, aye Andy." And she took his wife's hand and began walking towards the exit.

"...And you'll give me a list of people to call? If it gets too much?" she reminded Julie,

"If it gets too much, yes...good luck with the psychological assessment you nutcase." And they parted unsteadily.

Jo's knee was sore on the way home so Sue and Sam took her weight.

"I'm sorry about the gun business," said Jo, "...I was only..."

"No, Jo, you were only saying what happened and I've got nothing to hide...I just wish I hadn't had to do all that and...all this...It separates me somehow?" Jo shook her head, "...I just wish I was your old boring wrinkled mum again that's all."

"You'll always be old and boring to us Mum," said Sam and they all smiled and walked home in silence.

Adrian had developed a bit of a cough; the summer was definitely over.

The Mutton Renaissance Club

The next morning Sue woke up in her own bed in her own nightie with a firm mattress and soft pillows with the sun peeking through a crack in her curtains. She could hear one of her girls in the shower and the other one, Sam probably, was clumping around.

It should have been bliss but her head hurt and she felt a bit sick. She should've drunk more water before she went to bed. She could only just open her mouth because her tongue was almost stuck to the top of her mouth. She hadn't been that drunk. Who was she kidding, she couldn't count how many gins she'd had or how many glasses of wine. Poor Julie.

How must she be feeling with a day of more ringing round to do? She'd phone her later. She closed her scratchy eyelids for five more minutes. Four minutes later she got up, she was awake now.

The kitchen was empty and she quickly drank a large glass of tap water. When she filled her kettle and heard the swish of limescale. She emptied and refilled it. Her laptop was still on the dining table and she put her tea down and opened it up because that's what she always did, used to do. Jo walked in,

"Hiya Mum, you're up."

"Just about, what time is it?"

"About Half-Nine…Angela hasn't rung back yet?"

"No? Still, she's not one to ring when there's nothing to say is she."

"No? The lawyer rang. There's a special hearing about your Mental Capacity…" Sue smiled, Erskine was a good name for a lawyer,

"That was quick…well I s'pose she'll ring if she needs to? And Angela's on the case I s'pose" Jo nodded and paused, "…Oh they won't want me there, I'm just the subject. I'll only get in the way," said Sue, "…they'll ring if they have to." And a sigh slumped out of her nauseous tum. Jo wasn't comfortable with her mum's nonchalance. "…Alright love, let's not pretend. We can spend an hour discussing my Mental Capacity and ring a lot of people who won't pick up or tell us anything new. Or we can just get on with life and answer the phone when they deign to call. Talking about the Court wherever it is while we're sitting here in Chingford might make us feel like we're…involved or something, but it won't make a blind bit of difference. Look at Linda when she sued Thames Water." She took a sip of tea and looked at Jo over the brim of her cup. Jo sighed and said,

"Sam's gone to college, there's an Assessment or something…Do you want another cup of tea? I'm making one."

"Oh. Good. No thanks love, I've got this." And she sat back and looked at her desktop. She took another sip of tea and clicked her emails and deleted all the adverts. That left a cheery message from an old colleague asking for a reference. With a quick swig from her favourite mug, she cut and pasted their name into a reference she'd written for someone else and sent it off.

She sighed and drank some more tea. Rested her sore head on her hand. She sighed. She blinked. She sighed again. The tea was all gone. Should she make another to rehydrate? Was she bored already? Jo came back in.

"You alright Mum?"

"Yes love, just a bit hungover," and she smiled weakly.

"Not up to what I've Googled about Mental Capacity?" Sue shook her head, very gently. "…Okay, but it looks good Mum, they haven't followed the guidelines. Ms Bailey-Erskine is very optimistic." Jo was bursting to tell her mum about assessments and relevant circumstances and reasonable belief. "…do you know who your advocate is?"

"More guidelines, guidelines for this, guidelines for that. They're strangling me…Alfie's my advocate, No? Angela said it's her now? And…oh let me wake up a bit first love please." Why were young people so bloody enthusiastic?

"Here, this'll wake you up," said Jo and she leaned over and turned Sue's computer round and pressed and clicked a bit before swivelling it back. She had set up a YouTube video. The writing underneath said, '*Prince Charles Speech at Opening of the New Slaughterhouse in Moorcock, Yorkshire.*' '*Sponsored by the Mutton Renaissance Club*'. It looked like it had been filmed on someone's phone. The wobbling didn't help her head. There was His Royal Highness the Prince of Wales with his long face and that hand going up and down. Like a thing you find in a fairground, where you put a penny in the slot to get your fortune told. Sue passed Jo a look to show her that she was going to be a loyal subject.

"Ladies and gentlemen, I am so pleased to be able to join you here on the edge of the glorious North York Moors where sheep farming is such a major part of the social, environmental and economic tapestry," said His Royal Highness enthusiastically.

"Why am I watching this Jo? Am I mutton Gee-Emmed as lamb or something?" Asked Sue with her whole hungover face furrowed, "…I remember mutton, talk about tough…"

"Just watch," said Jo,

"…definitely provide the preferred taste and texture. And we have learned that it is essential to hang it for at least a couple of weeks – and preferably longer."

"Well, naturally…. Jo?"

"Keep with it Mum." Sue listened on,

"… After all, in truth, there is no exclusion, given that everything is bound by the benevolence of the Divine."

"That doesn't sound very Anglican?" Said Sue, Jo shrugged, she couldn't remember her Christening.

"Now I don't think you need me to tell you that we live in increasingly uncertain times. We are facing what could be described as a "perfect storm" – the combination of pollution and over-consumption of finite natural resources; the very real and accumulating risk of catastrophic climate change; unprecedented levels of

financial indebtedness, and a population of seven billion that is rising fast,"

"And this was in Yorkshire? How many people live in Yorkshire? It's the biggest county in England, I remember because…"

"Mum!"

"Sorry. just saying,"

"With an ageing population, and pension fund liabilities that are therefore stretching out for many decades, or longer, we need to do everything we can to preserve our land."

"Our land? Aging population? Is that me? Is that why you're showing me thi? Otherwise…I might be a Royalist Jo, but I don't actually listen to them, that would be…?"

"Mum, watch." Said Jo

".... you are promoting Divine Harmony, that has guided countless generations to understand the significance of Nature's processes and cyclical economy"

"This is sheep he's supposed to be talking about is it?"

"I know," said Jo, and they listened some more, *"Even as a teenager I felt deeply about what seemed to me a dangerously short-sighted approach, whether in terms of the built or natural environment, agriculture or healthcare. In all cases we were losing something of vital importance – we were disconnecting ourselves from the wealth of traditional knowledge"*

"Oh, traditional knowledge, I like traditional knowledge." And Sue sighed a thank-God-my-next-monarch-is-not-all-bad sort of sigh. Jo didn't say anything.

"... *that has guided countless generations to understand the significance of Nature's processes and cyclical economy. The principles of Harmony that I have long believed...*

Sue looked at Jo in an exhausted pleading way, Jo nodded towards the screen,

"We're not part of the cycle are we, well.... we're in charge of it aren't we! Doesn't it say that in the bible though?" Asked Sue, who had gone to a good comp but neglected her daughter's religious education and so received no answer. "...Be fruitful and multiply and replenish it and subdue it and have dominion over the fish? Even I know that. Miss Sims made us read that over and over in Ar-Ee? He's going to be the Head of the Church of England! He needs to read up... Oh what do I know? Each to their own." Sue was Church of England.

"*It has turned out to be a peculiarly hazardous pastime.*" the poorly filmed Prince smiled and the dutiful subjects in the Yorkshire room laughed politely, "*...But I have come to the inescapable conclusion that the legacy of Modernism in our so-called post-Modern age has brought us to a crucial moment in history. Why do we tip the balance of the Earth's delicate systems with yet more meddling in nature's harmony, even though we know in our heart of hearts that in doing so we will most likely risk bringing everything down around us?*"

"Tip the balance? What balance? Is Alzheimer's balanced? He's really getting to me now…"

"Just wait," said Jo,

"…*dominance since the Enlightenment has certainly enabled us to improve the material realm of the human condition. But let us also recognize that this progress was only possible because of an earlier and crucial shift which took us away from a traditional sense of participation in Nature to the claim of mastery and exploitation over the natural order that has reaped such a troubling and bitter harvest.*"

"He sounds like one of those…he makes Eco-types look sensible?"

"Extinction Rebellion,"

"Who?"

"You need to catch up Mum,"

"Yes well…He said there he's been saying it since he was a teenager? Are that eco-lot Prince Charles types then?"

"Someone in, one of the broadsheets, said something like that, said what he said was good," said Jo without taking her eyes of the screen, they were getting to the good bit,

"*The Ancient Greek word for the process of Joining things up was "Harmonia." So, "joined-up thinking" seeks to create harmony, which is a very specific state of affairs.*"

"…What? Harmonia? I thought that was a musical instrument. What is he on about?"

"*In fact, it is the very prerequisite of health and well-being. Our bodies have to be in harmony if they are to be healthy, just as an entire ecosystem has to be. This is the way Nature operates."*

"Yes, and nature killed Heather before her time!"

"Natural sciences like microbiology and genetics"

"Here we go,"

"...tell us very clearly that every kind of organism, be it big or microscopic, is a complex system of interrelated and interdependent parts – which makes each organism a microcosm of its local environment; the very essence of it, in fact. The sum of these parts builds and maintains a coherence – an active, harmonic unity – with no waste. No one part operates either in isolation or beyond the limits set by the whole." The Prince paused in what looked like a very nice pub and his mutton loving subjects murmured in agreement, *"...This creates what are called "virtuous circles." You can see this in the relationship between the waste, energy and water sectors where the waste product of one process becomes the raw material of another, thereby mimicking Nature's cyclical process of waste-free recycling."* Jo looked at her mum, Sue was scowling at her future King.

"A circular economic and natural harmony can be generated where wastes become resources. So perhaps, at the end of the day, it might be cheaper rather than pursuing the more expensive option of encouraging people to take yet more pills and treatments prolonging and extending life beyond natural boundaries. This interrupts the virtuous circle denying nature it's waste and turns harmony into, not another circle, but chaos."

"Is he talking about me? Am I chaos? Does he want me to be waste?" Jo shrugged again and turned her eyes back to the screen. ".... Well. That is definitely not in the bible...we need a...?" and Sue sighed and listened some more,

"It is why for a rather long time now, and not without criticism from some quarters, I have been attempting to suggest that it might be beneficial to also develop truly integrated systems of providing health and care. This wider role for medicine is supported by traditional wisdom which sees not only the patient's body, but his mind, his self-image, his dependence on the physical and social environment, as well as his relation to the cosmos."

"...The cosmos?"

"The cosmos."

"I know that mine is a somewhat wider definition of integration than commonly used,"

"You're telling me! Is there much more of this...this...""?

"This is where the Modernist paradigm needs to be called into question before the damage being done is irretrievable. You at the Mutton Renaissance Club are a model of truly integrated and holistic thinking and a beacon of inspiration for others to learn from –the remarkable potential of a new discussion. Consumers love lamb but a steady increase in demand for your..."

"It's as tough as old boots! Whose got two hours to boil it tender? And you're a, a...There's a cycle for you; another Mad King!"

...A renaissance of mutton won't change the world, but it just might make the difference between survival and disappearance and that, ladies and gentlemen, is enough for me."

"And that's enough for me as well!" That was all she needed. Her head still hurt, more even.

"Well, what do you think?" Asked Jo. Sue sat back fuming, "...I don't think he'll have too many fans in Buckingham Palace...that's what he's worried about, if his mum lives forever then he'd never be king?" Sue was too livid to speak. "...That's what the Daily Mail said, well hinted respectfully. The Sun said he was 'Baa'king', geddit. It went viral till they took it down but we'd already copied it."

"Have you still got the Daily Mail one? Oh no online. We should give the queen some of my Dee-En-Aye. Could they do that? "

"God knows." Answered Jo,

"Why doesn't he just keep his mouth shut, stupid man...bloody Cosmos...bloody nature's bloody Harmonia...is bloody Alzheimer's bloody harmonious? It's all right for him. Bloody Cornwall and half of bloody Transylvania of all places to faff about in and all the bloody mutton he can eat. Tough as old boots, that's why we stopped bloody eating it." Sue sat and stared red-eyed at the screen, mentally picking stringy bits of meat out of her teeth. "Does he want us all living in one of his model villages, living like peasants, dying of curable diseases to fertilise the, his, land? Who does he think he is sticking his nose in? What right has he got to tell people what to...?" She stood up suddenly and went into the kitchen looking in several cupboards before she found her Duchy Originals,

"Bloody cardboard any way. Talk about over bloody priced." She said and tipped the Prince of Wales' biscuits into the food composting-bin,

"Recycle that." She said to the bin lid flapping back and stamped away towards her shocked and smiling daughter as the phone rang,

"What now?" She said to the hall door and went to answer the phone in the living room. It was Ms Bailey-Erskine's clerk, Mr Harris. And she had answered in the wrong voice. She didn't care.

"Yes? Any time really…On the Thirtieth, Wednesday? Yes…what day is it today sorry? Oh." And she sighed. It was only Tuesday. "…Yes, not sooner? Okay okay." And she reached for Jo's notepad to write down the address of a psychiatrist on Harley Street. Jo walked in and Sue put her finger up and kept listening, "…okay, okay, yes," And out loud so Jo could hear, "…the appeal yes, yes. Okay? Have you contacted anyone yet? Oh. Oh." And for Jo; "…it was the Department of Health that won the injunction. Why? Why would they do that? Okay, okay. Do you know who the…?" My Protected Party advocate is?" And she looked to Jo who mouthed a name, "…I think it's Alfie Bester, or? But…Could you find out? Well, keep me posted…Will you be at the psychiatrist's. No, no why would you, sorry. Oh okay straight after." And she wrote some more details. "…Yes, Thank you." She hung up and flopped into the easy chair she had perched on.

"What? What is it mum?" Asked Jo sitting down.

"Well, they've sorted out an independent psychological assessment but…I have to go in tomorrow but, well it seems it was the Department of Health that took away my Mental Capacity…Mind you, the way I'm feeling I don't know if I want it."

"But Angela? Why didn't she know?"

"Out of the loop? Dunno…I'd better phone her. Why hasn't she phoned yet?" She rubbed her throbbing temples, "…Do you want a coffee? A real one?"

"Shouldn't we ring Angela first?"

"A few minutes won't make a difference and my head hurts. You know, I've only just got back and it's all Department of this and Department of that and Mental Capacity and lawyers…and the bloody Prince of bloody Wales and limescale in the kettle. Let's have a coffee first aye. I need some time to think. I had more time to think when I was running away. Now it's all this stuff."

Jo joined her in the kitchen and Sue banged some cupboard doors until she had made real coffee. Jo stared at her mug and Sue looked wistfully out towards her apple tree.

"They haven't got a leg to stand on mum, the Mental Capacity Act says they need to take *reasonable steps* to work out if you're mad or not."

"Yes, yes. It'll all get sorted out and Angela's on the inside. She'll be beavering away, she's very efficient," said Sue without looking away from her tree. They sat for a bit.

"Oh!" said Jo, "…post." and she pushed the pile towards her mum. Sue took out what was obviously her replacement debit card and searched for the separate pin number letter. She pushed the rest aside. They sighed.

"You heard from Jason?" She asked looking back and getting his name wrong on purpose again,

"Jacob. Yeah, once…he was just being nosy, really. You know, about you." Sue reached out for her daughter's hand.

"So, nothing about the money?"

"Oh, he said a few things, but I don't expect anything really. I mean I am trying but…"

"Yes, yes, I know but…if it stops you, you know moving on…maybe we should just forget about the money?" This surprised Jo, it was her mum's money really and she had been livid when Jacob had 'taken out the equity' on the flat and then done the dirty on her. "…but mum you worked hard for that money and and…"

"And you, we both worked hard…I've got a sort of plan for getting you back on your feet, and Sam…and we might be able to salvage something still." Jo sighed now, "…let's get your knee better and sort out this law business and then have a proper talk."

"Yes, yes with Sam, she needs to be 'in the loop' too."

"Yes, with Sam."

"I'm sorry about the kettle mum." And Sue shook her head smiling, another first as far as kettles were concerned. "…and the Prince of Wales I know how much you love…"

"Oh never mind that," said Sue, "…I've thrown away my Duchy Originals. And that's the good thing about the monarchy isn't it; you can just ignore them if you want."

"S'pose," said Jo who had indeed been ignoring them pretty much all her life. "…can't really see the point of them really." She was trying to play that old childhood favourite; 'Wind Your Mother Up',

"No? S'pose not," sighed Sue,

"We could just get rid of them, couldn't we," Jo said, pushing her mum a bit, but her mum just gave in with an "Mmmm." and she looked out towards her apple tree. She realised she was contemplating letting go of something she had had her whole life. Something solid and dependable. A part of her. The mugs and plates and tea towels. Monopolising the telly or spending half the day in the Elizabeth to watch births, marriages, anniversaries and deaths. It didn't seem like such a big deal and she took another swig of coffee. Jo was still in a playful mood,

"We could start a little revolution Mum, start a republic." She glinted. Sue was feeling playful too. Her head was fuzzy and she was reluctant to think about her Mental Capacity.

"Why not?" She smiled. Why not indeed. She'd had a few little revolutions in her time after all. There was getting rid of collective bargaining and nationalised industries. She had felt a part of that hadn't she. Even if Eddie, who still worked for BT, just, hadn't been as keen once the new working practices had kicked in. And personal freedom and the getting rid of the nanny state. Well that last bit hadn't quite worked out.

But there was definitely having a career after you got pregnant. Although that had sort of happened really, she had just gone along with that. But it was still a little revolution wasn't it. Her mum had just stayed at home and made things with mince.

Food was a little revolution too, anything you liked any time of year and all so cheap compared to before. And real coffee. And she had voted for the Blair revolution hadn't she? Reluctantly but the NHS, you know.

And there was the internet and mobile phones. She had lived through all that. Standing in a stinky phone box with a pile of two-pence pieces one minute. Googling the Hermitage Museum on the train the next. She could travel too couldn't she? Actually see that Rubens horse as Pegasus, in Russia. Could she? There was something about sanctions now wasn't there. Still. "…a little revolution?"

"Yeah Mum, we could replace them with a president. You could stand…President Jolly. I like the sound of that." Smiled Jo using her mum's maiden name. Sue smiled too

"Well. I'd need my Mental Capacity for that. Although?" And she sat up like Napoleon and said down her nose in her fattest, poshest voice, "…President Johnson?" A little revolution of a president to watch over all the other revolutions; 'staying in the game'-a kind of fear at work all the time. Not just her. That's what drove bloody Emma wasn't it, and everyone else; fear. Never mind collective bargaining, individual bargaining wasn't all that was it. Zero hours.

And normal houses costing a million pounds. And something vaguely worrying about China and non-doms and bankers and MPs who were too posh to sound Scottish and health and safety and political correctness gone mad and

Brexit Means Arsing about for three years, and dirty beds passing as art and immigration.

Mind you that last one was around when she was young, the first time. Her dad was always saying he didn't feel at home any more wasn't he. No, there was nothing anyone could do about that one. Whatever Government got in they said they'd do something, but people just kept coming. All of a sudden it seemed silly to her to keep trying to keep people out. And then when they did throw people out, they got the wrong ones and Angela had to pull some strings to keep her dad in his own home.

Sue found she didn't mind about immigration at all. Liked it even. Why was that? Not just Yusef and Yunis. Was she letting go of things, all of a sudden? Having some sort of clear out? She sighed. Polish or not, Aleska was spoiling that baby.

It was all just a genetic lottery anyway, where you started off. No, not all of a sudden. Nothing really happened all of a sudden did it? Not even little revolutions.

"Or President Corbyn," said Jo trying to look crumpled.

"Well, they should skip a generation any way. I for one don't want that bloody nutter on the throne," said Sue, adamant and eyeing her food recycling-bin.

"King William the Second," said Jo sounding it out in the air,

"Fifth Jo. God." Interjected her mum, not letting go of her horror at what were they teaching them in school nowadays.

"Fifth then…. Queen Kate? that doesn't sound right?

"They haven't been the same since Princess Di," said Sue, still shocked by the cocaine. That cocaine in the dead blood. The Queen of Hearts' heart had been beating very fast when she died. She couldn't forget that somehow.

"Katherine the Great," said Jo, still musing. Her education hadn't been that bad.

"No. She's a nice enough girl but Great? Well I s'pose it'll depend on how they spin her."

"I think Prince William is against all that Pee-Ar," said Jo,

"Yes, well. It killed his mum didn't it. Poor love. But I don't think they can avoid it now can they. I mean the genie's out of the bottle there isn't it?"

"Like you Mum. I mean what happened to you. You're a little revolution aren't you really? A gene genie!" And Sue looked down at her pert little bosoms and sighed and stared out at her apple tree.

"Not really love, just a genetic lottery player. Just like everyone else really…I had better phone Angela." And she took a swig of lukewarm coffee and huffed, "…after I've had a paracetamol…and a bath. Maybe I should do my Yoga?" Before she had run away Sue had been determined to look after herself more this time round.

She didn't get up but looked out at her tree. It had been in bud when she had gone to Switzerland with Jan. Jan had said all that stuff about the NHS and looking after her properly and locked her up. Jan was probably going to go to prison. Her own sister. She took a big gulp of coffee.

"I'm wondering mum? Should you? Ring Angela I mean? What did Ms Bailey-Erskine say?"

"Oh, she said not to call anyone about anything except her didn't she. But you can't let lawyers rule your life can you? Look what happened when Linda sued Thames Water, it's all she talked about for nearly a year...Yup. Yoga. Where's my phone? Probably evidence in Switzerland or something. I'll have to re-download the app, and it had all my settings. Oh I'll just do the bits I can remember. Better than nothing. What are you up to this morning?"

"Well, I was looking up the Mental Capacity Act Two-Thousand-And-Five...They should've talked to me and Sam too you know? Before doing it I mean...Did Ms Bailey-Erskine tell you if...?"

"Not now love please. I've only just got back after a hell of a trip. Heather's dead. My head is still wobbly. I should shake off this hangover before anything else," said Sue and Jo gave up for the time being.

"Later then. I s'pose I should do some exercise too actually, the doctor said yoga would be good. Gentle yoga. Can you teach me a bit mum?"

"Well I'll try I'm only a beginner myself. I've been a beginner for about ten years now. Should be all right...but you'll have to stop if it hurts," said Sue and they got up and went to find their mats. Jo's knee was a bit stiff when she got up from her chair but she was hardly limping at all by the time she got to the stairs.

The phone rang when Sue had looked for her mat in all her cupboards upstairs and was now in the cupboard under the stairs. She only just made it. It was Julie.

"Hello Julie. How are you feeling?"

"Better than you I should think," said Julie wryly,

"Was I that drunk?"

"No, not that drunk, just a bit tipsy."

"Well my head hurts…How's the phoning going?"

"It's done, well there's a few more people but Chris has got the day off, he's going to do them. And the funeral's booked and I'd already chosen the casket and the order of service and that… the wake is sorted so..."

"That hotel, the…?"

"County. Well it's something else now but it's all sorted. I'm a bit…fancy that trip into town? The only thing I need now is a hat."

"You sound perky?" Said Sue,

"Yes, yes I do feel better. I was talking with Andy last night after the pub and I think I've been grieving for years. Now it's all over its kind of a…not a relief. But…she was very bad towards the end; it was very hard. But now, well I'm sort of free, you know. I've done my duty, and it was a duty those last few months. She wasn't my mum any more. Just some old woman. And now I'm free and I'm going to live a little. I don't feel guilty." She was talking very quickly.

"Now she's not…?"

"In a way, I'm happy for her, not happy? Relieved. To be at peace you know? And she's gone now and I have to get on with my life. The life she gave me. Sometimes, in that room, in the hospital, I think she used to get angry with me for being there. You… I, she used to get frustrated with being so dependent, yes, but also for me having to be the one she depended on. I don't know, but… I've got this feeling now, to do things. Do things for me. You know it's been all kids and Andy and work and helping Mum and grandkids and now it's what's it called? Me Time. Is that selfish? I don't think it is?"

"No Julie, course not I…"

"I just know she's at peace now and well, she wasn't that easy to get on with when she was well and… Andy has been a rock. But I just want to breathe a bit. I…" Now Sue interrupted,

"I'm not… See, at this point I would usually say something to, not humour? Soothe you…and I do agree with you, you've definitely done your bit. We've all been saying it but you couldn't hear. But…before, I'd say something like 'well me and Jo are going to do some yoga' so you'd worry about us injuring ourselves and come over and show us how to do some yoga and calm down a bit. But this time I'm just going to say it. You sound a bit manic Julie. You've had to live a nightmare for four years more or less alone…and not got the understanding from people you deserve because it's a normal nightmare. So other people don't think about it unless they have to, and now I think you've gone a bit manic."

"Manic?"

"Yes, manic. It's normal after what you've been through…and you've seen me manic often enough haven't you and said something soothing till I came round to thinking I was manic. But this time. Now we're you know… what's the word? Mortal. And life is too short and we could be run over by a bus tomorrow so I'm just going to say it. You're manic and you need a cup of tea and a chat and to tell me and Jo how to do yoga or we'll injure ourselves as well."

"Life is too short, isn't it," said Julie, and paused for quite a while. Sue was worried, they'd been dancing around each other for 50 years and she was afraid she'd been too blunt with a manic person "…I'll be over in half and hour…But I still need a hat."

By the time Julie had found her mat and changed and come over, Jo and Sue had found their mats at last and changed and Sue was ringing Angela. She was leaving a message when Julie walked in. They hugged and Sue asked,

"So, have you had lunch?"

"Is it lunch time?" Asked Julie.

"Yes…have you had breakfast?" Asked Sue, switching to interrogator and eying Julie up and down. It was obvious she had lost weight.

"Neither have you Mum," said Jo, "…you both look a bit skinny if you ask me." She kept her eyes on Julie's hips but Julie knew her face looked haggard and old and grey.

"Well, you're not exactly obese are you Jo," said Julie. "…you've been sat at home with that knee and actually lost weight." Her eyes were shining.

"Alright, alright," said Sue, "… We are all secretly loving this conversation, none of us is too fat. We've all been 'battling' all our lives and now horrible things have happened and we have all got too thin without realising it. And all at the same time so no-one has to be pepped up. This is not necessarily a good thing?... But now we can live a little… I fancy a crisp sandwich. I haven't had a crisp sandwich since I was pregnant with Sam. I love crisp sandwiches…with white sliced bread and salad cream."

"Mmm," said Julie relishing the idea,

"Mmm," said Jo without the same enthusiasm. "…First she throws away her Duchy Originals and now white bread? You've changed Mum."

"You threw away your Duchy Originals? You saw it, that video?"

"Yup," said Sue, "…and I've thought about it, and I'm not that bothered really." Julie raised her eyebrows and said,

"Okay." and then furrowed her eyebrows and then raised them again, "…Lamb passander, that's what I fancy."

"Before yoga?" Said Jo,

"Okay, crisp sandwiches for lunch and a curry for tea? How does that sound?" Asked Sue. The other women nodded. "…Right. All we need is crisps, white sliced bread and salad cream. I'll nip to the shop."

"Well, maybe we could just have something from the cupboard, we've got some…?" Jo realised there was nothing in the cupboards. She and Sam had coped, but only just.

"Well why don't I make us some cheese on toast," said Julie, her cheese on toast being legendary as it was. Sue and Jo sighed knowing there was no cheese. Julie sighed. Sue said,

"God, we're boring ourselves here ladies, let's just…" The phone rang and she silently thanked God Almighty, even if it was Angela. "…I don't know, one minute I'm on the run from multinational drugs conglomerates with an oozy, next minute there's no cheese." She said as she walked to the phone. It wasn't Angela. It was Sam on her way back from college and wondering if they needed anything from the shop. While they waited, and with several, "Sit down I'll do it", "No, it's alright I can manage." "You're injured I'll..." s, they managed to put the kettle on.

"Well I for one think it's nice not to have anything to do for a change," said Sue, sipping her tea and sort of lying. Truth was, she was bored already. Life was short, she could be run over by a bus tomorrow.

"Would you like to see what I found out about the Mental Capacity Act Two-Thousand-and-Five?" Asked Jo filling a gap.

"Maybe when Sam gets back. You know to keep her in the loop," said Sue, "...What sort of hat do you want Julie?" Julie had sort of slumped again and she answered slowly,

"Oh? I don't know, something sophisticated...and cheerful. Mum would have liked that I think...There was this time back in... the Nineteen-Seventies sometime...and I had this copy of...Honey magazine? Do you remember Honey magazine Sue?" Sue smiled in recognition "...there was no internet Jo, no 'youth programming' well except for Top of the Tops. We only had magazines...and what we saw other people wearing..."

"And films Julie...James Bond and...?" Interjected Sue gently,

"Yes, and films and what the Dr Who assistant wore...anyway I had this copy of Honey magazine and there was this hat. It must've been the Seventies because it was sort of wide-brimmed and...more of a panama really... and a horrible shade of red. My mum was looking at it all wistful...I don't know why I thought of that?" And she sighed and no-one said anything. "...I remember thinking she looked so old, that hat would never have suited her. But she can't have been more than...Thirty-Five, or Six. She was only Thirty-Six but she looked so old to me." For Jo, 36 was still a whole decade away,

"When did she have you?" She asked.

"Young," said Julie "...very young, but that was normal back then."

"You'd've been what? Seventeen, Eighteen?" Asked Sue and they looked at each other and smiled for back then and all the years in between. Julie looked away too suddenly with a twist in her face she didn't want Sue to see.

Sue looked down at her hand on the table next to her tea. Smooth and pink and plump. Involuntarily, she looked at Julie's hand then looked away. Julie's hand was blotched and angry and had crinkled veins that writhed like green and purple snakes as she stroked her hair. Sue was a little disgusted. She was greatly ashamed. She couldn't remember how Julie had felt about her rejuvenation when it first happened, she hadn't cared.

She'd been so wrapped up in touching her toes and the place where her crow's feet used to be. She glanced back across at Julie who seemed so far away and a tear formed in her eye. She let it fall and blinked.

"Those hats are back in fashion now, it should be easy to find," said Jo optimistically.

"Yes," said Julie rallying, "…does Selfridges still have a hat department? Let's go there like we used to and try on hats and have tea and…people can think I'm your Mum." She laughed in Sue's direction. Sue didn't try and laugh. She looked out at her tree and stretched her hand back towards her friend's. Julie took it and squeezed.

"Makeovers! You could have a makeover Auntie Jules. They do those in Selfridges, you could get a personal shopper."

"Yes, I could turn up at Mum's funeral looking like Kim Cattrall. Andy'd like that."

"You already look like Kim Cattrall, Julie, actually better. It's not like your mum's day. She did look old at Thirty-Six. Now…now we've got washing machines and… Rohypnol," said Sue, finally turning around to look at her best friend.

"I think you mean Retinol," said Julie.

"She's got a bit thick round the middle, Kim Cattrall," said Sue

"Yes well, face or figure that's what they say. Face or figure," said Julie. "…we should eat." She added remembering her own again, "… When's Sam back?"

"Not long now…we could do our yoga in the garden, it's a lovely day."

Crisp sandwiches do not work with olive ciabatta and Kettle Chips. But luckily Sam had got some nice ham and a bit of Camembert as well. Then they had to digest. Julie especially, she ate nearly half a loaf of bread. Sue tried Angela again and left a text.

Sam got changed and convinced her auntie Julie that she didn't need a mat. The sun was glinting and a warm breeze rustled the leaves. No-one was cold. They arranged themselves in a sort of semicircle around Julie.

Julie had done a weekend team-building course in 2006 and got hooked. She didn't have a chakra or anything but she had kept it up; half an hour a few times a week. The yoga gave her a few minutes of 'me time', reversed some of the gravitational issues that her bum had, and the physical strength to lift her mum when she sat down suddenly in the road for no reason at three in the morning. This was the first time she had done it since her mum died and she did seem lighter somehow.

The Duggens lumbered and grunted while Julie glided through the moves telling Jo when to stop to protect her knee. Nor did she have to lean on her apple tree to stop herself falling over in the 'tree pose'. Or fart when she bent over. Sam was seriously out of breath by the time they sat down for 'staff pose'.

By the time they unfolded from touching, or nearly touching, their toes their breathing was back in sync. And the endorphins had kicked in for all of them. Each one had a sublime warm bath smile for the last few moves. Arms and legs all seemed to work together, like synchronised swimmers beached on the grass.

As they lay back finally for 'corpse pose' the sun seemed to get a little brighter and the wind tickled over their glowing skin and through the trees. No-one wanted to get up, no-one wanted to 'empty your mind', so they didn't. They looked up at clusters of apples, some glimmering sort of golden in the low sunshine, hiding among the leaves. Each one lost contentedly in her own thoughts. A blackbird began to sing obligingly. Lovely.

Julie was the first to sit up.

"My mind's made up. I am determined to get a hat," she said. The Duggens did not move. The Duggens reserved their energy for the 'best way into town' discussion that Julie was about to have mostly with herself. Julie didn't like taking the train in for fun things because it was too like her commute. She didn't like driving because of the Congestion Charge and there was nowhere to park,

"Let's get a cab," she said. The Duggens sat up briskly. Now all they had to do was enact the 'four women can get showered and changed in half an hour' protocol. They'd done it before, they could do it again. Sue was on her way to the phone to book a cab when it rang.

"Angela! Hello… Well I'm about to go out. Oh, oh! But I'm coming into to town, we could meet…? Well, Selfridges actually. It's a long story, okay, okay. Four-Thirty. Can I bring a friend, and maybe a daughter or two? Good…Well I'll see you then. Pardon? Yes? oh oh…good. Thank you, Angela. Yes. Bye, bye." And she hung up and shouted to the people all engaged in the getting out of the front door manoeuvres, "…Good News! Angela is my advocate! She got a special sitting of the Court and it's all under review. I've got to meet her this afternoon…" The phone rang again as various voices made various happy noises, "Hello? Oh, hello Mr Harris. Yes, I know. No, no she's a good person I'm pleased. Yes. Oh? Okay. Well thank you for letting me know…. Yes, see you on Friday. Yes?

No? Why would you…. Okay, okay. See you on Friday."
And Sue, who had not sat down, phoned for a cab and ran
upstairs to get changed with a… "that's an odd question?
Still these legal types."

It's the Drink What Did It

Julie and Sue, for that was the order in which their names were always said, 'twas ever thus, worked out that they hadn't done it for about ten years, when the kids were small, so it was only really twenty-nine years of trying on hats in Selfridges. In all that time they had only been asked to leave three times. They had dressed appropriately, that is up, and were not at all drunk so as to avoid a fourth time. They had never actually bought a hat in Selfridges. This afternoon would be different. Nor had they had ever done it with Jo and Sam and they had already silently agreed to initiate them once they got there.

"Now you don't look so...so...?" Struggled Julie, once she was sure the cab-driver had taken the right route, that is when they were nearly there.

"Distinguished?" Asked Sue sticking her nose and one elbow in the air from the back,

"Old?" Asked Sam,

"Sam!" Said Jo,

"Old and distinguished," said Julie, "...we had better be careful." Sam and Jo wondered about that but didn't say anything. They were as aware as anyone that this was some sort of 'oldies' thing. The fact that their mum and auntie were dressed to the nines and vetoed a couple of Sam's choices of dress had told them that.

"Now let's see if you are a hat person," said Sue as she got out of the cab.

"I'm a hat person and so is your mum, but some people aren't," said Julie to the two younger women who had never seen either of them in a hat.

Hats were scattered all over the shop nowadays, in with the clothes, shoes, accessories and finally other hats. It was hard not to get distracted by a nice top or dress, which Julie, the retail expert, explained was the idea. They all stopped and walked back to a rail or two, but Julie was attracted to the most things. She was pulled thither and hither by day, evening and holiday wear like a magnetised pin ball. First Sue and then Jo and Sam had to pull her away from some very brave choices. Despite working for a major clothing retailer nearly all her working life she was still mesmerised by all the lovely things.

She was also determined to 'get away with' puffy sleeves when Sue had been telling her for years that they didn't suit her. Julie sort of knew that Sue was right but ever since Deidre in the Fourth-Year had had that mutton-bone sleeve maxi-dress Julie had desired puffy sleeves at a level that quite possibly went below the id. But some people should never ever drink even a tiny bit of alcohol and Julie should never ever wear puffy sleeves, even in chiffon. Sue, Jo and Sam pulled her away from the black-and-white geometric print chiffon with some difficulty, saying,

"Hats Julie, hats." As gently as they could.

"Hats, yes, hats," said Julie sighing deeply,

Wherever there was a hat, they stopped and everyone tried it on at the nearest mirror; straight, tipped back, tipped forward, at a jaunty angle, or another jaunty angle. Jo and Sam had both seen the races scene in the film 'My Fair Lady' at some point. So they soon got the hang of the po-faces and posh poses so expertly demonstrated by their seniors.

While Sue and Julie could swap most of each other's clothes and they'd fit, Julie had broader square shoulders and a shorter neck. She was definitely a hat person but had to be careful she did not go for too broad a brim. The hat she had seen in Honey in 1971 had a very wide brim, so it was tricky. Sam was also a hat person and could swap clothes with Sue if they hadn't unanimously agreed that that was a no-no immediately she had reached Five-Foot-Eight like her mum a few years ago.

Jo was taller than any of them so she should have been a hat person. But somehow, she was not a hat person; nothing seemed to suit her somehow. By now they were in the actual hat department and Sue had to take charge of finding something for her flagging daughter.

"How about a Fedora?" Asked Jo desperately picking up a panama and nodding to a panting plain-clothes Aaron who had only just found them. He picked up a pink fascinator and looked at it very carefully indeed.

"Let's not give up just yet Jo…. you've only tried a beret, a cloche, a bucket, a cap, a Provence, a, a pillbox and a fascinator…. Here what about this?" She was still wearing a neat little porkpie and proffered a turban to Jo who, quite rightly, squirmed and looked around,

"Ah, a boater," she said picking up a show hat. Her mum put it down. "…this?" Asked Jo,

"That's a nice little Trilby," said her mum, Julie had taught her all the hat names over the years. Jo tried it on and looked into a mirror. Sue examined her from the side, took off the trilby and changed the dent from a diamond to a teardrop and put it back on her daughter's head; no. She tried a straightforward centre dent; no, a telescope took ages; but no. "…What about something with more structure?" She said reaching for a stingy-brimmed straw fedora; no. This was like that dress for that date with whatsisname in 2007 all over again. Jo was visibly shrinking. "…Okay, less structure," said Sue smiling and catching her waning daughter's eye. Jo managed a smile and Sue looked around for something in her colour, a mahogany felt, short-brimmed fedora with a telescope dent. Sort of. "…Oh yes," said Sue with relief, "…that looks great." And Jo inspected it and herself in the mirror,

"Well, I don't know?" She said, quite right to be suspicious. Julie came up,

"Oh yes, that's better," she said from under a maroon-ish red felt Dunaway with a dimple crease, looking great. "…anyone can wear a fedora." Aaron nodded approvingly.

Sam walked up and smiled at her sister in the mirror from under a trilby. Sue came in for a closer look and caught sight of herself and Sam together in their trilbies. So did Jo,

"That's spooky," she said, "… you could be twins." Sue quickly took off the hat to show her dark hair.

"What?" Asked Jo, "…me and mum? No. We're nothing like each other." And she pulled her mum closer, pulled off her hat and stared. Apart from the hair colour, the

270

resemblance was astonishing even though it was also not surprising at all. "...See," said Sam without irony, "...Nothing like each other." and a blue bowler caught her eye and she wandered off happily. Jo and her mum shared a look. Jo shook her head. Sue said,

"Do you want to try one with a broader band?" And Jo nodded,

"It's alright mum I'll find it...you need to decide." And she nodded into the forest of hat-stands. Julie still had the Dunaway everyone agreed was perfect in her hand, but was trying on another red wide-brimmed felt. It was a brighter red. Much brighter. The brim was floppier,

"It's....it makes more of your shoulders.... it's very bright," said Sue from behind Julie admiring herself in the mirror. Julie, whose mum had looked into her family tree before she went senile and found lots of Scottish ancestors, explaining the pale complexion, did not seem to hear her. "...What are you going to wear with it," said Sue knowing that Julie would most likely wear her purple jersey dress and her black mohair shrug. "...It's a brave colour," said Sue, "...Very brave," a little louder. Aaron who had been perplexed by a diamanté fascinator looked round and was visibly startled.

But Julie had made up her mind. She did not look away but pointed to some cloches. "...Ooh!" Said Sue and she fell onto a maroon-red one and replaced the trilby. It went with her face, it went with her bob, it would go with her new suit if she wore a reddish top, it would go with the neckline of lots of things she had at home, and lots of her shoes.

"It's definitely you." She heard from three different directions. It was definitely her.

"But red?" She said to herself and picked up a black-and-charcoal one in the same style. She was just about to put it on when she heard,

"Can I help you." In a tone she had heard many times before. She put it on,

"No thank you. I'm fine" she said and turned her head to one side; it was definitely her. But the Selfridges assistant was not going away. It so happened that she had found the hat she was going to buy, so had Julie, so had Sam and so had Jo. However, all four women suddenly became interested in a Givenchy fascinator, a diamanté covered Ben Hogan, a red felt show hat and a Chanel silver turban located at different ends of the hat department. The assistant looked from one to the other and stepped first toward Julie in the Givenchy, then Sam in the turban before striding up to Jo in the Ben Hogan and raising her eyebrows,

"Anything I can help you with?" She didn't ask,

"Just sampling your wares," said Jo smiling before putting it back. The assistant adjusted the hat on its stand without stopping her surveillance of all four women. She followed Jo towards Sue, who put the show hat back at a jaunty angle. The assistant straightened the show hat and looked sideways at Sue,

"All right ladies?" Said Julie and all four took their hats towards the checkout,

"We will need boxes." Sue called out without looking back at the assistant. The assistant made sure that the lady at the till had eyes on all four hats before she went to get four boxes. "…My treat ladies," said Sue hopefully, not sure if her savings had transferred yet. She got out her card and mentally crossed her fingers. It worked.

"Well, I'm getting the tea," asserted Julie, Sam and Jo said nothing.

Sue's card worked a lot; she quickly ordered a lamp-stand, four very large outdoor plant-pots and a new set of cast iron garden furniture to be delivered for a sort-of plan that might be beginning to form in her head, and because they were nice. Then, they still had half an hour before meeting Angela so they perched in their hats at the champagne bar and sampled its wares. Twice. Aaron sat on the other side of the bar and had an orange juice.

"Doesn't it bother you? Him, there, watching?" asked Julie after she'd offered him a drink just to be sociable,

"Who Aaron?" Said Sam looking at him and smiling, "… No, you stop minding after a bit, well… It can be a bit annoying when your shopping's heavy and they don't bother offering to help you carry it, just carry on lurking like their invisible. But, their harmless."

"And he thinks he's helping, which is strange?" Said Jo, "… It's not as if he'd be any use if someone did try and kidnap Mum or whatever."

"Well, we know his shifts and his routines, that's the main thing," said Sue and they clinked their glasses and knocked back their bubbly.

Up on the roof, after some tottering with empty hat boxes in posh Selfridges bags, they found Angela, who had already ordered the cream tea. They all kissed on two cheeks before they sat down.

Angela said nothing about the hats but smiled appreciatively. She looked a little elated like someone who has landed a new job and can't wait to get it into the conversation. Julie and Sue looked like they lived in Selfridges. Jo's nose was sweating and her eyes were pleasantly vacant. Sam's head wobbled a bit under her trilby into which she was already growing, and she had the hiccoughs. Julie poured.

"You look happy," said Sue to Angela in the hat that was definitely her,

"I am a little," said Angela, hatless, "…it's good news. On two counts. As you know, the Court, which has made you a Protected Party…"

"Which they shouldn't have. There's a procedure and they didn't follow it," said Jo in her fedora,

"That argument was made, they were able to claim that they couldn't follow procedure because you were both unavailable and un-cooperative. But it won't stand for long. It is only a matter of time I'm sure…the wheels of justice and so forth…in the meantime, the Court has to appoint an advocate to work out whether you can make important decisions. The judge has not overturned the Order, there is some pressure from within the Department of Health. You know it was the Department of Health that took out the proceedings?" Everyone nodded, Sam particularly, "…But they have made me your advocate while we wait for an independent psychological assessment, someone who is an approved expert witness, which is on Wednesday I believe?" Sue nodded.

"And you should get a statement off that Abigail Mc…something from the Security Services. She was very impressed with mum's Mental Capacity in getting home," said Sam,

"Yes, well she seemed to think that her type has the monopoly on pretending you're somebody else," said Sue,

"She should try working in retail for forty-odd years," said Julie in the hat that was definitely not Heather,

"Or anything," said Jo,

"Quite," said Angela, "…but you did show great presence of mind Sue and…"

"But what does you being my advocate mean?" Asked Sue, "I mean I'm glad it's you and everything…if I have to have one… But?"

"Well, I am to represent your interests as a patient and as the owner of the Dee-En-Aye copyright. You will not have to deal with all the legal business alone, I am here to ensure that your views, which coincide with those of the Good-Ole-En-Aich-of-Ess as you told Alfie and myself, are represented fully. And all it means in practical terms day to day that if there are any important decisions you should make, to do with money or contracts or well…there is something you should know…"

"Can't she buy a hat without asking you!?" Asked Sam all indignant.

"No nothing like that, it's about big decisions like buying a house. That's all. No, no, my being your advocate should not actually affect you in any way. The whole thing should be overturned by the time you want to make another big decision. As far as I'm concerned, it's almost a formality. If you do want to make a large financial decision or sign a contract while the Order is in place you will have to tell me that's all. And I will have to meet with your legal team to tidy up a few procedures. Is that okay?" Sue nodded, "…. It's just…Well; the less than good news is somewhat private. It might be that you want to discuss it privately." Sue shook her head,

"I'll only have to tell them later." She said. Angela nodded,

"Well, the Court has insisted that…well, if you were to contemplate any…intimacy…with a…a man…I am supposed to…advise you on…if you are contemplating sexual relations with anyone." There she'd said it.

"What!" Chorused the women-about-town.

"It's an established precedent I'm afraid, for protected parties who are considered vulnerable…to avoid exploitation or abuse of your human rights. I have to draw up a thing called a Care Plan."

"What!?" Came the chorus before a tirade of 'who gives you/them the right?', 'Does she look vulnerable?" "Where's the human rights in that?" and 'bloody cheek's.

"I know I know…and it may be that you do need support in light if the intellectual property rights that are at stake. Your De-En-Aye, exchange of fluids, and possible pregnancy, are important decisions, not just for you. Have you spoken to your legal team?"

"Well, Mr Harris said that there were some important things to discuss, he did ask if I was in a relationship at the moment come to think, and about you, but I had hats on my mind. Ms Bailey-Erskine's going to explain all that after the assessment."

"Good. And well, have you got any plans in that area? I'm sorry to ask but…"

"No I bloody haven't! It's none of your business I mean!"

"I know, I'm sorry, very sorry and it won't be for long. It will be overturned, probably, perhaps as early as Monday."

"So you just have to keep your knickers on till Monday Mum," said Jo and Sam and Julie laughed." Sue looked disapprovingly at her daughter.

"But the principle. I really don't like that. I really don't" She said, "…I'm Fifty-Eight years old. I can make my own decisions, even if I decide not to do anything or the wrong thing…I'm the subject, you said." Angela nodded apologetically. "…what's the other thing. You said two things?" She was suspicious now.

"And your principles are usually very sound Sue. You are a very principled person so this must really hurt?" Said Angela,

"Yes, yes it does. I mean I've done my best haven't I? Gave blood for years. Got the donor certificates. And…all I did was volunteer for some tests. To help people. And now I'm not allowed to sell the house or go to bed, or sell myself…. patent, that's what this all about, they don't want me to do anything with my patent but I'm not going to sell my patent am I…yet any way. I just want a normal life…"

And the most important people in her life all nodded. Julie squeezed her hand,

"And you can help people Sue. This will all be over by Monday, probably. You are still the same person. Your views are still the same on that aren't they? Your views on the public good, The 'good ole' En-Aich-of-Ess and your girls. You still can help lots of people can't you."

"Well, yes. I'm still the same person. But if I'm going to be treated like this I..." Out of the corner of her eye she could see Sam looking out of the corner of her eye at Jo. Jo looked at Sam and then Angela out of the corner of her eye. Then she leaned sideways into her bag while Sam looked out of the corner of her eye at Angela and felt for a sandwich. She leaned forward to Angela, all intent with big eyes while she bit and chewed and Sam got out her phone and pressed some buttons. "...Of course I haven't changed. I'm still the same person and I want to help.... And you will help...speak on my behalf won't you." Angela smiled her warm smile, "...Monday and it will all be over? Sorry, what was the other thing?"

"That? That is entirely separate, well, it's to do with your medical situation and highly confidential. Not just patient confidentiality but legally. Subject to the injunction you know. I should really discuss this with you alone Sue? And somewhere more..."

"What could be more confidential than 'that'?" Said Sue and she got up disgruntled, and moved to the next table, which was very close. Angela sat in the chair as far from the others as possible, not entirely happy. Aaron strained to look over from his lonely table and ensured whatever he was there to ensure before going back to his phone.

"…Well, it looks like the medics have found…but I have to be sure that the sex thing is understood?"

"Oh it's understood alright," said Sue to murmurings of agreement from under the hats behind her. She shot the other hats a look to say 'don't look like you can hear' The other hats turned round and up and looked nonchalant. "…and I'm going to talk to my lawyer about all this." She warned, "…What have the medics found?" They were all as sober as nosey judges now. Only Sue's keen eyes were actually on Angela though.

"Yes of course, it's a good idea. I can only do so much as an advocate. You will keep me informed, won't you? It is almost a formality. I did explain to the judge that you were highly unlikely…." Sue's face told her that her discussing Sue's sex-life with a man in a wig and gown was not at all form in her book. "…If you could just keep me in the loop. To keep the process as smooth as possible." Sue nodded with less enthusiasm than made Angela comfortable.

She looked around, they were the only people on the terrace apart from Aaron and a bored waiter, then she carried on speaking in almost a whisper. You would have to be really concentrating to hear from another table. Sam moved her phone next to Julie's plate, "…And you don't feel any differently about helping people benefit from what has happened to you?"

"Helping medically, yes. I know I'm just a lab rat to a lot of people but I know I'm not and I want people, people like Heather not to suffer."

"So your desires coincide with the 'Good-Ole-En-Aich-of-Ess'?" And Sue nodded sceptically, "…Good. The other thing is… the medics at Cambridge have done some extensive analysis of your blood samples during your illness. They think that they may have found a possible cause for your reaction during the trials. It was completely unexpected. But it is a new area of medicine." The hats were agog. "…As you know it was thought that your catching actual chicken pox had somehow enabled the modified chicken pox Helper Virus deliver the Ee-Four Cluster into your genes on a permanent basis? Sue nodded. "…Yes. Well, it seems that it may have been enabled to do that by sugars in your blood. It's a complex chemical process that they have only been able to reproduce once. They're fruit sugars. High levels of fruit sugars in your blood. All of them; glucose, fructose and sucrose. There's another substance that they haven't yet identified. The Cambridge team should be calling you soon. About your food intake the days before the trials. If they haven't already?" Julie and Sam looked at Jo. Jo shook her head. Sue was thinking back to the day before the trials,

"I didn't have any fruit, did I? I only like apples and…I. It was Julie's birthday, Julie…That's why I was still a bit drunk, Julie, did we have any fruit at your do?" She called,

"You might not have got it from fruit, other foods contain glucose, fructose and sucrose. They're added to all sorts of things…" Interjected Angela, Julie shook her head from the other table,

"Not really? I did those filo things, there wasn't much sweet stuff. We were all getting beach ready. Just that cake from Marco's you brought. Could that? No, it was red velvet cake that hasn't got fruit in it, has it? What else?"

"Fruit sugars, including cane sugar, are added to a great many…"

"Oh no. Julie does it all from scratch, she's a very good cook…What did I have for lunch that day? …it was a Sunday? I only picked at a slice to be…But I was going to eat later? …" Said Sue trying to remember, Julie was still thinking about her buffet, she was rightly proud of her buffets,

"…Some home-made coleslaw…oh but you don't eat that, it gives you…those vol-au-vents my mum likes, liked…. mini fish cakes, salads, home-made sausage rolls to go with the…." Another chorus,

"Cider!" All five women sat back in their chairs in a fancy that sort of way.

"And that apple brandy you make. That was lethal…well not…that's what was to blame for the alcohol levels I did tell the nurse…I don't think she wrote that down? She was a bit sniffy."

"That's your apples Sue," said Julie,

"I've got trees, apple trees." Explained Sue to Angela still sitting back. Angela had seen them from the kitchen window, "…Julie makes cider, and has a go at apple brandy sometimes. They don't keep that well and…well they aren't very nice in a pie, or jam or anything. Too dry.

Crumbly. They're good eaters, very good. But there's only so many you can eat. We get bushels…they're only any good for cider by the end of September."

"Homemade apple cider," said Angela thoughtfully, "…Would you have any of that left, from the same batch?" Sue called over to Julie to maintain the pretence,

"Have you got any left? Or the brandy? …from the same batch?" Julie shook her head unsurely,

"No," said Sue to Angela, "…. You see it's almost past time to make this season's…"

"Hang on?" Said Julie, "…there might be some of the brandy left, in the basement, but that's from the year before or four years ago…I'll have to check. Do you want it Angela?"

"Yes please," said Angela "…I can pass it on to the Cambridge team…and the recipe."

"Recipe? I haven't used a recipe in years? I mean it's different every batch," said Julie worried.

"Well, a list of ingredients will be fine I'm sure," said Angela.

"I can do that; apples, yeast, sugar and some citric acid, its special yeast though for cider-making."

"That's great, if you can just write down the type or brand it would be very helpful. And if you have any left over? Approximate quantities would help too. Presumably the brandy is more concentrated." Said Angela moving back to the original table. Sue, Sam and Jo nodded a lot and Sam said,

"It's more concentrated alright."

"Or did I use malic acid that year? Never mind, I'll write everything down. They can work it out…. more tea?"

"Yes please," said Angela, "…of course it might be something else, or a combination of things. And the researchers may find that it has nothing to do with the process at all," But the behatted ones had decided it was the cider that had made Sue young again so that was that.

"An apple a day," said Sam because someone had to, and they all laughed a little because they all had to. There was a silence and everyone took a sip of tea.

"It's nice to have an explanation at last," said Sue and her friend and family nodded. But Angela was a medical ethics expert, she couldn't give up,

"A possible explanation." She was also a very nice woman so she said it quietly.

"You're not going to get into trouble are you Angela telling us, me all this are you?" Asked Sue. "…I mean is it medically ethically alright, is it procedure? Not just all the Court Orders stuff?"

"Oh, yes. The procedures are guidelines, but patient care always comes first," said Angela, thinking of her mother's swollen ankles all of a sudden "…not that I work for the Em-Ar-Aich-Cee anymore. And my prime concern as your advocate is to keep you as informed as possible to enable you to…" But the women's faces had all fallen in an expression of sympathy on the assumption that she must have been sacked, so Angela added quickly "…I've got a new job…. At the European Institute for Ethics in Industry." Sue especially was surprised,

"Did you move on you know because of…"

"No, well yes, it was partly because of what happened to you…but…The European Institute for Ethics in Industry is the central body that oversees all research procedures and guidelines, in Europe. Under Ee-You legislation its ordinances have legal force across Europe and given your experience and my experience of your experience I am well placed to contribute to any revisions or new guidelines going forward," said Angela trying to hide her delight at having got the phone call this morning.

"Will you get more money? Is it like a step up?" Asked Sam,

"It is a step up. Yes," said Angela and she beamed. "…But your experience means that we will be having to review nearly all the Institute's ordinances. And quickly. My new position means that I am well placed to advocate your best interests Sue."

"What is it? The European Institute for Ethics in Industry?" Asked Jo googling on her phone, and Angela nodded,

"The Ee-Eye-Ee-Eye. So, it gives Orders that all manufacturers, including the Pharmaceuticals. have to follow? Zabtrex included, if it wants to sell in the Ee-you? And Fielding and Hardy?" Asked Sam and Angela nodded again,

"Not just the manufacturers. All public and private bodies have to comply with the Institute's Orders. Yes. It's the head of the octopus Sue. Independent of the influence of any particular government," said Angela smiling confidently, and Sue looked at her quizzically and said,

"But, what about Brexit?" and she lifted her head, "…Won't we, Britain be out of the Eee-You tomorrow or…soon? I've got some catching up to do. The Ee-Eye-Ee-Eye Orders, Ee-Eye-Ee-Eye-Oh? They won't apply to us then, will they?" Angela laughed, Sue thought a bit too sniffily.

"Oh, Brexit, if it happens at all won't make a difference in this sector really, it's just a bit of a hiccough, the posturing by the politicians has a role, but when it comes to Industry…Well, They, we, Britain and the rest of Europe have interests in common and will sign up to any trade agreements that serve their, ours and the Ee-You's interests. A country the size of Britain can't expect to maintain its position as an industry leader without cooperation. You've, your experience has actually been quite useful Sue, we, the You-Kay have been able to leverage quite a good position in the trade-negotiations with the You-Ess as well as the Ee-You."

"Oh, so she's a bargaining chip as well now, is she, said Sam,

"Whose she, the cat's mother?" Said Sue,

"Rest assured ladies, Sue's interests are paramount. And the Ee-Eye-Ee-Eye makes its Orders entirely independent of any particular Government…" but Sam interrupted her,

"Independent of our Government though, and Romanian Government. I bet Germany gets influence, or France. I bet big pharma companies…"

"No offence Angela," interjected Julie, "…but the reason we voted Brexit in the first place was so that

European institutions we've never heard of would stop making decisions independently of the Government, we voted for the Government to make decisions, we don't vote for the Ee-Eye-Ee-Eye."

"You? You voted to leave? You Sue?" Asked Angela, incredulous and in a tone they had not heard before, a slight tone of contempt? Sue nodded. Julie nodded. Sam and Jo shook their heads,

"Well, I'm beginning to think I should have done," Sam said, "...Why have we never heard of this institute before?" She asked, all suspicious again and Angela shrugged,

"I thought you'd have more, more...? Well it's a specific organisation within European government with a very narrow brief in the grand scheme of things. It's just its relevance has come into the spotlight because of Sue. I will be in an excellent position to advocate your rights as a patient, not simply as an asset." she said,

"Well congratulations Angela," said Sue, "...I'm pleased for you, we're all pleased for you aren't we ladies, and I'm sure you will stand up for me and you'll make industries much more ethical all over Europe, just like you have at home." And she raised her teacup and looked at her daughters and Julie to oblige them to do the same.

"Yes, congratulations Angela... I'm sorry, I didn't mean it. I'm sure... I'm sure you will look out for Sue, and us, over there in, will you have to move Brussels?" Asked Julie,

"They are based in Brussels but I'll have to spend a lot of time here, there and everywhere. At least in the beginning," said Angela, ".... once this issue, your situation is on an even keel." Sue had been staring very hard at Sam and Jo. Sam said,

"Yes. Yes? Er, I'm not really against er... I was just playing devil's advocate; you know with all the issues involved I ...." Jo helped out her sister and said,

"We all agree with you, Angela," and everyone nodded enthusiastically, "... about this issue and we're very happy you will be making Ee-Eye-Ee-Eye-Ohs and be in the head of the octopus and..." And Sue, who was their mum, and the issue that had made Angela's career said,

"Well what a lot of news in one day; Prince Charles wants to compost me and I've still got tentacles from the First, Second and Third Sectors want a piece of me. Angela's got a new job, which of course is good news, Sam, and Jo, are hat people, I'm not allowed to have sex without permission and Julie's cider, or maybe apple brandy is the secret to the secret of possibly eternal youth ...and yesterday wasn't much different, or the day before. Pass me over one of those scones I need energy." Julie passed her and everyone else a scone. Angela took a bite then looked at her watch,

"I had better go. There's a great deal of work to be done. I can talk to your lawyers?" Sue looked regretful for a millisecond,

"Course you can Angela, anytime, you've got their number?"

"Yes, at Court this morning. Well, I'll leave you ladies to it." said Angela briskly with a smile, "...if there's anything, anything at all Sue, if you just want to mull things over, anything…" Sue got up and kissed her, "… and there are other matters, private legal and contractual matters that I would like to discuss with you more privately… as soon as we both have time, no need to bother the lawyers," added Angela quietly.

"Thank you, Angela." Sue said and let her go. Once Angela had left the terrace, they turned round, looked at each other and finished their scones in silence. Julie took another scone, for her face.

Julie and Sue had seen people, lots of people, get promoted before. They had even been promoted themselves once or twice. Sue had to find a way to explain to the girls that they could not rely on Angela any more, if they ever could. She was still thinking of how to say it when Sam said,

"Oh!" And pressed some buttons on the phone that was on the table, '…It is just a formality. I did explain to…" it said in Angela's voice. Perhaps she did not need to explain. Jo was shaking her head,

"Even her," she said, and Sue slumped a little and sighed,

"She was so nice, good, good to us," said Sam, "…And now she's, she's shafted us, you, hasn't she Mum." And she looked at her mum, whose hand was in Julie's.

"Our one ally, gone," said Julie flatly, and then with more emotion, "…and her a Doctor of Ethics!"

"And a practicing Anglican," added Sue sadly.

"All for a bloody job in Europe," said Sam, who was getting angrier,

"Our one ally? Do you think she knew about it yesterday? Or even before that?" Asked Julie and Sue shrugged,

"Well, at least we know where we stand now," said Sue with a bit more resoluteness and a shorter sigh, "…and we're not alone are we, we've got each other."

"Yes, but, but we haven't got any friends in high places now have we, what have we got now?" Said Sam,

"What are we going to do?" Asked Jo, sounding younger again.

"Why did she do it? Why did she, she…?" Asked Sam,

"Side with the rich and powerful of Twenty-Seven, twenty-eight Countries and not a middle-aged light electricals designer?" Said Sue and they all sort of laughed, "…Oh she'll have told herself something about the good of the many over the good of just one person or some such, that seems to be the usual sell out line nowadays. Or maybe she really thinks my needs are the same as her bosses? That would be worse, I think."

"Yeah. And the fact that she's set up for life is just a coincidence," said Jo, "…They're all the same, it doesn't matter where they started out, once they get to that sort of position, they all go rotten, well, all the ones we know anyway."

"Rotten? That's a good word Jo," said Julie, "…I s'pose the religion and the ethics and that kept her a bit good for a bit longer than most, that's all?"

"Yes, and the love of a good mother. What would her mum make of it, I wonder? She wouldn't be best

289

pleased," said Sue. She and Julie let their hands grip a bit tighter while they missed their own mums for a moment, then they let go. All their mums; Julie's, Sue's and Angela's, were dead and might not have been sufficiently clued up any way.

"Yes, but what are we going to do?" Asked Sam, more emphatically this time.

"Yes, well, we're in a bit of a pickle it's true," said Sue,

"A bit of a pickle?" Jo almost shouted, "...A bit of a pickle? You've had your Mental Capacity taken away by your own side, your 'advocate', that is the woman who decides on your Mental Capacity has sold out for a job, there's European and Chinese and American multi-nationals all literally after your blood and...Oh you can walk about and buy a hat, have a nice tea, see how she left before it was time to pay the bill! But you have no freedom for anything important at all, no freedom at all...and pickle?"

"Well, who has? And they're not my side are they, that much is clear. You are my side, ladies, and, well I don't know what. But I have actually got my Mental Capacity, and a lawyer called Erskine and, and...you are my side and with you..." but Sue was interrupted by Jo,

"What? Two designers, an Art student, a retail exec' and a human rights lawyer opposing a decision made under the Human Rights Act, against; the Department of Health, the Department for Business, Innovation and Skills, the Judiciary and the Ee-Eye-Ee-Eye fucking Oh!" Sue took a sip of tea, but it didn't help. Sam took a sip of tea, Jo fumed and Julie rallied,

"Well, a lot of things have happened very quickly…we've got some mulling over to do," she said, "…and some plans to make. I fancy a curry." Some people put on a Stone after a loved one dies.

Mass Alzheimer's

The mulling took another pot of tea, a strawberry tart to keep Julie going, a cab ride to Julie's, a bottle of wine, phoning for more Lamb Passander and various accompaniments than it was possible to eat, some more wine, some fancy gin that tasted like normal gin and not quite the last of the apple brandy. It was a bit smoother after another year down in Julie's basement, but only a bit.

Andy was on Lates so they could talk freely into the night to work out the finer details of their plan. They would only need one other person, someone with the specific skills; knowhow. Luckily, Sue loved babies. They were still up when Andy came home. Well, Sue and Julie were, Sam and Jo were asleep on Julie's big soft sofa. Andy came in unsurprised and smiled.

"New hats?" He said and they smiled. He heard that they were back on the topic of student loans again so, "…Night," he said, and went to bed.

"Night love, Well, how Paul and Aleska can afford a baby I don't know. I mean you can't ask can you and we help them out where we can…but thirty thousand pounds just for Paul's student loan and a mortgage on top…and all the way out in Hornchurch. We didn't have all that did we." Was what Julie often said and said again.

"No we didn't Julie. But we didn't have a dishwasher or central heating either." Was what Sue said, also again, "Two pairs of shoes was all I…but? Well I'm just thinking Julie, was it our fault?"

"What was our fault?" They'd been up all night and Julie didn't feel like guessing what her friend was on about,

"I don't know…all this, the loans, the house prices, the staying in the game with individual bargaining…I mean we voted for it didn't we, for you know. All this."

"For what? We didn't vote for house prices!"

"No, but we didn't vote to build any either did we. We just accepted it. I mean we loved it didn't we…all that equity," said Sue,

"All that mortgage you mean…or the loans. I didn't vote for loans. Neither did you. We just accepted it that's all. No choice."

"Didn't we? No, I suppose we didn't…but we did vote for the getting rid of the state thing didn't we."

"Did we?"

"Yes. I remember…I've been thinking, you know I was on my own a lot and…and thinking about when I was Eighteen the first time and…oh I don't know…But I did then. I mean we were so sure weren't we…that we should get rid of the unions and it was all about 'the individual' and…and that. Was that such a good idea really?

"What?! What Sue? Have you forgotten? Power cuts and three months wait for a telephone and six months wait for an operation and two pairs of shoes, one for work, one for out."

"…and mince, all that mince. No, I haven't forgotten Julie. Well no more than anyone else. Haven't we all forgotten it a bit but…"

293

Kate Abley

"Well, I was thinking that, you know sitting with Mum all that time not talking. But who can blame us. It was so depressing, inflation…and the Eye-Em-Eff? didn't the Eye-Em-Eff have to bail us out back then? I was thinking that with all this Greece business. They called us the sick country of Europe. We were like Greece without the weather." Sue tried to remember something about the IMF, she put herself back on the settee with her dad, but nothing came. "…Anyway. My mum couldn't afford that hat could she, couldn't afford anything. When I look in a magazine, I can get the same whole outfit from Primark if I want. The only difference is the label isn't it, it's been tough competing in fashion retail let me tell you, it's all so cheap.

And my mum could only sit in her kitchen in her one nice Cee-And-Aye cardigan and dream about that hat…And the grave diggers, do you remember the grave diggers going on strike? Bodies piling up Sue. And the miners…oh we all feel sorry for them now with The Full Monty and everything but…or was that the Steel workers? Anyway, maybe they could have done that better I s'pose. I mean the Miners, Andy can tell you…but they were, the police were only doing what the Government wanted and well, the police always get blamed for doing what the Government wants don't they," said the policeman's wife. The painter's ex, whose photo was on a website made in Italy, was not going to go there, not tonight, but,

"Yes, yes, I remember and well, I didn't say anything about the miners back when they were striking, maybe we let that happen? Accepted it. Maybe we believed the ransom thing, you know maybe we thought they were

294

holding us all to ransom. That's what they said wasn't it, the Government. And the only people who said any different were so...so socialist and scruffy and stuck in the past and full of rubbish...But that's not what I'm trying to say, well maybe it is? But what I am trying to say is...What's the thing we all care about enough to bother to vote for nowadays? The En-Aich-Ess, the Good-Ole-En-Aich-of-Ess. And what's that? A huge big state monopoly like we voted against. Oh, there's partnerships and private contracts and, well, I told you didn't I, everybody treading on everybody's toes all the time. Isn't that 'state inefficiencies'? All these different initials with their fingers in the same pies... the money, as big as a small country I heard, all that comes from the Government in the end."

"That's different," said Julie emphatically. Sue tipped her head back from under her cloche to indicate 'oh yes?' "...it's different because...well it's not British Leyland is it. I don't know how it's different but...we've learned now haven't we? I mean fat cats and bankers and that...That's what my mum said once? She was out of it most of the time, but about two years ago and she hadn't said anything for months. Months. It was like I was on my own in the room in a way. Then she suddenly said, the news was on, just for background you know...and I can't remember what was on? Something about bankers or the one percent or something...and she suddenly said 'trickle down. Trickle up more like.' And then she was gone again?" And they went quiet for a bit,

"That's really weird?" Said Sue eventually,

"Yes. But I knew what she meant…and that happens sometimes, you know, moments of lucidity they call it."

"You never said?"

"No? Well I was on auto-pilot wasn't I. And you had that conference." Sue nodded in acceptance, "…and she was right wasn't she, about trickle down I mean. She was sharp my mum.…it didn't happen though did it…I think that's what we voted for wasn't it? Trickle down. There'd be entrepreneurs and they'd make loadsamoney and something about boats all floating upwards or something and it'd trickle down and we'd all save up for education, did we ever think about that? I don't think so? Or pensions. But there never was enough to save up?

Oh we were alright for a bit but then there was always something wasn't there. And the equity! What did we do with the equity? The kids and a few holidays. Don't we deserve holidays? We just took out some equity for a holiday when we were so knackered from the Nine to Five. Hah.

Do you remember Nine to Five Sue? We did used to work Nine to Five didn't we back then? And sit down and have a coffee in 'breaks', remember breaks? Nine to Five, then Quarter To to Quarter-Past, then Half Past, then Six and just popping in at the weekend or up half the night for a bloody presentation. We just accepted it. It all just trickled, evaporated up and collected in someone else's pocket. But us? We just worked harder and harder and never seemed to get anywhere.

There was always something…A school trip, a new mattress or a sofa, the fashion changing too much to get away with that old suit just to what you say, stay in the game…and we needed a car for work when Andy got transferred. … and the mortgage always the mortgage…and now there's helping out with Paul and Aleska; Em-Oh-Tee, Insurance, nursery. The price of that nursery! …we talked about me taking early retirement and looking after the baby but my mum you know. But we talked about health insurance didn't we then? Back then. I had Bupa for a while."

"Did you?"

"Yeah, back in the early Eighties…For a year or so. But I never got anything and then Paul was born and I couldn't afford it. And why pay twice? Good-Ole-En-Aich-of-Ess. I don't care if it is…actually I do care…I want a state-run health service. Do you want private health Sue? I mean you saw in Switzerland. What was it like?"

"I don't think the private health sector handcuffs people to their beds as a general rule Julie. That was a one-off."

"But you were in that hospital and no-one knew. Say what you like about the En-Aich-Ess, but they'd know if you were in…"

"I am for the En-Aich-Ess Sue, I only went to Zurich because of all the initials and the greed but…How come I don't know so much about you? After all these years? Why didn't we talk about these sorts of things?" Asked Sue,

"Well we led different lives for a bit didn't we. We didn't see much of each other when you went off to college…and Steve…then Andy. And work. Then it was the kids wasn't it."

"And then Heather got ill. God, you've really been through it haven't you Julie." And Sue leaned over and hugged her friend again.

"Haven't we all Sue," said Julie gently from inside their embrace. "…and we can talk more now can't we." And she pulled herself away and straightened her hat and added, "…and, well I've been thinking too. You know I had plenty of time sitting with my mum and worrying about you and everything and…well, you know what you said before about forgetting, we've all got a bit of Alzheimer's haven't we?" And she smiled,

"Have we?" Sue smiled back,

"Yes, you know, we forget things, lots of things. What our mums went through, stinky buckets of terry nappies all over the place…and our dads. And like you said, what we voted for and that. We did used to think about those things, not just at election time but you know. Well more than now. And we were passionate? Is passionate the right word? But we really cared and we argued and things. But now? Now no-one talks about those things do they and, well my mum was always banging on about before the War and after the War and she was only a kid. But we don't do we? Any of us. Before Thatcher and after Thatcher, sort of. It's like we've forgotten too? You know, when she got dementia Thatcher, we all forgot too? Maybe it's catching?" And she tipped her head and Sue laughed. "...Mind you, now I say it out loud, there's other things too?"

"You didn't talk to Andy?"

"Him? No, well I might've, but he doesn't really listen does he, not all the time" and Julie was feeling bold from all the drink and saying something her cleverer friend hadn't thought of, "...like you." And she grinned cheekily.

"What? I don't listen? To you?" Asked Sue, a bit incredulous.

"No, not all the time. You know, you start listening and then you can see your mind wandering off, like with the immigration thing the other night." Sue thought back and remembered vaguely. She looked at Julie for the detail.

"You know. When you said that stuff about immigration and Andy was so shocked. He didn't like that, did he. He thought you were his 'last ally', with that you know." Sue didn't understand, "...well, you know we didn't just forget stuff did we, we changed as well, well you didn't, well you did but not about immigration. You kept banging on about it while the rest of us were more, more, understanding? Is that the right word?" Julie looked at Sue, who widened her eyes. "...Or welcoming, or something? I don't know. But I do know that me and Linda, the whole gang, we saw the good things about immigration. You know we used to say things to you about people. You like Aleska and so me and Linda, and Mum's nurses, you liked them so me or Sam or Jo, would say something about how good it can be, immigration I mean and you wouldn't listen...and... You used to say being anti-immigration is not the same as being Racist, remember that? And every time, every time you said that then one of us would say 'but it can be', do you remember.... You're doing it again! Zoning out." Julie's voice showed kindness and hurt at the same time.

"No! No, I am listening. I was just thinking at the same time!" said Sue, but Julie didn't believe her. "...No!

Really. You're right, I didn't listen. And me and Andy used to look at each other when you'd start banging on about food or music or…? You bring it up all the time?!"

"Yeah, well it's important, and you know, you're a really nice person and I love you and... well no-one wants a best friend who's a Racist do they?" She smiled and put her hand on Sue's. Sue leaned into a hug she needed and Julie gave it to her. Their eyes got wet.

" God! You are such a good person. I've been a terrible friend and... I'm so lucky to have a friend like you Julie."

"God Sue, don't wallow for God's sake. And you are a good friend. My best friend. You've been with me all the way with mum, nearly," and she sniffed and laughed, "...but God! Brexit Sue! The things you said!" and she laughed again because you've got to. Sue sat up and looked for her glass and took a big swig,

"Am I a Racist Julie?" Sue was, quite rightly, concerned. Julie nodded apologetically,

"A little bit Sue." But Sue was not reassured, she knew you can't be a little bit Racist like you can't be a little bit religious, you either believed or you didn't. "...not nastily Sue, you're really nice to all the black people and Eastern Europeans and everything, you know, normal with them. But, but when you're down the Elizabeth, with Andy especially, or when it was Brexit, voting. You vote Racist even if you're not actually Racist to real people." Sue was not consoled, since Brexit, she had realised that a person's vote could, possibly, count.

"I'm a Racist? I have said 'I'm not Racist but' haven't I. You used to laugh when I said that?"

"I didn't have much choice Sue, you're my oldest friend...and Andy's worse."

"I'm a Racist. Do I think I'm more British than other people? I don't think that, really," she said quietly, "...Am I Racist like I'm Church of England? I mean not really? I don't really believe it do I? I never go to a Church or to any of those rallies you see on posters near the station. I hate those Ee-Dee-Eff and Youkip people, they're nasty and backward and, well I won't waste my breath on them... And I just tick the Cee-of-Ee box on the forms, it doesn't mean anything. And Gay marriages must be really lovely, how can the Church of England be against gay people, They're all gay anyway? " Julie could not see what Sue's Racism had to do with gay marriage but she went with it. "...So are most of the black people I have ever met, not gay, I mean, really lovely. Normal. Those nurses! Saints the lot of them. Yunis saved my life and, well Angela's just posh isn't she," Julie nodded a what do you expect from posh people and Sue nodded another acceptance of her best friend's wisdom. "...That lot just look after themselves don't they, whatever colour they are. But black people in general are just normal, like us, and Eastern Europeans. But it's like religion...is it. I mean I don't really believe in it anymore, well?... But, do you remember when a Mum and Dad not being married was shocking? You weren't allowed to bring that Katie home for tea were you, your mum called her a bastard..."

"Well, she called a lot of people bastards, my mum." smiled Julie weakly, Sue joined in and squeezed Julie's hand remembering the awful things Julie's mum had raved as the disease took hold of her. Sue went to hug her friend and say something about God and Heaven, but Julie wanted a night off all that and squeezed her hand to tell her to go on.

" I'm having another bloody revelation here!" Smiled Sue in gratitude, "... We have changed so much haven't we. And it's good if I don't care if some one's black or if they're a bastard. Maybe I'm just used to being a bit Racist out of habit, not really thinking. Or maybe I was Racist, I did believe in God once too, I think, but now…. I just recite a few old words out of habit, mantras is sort of the right word strangely, 'Our father who art in heaven' or 'they are taking up hospital beds' because it's comforting, no not comforting …lazy, easier…to have someone to blame? Some-one who's easy to spot, not hidden behind a lot of initials…?" And her revelation ran out of steam and they both sat and wondered for a bit but nothing came. Julie picked up her glass and perked up, she remembered something else she'd thought a while back.

"I know who's to blame alright! Fat cats! Them! And Angela and her mates. "My mother was right! Oh you say they're all at each other's throats the whole time and that's true. But when push comes to shove, when they're up against it, they're still just one big club and, one percent and and….look what's happened to you! It's us wo gets our Mental Capacity taken off us. And my mum before she went into the hospital, where was the En-Aich-Ess? No, it was me cooking and shopping and cleaning her up and trying to, to help her. They only got involved when she was almost a vegetable!" And then Julie's revelation ran out of steam and they both sat and hugged and cried for a bit. Then they wondered for a bit more but nothing came, then Julie said, kind of depressed,

"But Corbyn?" and Sue made a face like she'd just swallowed a fly by accident. Julie laughed,

"...You're face," then she said, "...we have changed a lot, accepted a lot of things, some bad, some good. but, maybe that's why, well Andy, why he hangs onto the racism? Maybe it's all the accepting he's had to do with everything else. And the racism is just being bloody minded?" and Sue nodded because she'd heard someone at work, or on the radio, say something like that and now Julie was saying it so there must be something to it. She could see Julie struggling through the drink and the grief and the drink. She put Julie's glass in her hand so that she could think, it is the British way. Julie drank, Sue drank.

"We all accept too much!" said Julie. Was that it? No there was more, "...it's too depressing accepting all these things. Why did they give all that money to to, was it Ar-Bee-Es? Why didn't they just give it to the people with the mortgages or the savings or whatever? They gave it to their mates and we just put up with it and thought 'what do we know it's hard sums'," and she waved her hands about and wiggled her head like some dippy girl, "...and then they called us...when we voted to leave...they called us Racist! And, well you are a Racist, well maybe not now, but Andy is definitely Racist, but, they called all of us Racist! All Fifty-Two percent of us. And we took it! We just took it! We're the ones who actually live with immigrants and we get on fine most of the time, and... we don't mix as much as we should but we're not bloody Racists. All we wanted was a bit of democracy, so some European thingy doesn't decide things without us even knowing and they called us Racist, so we took it. Again."

"That's really true Julie, really true...and they're the ones making Yunis a criminal, keeping out the black people, in the Camps, actual camps, that's quite Racist really? Watching people drown. ...Well, maybe it's like you said, it's too depressing just accepting all these things.... or maybe it's denial? My, Alfie, is big on denial? And you're right, but..." But Sue didn't really have a but so she took another sip of whatever was left and so did Julie. Then Sue perked up, "...Look on the bright side Julie, you said it yourself didn't you...no more tinned mince...and loads more hats, Julie, hats." And Sue flicked her best friends brim. They smiled, then they smiled some more.

"Well you've got to laugh haven't you," giggled Julie. And they began to laugh. Laugh and laugh and laugh. Because they had to. And they'd had a drink so they could. So Sam and Jo woke up to almost hysterical laughing and Sue pointing at Julie's cheeks and spluttering,

"There's your trickle down, Jules." Before the next wave of laughing hit.

But a noise came from upstairs, the noise of a grumpy man who's been on Lates. They stopped laughing and recognised that the end of the night was something else they would just have to accept.

"Seriously though Julie. Shall we pay off your mortgage. You know with the research, money? When it come…if it comes?" Sam and Jo nodded vigorously and Julie laughed and hugged her friend,

"I was wondering when you'd get to that Sue." She said, "…of course we can't take your money but you are a wonderful person for offering." And she smiled openly, while Sue and Sam and Jo began a silent plot to change her mind.

"Well, talk to Andy about it," said Sue not saying anything at all about how he was 'supplementing their income' by betraying his wife's best friend to some sleazy hack and he was a Racist, because she wasn't going to let him spoil things. Jo and Sam echoed her. "…But we need sleep for tomorrow don't we." and there were lots of hugs by the front door and the Duggens went home. Adrian's cough wasn't getting any better.

They were walking arm in arm, with Sue in the middle and the autumn chill settled on their necks so they could huddle a bit more with justification. Sue asked quietly,

"Do you think I was ever Racist girls?" The girls were silent. Whenever anyone else they knew had stopped being Racist no-one said anything, it was just accepted and everyone carried on as if they had never been Racist in the first place. "So that's a yes then is it."

"Well yes Mum, a bit, but what you said down the pub the other night that was brilliant, about immigration I mean." said Sam and Jo squeezed her mother's arm in agreement.

"Well, that's another thing that I'm going change," said Sue emphatically. First Sam, then Jo put their heads on their mother's shoulders and nuzzled as close as they could without falling over.

So Thursday ended up being another busy day. Jo had her follow-up appointment for her knee, practiced the Selfridges logo and then went food shopping with a proper list. Then she cooked. Sam read everything out loud to her mum and did the black felt penning. Sue sifted through the post she had received over the last two and a half months. The only important letter was a voluntary redundancy notice from work. She could vaguely remember a conversation with Aich-Ar when she was still covered in welts and up to her eyes in painkillers. Then she remembered that bloody Emma had had a bit of a thing with Clive from Aich-Ar. It had raised a lot of eyebrows.

If she had been sitting at home all this time, she would probably have been furious. But the only sitting around she'd done was handcuffed to a hospital bed in Zurich. She was relieved at the letter as she re-read it. And very happy about the BACs payment, which explained how she had been able to afford all those hats and the necessary big boxes, with next-day delivery, for the plan. Enough to call it hush money. Enough to last a couple of months. Julie went back into town on the train in her black business suit, that is invisibly. She got a cab home, where Jo was waiting to spray the Selfridges logo onto the boxes. Then, Julie and Jo tottered round to Sue's with the boxes at exactly the same time as Sue's genuine order from Selfridges arrived and a particularly chatty and cheerful Sam gave Aaron his elevenses and some cough sweets for Adrian.

By lunch time they were all back in Sue's kitchen wondering where Aleska was. Aleska's baby, Jacob, Julie's grandson, had a rash on his cheek. He hadn't slept well either and he looked pale. Aleska thought it was just teething trouble but the nursery had refused to let him stay in case the rash was an infection. They had told her to take him to the Doctor because he was very pale as well. The Doctor said it was teething trouble. Jacob was half English and half Polish so of course he was pale. Still, it did give her a good excuse to tell work. And Sue got to play with the baby who had had a good sleep in the Doctor's waiting room.

She said nothing to her girls because she didn't want to pressure them. Being a Mum is a complete joy but also a horrible slog. She wanted to be a Grandma. Julie was a Grandma. Her mum had been a Grandma by this age. Sue might wait another ten years to be a Grandma. Being a Grandma is better than being a mum. A complete joy. And you can help with the horrible slog. Jacob did not find hiding his face in Sue's hat and then throwing it aside repeatedly for 15 minutes at all repetitive. Neither did Sue. It was a complete joy.

Aleska had a lot of knowhow but she had never actually set up anything as simple as a scanner before. Julie had, and Sam had one like it at work. So it only took an hour or so. The job itself took 20 minutes. Aleska ran through what they'd have to do tomorrow for five minutes while the baby played with her necklace and stuck his fingers in her mouth. Sue felt like it should have taken longer, or been harder to do. It was a big thing and big things needed to be hard or take a long time or both. But they don't always so there you go.

There was a grey rain drizzling out of a grey sky when Julie and Aleska left at about three o'clock. Sue went to clear up the kitchen but Jo and Sam were talking excitedly about the plan while they did that. Sue paused at the door to watch them witter and laugh. Like her and Jan when they were younger than that. She left them to it and went and sat in the dining room.

A cold breeze was shivering through her garden but her trees couldn't shake off the rain that she couldn't see fall. It had been raining the day she left but then the leaves were light and lush. Now there were grey shades creeping everywhere outside. It was definitely autumn now. Winter was not far off. Inside was cheerful, light and hopeful. They had a plan for the future.

This would be her second winter without that trouble in her hip and her thumb in how long? She couldn't remember. Old age did just sneak up on you it was true. That hardly noticed nag once in a while morphing slowly into a nasty pain you only noticed when it got sharper every so often. Blending in with all the other troubles, one morning your neck wouldn't turn without sounding like the rigging of a battered ship. Or a noose. Another day your elbow wouldn't stretch out without a gripe. Your left knee one week, your right knee the next. Then both. And it tired you out all that aching. Then you went to the doctors and they said sentences with 'your age' planted in them. Not her though.

Not anymore. Or not again for how long? She could stay like this forever, or start to age again slowly or fast. no-one knew. Finding out that all this had happened because she had got drunk and hadn't had chicken pox made everything even more flimsy. Then there was the big C that could be eating her up as she sat there watching leaves bounce about in invisible rain.

She realised she was looking down at her hand, turning it round in front of her. Wiggling her pink nimble fingers. Like she had for hours and hours when it had first happened. Her face was the thing that other people noticed but her hands were the things she saw whenever she worked, or tapped her Oyster Card or turned on the remote. And there they were; smooth and pink and nimble and hers. The same brain operated them and they worked the way they always had; she could still draw. And she still drew like she had been doing it for 50 years. Sometimes, when she was working on a kettle redesign for the umpteenth time, she could watch her hands drawing almost on their own. She had good little hands and now they were pretty again too. Not like Julie's. The guilt of the disgust she had felt looking at Julie's hand the other day buffeted against her chest again.

Her hands dropped and her eyes were on the sagging garden again. Then a big burst of young laughter bubbled into earshot from the kitchen. She hadn't thought it for a good six months. It was just too scary. And that insensitive comment from Linda back at the Elizabeth in January had not helped. Would she outlive her children? Would she watch them marry and have kids and age and die while she just kept on living? Even with the money they might save on child-care it was too cold a thought. She forced the reassurance she had made for herself into her mind. It was a cold thought too, but better than the alternative. She would not outlive her children.

And she would not be antisocial about it. These people who jumped in front of trains or slashed their wrists in hotel rooms ought to be ashamed of themselves. The poor train drivers and maids could be scarred for life. If it came to it, she would make sure her affairs were in order and that it was a stranger who was used to death who found her body. She could take an overdose and then go and sit in the A&E waiting room with a minor complaint. By the time any one was available to deal with her she'd already be cold. How many more winters would she have? Should she talk to the psychiatrist about that tomorrow if it came up? She would make sure it did not come up.

A splatter of rain dashed at the window and made her jump. She saw it now, dull monochrome droplets dripping down the grimy windows. She should get a cloth out the next time she had a minute and it wasn't raining. Things always looked better through clean windows. Shinier. Even when winter was stripping out the life and the colour like an angry toddler with a cold dirty paintbrush. Then it would cheer up and be spring again before she knew it. Like winter had never been. The seasons came and went so much faster nowadays. Her final winter was coming. She just didn't know when. Sue wondered how many episodes of Game of Thrones she had missed and went into the living room to catch up.

Mental Capacity

A quiet and early night had done Sue the power of good. She was worried she was getting too used to cabs. The expense. But not being stressed and so being psychologically prepared for getting her Mental Capacity back justified it. The Harley Street office was in a big, intimidating white building but inside was spacious and warmly decorated.

Dr Marx looked like Sigmund Freud except he was a bit fatter and his hair was only just not all over the place. He was also in colour and had a cheerful twinkle in his eyes. But he did have a slight German accent and a soft tone that showed he was used to being very nice to crazy very rich people. Sue was a little bit elated; a lawyer called Erskine had fixed her up with a Harley Street psychiatrist who looked like Sigmund Freud and had a slight German accent. And none of it was costing her a penny. She was living some sort of dream. She brought herself down with a reminder that she was there because the N H of S had taken away her Mental Capacity after a botched drugs trial had left her worth so much money nobody bothered putting a number on it. She could get run over by a bus tomorrow or outlive her own children. She had gone over her suicide plan only yesterday.

She was still sort of disappointed not to be asked to lie on a couch. She could see a couch in the large consulting room but Dr Marx offered her a comfy chair and the receptionist brought her a cup of tea and a biscuit to put on the mahogany coffee table.

"So, you are Fifty-Eight." He said sort of awestruck and fascinated at the same time. Sue had seen that look a hundred times before she ran away,

"Yes…I know it can be hard to remember when we get talking Dr Marx, but we must be about the same age," said Sue to the man who was obviously at least ten years older than her. He twinkled to tell her he knew how old he was.

"Well, if they do develop an anti-ageing treatment you could lose me about a third of my business." He chuckled. His chuckle was infectious. "…and be assured, I will not be basing any judgements on your age, apparent age, appearance or assumptions about your 'condition'. Nor is your behaviour or choice of action previously or now going to affect the outcome. I am only interested in your ability to make a rational decision." Sue smiled; Jo had shown her that Mental Capacity Act checklist on the laptop. "…So, if you are comfortable, we should begin," he said and Sue nodded, "…Good. I am Dr Marx, a psychiatrist and am acting as an independent expert witness for the Court and the civil Court?" Sue nodded, "…Although your legal team appointed me, both sides of any legal dispute will usually accept my judgement. Either party can request another assessment but, in my experience, no one ever has. Or both parties can ignore my findings."

"I see," said Sue sort of seeing,

"I have to assess your Mental Capacity under the Mental Capacity Act Two-Thousand-and-Five. Mental Capacity means your ability to make rational decisions. They don't have to be good decisions; they just have to be rational. I am of the opinion that reason always exists, but not always in a reasonable form...." And he twinkled again. "...So. The Ministry of Health asked the Court to make you a Protected Party..." And he paused, "...Your lawyer has explained what a Protected Party is?" Sue nodded but that wasn't enough for Dr Marx,

"A Protected Party is someone who has an impairment of, or a disturbance in the functioning of the mind or brain."

"Very good," said Dr Marx momentarily exposing the fact that he was entirely used to talking to mad people as if they were sane. "...Now, there are specific tests that need to be applied and procedures to follow for the Court to decide whether or not you have such an impairment. The law does not like people to be without the ability to make reasonable and rational decisions. The principle of the rational man, and woman, is central to the functioning of the law, without rationality there can be no guilt. And English common law has centuries of experience in judging people who most people would think are as nutty as a fruit cake to be entirely sane. The Two-Thousand-and-Five Act is based on common law. So, the law is on your side Sue." He saw doubt in her face and paused,

"You'll let me be the judge of that," she said and she smiled broadly,

"Excellent," said Dr Marx in his slight German accent and soft tone so that now Sue twinkled. "…I am not here to discuss with you whether those tests or procedures were carried out correctly when the application was made. That is a matter for your lawyer. But I will ask you questions in order to try and judge if your mind was impaired at that time. Is that clear?"

"Work with you. No moaning," said Sue and Dr Marx chuckled again,

"Well, as your doctor I cannot discourage moaning altogether," he said and Sue chuckled, this was going to be alright. Unlike Alfie, or anyone else she had had to deal with over the last few months, Dr Marx appeared able to listen, talk with eye contact and take notes all at the same time, "… I need to assess four things. All four things, and this is most important, are time-specific in that they concern when important decisions have to be or have been made. Temporal specificity is essential in order to…"

"I haven't made any important decisions," lied Sue, "… except to get out of that hospital…you do know my history, don't you?" She was mightily relieved when Dr Marx nodded, "… And decided who to trust, mainly. I'm a sucker for a nice lady about my age. I am considering downsizing and…well at some point I will have to decide what to do with my patent…of me, my Dee-En-Aye. You do know I had to patent myself?" Dr Marx nodded again,

"Interesting," he said slowly, he had actually said 'interesting' slowly in a soft German accent, and then, "…very interesting." Sue nearly wet herself with joy.

"…So, you are unaware of any decisions or contracts pertaining to your patents?"

"What decisions or contracts?" Asked Sue, joyless, alert, angry. Dr Marx paused before he spoke,

"This assessment is very important and I have to do everything in my power to maximise your…latent or otherwise, decision-making capacity. But it is possible that what I am going to say will make you angry," and he paused again. Sue joined in pausing and then said,

"I have made some very good decisions while very angry indeed…I know Americans say mad when they mean angry but I'm British and…although I have been through some very stressful situations, I have never entirely lost the plot. When there's been a plot that is."

"Very well then." And he sighed, "…I should tell you the four tests first, so that you can respond in an informed way. You need to understand the information pertaining to the decision, retain that information, be able to weigh up that information and communicate your decision. That is the test of Mental Capacity."

"Okay; understand, retain, weigh it up and decide. Okay." That checklist was on the same webpage Jo had shown her this morning.

"Okay. Then, if the Court decides that you lack Mental Capacity it must appoint an advocate to help involve you in any important decisions as much as possible. If they are unable to involve you, and there are specific criteria for that inability; they must first consider if the decision can be delayed until such time as you have regained your Mental Capacity or can be involved. If they cannot delay then they must consider your past and present wishes and feelings, your beliefs and values and consult any other people that you would have considered in any decision," and he paused for Sue to say,

"Right...but I'll need to write that down or...it's a lot to take in..."

"I am here to keep all the procedures uppermost in your mind. I will draw your attention to the relevant aspects as we proceed. That is my job." Sue nodded but still got out a pen and her little notebook.

"It helps me think," she said finding a clean page. Dr Marx waited until she had stopped writing.

"So. Two days ago, on your return to London and after counselling with your then advocate Mr Alfie Bester, a contract was issued to the Department of Health granting a licence to use your original and modified Dee-En-Aye for the purpose of research into several treatments for the effects of aging. It is what they call open ended research but the possible treatments include, Alzheimer's Disease, degenerative heart disease, arthritis and burns." Sue was speechless. Burns?

"And you had no knowledge of this? None whatsoever?" Sue shook her head wide-eyed and still speechless. "...What did you talk about with Mr Bester?" He asked and Sue looked around the room quickly,

"He just asked me how I was feeling? About why I left? Why I came home? How I felt about the En-Aich-of-Ess. He asked a lot about that...if my feelings had changed about the En-Aich-of-Ess. benefiting... you said feelings, right? … the money…for the public good? … sneaky bastard." Sue was mildly impressed at Alfie,

"Sorry, En-Aich-of-Ess?" checked the well-paid doctor,

"Oh that. Yes. Well I just call it the Good-Ole En-Aich-of-Ess. You know, it's like another country isn't it. Very hospitable but a bit strange really; its own language that only looks like it's English with all that jargon, what's health care and what's social care? Its own time zone, different hours; never night, never day, some hours very slow some very fast… and its own laws, if you're five minutes late you have to rebook and wait another month for an appointment if you're lucky but if they're late you just have to wait and wait, if you're overweight it doesn't matter what you've got it's your fault, and as for the economy, well anyway….I s'pose I did wonder why they sent him, you know kept him on, after I found out that they probably knew about that thing…You know he and I had a bit of a…thing you know. Just for one night." Dr Marx did not know and scribbled without interrupting, "… But I've had a lot on, my friend's mum died…and we had to buy hats. It sounds silly but it was important to her, you know. Rational. And me…But when I saw him at the station, I just assumed they didn't know. But now I think they must've known and he had to or they made him do it. He's a nice boy really…that's why he was sweating! And I thought it was because of that night…"

"And he mentioned a licence, a contract?"

"Nope, not a word…sneaky bastard."

"Who is they?" asked the psychiatrist blandly, not for the first time in his career,

"Oh, I don't know. You know. That lot up there." Sue saw Dr Marx's eyebrows arch,

"Could you a be a little more specific?" He asked,

"The Security Services, Bigwigs. The ministry. Whoever is the Minister at the moment...Oh! It's not a conspiracy or anything it's just a lot of greedy people without much of a...footing on anything, trying to get in on a good thing that's all. And there's a lot of them and just the one me.... They... the Department of Health probably just wanted to get their foot in the door before the Dee-Bee-Eye-Es did some deal with Fielding and Hardy. Then there's all the Zabtrex business that'll've made them all a bit jumpy. I don't know. Why aren't I angry? Shouldn't I be angry? Is that denial?" Dr Marx sat in his chair, "...They...the Department of Health have taken away my Mental Capacity so they could cash in on my genes...the research. Why aren't I angry? Am I in denial? I'm quite good at denial. Been doing it for years."

Sue sat in her chair and took a sip of tepid tea. She wondered if the plan had anything to do with not feeling angry. Probably. She wasn't going to tell Dr Marx that. She needed him to get her Mental Capacity back. "...You know that thing you said about rational decisions...it doesn't have to be a good decision just a rational one?"

"Yes?"

"Oh nothing. Just weighing up the information." And she looked at Dr Marx, she could probably trust him with the plan. "...But why complicate matters any further....I am very angry," said Sue, "...very angry indeed." And she nodded to him to write that down, "...with Mr Alfie Bester...and Dr Angela Carter, my current advocate. She asked me the same sorts of questions now I think about it, about changing my views, the day before yesterday."

"Did Alfie or Dr Carter say anything about a contract or licence, or payment for use of your genes?"

"No, nothing like that. Did they? No. Stuff about security for my daughters? Have they started researching already?"

"I don't know."

"Payment? Do you know how much?" Dr Marx shook his head,

"I'll have to check my balance? Have they paid me yet?" Dr Marx didn't know that either, "...That's why I could get all those hats. I thought it was the redundancy money."

"Now we know that this decision was taken without involving you explicitly, and in circumstances very far from your choosing. And you are angry. But I would like you to think carefully, how do you feel about the decision that has been taken in your name? Do you think it was the right decision?" He asked,

"What does that matter, it wasn't my decision...I don't know. Would I have signed, if I'd had the chance? I don't know. I don't want anyone to suffer like Heather, or Julie? There's got to be some sort of research ...And maybe... if people want to feel young again, is that up to me? That's what 'burns' means doesn't it? Skin treatments?

But…And if there's money to be made shouldn't it go to you know, people…. You know if it's a choice between public and private benefit…You know, no-one likes the big pharmaceuticals, not just Fielding and Hardy or Zabtrex. You should see my sister's house…remote-controlled curtains….Public is better surely…but they're so muddled up now, it's hard to tell which is which…I mean there's Government departments and Government Research Departments but they haven't got any money so they work with Independent Research Departments who get their money from the Government and Fielding and Hardy or a charity sometimes and sometimes the research departments are in Universities but they work for the Government or they can work for Fielding and Hardy or a charity…then there's Fielding and Hardy's Research Department but they got a contract from the care data people who are Independent. But Independent is mainly really Government but not so much. Or sometimes charities, and the charities lobby the Government departments for the independent departments and-or Fielding and Hardy and they all have very nice clothes. I mean very nice. And nice teas in the House of Lords and well, I never got invited. Just heard about it from Angela…that's why I left in the first place…. it's a mess and nobody can ever make a decision and…"

"But they have made a decision…"

"Well now they have. The wrong decision …There must be a big pressure from somewhere for that to happen? They're like headless chickens most of the time, then they go and overreact…It's either Dee-Be-Eye-Es or Fielding and Hardy… or Zabtrex… or all of them or someone just pushed the panic button because they were confused, and who can blame them," and Sue paused to let Dr Marx catch up with his note taking.

"...But...The important thing is the results of the decision, if they've thought that far ahead, and that is not necessarily high on their priority list; thinking ahead. Actual drugs for actual people. It's all about their own career paths. ...But I'm people too aren't I? And the Department of Health has no right to...I mean tricking me like that? ...Taking away my chance to think about it all. I mean I know it was only luck that put me in all this but I should still have a chance to think about it at least...and what about the people who've got Alzheimer's or heart disease or people who love them, shouldn't they have a chance to think about it, I mean these big charities say they are speaking for those people but they're too busy having nice teas with Lords most of the time. And have you seen the dresses those charity Heads wear I mean. I saw this one woman.... How many test tubes could you buy with a Versace handbag?"

"And what about you? Would you like a Versace handbag? Or your daughters?"

"Well, not Versace... Well why shouldn't I have nice things?" And Sue straightened her Paris skirt with her hand. "...Or help the girls buy places of their own, they need to not live with their Mum...is that much to ask? They're grown women...and what about pain and suffering? I should get something for that...."

"So, the money is a determining factor for you?"

"Of course the money's a determining factor, is that bad, Dr Marx?"

"Good or bad does not come into it Sue, it is simply that in my experience, money is always a determining factor."

"But with this, I mean the possibilities… I mean. The numbers are so big no one ever mentions them. It could be a win-win situation. We could have nice places to live and nice things, me and the girls, and they would, could do their own art as well as work, they'd have the time…so could I?… and people could get all sorts of treatments and live long and happy lives. And look young, why not?

And all the researchers could win awards for researching and the charities could win awards for having cups of tea with the right Lord and the Department of Health and the Department for Business could get more money and there's the taxes too and they'd look good… get re-elected. They didn't need to be so heavy-handed. I'm a reasonable person."

"You could make the right decision for something so complex? The people at the Department of Health they have expertise?" And he paused for a response,

"Expertise! Hah! They don't know what happened to me. None of them do. Oh they can describe things with long words all right but that's not the same as knowing is it. They don't understand it. The latest theory is that I drank myself young again you know…on Apple Brandy." Dr Marx's full eyebrows arched and he cocked his head, "…I'm not allowed to talk about the Brandy, there's an injunction."

"It's a big decision, however, to have control…power over something so important. You feel able to make such decisions?"

"Well not on my own but I could contribute…oh I know I just draw kettles but I'm not a moron and if they don't tell me what's going on because I'm a Protected Party how can I even know if I can make a decision? And you said it didn't have to be a good decision just rational didn't you."

"Well good decisions are better than bad decisions. You said 'not on your own'?"

"Yes?"

"Your advocates, Mr Bester … Alfie and Dr Carter, you have known them for how long?

"Well Alfie…about Eighteen-Months and Angela…" and she pressed down on some imaginary keys to count with her fingers, "…about Ten or Twelve months"

"And prior to their being your advocates…"

"Well they were sort of my advocates before really so…"

"Yes. So, before they were your official advocates you talked about these issues, on patents and so on?"

"Yes, it was Angela who…well?" And she sighed, "…Dr Carter was the person who informed me about patenting my genes in the first place." And while Dr Marx wrote that down, she quickly added, "…But she's in the same position as Alfie really, now I mean…she probably got a lot of flak for helping me and needs to show she's you know 'on side'. She's an ethicist for the Government, well Europe now and well she's got a mortgage to pay and you know…" Dr Marx did not appear to know. "…she's worked hard to get where she is and doesn't want to be side-lined at just the time when she could…do more ethics or whatever and, well there's the money as well, even for her…I don't like saying that but you know…"

"Are you concerned that they do not act in your interests?"

"Yes, not any more, now, well I'm a bit angry, but you have to move on… now I just know they don't act in my best interests and I've got a p…a lawyer of my own… and you maybe?"

"I am simply involved to assess your Mental Capacity, nothing more Sue. You do not believe that your advocates are working in your interests?"

"No, not unless my interests are coincidentally the same as the En-Aich-Es and the Dee-Be-Es…or the Brexit negotiations, or the European Union, if they can work that out. Any way what if they are the same, why can't I decide?"

"Do you think that Alfie and Angela understood your wishes and feelings…and your beliefs and values. These are things that must be considered by your advocates when making a decision on your behalf."

"Well roughly yes, I suppose. Well we agreed really you know on helping people."

"So it would be reasonable to assume that they made a decision that you agree with."

"I don't know," said Sue frustrated, "Roughly, I suppose I was thinking that it would be better for the En-Aich-of-Ess to do… or keep control of the research. But what is the research exactly, open ended? And where does the money go? ...the devil is in the detail Dr Marx." He showed her by waving his pen that he was aware of that,

"So you think that you do not have enough information to weigh up the decision?"

"Well no-one does do they? They don't know what happened and no-one knows what's going to happen. They think that they control something like this but it's too big, no-one can control it really, the genie, the gene genie me and my girls call it, is out of the bottle. Like the internet?... I don't know... open ended research? What if they? They could do things with funding couldn't they so things, you know possibilities, that could really help...don't get the money? ...Who pushes these things along? And once the Government gets the money who knows what they'll spend it on, is there a clause or something so it gets spent on doctors and nurses or who knows what they'll spend it on? More wars? ...and what if I'm the research again, they could just...what could they do to me?"

"You feel you do not have control over the situation?"

"Well, No," said Sue without adding 'well duh' out loud. "...they've taken away my Mental Capacity haven't they. That's why I'm here."

"And if you had your mental cap...if the Court's decision was overturned you would make a different decision?"

"I don't know, do I," said Sue, getting a bit fed up with saying it,

"But you would have control?"

"Well, it's not like anybody really gets to have a say is it? Not unless…." but Sue was not going to share her plan with a psychiatrist, that would be irrational. "…What if they just sell whatever it is to vain rich people? And nothing else. There needs to be something in the contract about where the money goes. I will need more detail, more information. I haven't seen these contracts. I need to see these contracts and have a lawyer, not a psychiatrist, no offence, …and to have a say in where the money goes, and people who are ill and the people who love them they need to know as well…but that'll be Ms Bailey-Erskine's department…I do know it wasn't my decision, that's what's important to me at the moment…at this specific time…. shall we get on with the actual tests so I can get on to Ms Bailey-Erskine?"

"Soon, and actually this conversation is very useful in the assessment. You are doing very well Sue….is there anything that could be done by anyone to help you feel more in control, more involved? By anyone?" Sue thought for a minute, her silent answer was 'Yes I could feel more in control and something can be done by me and Jo and Sam and Julie and Aleska' But she needed a consistent defence case, just in case. So she said,

"Information…I need to see this contract or the licence or whatever…paper trail." She remembered suddenly from a management training day in Two-Thousand-and-Eight. "…and the Court Order and everything, who said that was okay? … I need to see the paper trail."

"Okay," said Dr Marx as he continued scribbling quite a lot down and looked up, "…I think have almost enough information to assess your Mental Capacity. I need to ask you some questions about your daughters, if they were consulted, while you were away or since then? …And I believe that you have Mental Capacity at this time. I would also like to ask you some more questions about your…trip to Zurich and your return in order assess your Mental Capacity at those times. Your reasons for leaving and why you got out of the car on the way to the Ministry?"

"Yes. But I thought you said you weren't going to look at those times, just this time?"

"Yes. I did. Another example of the ability to retain information," and he chuckled. "…Having assessed your capacity now, and having found you most competent, I am hopeful that I can assess your capacity in the past. It will help inform the Court, I think."

"Okay then," said Sue stretching her neck from side to side like a boxer about to enter the ring,

"Okay…Now I have a favour to ask you."

"What?" Said Sue suspiciously, some of the favours she had done for medical types not having worked out so straightforwardly in the past,

"You are an interesting subject, Sue. A mature and experienced woman who looks to others… is perceived as an immature and inexperienced one."

"Tell me about it," said Sue sighing deeply, "…they've been treating me like a child since all this started really. Even Angela...Spoon-feeding me what she thought was…? I've been seriously managed! And Albin…the government agent sent to…you know about that?" Dr Marx nodded, "…well, if he had treated me like a grown woman, and Oskar! I probably wouldn't have been able to…they wouldn't have been so sloppy. Maybe?" Dr Marx wrote something down, "…and would you tell me you know your assessment…if you found out anything interesting I mean."

"I would share any findings at all times… It might mean a few sessions?"

"Oh, I don't mind that, I've got time," and she chuckled, then her face furrowed, "…I have got the threat of Cancer hanging over me though. You know that's a big thing too."

"We could talk about that too if you like? Perhaps when you have resolved some of the legal issues surrounding your capacity. That is, as you said, the most pressing?" Sue nodded and huffed,

"Okay Dr Marx, the subject is ready. Shoot." And she sat back in the chair and tried to get comfy,

"Would you like some more tea?" Sue shook her head,

"Do you mind if I lie down, over there? On that couch?" She asked. Dr Marx shook his head and sighed and Sue went to lie on the couch.

"So" He said almost wearily, "…Tell me about your father."

Sue Jolly Limited

She went straight to the cashpoint after the consultation. She felt a pool of guilt for lying to Dr Marx, especially since she did feel much better after talking to him. Much more confident about the plan that she hadn't told him about. It was rational and good. But she had to carry on as if she wasn't going to do the plan otherwise, she, and Jo and Sam and Julie and Aleska, could get into a lot of trouble. And she needed her Mental Capacity back off the Government and Dr Marx was necessary for that. She could not take the risk of honesty.

She pressed the button for Balance and Withdrawal and her eyes nearly popped out of her skull. Finally, a number. A great big huge no more worries ever could be construed as hush money number. She withdrew a tiny percentage for expenses and went into the branch to set up a new account just in case 'they' tried to take it back.

She intended to move the lot into an account in her maiden name. But the nice young woman in the bank explained that people aren't allowed to move great big huge numbers, or even moderately sized ones, without a lot of kerfuffle involving ID and proofs of address just in case they are drugs lords or ladies or terrorists. It didn't matter that her illegal drugs career of once taking one of Julie's diazepam because her back was killing and her stealing some circulation medicine for Yunis's mother in-law's foot had been entirely not-for-profit enterprises. It did not matter that she was, technically, Church of England. All Sue's legitimate IDs showed a well-preserved Fifty-Eight-year-old woman. She thought briefly about asking Aaron to verify her but it didn't seem right. She was very near Oxford Street, very near indeed. But she couldn't think of anything she wanted. And she had to be at the lawyers at two.

She stopped for lunch in a very posh café near Regent's Street with the full intention of having whatever she wanted no matter the cost. But she wasn't that hungry and still pining for a proper crisp sandwich so she just chose the one on the menu with the longest name and some kettle chips. *The Air-Dried Bresaola from Organically fed Gloucester Old Spots Raised at Maids Farm Suffolk on Stone-baked Organic Whole-Grain and Rye Sourdough with Homemade Spiced Organic Locally Sourced Vegetable Chutney* came with some Rocket and Tomatoes without provenance on the side. Spending £22.49 on a rather small ham and pickle sandwich and a bag of crisps would have made her feel awful just a few hours ago. Now it felt strangely exhilarating, and it was really rather tasty.

She sipped the water that was, she estimated, about 30p a sip and rung home with the good news but no-one was in. She texted the girls and added that Dr Marx needed to talk to them. Then she left a £100-pound note as a tip because the young woman who served her had been really nice and not because she had always wanted to leave a £100 note as a tip, that was sheer coincidence, and went to find out if Ms Bailey-Erskine was still pro-bono.

Aaron didn't see her come out of the café and she had to slow down for a bit. Her walk had changed, she felt lighter somehow. No more mortgage. Ever.

S. Jolly LTD hailed a cab outside Ms Bailey-Erskine's chambers with a swathe of paper bulging in her bag. It was only half past six but already dark. She wasn't tired so much, more full up. She had relented and was going to serve suits on everybody Ms Bailey-Erskine could think of, mainly to look innocent in the future. If she played the victim then suspicion about tomorrow's activity might be deflected away from her now. Victims were rarely seen as pro-active.

Not that she told the lawyer that. Would she need another kind of lawyer if tomorrow went bad? Would they take all that money away? They'd have to prove it was her who had done it and Aleska was very confident that they wouldn't be able to. She really was a whizz with IT.

Tomorrow would be another busy day with everything changing. And now she was going to pick Sam up from a job helping one of her lecturers hang his show. And Jo would come straight from work. Her first day back after her knee operation. Then she'd have the weekend to recover if it was still a bit sore. Would Sam and Jo argue about pizza or Chinese? At least they were agreed about tomorrow, had been from the start.

Sue suddenly felt very small thinking of her daughters; tall and strong and beautiful and full of life. And she felt small under all the other things she was supposed to be carrying too. Angela had been 'protecting' her from the beginning really, keeping from her the full impact of what had happened. Feeding her information as and when she thought it was 'in her best interests'. She meant well enough, but she wasn't the friend Sue thought she was. There was no-one 'on the inside' she could really talk to and she couldn't be honest with Ms Bailey-Erskine or Dr Marx in case they dobbed her in. It was only just about not too much to handle. There was a nice-looking Tai restaurant. Would the girls agree on Thai?

The quiet in the back of the cab stuttered through the Friday night clash of hundreds of people's intentions in the dusk. A chilly breeze rustled through a bus stop full of irritable people mainly clinging to summer by leaving their jackets at home. An odd bit of laughter from young people in their work suits and heels percolated in behind a swearing cyclist. And the lights began to twinkle optimistically. It never got really dark in London.

This time last week Yunis had pointed out to lights on the land but all she could see was a great big gloaming sky and loads more ocean. That was dark. This time last year she and Julie were eating steak and chips in the Elizabeth talking about bloody Emma again and Heather's care plan and that nurse at the hospital. And the apples were all in and Julie had already made the scrumpy.

She should get those apples picked as soon as possible; it would have to be Sunday. Unless she was in prison or something. She stretched out her non-turkey neck. First, she would have to get through tomorrow. It really was only just not too much-all this. Maybe she could talk to Dr Marx about it in their next session? The cab came to a halt too soon, outside a posh gallery on a backstreet. Onwards, always onwards, and she huffed out onto the street.

Sue hadn't been sure about going out to eat with Sam's friend and her lecturer and his friend. She couldn't talk about more money than they had collectively dreamed of in front of strangers, but they were nice. Jo had brought her friend Sarah from work as well.

Both the, not 'oldies' this far West, 'grown ups' were artists. Both doing as well as can be expected. And she had liked his, Ian's, sculptures so she hadn't had to lie. He was just a bit younger than her and had kids of his own. Divorced for a long time; his baggage appeared sorted with a sensible quantity taken to the charity shop, one or two choice pieces still in use and the rest neatly packed away. He read the papers too so he knew vaguely about the trials and didn't stare at her all goggle eyed. Unlike his friend, Dave, who kept gaping every so often,

"So, you're Sam's mum?!" He had said more than once, as if the answer would change if he kept asking. Dave was only Thirty-Five. Neither of them had a beard, thank God. Sam's friend Gus had a beard and was a bit quiet really. He did sculpture like Ian. Sarah was vivacious and witty and did the marketing at Jo's work.

They talked about rubbish mostly, and laughed. Sue needed a laugh and Ian was funny. The meal was so much fun that, apart from Dave who had to get back for the kids, they decided to go for a quick drink in a quaint little pub in another back street.

Ian got the drinks in and they sat babbling about the body in contemporary art and Game of Thrones and the price of renting let alone buying. Was it him who brought up beauty not being so important in art nowadays?

"Well it's everywhere nowadays isn't it," said Sue dismissively expecting the remark she'd thrown away to be recognised as such,

"Yeah, Mum's got a theory about beauty haven't you Mum," said Sam,

"Have I?" She couldn't remember having a theory of beauty.

"Yes, you remember…what did you say? …When most people had horrible diseases and worked out in all weathers…and starved."

"Sounds a bit economistic?" Said Gus quietly to no-one in particular, perhaps no-one in particular knew what 'economistic' meant.

"Oh that, well I don't know if that…" But everyone was looking at Sue, "…Well, you know how it is. You know on the train. You'll see sometimes three really beautiful women in one commute, or stacking shelves in Tesco's. I mean as beautiful as in an old master at least. Those Somali girls. How many of them don't look like Goddesses? In ebony…In Zurich I had this guard, Yusef, very nice man he turned out to be, anyway it was like being watched by a black Adonis…." And Jo said,

"Oh yes?" And Sue said,

"Yes." And winked at her daughter, "…and maybe, in the olden days when people weren't so well nourished and work was you know so physical…and dentists, they didn't have dentists, maybe then seeing a beautiful woman, or man, was more of a rarity? That's all." No-one said anything but kept looking at her, "…and then, well my sister made me think of it the other day…when we were young. I'm Fifty-Eight you know. When we were young there were all these rules about what was beautiful; you had to have this shaped mouth and that shaped nose, first it was hourglass then it was 'twiggy'…be this shape and with that colouring…"

"An ideal of beauty," said Ian,

"Yes, and now there's loads of ideals aren't there…now you can be any kind of beautiful and people are allowed, they'll be able to see it. Beauty, all sorts of beauty…All you have to be is too bloody thin! Do men really find all those ribs and hip bones sticking out attractive?" She asked for the umpteenth time, Ian and Gus shook their heads for the umpteenth time.

"And young," said Sam, "…skinny and young." And mother and daughter looked at each other for a moment, and Sarah, who had big thighs, sighed, and Jo who was talented and employed and had thin thighs but still got burned by that bloody Jacob sighed, and they sat and shared the burden of youth that Sue had forgotten for a few decades.

"Yeah," said Jo, "…or have a big bum." A mental image of a massive shiny woman's bum that had so thoroughly done the internet rounds that even Radio 4 listeners had seen it came into most people's minds and a few of them winced.

"Yeah but Sue was talking about rules. Rules of beauty. Not passing fads, this year big bums, last year thin eyebrows, this year bushy," said Ian. Sarah, Sue and Sam reached up to their eyebrows and stroked them protectively, "…not bushy. Full," he corrected. "…but rules are different, it's interesting what you say about Somali women, it's hard to remember but white Europeans saw black skin as simply ugly not so long ago. It used to be the paler the better. Can I even say 'used to be'?"

"Before your time maybe Ian? ...Things move fast...Peaches and cream...mainly cream. I remember," said Sue, and she sat quietly for a moment and heard her dad say that other N word, the British one; 'nig-nog' and sneer at a lady in the Royal Academy one Sunday afternoon when she was Seven or Eight. "...it wasn't so long ago," and she heard the horrible word coming out of her lovely dad again and saw all the naked pink ladies in the paintings that had made Jan with her 'rose bud' lips and 'little pearls' for teeth giggle. Sarah, Sam, Gus and Jo sat quietly and remembered their degree course work with furrowed brows.

"It was quite a long time ago mum," said Sam and Jo nodded. Sue put her elbow on the table and supported her head a minute, feeling the burden of age on her own.

"So, there were rules, there's no strict rules anymore?" Asked Jo kindly, Sue nodded unsurely, "...So we don't need it in art any more so much, beauty? Because we can see it on the train to work?"

"Maybe? But, well people still flock to the old masters' exhibitions, don't they? I mean maybe we get side-tracked always thinking about the subjects? Those old masters, well not all of them...we've all got a favourite haven't we, even when there's no women in them, they're still beautiful aren't they? All the line and colour and form and that I mean...I mean what do I know I just draw kettles...drew kettles," said Sue and she went quiet again.

"Or date her," said Ian slightly out of sync with a brief look at Sue," ...Does anyone want another drink?" He asked getting up with his eyes on the near empty glasses.,

"Oh no, it's my round I think," said Sue cheerfully, getting up so Ian sat down, "...Same again everyone?" And everyone nodded,

"I'll help," said Jo and got up too.

At the bar, after the usual 'ice in the third from the left gin, lime not lemon' blah blahs, when there were three drinks already done on the mahogany, Jo asked,

"So..." and she looked at her mum smiling,

"So what?" Asked Sue surprised,

"So.... will you be applying for permission off Angela then?" Said Jo as she picked up the triad of glasses with two hands,

"What? Oh...do you think?"

"Oh yes Mum...I think you should go for it."

"How?" Asked Sue, but Jo was already walking back to the table. She turned back to watch the barmaid getting the rest of her order.

She saw her reflection through the row of gin bottles and wondered, should she go for it? He was nice, very nice. A bit intense maybe? No. He was nice. But how do you 'go for it'? The Alfie thing had just happened in the cab on the way back from that bar. Yusef was just being friendly. Forty years ago, Steve had got out a bottle of cheap wine after a late-night sitting. That was the sum total of her 'going for it' experience and she hadn't done the 'going'.

Or date her? That's what Ian said. Had she ever been on a date let alone ask someone on one? Or were you

337

supposed to do the, so-called but actually quite hard work, passive thing and manipulate yourselves into a situation where he asked you? She could do sneaky at work, but it didn't seem right for a date. And dates were a new thing weren't they? New-ish. American. British people just used to get drunk and sort of fall on each other.

No. It used to be more sociable; you'd say something to his friend or he'd say something to yours. At the pub, or a party or whatever, people who thought it was a good match would kind of steer things. People who didn't think it was a good match would kind of get in the way; tell you something unpleasant about the other person or something. Then, you'd get drunk and fall on each other. Then, and only then, if it had been fun, or not too dreadful, you went out for a meal after some non-desperate time had elapsed. Afterwards.

Dates before were weird. Mind you, it would be one in the eye for Angela. There was no way she was asking or even telling her. Protected Party hah. She picked up the glasses and went back to the table with a view to finding the right moment to ask Ian on a date. Somehow.

Jo had moved seats. Sue sat next to Ian. That warm feeling bubbled up in her tummy. Fast.

"Cheers," she said and Ian said,

"Cheers," too and they shared a moment's significant eye contact. He was British. He was Fifty-Seven. He knew how. Someone had told her that she needed permission from a third party. Dr Marx said she was rational, she could be run over by a bus tomorrow, she had to be fast. She was rational and fast. She smiled and said,

"So, how old are your kids?" And twinkled. He twinkled back and told her about two boys, who were younger than Jo and Sam but 'almost over the worst of it'. He was beaming,

"Can I be honest with you?" He asked just as Sue realised that a significant part of the stirring in her loins was actually the need for a pee. She gripped and nodded, "…it's great to be able to have a grown-up conversation with someone who is also so young looking…attractive in a young way. Is that shallow?"

"Can I be honest back?" He nodded a yes, "…Firstly, yes it's probably a bit shallow but I'm a bit shallow too and it's nice for me to have a grown-up conversation with someone who is also very handsome. There's all that men and women age differently thing we could use as an excuse?" She said quickly and smiled, he smiled too, broadly, "…and Secondly, I am dying for the loo…I'll be back in a minute."

The stairs down to the ladies were quaintly narrow and windy. Thankfully, the loo itself, although very small, was also clean. Also pot-pourri'ed and pink like an old two-star hotel. A tasteless woman's touch. There must have been a landlady somewhere. And there was a poem on the back of the door in a frame. Winner of the BBC's UK's Most Popular Post War Poem competition 1996. Sue remembered voting for it. It was a good idea to have something to read while you peed.

'Warning.
When I am an old woman I shall wear purple
With a red hat that doesn't go, and doesn't suit me,

And I shall spend my pension
on brandy and summer gloves…

Sue finished reading, smiled and leaned down to wipe her bum with the soft pink loo paper. Her period had started. She burst into tears. Floods and floods of tears. Not just because she didn't have the guts to buy a red hat like Julie did. Julie had always always had more guts than her. Not just because she might never get to wear purple and a hat that doesn't go. Bloody Cancer. Not just because back in 1996 when she voted for that poem Steve was going to be the one eating the three pounds of sausages and they would be old together and have grandkids by now. Not just because he ran off and made her feel old before her time and now she was having to worry about dates before and going for it. Not just because looking Twenty had made Andy betray her. For what? A few hundred pounds and to stay in the game. So cheap, that really hurt. The cheap, dirty London game. Not just because her own sister betrayed her because of some stupid bloody wrinkles. She'd age faster in prison. Her own sister in prison. And looking down on Jan all those years and spouting all those big ideas and believing them and voting like a maniac for Norman bloody Tebbit and now not even bothering with IDS because he didn't sound Scottish. What kind of a person didn't vote for someone just because they were posh? And they were all at it. So greedy and blaming anybody but their own stupid ideas. She was just as bad with immigrants and don't get her started with scroungers. Sneering down when she should be looking up. Just like IDS. Just like all the rest. All the rest. And Angela was the same as all the rest as well. And Alfie stupid boy. All the bloody betrayals for a few stupid wrinkles. And poor Heather. No-one really cared about Heather except maybe five people. Poor Julie so sad and married to a bastard. Not just because she couldn't spite Angela who had bloody betrayed her to stay in the game in bloody Europe. Head of the octopus? Rubbish. There was no bloody head just a load of writhing bloody tentacles strangling her. Not just because she'd loved, really loved, not having periods any more. All of it. All of it together was just too much.

That bloody Dr Marx dragging everything up and making her think about things she didn't want to think about. She didn't ask for any of it. Not circumstances of her choosing, that was some bloody comfort. And so much had happened so bloody quickly and before that so bloody slowly and she'd missed half of it somehow even though she was there. Her mascara was probably down to her blusher by now. And this time last week she hadn't washed her hair for a week and been floating about the Atlantic in a tiny boat with very nice Somali pirates and an Oozy in a hold-all not a wheeled suitcase and she'd forgotten to give the girls their pressies and they were rubbish pressies and too much Gin always made her sad. So sad. And she hadn't even had that much. And tomorrow she'd have a hangover while she tried to so break the law, again, and probably get caught and her daughters would go to prison for aiding and abetting and have a criminal record and she didn't want to but what else was she supposed to do and any way she was a Protected Party and wasn't even allowed to 'you know' with a very nice man who probably wasn't too intense and had kids too.

And he was really funny and nice and didn't think her ideas were stupid or maybe he did and he just wanted to 'you know' with a young-looking woman without feeling bad about child-snatching or her ideas were stupid and so was he and she was stupid for even thinking he was nice. And now she was a drunken twenty-something looking woman weeping in a West End pub on a Wednesday night and she hadn't even had that much and so she wept some more.

By the time the snot reached her top lip, however, she had stopped. She only looked 20. She put her head back and blinked and wiped her face gently with pink loo paper. She sniffed loudly.

"You in there Mum?" Asked Sam,

"Oh hello Sam, yes it's me…I won't be a minute." She said in a perfectly normal voice. She muffled a big breath, "…There's a nice poem in here Sam, you should read it." She said as she finished what she had to do.

"So Mum...?"

"Yes Sam" She answered as she flushed the loo,

"Are you going to…maybe you should ask Ian out?" And Sue unlocked the door and they faced each other as they shimmied past each other.

"I might, what do you think? Would it be a problem at college?"

"Oh no, he only teaches one class and…you alright Mum your face is a bit red?"

"It's the gin ducky," said Sue talking like her mum used to,

"Oh okay, well I think you should go for it Mum. Ian's really nice." And Sam closed the door and Sue washed her hands and looked in the mirror. Still bloody twenty. Twenties were awful. Things didn't really pick up till you were thirty did they.

"What about you and Gus?"

"Oh, me and Gus yeah," said Sam confidently. "…we see each other now and again. You know… Is it okay if he comes back tonight?" So, it was Gus's ineffectual tip-toeing very late and very early that had so intrigued her for all those months.

"No problem. You do know that 'friends with benefits' means that one of you is in a sort of agony don't you Sam?"

"Huh?" Poor Gus. But from a mother's point of view that was fine.

"Well, just be kind to him, that's all love," said Sue wondering if she had gone too far. Probably. She wound back up the little stairs to 'go for' a date before.

Jo and Sarah were laughing about something. Gus was pressing buttons on his phone. Ian smiled as she came to sit down. She couldn't say, 'I'd shag your brains out if I wasn't bleeding like a drain.' So,

"So, what are you doing next weekend?" She said. It was that easy. He looked slightly stunned. The really quite hot bubbling in her tummy welled up to meet a cold rock sinking in her chest. Had she paled, she felt paler? He still hadn't said anything. It wasn't that easy.

"Well, I was hoping you'd come to my opening on, next Wednesday night," said Ian, "…then maybe we could get something to eat afterwards?"

"Oh! Oh. Yes of course. That'd be lovely. I mean I'd love to. I mean if…"

"Great," he said smiling at last. The rock dissolved instantly. He was nice, very nice.

"Great…we should swap numbers…just in case…"

"Good idea," he said and got out a little notebook the same as hers. They smiled and scribbled and tore and swapped. "…it's a date," he smiled. She smiled,

"A date."

Sam came back and sat down and smiled and muttered something to Gus who beamed.

"Well. I've got a train to catch." Ian announced,

"Oh yes! And I've got a busy day tomorrow. What time is it?"

"A Quarter past Ten," said Gus, as disappointed at the Wednesday night with free drinks and it wasn't closing time yet as Sam and Sarah and Jo,

"Well, look," said Sue, "…and this is a one-off…" She said reaching for her purse, "…I'll give you lot your cab fares so you young people can stay for another, okay?" The young people nodded and Sam pocketed the rather large wodge wondering what had got into her mum. "…I'll explain later," said Sue quietly meaning that she would tell Sam about the millions and millions of pounds in her bank account when they were in private. Sam thought her mum was still in going for it mode and lifted her eyebrows knowingly for a split second and then smiled. "…Don't be too late back," said her mum.

She and Ian walked up towards the Tube Station in a happy silence after the 'nice daughters' conversation. Adrian really needed to see to that cough. When they were nearly at the station Sue started the 'looks like it'll be a good show' conversation and she and Ian parted with a fond kiss on the cheek,

"See you in a week," he said, "…I'm actually looking forward to an opening." He added as he was walking down the steps. Sue waved and saw a cab coming and hailed it and dozed nearly all the way home. That cry had done her good and she had something to look forward to. Of course, she might not have a date with a really nice man on Wednesday because she could get arrested tomorrow. But that was tomorrow.

Tomorrow

Well, it was a good day for it any way. The sun shone almost as brightly outside as Gus did inside, finally staying for breakfast. Well, tea.

"Morning Gus. Where's Sam?"

"Morning. In the shower." Beamed Gus from his phone.

"Do you want some toast?" Gus nodded brightly. When Sue went to the counter, she saw from the stains that he had made his own tea. "…Actually, I fancy a bacon sandwich. Do you want one?" Jo came in and said blearily,

"Ooh bacon, just what I need…I thought we were…there's that…thing…don't we have to meet Julie this morning mum?"

"Well there's always time for a bacon sarnie," said Sue, "…if we're quick," and since she was already heating the pan and opening the bacon packet Jo made herself a cup of tea.

"Ooh bacon!" Said Sam with her hair still dripping, "…but aren't we…in a rush this morning?"

"There's always time for a bacon sarnie." Glinted Gus from behind his phone.

"I have got a lot to tell you girls…but it will have to wait till we're in the car."

"But," said Sam, "it's already nearly Seven-Thirty, we should get going. All of us. What time is Julie picking us up?"

"Not till Five-past-Eight...this won't take a minute Sam," said Sue laying strips of bacon in the pan, "...do you want some?" Sam shook her head and used the just boiled water to make herself a tea.

"I've got to dry my hair." She said and left with her tea. A small dark cloud fell on Gus who kept swiping on his screen. Teens are awful. Sue's phone rang,

"Hello Julie...yes, we're all up, just having breakfast, and I've got some news for later...no, it's all organised, I've got the...things and...Be..., yes. Yes, I'm sure...no, no there won't be that much traffic, it's, well if you...no, it's alright Julie everything's...yes..." And she turned the bacon over, "...well I can't talk now, no, no, secure what? No, it's just.... Look, why don't you come over now if you're worried...no it'll be fine. Yes. Do you want a bacon sandwich? .... Don't worry Julie it's not even Seven-Thirty yet...okay it's Seven-Thirty, just...Look come over and the it'll be fine, okay." She hung up, "...Auntie Julie's in a bit of a twist...about traffic...you know she wants to get there before the crowds. She's coming over." Jo understood,

"Brown or red?" Smiled Jo to Gus. "...I'm afraid we've only got white ciabatta." And she pointed with a butter knife at brown sauce, ketchup, mayonnaise or butter.

"Just brown sauce please," said Gus gloomily without looking up.

Sue had only just finished dishing up the bacon when the doorbell rang. She and Jo froze. Sam must've been halfway down the stairs already. They heard her clump down the last few steps and open the front door. Sue and Jo and Gus did not look at each other as they slowly raised their sarnies to their mouths and bit nonchalantly. Gus looked a bit confused as well.

"Mmm," said Gus appreciatively, Sue and Jo smiled a bit. Sam and Julie came into the kitchen,

"That was quick!" Said Sue a little shocked but also very happy. "…Do you want some tea? I've done some extra bacon just in case?" Julie looked at Gus and then at Sue and then at her watch. She did not say hello, she did not sit down. Sue got up and put some real steam in the air to match the metaphorical stuff that was coming out of Julie's ears. "…Sit down Julie, have a cup of tea." Julie sat down and glared at Gus, then Jo, then Sam and then Sue. Her eyes stayed on Sue as she made her friend a cup of tea. Gus put his phone in his pocket and finished his sarnie before the kettle clicked.

"Thank you very much Mrs Duggen…Sue, that was very nice…I've got to go now…it's getting…I'm…doing something…See you at College Sam." And he lurched into Sam, who wasn't getting up to say goodbye, to kiss her on the cheek and missed and left.

"Bye Gus, nice to meet you," said Sue to his back,

"Bye Gus," said Jo,

"Bye Gus," said Sam. They heard a muffled 'bye' and the front door closed,

"Bye Gus!" Said Julie, still fuming, "...who was he?!" She asked indignantly, "...we're supposed to be...he's a witness...what are you all doing here just sitting eating when we've got to go? Where's the tablet, where's the phone. You're not even ready." She almost shouted. All the Duggens knew not to say, 'calm down' or 'just relax' so there was a silence, "...this is important you know! We could all wind up in prison...my husband's a Policeman! How can you be so, so...nonchalant?"

"It's all organised, the tablet's in the case, the phone is in my handbag and it's not even Twenty-to... we don't have to set off 'til eight," said Sue putting down Julie's tea.

"I said Eight was too late we'll miss them. They set off early you know. Have you checked? Now there's a witness. What if...the batteries have you checked the batteries?"

"Yes, there's a witness to a pair of old friends going into town for some culture. I've booked the National tickets, we'll have to get the others at the door, the site was down...but we'll be nice and early so it won't be a problem...

"But the alibi! If we don't get tickets we'll...."

"So we buy something in the shop on a card. The receipt can be our alibi. The things were all on charge all night, a hundred percent. Everything's ready we just have to..."

"Okay, okay, what about...what if there isn't a coach party? We only see them some days, don't we? What if they catch me putting the case...?"

"The coach party part is just an added extra to be on the safe side you know that Julie. If you don't want to do it then we can just skip that part. Put the tablet in Mesopotamia, the Mesopotamia section next to the relief 'Queen of the Night' like Jo wanted? Do you want to skip that part?" Asked Sam

"No. No I don't want to skip that part! We should stick to the plan."

"Okay. The plan is to leave at Eight and drop you at Bedford Square while I park, do the thing with the coach party and then go to the British. Then we send the signal from the National any time after," said Jo,

"We said Two. We should stick to the plan," said Julie, "…in your hand bag? You should give me the tablet, we need to check it works, and the signal we should check…"

"We have checked haven't we, with Aleska, remember, and I turned them both on this morning. They both work. Please Julie, we're all organised and now we just have wait for Eight o'clock. You're making me nervous now," said Sue nervously biting into her bacon sandwich with her eyes on Julie,

"Okay, sorry but…what time is it?"

"Coming up for Twenty to," said Sam,

"Okay, and all our phones are off, right."

"Not yet, we don't turn them off till we get near the National, so as not to interrupt the talk, remember," said Jo with her mouth full,

"Okay, okay," said Julie and she took a sip of tea. "Alright I'll have a bit of bacon, if it's going. Sorry." And

Sue got up to fetch it, "…but we should put the tablet in the suitcase. Is the tablet in the case?"

"Yes, it's in the case," said Sue buttering Julie's bread," …and look, well, I couldn't say anything last night…or this morning with Gus here but I've got some news."

"What? What's happened? Are you okay? Are you feeling okay? Is it Angela? Has she got wind of…"?

"It's good news, well…it's good news financially. Very good. Amazingly good. Lottery good. And Ms Bailey-Erskine says I'll get to keep it if it all goes according to plan, her plan…get more even…" She put the bacon sandwich down in front of Julie, who picked it up but didn't bite. "…You know the Department of Health made me a Protected Party…" Everyone nodded, "…well, without properly consulting me or my family, you girls are going to have to speak to the psychiatrist and Ms Bailey- Erskine by the way, they sold a licence in my name to Fielding and Hardy who paid me Twenty-Three point Five Million Pounds…it's already in my account." Julie bit into her sandwich with eyes as big as saucers, Jo spluttered on some tea and Sam sat back in her chair.

"That's a lot of money," said Sam.

"A lot of money," said Jo wiping her mouth with the back of her hand. Julie chewed her bacon with her eyebrows as high as eyebrows can go.

"Yes," said Sue, "…a lot of money…but it won't last forever, and I might. We will have to be careful…but maybe a holiday?"

"Twenty-Three point Five Million Pounds," said Jo.

"But if we do this thing?" asked Sam, "…won't…?"

"There is that risk, yes, but we might be able to have our cake and eat it too and…"

"We have to be careful, very careful," said Julie, her eyelids lowering slightly. Her eyebrows weren't going anywhere, "…Twenty-Three point Five-Million pounds. It might not sound a lot to them, not compared to how much the En-Aich-of-Es has got to spend altogether, but, it's still a lot of money, even to them." Her eyebrows stayed firmly up.

"Twenty-Three point Five-Million pounds? For a licence for your patent? Of you. Is that it?" Asked Jo just to be clear,

"Yes, well there is a lot of money to be made potentially and well they messed up didn't they. I think part of it is hush money. Ms Bailey-Erskine says probably none of this will get to Court. I can push for going to Court maybe if I want but it would be more for the principle of the thing. And the judge might make me pay costs even if I win, though she says she's still pro-bono now there'd still be costs. And the Department of Health would spend a lot of money on costs she said. She says usually people do deals and then it doesn't get public so no-one is any the wiser."

"I think you should go to Court Mum. Even if they take the money away," said Jo all haughty,

"Well? People should know about it shouldn't they, I mean that's why we're doing the plan," said Sam, "…but…well it's a lot of money," Sue could almost see Sam's brain scrolling down her Amazon wish list.

"Well. We could get in a lot of trouble…I bought that computer, they might recognise me," said Julie with the outsides edges of her eyebrows coming down a bit,

"Yes, and that's why I still think I should do the plan on my own. I'm already in a lot of trouble and you don't need to get involved with it really do you. I can say I looked it all up on the internet by myself and they shouldn't judge me, think I can't do internet and computer things just because I'm fifty-Eight."

"Yeah but Mum, you can't do internet and computer things and under questioning they're going to… they might work that out…"

"Well then I just don't say anything Jo, as long as there's no evidence. I've been asked a lot of questions, sometimes in very stressful situations over the last few months and they can't torture me can they. Just threaten to involve you lot…" She left a pause to let that sink in. "…But as long as there's no evidence. That's why the coach thing is useful, I know Aleska said it was untraceable but doing it in a busy spot and all that I think it's better. Well, we all do… and Aleska's not even in their radar is she. I never said a word to Angela or Alfie about her. No offence but I don't think about her that often, she's a nice girl but…all I've said is that Julie's a grandma. You lot are in their radar and I should do it alone."

"Sue," said Julie emphatically, "…We should stick to the plan."

"Yes," said Jo, "…we are all involved. You're our mum and our friend and we want to be involved. You had to get out of Switzerland all on your own and we want to help this time. We have been over all this and we should stick to the plan." Sam and Julie nodded sternly at Sue,

"Alright. It's very nice of you…well wonderful…but I'm not happy. Not happy at all," said Sue not at all happy, "…eat up it's nearly time to go." She added to make sure they knew she could have some control over something.

"Twenty-Three point Five Million pounds?" Said Sam,

"Twenty-Three point Five-Million pounds," said Jo.

They set off early in Sue's car. Aaron's engine spluttered to a halt on the roundabout, which made Jo feel guilty for a minute,

"I should've used more sugar." She said looking back.

Sue drove quite fast to stop Julie from exploding and the streets were clear so it was actually only 8.30 when they got to Bedford Square. There were three tourist coaches to choose from so Julie nipped out at the lights and went for the one with Germans.

"I've been asked if I was German on holiday that many times…go on stick to the plan," she said as she wheeled her black case down the road. Sam got out too, found her phone and sniffed a lot.

Julie smiled benignly as she muddled into the crowd of tourists handing their baggage to the driver to put in the big boot on the side of the coach. He gave her a second look as he took the bag,

"Dunker," she said, and then getting into all this she smiled and asked like the chatty Fifty-eight-year-old white lady she was, "...Spekenzi Doich?" He shook his head, which was lucky as she had done French with Sue a very long time ago, and he put the suitcase in the trunk with the others.

She wandered back towards the hotel the tourists had come out of with an "...Ooh" As if she had forgotten something. Then she put on her red hat with the brim and walked quickly away. Sam walked to just outside the coach and stopped to text something urgently. After a long minute, she heard a muffled,

"Is everybody here?" And some cheerful German voices and the coach's engine started. She turned back and walked to the designated Starbucks opposite the British Museum. Sue had just got her a latté and Julie was a bit flushed but smiling like a loon. It was quite crowded already and they all had to squash round a small table. But they had chairs. Sue glowered at the hat. Julie didn't care.

"It was so easy!" She said, "...you were right Sue, it was like I was invisible...I could rob a bank and no-one would see!"

"Easy tiger," said Jo, "...one 'job' at a time." And they all giggled like schoolgirls.

"It is exciting isn't it," said Sam, "...all this. But what time is it."

"Coming up for nine."

"It was so quick!" Said Julie, "...Then it was done! I can't believe it? I just wandered into the crowd and gave the driver the bag, all the others, the tourists didn't even notice me they just kept talking to each other...Oh I think they're going to Stonehenge, I think I heard Stonehenge a couple of times and Salisbury."

"That's nice," said Sue, "Salisbury's lovely...we went there when you were small, do you remember girls."

"I remember Stonehenge," said Sam, "...big sky and the plain...it was very windy. Stonehenge. The stones were very far away?" And Jo nodded,

"Like the model in that old film 'Spinal Tap'."

"You've seen Spinal Tap? Oh well. Yes, well, you could climb all over it when we were young Sue, do you remember?" Said Julie,

"Oh yes...and do sacrifices on that stone...you know playing, did we go together?"

"No, I don't think we knew each other then," said Julie trailing off acknowledging the threatening boredom on Sam and Jo's faces, "...what time are the tickets?"

"Not till Ten...well I couldn't book those, the site was down, but that's when it opens, Ten...we've got an hour." And she took a sip from her ceramic bucket. Julie took a sip from hers. Sam and Jo sipped theirs, "...does anyone want a muffin?" They all shook their heads.

"Where's the car parked?" Asked Julie. "...Museum Street?"

"No, it was closed for some reason...I had to use the one in Drury Lane, that was nearly full. We had to nearly jog to get here didn't we Jo." They looked around at the bustle in the café. Jo took another sip of coffee.

"Cake? I saw a nice lemon drizzle...?" Everyone was already shaking their heads. Sue took another sip of coffee.

"So, is this exhibition any good then...what's it about again?" Asked Julie,

"Oh, it's great!" Said Jo, "...it's about The Myth of Troy, there's a Judgement of Paris on an Etruscan Tomb and a lovely Death of Hector on an urn," Julie nodded diligently, "...And then there's pictures of Troy, what they thought it looked like later..."

"Oh I didn't like that room so much," said Sam," ...I preferred the earlier stuff, you know the actual Greek..."

"So you've seen it then?" Asked Julie, "...have you Sue, as well?"

"Not yet, I've been away. But it looks like I'll need to go a few times, and I can afford it now," said Sue, "...but you know, we're quite arty and well, are we still all living with that Greek ideal in a way really? What with..."

"So why are you seeing it now? Asked Julie, who was not quite arty.

"Well that's the way we...to do the coach thing and have an alibi?" Said Sue beginning to see a flaw in the plan. She was not the only one and Sue's worried expression was being picked up on and elaborated by the others. Going to the exhibition would place them firmly near the scene of smuggling away the suitcase.

"But...they won't find the suitcase at all prob'ly.... Will they?" Asked Sam, "...It was quite late when we thought of that part of the plan wasn't it...well nearly morning."

"Yes, and we had drunk quite a lot of Julie's Brandy," said Sue,

"Well, we'd been drinking since just after lunch time really," said Jo. They all took another sip of coffee.

"It's harder than it looks, all this, I bet Tim Berniers-Lee didn't have all this trouble," said Julie, "…Well, lucky the car's parked so far away really isn't it." Sue nodded,

"It's not that far," said Jo, "… it only took us a couple of minutes to get here."

"But we did nearly run didn't we?" Said Sue. They all took another sip of coffee.

"Good job the booking site was down," said Jo. They all got up and walked very briskly away from near the scene. They were led by Sam who had memorised, roughly, all the CCTV cameras from a map she had found on the internet at College, just in case. She avoided whole streets because no-one was sure of the cameras' range. Sue and Julie veered away from cashpoints sometimes so violently that they got in the way of a tourist or two. no-one felt guilty about that. Then they were on Oxford Street and everyone was breathing heavily and staring in disbelief at Sam. Oxford Street was strewn with CCTV cameras, everyone knew that.

"This is not the near the scene." She asserted, "…this is where a woman with Twenty-Three point Five-Million pounds suddenly in her bank might reasonably go."

"We parked in the En-Cee-Pee carpark in Drury Lane at Eight Thirty-Six and got a bit lost and looked in shops on the way and went to Oxford Street by...?" Said Sue, trying out the alibi with a huff and looking at her watch. "…Nine-Twelve…that works. With a bit of window shopping, someone could drop their phone to slow us down? But why so early? Who goes shopping before the shops are open...Parking, we wanted to be sure of the parking...and a nice breakfast we all wanted a nice breakfast...but the bacon!?" She was all hot and bothered from walking so fast.

"Let's not over-complicate things, we said the other night not to over complicate things," said Julie fast and breathy,

"What now?" Said Jo, "...maybe we should review the rest of the plan in the light of this...issue."

"Well I've already booked the tickets for the National Gallery Tour and I've never been on it and I want to go. I have wanted to go for years," said Sue, almost petulantly, "... And I want to let the gene genie out in front of my Rubens and..."

"What time is that for?" Asked Julie, she was the only one still out of breath and really quite red.

"Two," said Sue, "We said Two it's in the plan. But the tickets aren't an alibi they're evidence against us. Why did we..."

"The rubbish plan," said Sam, "...we should've reviewed the plan before. Why didn't we go over it before? Issues!" And she huffed,

"We did go over it...with Aleska...she didn't seem that bothered. Did she understand about the tickets? Did she let us.... where does she work anyway?" Asked Jo suspiciously,

"Alright, hold on, hold on," said Julie defending her daughter-in-law." ...she doesn't think we need to do any of this. She says it's untraceable. She's the Eye-Tee person and... so far, we are okay. Let's calm down let's...let's..."

"Let's stop panicking on a street corner. Let's get a coffee or a drink or something." Jo looked at her watch, "…a smoothie or something. Sam." Sam knew the West End best so she led the silent way to a nice little coffee shop in a side street where they ordered tea.

"How long does it take to get to Salisbury on a coach?" Asked Julie once they were all sat down. "…I'm just thinking that they might wonder about the suitcase when they get to the hotel, then the driver might remember me." And she took her hat off. She was still red and starting to sweat. Sam was already googling,

"Two and a Half hours," no-one said anything as the waitress set down the four teacups on four saucers and two small teapots and two little milk jugs and a jug of hot water. She smiled and they smiled and watched her walk away,

"A couple of hours?" Said Sue. "…The coach left at say eight thirty-five so that's Half-Past-Ten…We need to have sent the signal by Ten Thirty." Jo sat back in her chair and rubbed her knee, she was usually in bed 'til 11 and she'd done her first day back at work yesterday, then there was the pub. Her mum read these things on her face and squeezed her hand.

"And it's Twenty-Five past Nine now," said Sam, "…that's an hour, probably a bit more with traffic and by the time they park and get out all the bags and then there's no reason they would try and open it straight away any way is there. I reckon we've actually got an hour-and-a-half minimum. They might just put the suitcase somewhere in the hotel and wait for someone to remember it or call the hotel in Bedford Square, or…Is that where the poisoning was, that old Russian spy? And the park-bench people? Call the police or Porton Down…or the bomb squad, all that would take ages." But the loss of faith in the plan was evident from the despondency round the table. "…well why don't we just do it now? Aleska said it was untraceable. We don't need to do all this do we. Really." Sue and Jo shifted positively in their chairs.

"Aleska is a configuration analyst for Eff-Cee-Oh," said Julie slowly. "…I think Eff-Cee-Oh is a private company but it stands for Foreign and Commonwealth Office, which I thought was the Government, she did it explain it once but I didn't take it all in. I was so tired." And everyone saw her mother's long illness and death push her head down towards the tea that Sam had got round to pouring. Jo leaned over and squeezed her hand.

"So, she knows what she's doing," said Sue, "…And it is probably not traceable and we made a mistake about an alibi we don't need and this is just for fun." She got some looks, "…Or to be on the safe side. We've got to do it somewhere now the tablet's going to Salisbury…and a busy place full of people and signals is here and just in case any way. I just wanted to do it in the National Gallery that's all. I don't know why. Maybe I just wanted a look round again…cos I was missing home? But we can just do it now. It's busy enough."

"Well why don't we just do that then," said Jo to a group of women who didn't seem to know what that was. "…We can get to the National in ten minutes in a cab and you can go and do the tour after some shopping and a bit of lunch mum," said Sam, "…then your alibi is that the signal

361

was sent at Ten or Eleven even, and you weren't there 'til two."

"Cee-Cee-Tee-Vee," said Sue,

"Hats," said Julie,

"And sunglasses and make up and entirely different outfits…Makeovers! I've always wanted a makeover," said Sue and she was already standing up and throwing tenners at the table. "…Come on, it's not Half-Past yet. And Sam's probably right we've got an hour at least."

"We can go to Selfridges and get all the things we saw before…pay cash. Have you got that much cash Mum?"

"Oh yes. I got it out bit by bit every time I got a cab too…in different places." And the ladies left another café very briskly without having finished their beverages

It's the Hats

The lady who was going to lead the tour at Two was already leading a tour at Eleven-Thirty. Three large-brimmed hatted and sunglass'ed ladies in designer wear went and sat on the bench across from the painting. One large-brimmed hatted lady in sunglasses pushed close to the little crowd, pressed a button on her mobile phone, wiped it with a silk scarf with the label still on and slipped it into the backpack of a tourist listening very closely to the tour guide,

"The Trojan Paris was charged by Zeus to give the golden apple 'to the most beautiful'. This painting is based on the Roman version of the Greek myth which sets off the chain of events that lead to the Trojan Wars. The Goddess Eris, here looking mischievous, took the golden apple, said to be the source of the Gods' eternal life from the orchard of Hera who grew…" The large-brimmed hatted lady took a sharp intake of breath and returned to her friends and whispered,

"That was fun!" Shivered Jo, "…Thanks mum…did you hear what she said, the tour guide?" They hadn't, "…That apple in your picture, the Rubens… it's an apple of eternal life! Did you know that?" Sue shook her head.

"Well I never," said Julie only just audibly, "Just like yours Sue!"

"I never looked into it, well I knew it was the Goddess of chaos who gave it to Paris and that he had to choose and give it to the most beautiful but I never thought to ask about the apple."

"Well, why would you." Whispered Jo, "…It's kind of weird though isn't it…I mean you've been coming back to this for years haven't you…you came here with your dad, didn't you?" Sue nodded,

"And Janet, Mum sometimes too. But Jan was never that into art, bored really. She used to giggle at the titties and willies."

"But then, now there's our apples aren't there and they're what caused it, you I mean!" Whispered Jo all excited.

"Well it is a funny coincidence," said Sue quietly, "…but. Well, it means so much to me that picture; Dad and art and…Mr Smith and…Something so beautiful. I don't know?"

"Did you know the story mum? Way back then I mean, when you and Jan used to come? I know you used to tell us," said Sam tilting her head to one side so her wide-brimmed hat nearly fell off.

"Oh yes, Dad knew all the stories…that was the only bit Jan was interested in. Like they were illustrations in a book. Other people used to listen to him, you know just stand near like he was a tour guide, it made me feel so proud…a clerk being listened to by…and Mum. Mum liked Dad being listened to and…"

"So do you think that's why Mum? Why you liked it so much, because of your dad or maybe because of you and Jan? Her being prettier I mean?" Asked Jo,

"I don't think so...I don't really remember...And I've loved it for so many reasons over the years you know, you know like loving a person?" And she turned to Julie, who had loved Andy almost continuously for 31 years and so knew what she was talking about. "...Or a child? No, well sort of. You love people as they grow and change. But this, you change and what you love changes, the subject or the skill or the light. Sometimes it's just the way the little putti clings on to Aphrodite's I mean Venus's leg God knows why.... Do you two ever...? I mean..." She asked turning to her daughters. It was hard to see their eyes in the sunglasses.

"Oh no," said Sam,

"Well sort of," said Jo, "I mean we all know that Sam's the prettier one but, well I'm not so bad am I." She smiled. Sam shook her head in disbelief,

"And so are you Mum, beautiful I mean. Maybe back then because you weren't blonde and your face is quite long," said Sam, "...you know what you said last night about rules..."

"Well I don't know what you're talking about," said Julie "...but you're all gorgeous and you should stop complaining."

"We weren't complaining!" The Duggens chorused. The tour group was already moving off and the women were able to see the picture. Well sort of see it, other people kept walking past it, some of them lingered for a moment. And the ladies were wearing sunglasses indoors.

There it was again. The luminous pink soft skin. Buff Paris handing over the apple. Venus reaching for it but not really that bothered. And the putti clinging to her leg for no apparent reason. Shafts of light piercing down from behind a tree.

"So, which one is which again mum?" Asked Jo dutifully,

"Well the one on the left, the cross one is Juno, Hera in Greek…Married to Zeus the top God."

"No wonder she's cross, it's her apple! From her orchard, that lady said. That other one, Eris, nicked it," said Sam.

"Well yes I suppose so…the one with her back to us, she's Minerva, Athena in Greek…."

"And what was she God of again…?" Asked Julie,

"Minerva? Athena: War and Wisdom. Juno slash Hera; marriage and family, very jealous her, and Venus slash Aphrodite, love and beauty," said Sue looking hard for something in the picture.

"And Paris had to choose…?"

"Yes, they all made all sorts of promises, you know bribes…err…Juno-Hera offered him power, Minerva-Athena: wisdom, and Venus-Aphrodite; the most beautiful woman, mortal one, in the world. That was Helen of Troy and she ran off with him but she was married, to a much older man, and her brother-in-law was a nasty piece of work and organised to get her back and that was the Trojan Wars." She sighed,

"What's the matter Mum?" Asked Sam,

"I don't know…. It's not…now I see it again I'm not getting… I think I've gone off it somehow." Everyone was quiet for a moment.

"Well I've never liked it," said Julie abruptly and Sue turned to her shocked,

"What never?"

"Never."

"But?!"

"Oh it's alright…and I love coming here, I like the Caravaggio down there and the horse rearing up drawing, but this…" And Julie sucked a breath in and said, "…It looks like they've all put lipstick on their tiny weeny nipples…they're bright red. It's distracting." The girls laughed in acknowledgement and Sue turned back to the picture,

"And they're not that good-looking really are they. I mean for the Goddess of beauty she's a bit heavy in the hips that Venus isn't she," said Sam,

"Well they liked them like that back then didn't they," said Julie,

"Mmmm…I think it was the skin they were into…they never got to see any and when they did it wasn't like that," said Jo, "…you all right mum?" And Sue thought,

"Yes." I am all right…. Actually, more than all right. I feel really free. The signal's gone out. Now no-one will have to bother me anymore and anyone can do what they like with it…and well, there's not a shortage of pictures to love are there. I will have to hunt down another favourite that's all…but you are all a bunch of philistines by the way. Lipstick on the nipples! Julie." Julie put her thumb and forefinger together and mouthed 'tiny weeny nipples', she didn't mind being called a philistine. "…So, none of you have ever liked it?" They all shook their heads, Sam shrugged,

"Sorry."

"So you were just humouring me then? All these years!" They all shook their heads again, vigorously,

"No, no, Sue. Don't be like that," said Julie quickly, "…We knew you liked it, loved it, and well even a philistine can admire the skill." Jo and Sam nodded vigorously some more,

"Well, all right then…But I've booked the tickets now," said Sue disappointed,

"Oh there'll be other pictures on the tour…you might find a new favourite...come on let's get a cup of tea, and finish it this time," said Julie. Sue didn't say anything. They got up and Julie led them to the café. Her favourite part of the gallery. "…what's the tour anyway?"

"Rubens' The Judgement of Paris: A longer Look," said Sue flatly,

"Aah," said Julie,

"Oh it's all right. It's not like I hate it or anything, I'm just not in love with it any more…are we having cake? I fancy some cake. Elevenses!"

"I must say, you're coping with all of this very well Sue."

"Well it's been a busy week. But I'm coping Julie? Your Mums just died."

"Well, all this has helped me take my mind off it…and it's not like we didn't know it was coming…I've had years to grieve really."

"But still," said Sue and she linked arms with her best friend and got as close to her as their wide brims would allow. "…should we stay here? For tea I mean, shouldn't we split up like we said we would?"

"It's all right Mum," said Sam, "…we're in disguise and any way Jo's knee is bad, look."

Sue saw Jo was limping a bit,

"Yes, and I'm gasping," said Julie, "…and besides. There's not a Court in the land would convict us. It's a public service."

So they went to the gallery café and ordered tea and cake. Sue passed Jo a paracetamol and beamed from behind her sunglasses,

"I feel so freed!" She said, "…the gene genie's out of the bottle and I am free." and they lifted their cups and said,

"Free." Altogether,

"And rich," said Sam, "…Twenty-Three point Five-Million Pounds." And they lifted their cups and said,

"Twenty-Three point Five-Million Pounds." Altogether,

"And you never know," said Julie, "…the cure for Alzheimer's might be just around the corner, "…We could all have our cake and eat it too." And they lifted their cups and said,

"Cake." Altogether, and giggled and ate cake.

Some Chinese people were looking at them from the next table. Then they talked to each other in Chinese quietly but quite excited, exposing the one problem with a multilingual city; the inability to eavesdrop accurately or at all. It can be very frustrating. Jo tested the situation,

"Cheers!" She said to the Chinese people, raising her cup. They smiled and raised their cups and said,

"Cheers." In perfect, somewhat Americanised, English and went back to their cake, content.

"They think we're English eccentrics… it's the hats." Surmised Jo,

"Did you know more Chinese people can speak English than there are actual English people?" Said Julie. They did all know that, Julie told them every time anything to do with China came up. "…and Twenty-Percent of our socks are produced in one town in China…that's one in five…" They knew that as well.

Julie's phone rang just as Sue's phone rang and they smiled and reached into their bags and rummaged in a sort of race,

"You left your phone on!?" Said Jo,

"Oh it doesn't matter," said Sam, "We'll either get caught or we won't. And there's not a Court in the land will convict us. Probably."

"So are you going to take your hat off then?" Asked Jo taking another bite of cake,

"No," said Sam, "…I'm a hat person remember…but that one looks good on you as well." And she took a bite of cake and Jo adjusted her brim while Sue and Julie took calls from Angela and Andy and tried to sound shocked, "…that was quick."

"Yes, bloody quick," said Jo, and she stage-whispered to Julie and Sue, "…say we're on our way to the

National…we've been shopping." Her mum and Julie nodded and listened to Angela and Andy some more with some 'oohs and ohs'. "…so what do you think Mum should spend the money on?"

"I don't know…she can pay off the mortgage…maybe pay off our loans?" They ate more cake and contemplated a life without debt for a moment. They both started smiling and took sips of tea and grinned. Then they burst out laughing.

"Girls! I'm on the phone…sorry Angela, they're very happy about the money, we're just out shopping…. I…oh? Okay. Well thanks for letting me know and…well I'll see you in Court…yes, bye, bye, bye." And she pressed end call." …Cowbag." And her phone was put away, "…apparently they're calling it Genie-leaks!"

"Bye love," said Julie, "…that was quick! Apparently its already got a name, Genie-leaks…how long was that?" Sue looked at her watch,

"Half an hour? Maybe forty minutes…That's not very imaginative is it, 'Genie-leaks'. Angela's not happy. Not happy at all."

"Well tough," said Jo, "…she should've been more ethical."

"No-one's got a clue. I mean her end…She says it's a matter of time though. Fielding and Hardy are livid apparently." They sipped their tea, Sue topped up anyone who nodded, and asked,

"So, Julie. Is it too soon to talk about early retirement and a life of leisure?"

"Well we've talked about it…but Andy's still quite happy at work and well, you know what people think about coppers who take early retirement…" Everyone nodded and knew that coppers who took early retirement were very bad men who were getting away with something. "…I might though? But I was thinking more of a mini-break really. My mum's money will only go so far and we wanted to give her a good send off so…I've always wanted to go to Vienna."

"Vienna? More stuff I don't know about you Julie."

"Yes, Vienna…to see the sewers…you know from The Third Man. That film. I love that film. But Andy doesn't want to go… I was going to ask you Sue."

"Oh yes! I'd love to go! They've got more Rubens there per square foot than…and other stuff, beautiful palaces…and cake! They do great cake."

"That's settled then…after the funeral," said Julie,

"When is the funeral again Auntie Julie?" Asked Sam,

"Next Saturday," said Julie, and she puffed, "…it's all sorted…and it'll be a good turn-out I think. Lots of people keep ringing up. But I need something for afterwards you know? Something to look forward to…a trip to Vienna!?"

"A trip to Vienna…to start with," said Sue, "…That's what was good about the last few months…"

"Good?!" Said Julie and the girls together.

"Yes. Good." Said Sue," …I got to see a lot of places. Properly. Not like for work where you see a lot of airports and hotels that all look the same. Puerto Rico is lovely, not like I thought it would be at all. We could go there Julie?" The girls shrugged and Julie said,

"Maybe." But everyone heard 'No',

"Or New York. See your dad...And you know what else I liked? Well not liked...not then. But I can appreciate it now. Now I'm back and I don't miss you and I can come back when I like?" Said Sue, "...I liked being on my own...I've never really been on my own...except for the commute and that doesn't count. I liked being on my own and...thinking about things. Not talking." Everybody thought about that for a second,

"I like being on my own too," said Sam, "...just you know pottering about and pondering things...it's nice." So that's why Sam was always in her room. That was a relief.

"I don't," said Jo, "...I like to be with people." Slightly superior,

"Me too," said Julie, "...I hate being on my own" And she went quiet thinking about how being with her mum towards the end was like being on her own, then she huffed, "...But we should...you can have a bit of 'me time' now Sue can't you. We're still going to split up now though aren't we? That bit of the plan's alright isn't it and...well. Do I have to go to the Longer Look at Rubens?" She pleaded through her sunglasses at Sue. Jo and Sam joined in.

"We could buy things on our cards for an alibi," said Sam optimistically. Sue smiled,

"No. I'll go...on my own...but how'll you get back?"

"Well us non-millionaires can take the Tube." Smiled Jo,

"I might take a bus actually," said Sam, "...or two."

"Or five Sam," said Jo, "...the En-Twenty-Six only works at night, it'll take ages."

"I don't care," said Sam, "...I fancy a wander."

"I fancy a wander too," said Sue, "I'll come back at Two...Shall we go?" And everyone, some more grudgingly than others, got up and hugged and left separately by the agreed exits.

As soon as she was down the steps and onto the street Sue took off her hat and sunglasses and tossed her head like she was in a shampoo advert. She took a deep breath of free air, put in her headphones for some music and started walking. Alone.

She turned up the street and was partially blinded by the autumn sunshine. It was a great day today, but it wasn't today, it was tomorrow.

She was old with good knees. Old and free and single. She rummaged in her new bag for those sunglasses. The Genie-Leaks were happening and Alzheimer's might get cured by a scientist from anywhere in the world. They'd say goodbye to Heather next Saturday with some kind of hope. She could clean the windows anytime, She had a date on Wednesday with a very nice man. She was going to get her Mental Capacity back. She was going to downsize or upsize and she and the girls would both get nice places of their own. She was going to go back to her maiden name when she sorted things out at the bank full of her millions of pounds.

She could put ads in all the papers about the camps and how good immigration was. Or just vote for more immigration in a country where her own Government made the decisions. And less initials, she'd vote for less initials and no more public- private Octopuses. She found her sunglasses and slipped them on. Should she go into that church opposite, she'd never been in it after all these years?

She'd finally remember to give the girls their pressies from Paris this afternoon. Get those old pads belonging to them out of the loft. And pick those magic apples. She'd put a good word in for Jan at her trial if she had one. She and Julie would take early retirement and they'd go down the sewers in Vienna and wear purple. She could go back to college next September and draw and paint from morning till night if she wanted. She might get an exhibition. She might sell. And she had a date on Wednesday with a very nice man.

Her bag slipped a little off her shoulder and caught her headphones, pulling one out of her ear. She lifted her knee to prop up the bag without stopping and pulled the lost headphone up by its wire to put back into her ear. The thrill of such flexible knees had not quite disappeared as she stepped off the curb and she smiled to herself. She was free.

It wasn't Wednesday yet. It was tomorrow. The first she heard were the screeches of the number 23 bus's massive breaks. The next thing, a nice lady about her age was asking if she was alright as she sat flat on her bum at the curb. She didn't get up immediately, just nodded and smiled. If her headphones had been in, or her knees had been older, she'd be dead. At 58. Luckily, they weren't and she wasn't. Which was lucky; she had a lot to do.

If you would like to,

- read the whole text of Prince Charles' speech
- or Dr Angela Carter's full report to the Select Committee,
- get readers' questions,
- find out about my next story: Hausa Blue
- or read my diary of a self-publisher,

then please go to https://www.kateabley.com/ and subscribe.

About Kate Abley

I am Kate Abley and was accidentally born and intentionally live in London, England, where, amongst other things I have been an awful front woman in a terrible psychobilly band, good dish-washer, bad shop assistant, officially outstanding Early Years teacher, adequate child consultant, nice charitable fund-giver, passable event organiser and failed political activist.

Last century, I wrote the useful non-fiction book, 'Swings and Roundabouts: The Dangers of Outdoor Play Safety' (1999), Sheffield Hallam Press.

Nowadays, I am a respectable and happily married woman with two children who have grown up pretty well and have turned my hand to killing plants and writing stories. I have nothing against cats, fear all dogs and quite like Marmite.

Look forward to my next story; 'Hausa Blue'

www.ingramcontent.com/pod-product-compliance
Lightning Source LLC
Chambersburg PA
CBHW060347260626
47160CB00006B/2234